THROUGH THE VISION-GLASS

Through the glass, Tyrus stared at a shape which was rising to fill the center of the chamber. The wizard Vraduir was addressing the shifting, smoky form, bowing to it. He was groveling, all his pride put by.

It was never still. And always cold emanated from it, reaching across space, through the vision-glass, to wrap icy fingers around Tyrus and Erejzan. It was omnipotent, past human fathoming. Tyrus shivered, his mind dizzy with awe. He could never cope with that terrible presence. Without comprehension, he saw Vraduir looking directly at him, as if the wizard could follow the deadly cold, tracking it to where Tyrus stood.

"He senses we are hunting him!" Erejzan yelled. "Now he is going to hunt us!"

The Death God's
Citadel

Juanita Coulson

A Del Rey Book

BALLANTINE BOOKS • NEW YORK

A Del Rey Book
Published by Ballantine Books

Library of Congress Catalog Card Number: 79-57464

ISBN 0-345-28089-X

Manufactured in the United States of America

First Edition: June 1980

Cover art by Douglas Beekman

Contents

THE PROVENCE OF CILARIQUE

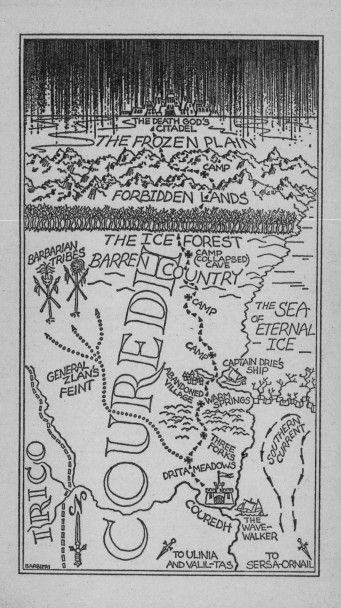

I

The Bazaar of Couredh

As the cargo vessel rounded the promontory, her seamen scurried to reef the sail and adjust its braces. The steady wind off the North Clarique Sea dropped to a good breeze as the ship entered Couredh's harbor. Familiar with these winds and waters, the helmsman anticipated his orders and steered clear of the treacherous outer shoals without trouble. Safely past those and a breakwater, the ship headed directly for the western shore.

Couredh's harbor was busy with fishing craft and many cargo ships. A few military vessels, outfitted to patrol the coast and hunt for pirates or any unlikely sign of invasion, waited at the quay or were rowing out past the incoming ship from Sersa-Ornail. Losing way at a planned rate, the new arrival made her way through the roads. She was in shallower waters now, and her lookouts stood to the rails, crying warnings when she bore close to obstacles or smaller boats.

Two men who had earlier been helping work the lines left the task to those who knew the port better and went forward to watch the final approach to the docks. Couredh's capital was built upon a small estuary. The harbor was embraced by rocky arms which protected the city from invasion and severe storms. Its realm was also blessed by a warm southern current which held back the worst weather of this extreme northern region. A pocket of greenery at the edge of perpetual ice, Couredh was basking in the return of spring and the lengthening days. Trees and vines lined her shores and river banks, and flowers dotted the rolling hills beyond the city walls.

The captain roamed the deck, supervising his crew, but he stopped to chat with the two passengers near the bow. "Here we are, lads. Did I not promise my *Wave-Walker* would bring you safe to Couredh in good time for Hetanya's festival?"

"Very good time," the taller young man agreed politely.

"Ai. And never a danger from those pirates we spotted yesterday." The captain glanced seaward and scratched his beard, puzzled. "The gods must have made them look the other way. I cannot guess how they did not spy us and come chasing to plunder us."

"Indeed?" The passengers smiled slyly at one another, a secret exchanged between them. Then the tall, fair-haired man said, "Hetanya's festival. You say that goddess is much revered in Couredh?"

"She is life to them, as to the Irico, for she brings the warmth to melt the snow." The captain studied them and asked, "Do you not worship Hetanya on your island?"

"Oh, she is honored by us, of course, but . . . Gros-Donaq's sons are more in our thoughts."

"You fear storm and raging seas, as we do, eh?" the captain said jovially. "Here in the north, you must learn to pray to Omaytatle as well, the great Irico god, Lord of Blizzards. Ah, but now is the time of Hetanya. I would guess where *you* came from, it was warm every season and no need to beg Mother of Earth to send the sun back in the spring."

Again the younger men smiled cryptically, letting him believe what he would. "When we land, may we go ashore free, Captain? Have we worked our passage?"

The captain blinked at the shift of topic. "Ai, certain you have, lads. And any time you take ship, welcome to sail with me. Are you sure you are not seamen?" Like questions about their home island, this was a query he had made often throughout the voyage, only partly in jest. The captain knew they were not members of the sailors' guild, for neither passenger bore the ritual scar of the crescent moon demanded by all such. Yet they had known their way around a ship most skillfully, arousing his wonder. "I vow, you spelled my helmsman past a bad chop or flaw as cannily as can be. And *you,* you climb to the yard so quick we can scarce see ye move . . ."

The second man shrugged and sat on the bow rail. "It is a skill I have. Acrobats must."

"And I am a simple conjurer, no more," the other added. "Erejzan and I are not seamen, though we thank you for the compliments. Just . . . amusers. No more. No more." His gaze was distant, his hand curved as if using a tiller, a man raked by longing to rule a ship as of old. "There *was* a time . . ."

"Tyrus," came softly, in warning. The captain waited, hoping to learn more. But the mood which had loosened Tyrus' tongue had been broken by his friend's reminder.

Disappointed, the captain turned, intending to go aft. Tyrus suddenly held up a hand to detain him a moment and said with feigned worry, "Your pardon, but if audiences are not generous here, are there ports north?"

"Oh, a perilous cove or two, perhaps, fit only for a ship running from death in the ice or storms. But for any chance of provisions, Couredh is the last landfall. Forget any plan to go further north, lads. Couredh is the end of the world!"

As he left them, Tyrus sat on the rail opposite Erejzan. He watched the dark waters, warm with southern current, curling into a froth and rolling along *Wave-Walker*'s well-weathered hull. Salt tang and ocean smells were being replaced by those of city and harbor traffic and the heady scents of flowers and young grass. A quay and a series of wooden piers extended from the river banks and the stone wharves near the city walls. The docks teemed with tradesmen and laborers and seamen. Rafts of Irico logs, come down the thawing river, bobbed among the barges and ships. Vessels flew the flags of nearby Clarique islands and the cities southward along the coast; but the banners with the crossed pikes of Couredh dominated all the rest. Gay pennants fluttered from watch towers and battlements and poles, signs of the on-going festival. Together, Tyrus and Erejzan surveyed this scene with tangled emotions —anticipation of journey's end and apprehension of what they might discover when they disembarked.

The captain and crew of *Wave-Walker* must have known they were not seamen, even without the proof of their scarless foreheads. Their speech had an outlander tinge and their shabby cloaks and tunics were cut in the fuller south island style. Erejzan wore a breechclout, as did many seamen, it was true. But Tyrus dressed in trousers, like a landsman, though he did not bind these in the local fashion. Besides their accents and clothes, there were other differences as well. Tyrus was taller than most Clarique. Long-limbed and very fair, he was handsome in face and body, and his humble attire did not disguise a regal manner. Even among Clarique's tall blond peoples, he drew attention by his height and demeanor. Erejzan was of more ordinary stature and commoner features, muscular, with coarse reddish hair that had earned him many a friendly teasing. He had the easily burned skin that often accompanied such coloring. Both men were bearded, Tyrus' whiskers neatly trimmed and Erejzan's as tousled as his hair tended to be.

"You should not have said that," Erejzan remarked after some minutes of silence. He kept his voice low. "About remembering. You were going to mention when you commanded the fleet."

With a sigh, Tyrus admitted, "I was. Riding a far better ship than *Wave-Walker,* besting pirates. I wonder what the captain would think if he knew I blinded *his* pirates to his presence and that is why they did not chase him?"

Erejzan frowned and surreptitiously indicated several sailors working nearby. "Care. They might hear us."

"They suspect nothing, mai fiyel. Besides, street entertainers and amusers are *supposed* to talk strangely and posture like lords."

"Or like princes?" Erejzan said chidingly. His knuckles whitened where he gripped the rail. "Or like outcasts. Playing a scheme they were not born to, pretending to be amusers, and pretending we cannot remember . . ."

Tyrus took his shoulder, shaking his friend lightly. "If they will be avenged, we dare not yield to our grief and sorrow."

That dangerous glint in Erejzan's green eyes faded. "You are right." He grew sheepish. "I chide you for remembering, and I dwell upon the past myself. Yet . . ." He noticed Tyrus looking toward the city and asked hopefully, "Vraduir?"

Tyrus was intent on a search few mortals could comprehend. He touched his breast, feeling a hidden magic glass he had bound close to his heart—a thing of sorcery which linked him with their long-sought enemy. Erejzan busied himself shaking splinters and water droplets off a frayed little pack. It was the only baggage either of them owned. The pack had been sitting on the deck; now he offered it to his friend. Absently, Tyrus took it and slung the tiny satchel snugly under his right arm and then draped his cloak to cover it. It was filled with possessions far more important than spare clothes or bright metal, with more tools of Tyrus' arts. After a long moment, he met Erejzan's unblinking gaze and said, "He is close, now. I can easily touch the fringes of his sorcery."

Erejzan clenched and unclenched his fists and exclaimed softly, "He *must* be in Couredh. He can run no farther, surely."

"Patience. There is Irico to the west. And to the north is the region of darkness, the Death God's forbidden realm." Tyrus did not like to dash Erejzan's hopes, for these were his own. Yet he was compelled to deal honestly with what they faced.

Erejzan's voice fell to an aching whisper. "I . . . I think I sense his presence, too, perhaps because of what he did to me. I pray the gods this is the end of the hunt. Do not let Couredh suffer as Qamat did." At that, they both stared shoreward, searching for a volcano. This was the mainland, however. There were no cones with plumes of fire and smoke or showers of fine cinders, none of the potential disaster that had been branded on their minds and hearts. The hills beyond Couredh's walls were low and green, not broken by volcanic peaks. The sky was cloudless and almost hurtfully bright. Iesor-Peluva's golden burden shone down warmly on the land. But Tyrus' eyes were drawn to an ominous line of darkness on the northern horizon. The gray curtain seemed, to him, to portend sorcery.

Wave-Walker nudged her way into a berth, outmaneuvering other ships. The losers' crews shouted obscenities, but the arguments did not come to blows or weapons. With a sodden smack, *Wave-Walker* fetched up against the pilings. Sailors scrambled up to the pier and secured her. The captain and his men sent prayers winging to Gros-Donaq and his sons, thanking the gods of sky and sea for the calm waters and good winds that had aided their voyage. That ritual thanks given, the sailors began unshipping the cargo of exotic foodstuffs and delicate pottery from the famous kilns of Sersa-Ornail. Merchants came to the dock's edge and struck up a lively conversation with the captain. Similar loud bargaining was taking place all along the docks and quay. The merchants' big-sleeved cloaks flapped and the captains swore and everyone dickered for the best price or barter.

Tyrus and Erejzan climbed up to the dock and paused to wave a farewell to their former shipmates. "Good trade, and a safe journey back to your island," they called.

"And much coin to you, amusers. Be sure not to trust these Couredh-yan overmuch. Many are from the Rasil tribes, and they are half Irico, not true Clarique like us Lorit clans. And watch out for the women! Those Irico and Rasil-yan keep several wives and are murderous jealous. Hai! Bite the silver, but the gold you can spend free . . . !"

"As they constantly told us," Erejzan muttered. He and Tyrus left the shouted advice behind, heading toward the city gates. "Gold and grir fur. All they could talk about on the voyage, getting the best pelts and gold . . ."

"When I was a boy," Tyrus said, "I wondered where that luxurious grir fur came from. Now I am here. And their gold is supposed to be the purest in Clarique. A rich little realm, this Couredh. We have much to learn in a hurry—how they divide that gold into coin, how long they count a measure of distance, tools to help us find Vraduir, once we know the local customs."

They wended their way through a jumbled open-air

storehouse of bales and boxes and heaped grir furs. The merchants dealing in these were tended by well-armed bodyguards and private police. These eyed Tyrus and Erejzan with suspicion. The newcomers opened their cloaks to show they carried no blades bigger than the harmless eating knives at their belts, but the guards kept staring at them, just the same. "They are looking at us as if we were robbers or cut-purses," Erejzan grumbled. He squinted at the sun and mopped his brow.

"Which suggests the wares they guard are precious indeed, if they worry about every stranger in port," Tyrus said. He sighed and went on, "I hoped if I wore no sword, the authorities in Couredh would ignore us. Going weaponless has served us well in other realms."

"Well, we have turned and landed on our feet in many a realm. We shall here, too." Erejzan unpinned his cloak and knotted it loosely about his waist. "If we act like harmless fools, they will forget about us."

Tyrus stared up at the city's watchtowers, noting the fluttering standards. "It seems the monarch is in residence, and many of Couredh's nobility are here as well. It must be for the festival."

"Amusers would drool with greed to think of such wealthy patrons. I would not mind earning a few coins to buy better fare than we got on board . . ."

Tyrus murmured an agreement, continuing to look around. "The monarch of Couredh is fortunate. Goods ships and much trade, a thriving and prosperous people . . ."

"That describes Qamat," Erejzan said somberly.

Nodding, Tyrus walked on toward the gates. It was plain Couredh had little fear of attack, for her gates stood open wide, inviting the travelers and seamen newly arrived in port. Guards were posted at the portal and patrolled the walkways of the towers and walls.

But these soldiers had that relaxed air of men whose realm had not known serious war for many seasons. At the gates, the guards inspected Tyrus and Erejzan casually, asking them only a few harmless questions before waving them on through. Less easy to please were uniformed men, not soldiers but police hired by the merchants' guilds. They were stern and suspicious and wore an impressive array of weapons. For several lengths, three of these policemen stalked Tyrus and Erejzan, past the city walls and through the inner defenses. They lost interest in the newcomers slowly and at last turned back to the gates, apparently intent on spotting more likely prey.

The two friends behaved as if they did not know they were being followed by these uninvited attendants. But as soon as the police left, Tyrus and Erejzan peered over their shoulders, their thoughts the same. The redhead muttered, "Those must be the local thief-takers."

"Then they should not trouble us. We are not thieves."

"That did not prevent the guild police on Bendine and Tor-Nali and Atei from stinging us with their questions." Erejzan had been watching the departing policemen and lagging far behind Tyrus. Hurriedly, he took two steps for every one of his friend's, saying, "Thief-takers would pay us less attention if you did not march along like a visiting Sirin or lord."

Apologizing, Tyrus slackened his pace. "Old habits! As to thief-takers, we will avoid them, this time, by being more careful, mai fiyel. We must gauge well who we ask about the enchanted ship or strangers seen prowling near the island's treasures . . ."

"Remember, Couredh is on the mainland, Tyrus. Hai! And the sailors were right! This city *is* half Irico blood, and some of these men *do* keep several wives," Erejzan said, gawking.

Tyrus was equally fascinated. Two provinces and

their tribes touched and mingled in Couredh. He remembered studying maps of Clarique and noting absently that Couredh was little more than a tiny mark, almost off the charts. Couredh was a wedge of the island province separating Irico from the last open waters of the sea, at a place where Irico's border ran very near the ocean. So closely linked, these peoples had intermarried to some degree, with striking results. The yellow hair and fair coloring and height of the Clarique joined with Irico's snowy manes and pallor and still greater stature. There were dark-eyed and dark-skinned folk in the busy port, though. Tyrus saw men and women with Krantin's heritage in their blood. As yet, he had noticed no Sarli but he would not have been surprised if some of those small, curly-headed people from that far land had made their long way north to Couredh. The coastal kingdom seemed a crossroads, its population further swelled by the spring festival. The crowd was diverse but seemed affable for the most part. There were a few inevitable squabbles over prices and trading and differing customs among them. However, such noisy encounters settled quickly, without need for summoning the merchants' police. In fact, Couredh struck Tyrus as remarkably civilized for a frontier realm on the edge of nowhere.

There was a bewildering jabber of dialects. At first, Tyrus feared he and Erejzan would sound too much like outlanders. But now he forgot that worry. With so many varying tongues and accents here, no one was likely to remark on two newcomers speaking with the distinctive lilt of Clarique's southern reaches. Tyrus listened, but he heard no other speech quite like his and Erejzan's. That likely meant their quarry lay further afield. Captain Drie and his crew—and their powerful master!—could not have lost all trace of Qamat's sweet tongue in a scant year. They must search until he and Erejzan found that familiar accent, and the men who owned it.

"Sometimes I wish . . . how simple it would be if I could drop our protection and ask openly if any had seen a man who looked like me, except older in years," he said wearily.

"Vraduir does not look like you," Erejzan countered, watching him sidelong. "Not any more." Tyrus remained somber and his friend pressed the matter gingerly. "Once, it is true, you much resembled each other. Evil has changed him past all recognition."

"To you and me, perhaps. To one who had just met him, it would be obvious blood called to blood," Tyrus said with great bitterness. "I cannot deny the life he gave me."

"And tried to take from you," Erejzan finished with a growl.

"We must find him soon, mai fiyel. I dread what he means to do. He lost on Qamat. But his ambitions . . . it terrifies me, Erejzan. I know what skills he commands, what a lust for rule he has . . ."

"We will find him," Erejzan said. Then, to distract his comrade from such gloomy thoughts, he went on, "What a place is this Couredh. I think I like it. Nobility in grir fur and pearls and peasants wearing untanned motge hides! Stone axes and swords! Did you see those thin blades the merchants' police were carrying?"

"That is the Irico sword," Tyrus said, and Erejzan listened with interest. "It is as deadly as a thicker Clarique weapon or the double-edged Krantin-yan steel, I am told."

They had come abreast of a wool trader, who was haggling over fleeces beneath the archway opening into the city's central square. A noisy bazaar lay beyond. But for the moment Tyrus and Erejzan were intent on the discussion the wool merchant was having with a group of peasants. They pretended annoyance at being

delayed by a pack train of ponies and eavesdropped.
The merchant was displeased with the low count the
peasants had brought. One of the country folk said,
"If ye want the fleece of the mountain woolbacks, ye
can go fetch it yersel', dwelter-man. We go no more
north!"

"Ai!" another put in, nodding vigorously. "Demons
up there has taken whole clans away, into the Death
God's realm beyond the Ice Forest . . ."

"Superstitious babbling!" the merchant scorned them.
His guards nudged each other and laughed at the
peasants' wide-eyed fear. "In truth, you are too lazy to
make the hunt up into the hills. I have warned you, if
the fleeces are not gathered in early spring, they are
worth less. By fall their coats will be ruined by brambles . . ."

"Dwelter-man, pay us our measure," the peasants'
spokesman insisted stubbornly. "We go no more north."
There was a flurry of yelling and arm waving and many
curses. But Tyrus and Erejzan had no excuse to linger
now. The caravan was past. Since talk of happenings in
Couredh's northern regions had been buried in haggling, they had no further curiosity in the talk, anyway.
Wondering if these tales somehow involved their enemy,
they crossed under the arch.

To others in the throng, Tyrus and Erejzan seemed
to wander the bazaar at random. They appeared to be
studying their competition among the amusers, no more.
But they were searching, each man hunting in his own
fashion. A bond of the soul, forged amid holocaust,
linked and guided them.

They watched jugglers and dancers vie for the crowd's
attention. Animal tamers displayed caged golhi and ecar
and other wild beasts. Merchants brayed the worth of
their offerings. Gamblers tried to lure the gullible into
their games. A few fur-clad barbarians, those from the
more peaceable of the Couredh tribes to the north,

mingled amiably with the townsfolk. Jades prowled, looking for clients. One comely harlot accosted Tyrus and Erejzan and flaunted her charms invitingly. With courteous regret, they explained they had as yet earned no coin to purchase her wares. Sighing, she went away, seeking other buyers. Slowly, the friends went on through the bustling marketplace, now and then whispering to one another regarding their hunt, or chuckling over something they had witnessed.

When the priests paraded by, business and entertainment paused to do reverence to Mother of Earth. The holy men, too, seemed happy as they displayed Hetanya's sacred relics, the Adril-Lur, for all to admire. The citizens cheered, and Tyrus and Erejzan willingly joined in the ritual cries of, "Hai! Niyah! Hai-yan Hetanya!" The phrase was prayer and battle shout to enemies who would dare challenge Couredh's patron goddess. In the southern realms Tyrus and his friend had left, Mother of Earth was called Ethania and was less powerful than the nature lord, Arniob. Here, in Hetanya's region, they did not hesitate to hail her as supreme. Mortals must honor the gods of the realm. It was so everywhere, lest humans earn the holy ones' anger. They had learned many a new praise to gods and warlords unknown to them ere Vraduir destroyed their home. Yet in none of their travels had Tyrus felt more at ease than among these merry celebrants of the far north.

Erejzan was in agreement. "How they revel!" he exclaimed.

"Perhaps it is to forget rumors of kidnapped peasants," Tyrus said, growing solemn.

"That merchant did not believe the tales. Do *we*?"

"Stranger things have been known," Tyrus said. "A ship that sails stormy seas unerringly and cloaks itself in magic, stealing prizes from under the noses of the most vigilant guards, carrying them off to Vraduir ..."

Erejzan's ruddy complexion flushed deeper with anger. "I want Captain Drie and his crew almost as much as I want Vraduir! Traitors! My own kinsmen!"

They fell silent then and proceeded cautiously, gradually absorbing the customs of this mainland city. In other places, their questions and inquiries had sometimes aroused suspicions. They worked to avoid that mistake here in Couredh.

Festival had brought forth everyone in gaudy array. Wine sellers were doing a good business, pouring from jars slung on their ponies' backs or from booths in alleyways off the main square. Itinerant musicians added to the din. Horse traders loudly extolled the merits of their animals, earning an interested glance from Tyrus and Erejzan. They were used to the dredis breed, those red-coated horses common throughout Clarique. But in Couredh, traders also dealt in Irico stock, dapple grays and whites, and even sold a few roans and blacks brought from Krantin province. Again, the friends begged poverty, brushing aside the traders' earnest pleadings. They went on by a merchant displaying whantola cocks and hens and another selling strange, furry little travesties of men, cunning creatures he claimed nested in trees in far Sarlos and could be trained to do tricks.

A bit beyond that peculiar offering, they came upon a skinny gem merchant advertising his wares. Tyrus was tall enough to see over the customers' shoulders, listening curiously as the merchant boasted, "Pearls from the seas' icy depths, emeralds, the famed pure gold of Couredh, the precious silver of Krantin and the Bendine islands! And here! Here the birthlings of the Fire God's pits—the legendary white crystals which no blade or stone can mar!"

Most of the customers were obviously wealthy. Beside their garments of broidered fine wools sewn with gilt thread, Tyrus and Erejzan looked like beggars. The gem merchant's guards fingered their cudgels and glared at the young men. Tyrus took a haughty tone, demanding, "Have you no better jewels than these? Is there no black pearl, large as a man's thumb-tip? Or an emerald in a tiara of carven gold? And what of those rare stones of blue ice, the ones they say are set in a chain of gold, studded with carnelians?"

"Listen to the outlander!" The merchant wavered between outrage and hilarity. "Are you speaking of Hetanya's crown? How dare you! I do not traffic in pirate loot."

"Oh? Has the sacred crown been stolen from Sersa-Ornail?" Tyrus asked in naive wonder.

"All Clarique knows that it has, insolent dog! Begone, ere I set my guards upon you!" The merchant shouted with more heat than the situation seemed to warrant. "You and this scruffy handri—away!"

Erejzan bristled at the term handri, a slighting reference to his hair. Forcibly, Tyrus led him aside, only releasing him when they were at a safe distance. "I could have bested those bodyguards," Erejzan growled. "They were all fat. Not a real bone or muscle on them."

Tyrus quieted him with a sharp gesture. He said softly, "They knew of the theft of Hetanya's crown. I was watching their faces while I described it. Do you understand the significance, mai fiyel? The crown was stolen but a moon ago, while the enchanted ship was seen near the cliffs off Sersa-Ornail. If tales are true, the ship sailed toward Couredh . . ."

His momentary anger fled, Erejzan nodded. "Do you think the gem merchant helped in the theft? Is he one of Vraduir's minions?"

"No. I skimmed his thoughts. He is afraid of witchcraft and of being accused of blasphemy, for stealing the goddess's crown was certainly that. Yet the merchant had heard much, stories of a mysterious ship putting in at a cove, possibly to the north of the city. And when

I feel Vraduir's touch, it seems to emanate from that direction."

Erejzan grimaced. "We have chased Vraduir so long, Tyrus. When shall we corner him?"

"Soon, I am sure. I cannot yet tell precisely where he is hiding. We need to know more before we venture north. It is time for us to put on one of our shows," Tyrus said suddenly. "We will play the amusers, as we have in other ports and cities. When the people are amazed and laughing, they gossip more freely."

They walked deeper into the bazaar, squirming through the crowds and examining a number of likely areas where they might stage a performance. Finally Erejzan pointed to temple steps that seemed deserted and said, "That looks like a good one . . ."

"Bogotana, but it is not!" The speaker was a Krantin whose dark hair was beginning to gray. His face had been ravaged by plague and he hid the worst pocks with elaborate mustaches and a well-oiled beard. He was perhaps ten years older than Tyrus and Erejzan. The guttural Krantin accent had been softened by long living in other lands. He had given up the Krantin-style side sheath for his sword and wore instead the baldric preferred by northern peoples. His clothing was a dizzying blend of fashions—Krantin jerkin, loose-cut Clarique blouse, and thong-bound breeches in the Irico manner. He was also missing several lower teeth, and those that remained were jagged and predatory. He was grinning wide and wolfishly.

"Why is it not a good place?" Tyrus asked.

"Because it belongs to the furrier Stratai. He would take it much amiss if he found you there. Of course, you would mean no offense. But he is a thick-head and would set the thief-takers on you." The lean stranger, who was Erejzan's height, peered up at Tyrus and preened his mustaches, his black eyes sparkling. "And Stratai owns two of the bloodiest guards you would dislike to meet. Well and at that, we must find you another place to perform. Come along."

Fascinated, they obeyed, one walking to either side of him, a canny tactic that amused the stranger. He went on cheerfully, "Amusers, eh? What do you do? Let me guess. You—juggling? No? Not juggling? Ah, I have it. You are one of those limber devils who can twist and leap and fly through the air—a tumbler! Ai! And you? I think you are one of the wizard kind, a sorkra."

"I am only a magician, a charm-weaver," Tyrus said hastily. He used the inflection that marked him as a mere sleight-of-hand trickster, not a genuine wizard. "I fear you have the advantage of us," he added, adopting a broad theatrical tone, suitable to his pose.

"So I have." The stranger mocked Tyrus and bowed elegantly. Then he doffed his small plumed cap. "I am Rof, and I rule far more of this bazaar than does that prating gem merchant back there, the one who so interested you. What were you looking for? A chance to rob him? Ah, that is too bold, and you so newly come to Couredh, too. You do not *seem* that stupid."

On the defensive, the friends conferred silently with a glance and Tyrus said, "We had no intention of robbing him. If you mean to inform on us to the thief-takers, you do us an injury."

"Inform?" Rof laughed raucously, his arms akimbo. A few people turned around to look, attracted by the sound, thinking it might mean some entertainment. When they saw who was laughing, many of them made haste to leave the area, as if they knew who Rof was. Rof stepped in between Tyrus and Erejzan once more and flung his arms familiarly about their shoulders. He began guiding them across the bazaar. "I assure you, I am not an informer. For one thing, the merchants' police and thief-takers think you should inform for the common weal, not for reward . . ."

"And you work only for coin," Tyrus said, winking at Erejzan.

Rof slapped him on the back so heartily the tall young man choked for a moment before he could regain his breath. "Ha! I *knew* you were a pair of sharp ones. I saw it at once."

Tyrus and Erejzan were wary, anticipating some trick or snare. They could have combined their strength and twisted free of Rof's grasp easily. Yet they did not. The dark-eyed man disarmed them with jesting mien and cordial dishonesty.

"No, if you wanted to rob that scrawny gem merchant, let me tell you how to go about it. You must catch him alone in his dwelling or when he journeys with his caravan to Ulinia or Valil-Tas, down the coast. But that is dangerous. He is too cowardly to travel without a considerable escort. Best to strike at his house. Of course, there are his guards and the barely-tamed wolf-dogs he keeps on loose chains. No, too difficult. Choose smaller prey, that is my suggestion."

"You speak from experience, I trust?" Erejzan said sarcastically.

Utterly without shame, Rof grinned, flashing his yellow teeth. "Oh, a very great deal of experience, tumbler! Whatever you need to know about Couredh, I am your man." Rof stopped short and pointed to a vacant area beside some pillars and an overhanging roof. Three filthy youths were squatting there, gambling on the stones. When Rof hailed them, they acted like three cubs caught raiding a butcher's storeroom. Cringing, they awaited his command, then scampered away when he waved negligently to them. "Be off! I am giving this place to my new friends . . ."

He paused significantly, expecting to hear their names. With some reluctance, Tyrus and Erejzan identified themselves. Though Tyrus had long ago cloaked them in a form of anonymity that should protect them, they were most uncertain about revealing themselves to Rof. Rof brightened and repeated the names thoughtfully while Tyrus walked around the newly vacant space. No one rushed to claim the spot the boys had left. The location was a good one, near the main intersection of traffic across the bazaar.

Erejzan cocked his head and asked Rof, "Why do you favor us so? You know we have no coin to give you."

"Not yet." There was an undercurrent to his affable manner. "No doubt you will earn coin, but probably not enough to interest me. I have a big appetite, as you will learn."

"Shall we?" Tyrus said. "A fee for donating this space to us? Shall we repay you later in the day?"

Rof made as if to refuse the offer, none too convincingly. "Well and at that, if you are such honest fellows, meet me tonight at the Inn of the Cutpurses."

"It sounds like a merry hostel," Tyrus replied, playing the game.

"Merry indeed, if you are no thief-taker or merchants' police—and you are none of them. You will find good ale and spiced mutton and porridge and a wench or two most skilled in pleasing a man. Good fare, eh?" Rof jabbed an elbow sharply into Erejzan's ribs.

Erejzan countered with a mischievous and stunning poke at Rof's lean belly. Rof gasped in surprise and clutched his midriff. When he recovered a bit, he took the blow fairly, returning Erejzan's impish grin with his own. Erejzan flexed his muscles and tossed aside his folded cloak. He counted time to himself, an acrobat planning the space he would need to execute some run or leap.

"Stay a moment," Rof said. "I have not done telling you about the Inn . . ."

"Have you not?" Tyrus reversed his cloak and sat his small pack atop Erejzan's discarded mantle. The other side of his robe was daubed with magical symbols and arcane drawings, such as a charm-weaver would wear. "You told us clear enough—the Inn is a den of pickpockets and throatslitters, where no king's men are welcome."

Rof made a face. "You disappoint me, charm-weaver. There is no king in Couredh. We have a queen, LaRenya Jathelle. She is ruler since her sire's death last winter. Such clever fellows ought to have known that."

In truth, the young men *had* heard this mentioned, ere they took ship from Sersa-Ornail. But Tyrus said in apparent surprise, "Dead? How did he die?"

"How?" Rof searched his memory for that unimportant fact. "Of some sickness in the lungs, I was told. He was long afflicted with it, ever since his campaigns battling barbarians on Couredh's frontiers."

"A natural illness, then? Not sudden? Not a . . . peculiar accident?" Tyrus could not quite conceal his relief at this news. Rof eyed them with fresh curiosity. "Then long live his daughter. LaRenya Jathelle, you say?"

"Ai." Rof would not let the matter go. He absently reached under his cloak and brought forth a whip he had hidden at the back of his belt. It was less a thing to threaten the friends than an object to busy his hands. He flicked debris out from under the porch adeptly. "Peculiar accidents? Such things interest you, eh?"

"Perhaps, as oddities to amuse our patrons."

"Mm. Oddities. None here in Couredh. No fabled flying ponies, as they claim dwell in far Sarlos. No dragons haunt our little pocket of the ocean. Oh, there are stories of evil spirits haunting the northern reaches of the realm, true, tales of demons in the Ice Forest, stealing peasants." Rof spat and dragged his whip's trophies across the wet smear. "I have been to every province and to the Ice Forest, and scoff at such stories . . ."

"Rof, of course, is afraid of nothing," Erejzan cut in slyly.

A brief spark of anger gleamed in those black eyes. Then Rof chuckled at his own boasting. "I can be afraid, but it takes more than a few rumors of kidnapped peasants to make me so."

"*Have* there been disappearances?" Tyrus did not look at Rof. Instead he gesticulated, drawing the attention of a few passersby who hoped this was but a prelude to some entertainment.

Rof watched him, particularly Tyrus' hands, as he spoke. "Perhaps there have. Strange events northward. But it is not new, this rumormongering. Some seasons past the peasants have been spreading that tale."

Tiny red and blue smokes emerged from Tyrus' fingers, dribbling down through the air, interlacing and turning to purple mist. Abruptly, the smokes evaporated into nothingness with a loud report. People started and then turned toward him, gathering into an audience. For the ears of Rof and Erejzan alone, Tyrus went on while he smiled charmingly to the assembling spectators. "I am curious about such strange events. A charm-weaver can always use these as part of his act. Say . . . a story about a magnificent stallion fit for a hero-king. Or Hetanya's crown. Or the priceless silver net of the man-fish of Bendine. Or a musician who can seize the soul of mortals and gods, his harp luring birds from their trees . . ."

Stroking his sharp little mustaches, Rof added, "If we are talking of such plunder, best mention the tapestries of Maitu. Ai! I have heard of their taking two winters past, even this far to the north of the Arniob islands."

"That too." The game was now parry and thrust, and all three men understood its dangerous rules. Rof seemed delighted to find himself matched in the war of wits. Continuing in the same bored tone, Tyrus said, "Do you know of such things?"

"Perhaps. Come to the Inn of the Cutpurses, as I bade. We will share this and much more . . ."

"We are not thieves," Erejzan protested. When Rof did not answer, he said irritably, "And we have no more time to waste if we are to earn food and shelter for the night. Stand aside!" He went leaping toward the pillars and jumped up, swinging from the edge of the roof and sailing through the air in several masterful somersaults.

Tyrus abetted him, weaving more smokes and noise from his fingers. He formed the smoke into large rings and Erejzan tumbled through these while Tyrus said loudly, "Lords and ladies, gentle folk! Attend us a moment or two! We shall please you and mystify you and astonish you . . ."

As Erejzan launched another sequence of leaps, Rof grasped Tyrus' shoulder in a commanding way. "I insist, conjurer. You and the fihar come to the Inn, tonight. It is to your benefit, or your sorrow, if you refuse me."

Tyrus turned to Rof and was surprised by a sudden shift in the bandit's expression. His confidence was replaced by a furtive look. Rof hastily recoiled his whip and tucked it out of sight, then drew his cloak tightly about him, concealing his sword and other weapons. Without another word to Tyrus or Erejzan, he disappeared into the crowd and was gone.

Erejzan completed a spectacular jump and landed, panting, beside his friend. "Where is the brigand vanished to?"

"I do not know. He went into the bazaar like a cur with its tail between its legs. I wonder why." Erejzan was holding his arms high and smiling at the growing audience, soliciting and receiving their applause.

From the corner of his mouth, the acrobat muttered, "The rascal must be fleeing from thief-takers."

"I think not." Tyrus saw none of the uniformed guards or merchants' patrolmen. There were, however, two new arrivals joining the little crowd around Tyrus and Erejzan. These young women squirmed to the forefront of the spectators, very interested in seeing the show.

II

Jathelle and Ilissa

━┅━┅━┅━┅━┅━┅━┅━┅━┅━┅━┅━┅━┅━┅━

"BY HETANYA, 'TIS A CONJURER!" ONE OF THE PAIR
exclaimed. She spoke in a broad, somewhat exaggerated
rustic accent. When those about her gawked, she
gripped the bronze dagger at her belt as if daring them
to contradict her.

She was tall, dressed like a barbarian in leather tunic
and breeches and a fur-trimmed cloak. A necklace of
wolves' teeth was her only adornment. She carried a
sword as well as the crude dagger. A fringed hood and
half-mask hid much of her face. Yet sun-streaked,
honey-colored hair peeped from the edges of the hood.
To Tyrus' judgment, that hair was too clean to mark
her a barbarian woman. Her skin was fair, her eyes a
vivid blue and bright with intelligence and much spirit.
She struck a defiant pose, her head high. With a wide
smile, Tyrus swept his decorated cloak across the dusty
pavement. "Welcome, fiery battle maiden from Couredh's frontiers! And welcome also to your companion,
this lovely temple dancer!"

Both of them were surprised. The hoyden in leather
said too quickly, "I do not know her. She is no companion of mine. We are . . . acquaintances only."

24

"Ah! Forgive my confusion, battle maiden. I saw her clinging to your mantle and sheltering in your shadow and I thought . . ."

The smaller female whispered an apology to her friend. But she did not let go of the other's cloak. Sighing, the hoyden said, "We are . . . cousins. Nothing more, conjurer."

Unlike her swaggering "cousin," the temple dancer was swathed in layers of diaphanous veils. Bangles swung at her ankles, waist, and wrists, and a talisman of the goddess Hetanya fastened her headdress. Breezes plucked at the many-hued veils, outlining a slender body. Her hair appeared to be very pale, almost Irico white. Tyrus suspected that her eyes, could he see them plainly, would be mates for the battle maiden's. She cowered behind the braver woman, peering out timidly at Tyrus and Erejzan.

"She . . . she is shy," the battle maiden said. She put a comforting arm around her trembling companion. "They will not harm you. They are amusers."

Several slips in her outlander accent told Tyrus much. Though she strutted and talked loudly like some tribeswoman from the far mountains, her well-bred tone had betrayed the hoyden. The disguise aroused his wonder. Was the temple dancer also in disguise? Were the women truly cousins, or was there a closer relationship here? And why had they put on disguises at all?

He bowed again, most respectfully. "A modest behavior pleases Hetanya, I am sure. The Mother of Earth and her minions should delight in your arts, as we now shall strive to delight you."

Erejzan nudged him sharply and whispered, "Find out who they are!" The acrobat was staring at the veiled woman, his expression rapt.

"In good time, mai fiyel," Tyrus soothed him. "First we must catch the audience in our net. A few more leaps and tumbles, if you would."

"Watch!" Erejzan's enthusiasm alarmed the young magician. The nimble fire-hair twisted twice and three times in the air during his leaps and bounded so high the onlookers gasped. Some called warnings to the "handri" and plainly feared Erejzan would mistime these wild stunts, to his hurt. Though Tyrus had requested these antics, he was worried, too. Rarely had Erejzan taken such foolish chances during their performances.

Erejzan seized a slender pillar supporting the nearby canopy and spun his length around it horizontally. As he somersaulted free and came to earth beside his friend, Tyrus steadied him and scolded, "That is enough. If you crack your skull, you will never learn the temple dancer's name." Erejzan gulped and smiled like an unrepentant boy but promised he would be more careful. Doubtful, Tyrus let him go and said, "Now I will continue what you have so well begun."

Tyrus called on a pantheon of spurious arcane spirits. All the horrific names and incantations were sheerest gibberish. But he had discovered that spectators enjoyed such mysterious jargon, the more so if it sounded terrible and made them afraid. He deepened his voice and rolled each syllable dramatically. The two young women, among others, leaned forward expectantly and their eyes grew wide. Tyrus clapped his hands, and there was a flash of golden light. People squealed and started with surprise. When the light dissolved into a rain of dancing motes, they marveled, seeing two doves perched on Tyrus' hands.

"How did he do that?"

"He . . . he must have hidden them under his cloak."

A rough-featured man grabbed at Tyrus, searching for secret pockets in his mantle. Erejzan lunged to stop him and a nasty quarrel might have resulted had not Tyrus intervened. "Wait, Sirai. Please, examine my cloak, and tell everyone what you discover." Tyrus slipped off the garment and gave it to the astonished townsman. With ill grace, Erejzan smothered his annoyance and watched in disgust while the man picked through the cloak, turning the sleeves in and out.

"I . . . I can find . . . nothing," the man admitted at last. "It is just a threadbare cloak."

Tyrus smiled and rolled up the sleeves of his tunic as well, to show that these, too, were empty. "You may keep the cloak a few minutes, if you would, Sirai. Perhaps that will prove it has nothing to do with my magic."

"N—not Sirai. I am no lord or noble . . ."

"Nor any man of wit, either," Erejzan muttered.

The woman disguised as a battle maiden cried, "Show us more conjury. What else can you do? And what wonders can the tumbler do past what he has already done?" Again, unconsciously, she used terms no frontier woman would know.

"Why, many things, warlike maiden. Observe!" Tyrus paraded a rapid series of illusions and tricks. He pulled coins out of onlookers' ears and hair, created an explosion of scarves and feathers from a dirty pebble, a barking litter of pups that turned into fluttering moths, a rain that became bits of cobweb even as people shrieked and covered their heads, expecting to be drenched.

The spectators buzzed with amazement and Erejzan capered around his friend. "Behold a master charmweaver! You *have* been watching? Will no one fathom the hidden art? Surely some among you have solved the riddle?" His acrobatics were not so wild as before but he was quite energetic enough to spellbind them and hold their attention with ease. A few remained skeptical, but they were at a loss to explain Tyrus' magic.

Deftly, Tyrus started to blend common thimblerigger's tricks with genuine wizardry. Whenever someone scoffed and said he had seen a particular illusion elsewhere, Tyrus would follow that simple conjury with something so bewildering the most stubborn doubters fell silent. Tyrus took up the theme from Erejzan, gently taunting his audience. "Watch! You are not watching closely enough, or you would have caught me by now. It is not in the cloak. What then? Where are the secrets? Where do I keep them? How is the magic accomplished?"

He held out his hands and demanded, "Bind me! Battle maiden, will you tie my hands? Prove to these good folk I do not achieve my magic by any sleight of hand or gesture."

She hesitated a moment, then came to him. Part of her half-mask had pushed aside, revealing a dimpled chin and a hint of an attractive mouth. What Tyrus saw suggested she was indeed very comely. Those blue eyes were bright with impish anticipation. She rose to the bait Tyrus had cast forth. "So I shall, conjurer. I will bind you like a woolback destined for market," she said, jerking a rawhide thong from her belt. She wrapped it about Tyrus' wrists. Though she was not so cruel as to cut his flesh, she knotted the thong securely and tested it to be certain he could not wriggle free. So vigorously did she labor that more of her silken hair escaped the hood, curling about her fair brow and high cheek bones. Tyrus looked from her to the temple dancer and back again, skimming the surfaces of their beings with his arts, smiling to himself.

Erejzan seized an opportunity he patently had longed for. "And should his eyes not be bound as well? Lovely dancer, if I may impose on you? We need a finely-woven cloth, doubled and redoubled so that no trace of light may penetrate its fabric." He reached out but did not touch the dangling ribbons of her garment, waiting.

She shrank from him, but not too far, and she seemed tempted by the request. The battle maiden chided her gently. "He means you no harm. Give him the sash. I want to see how the conjurer creates his spells when he can neither see nor use his hands."

Slowly the dancer obeyed, her lashes lowered, then fluttering open as she peered shyly at Erejzan. He took the sash she offered and dared to press her fingers a moment longer than necessary. She did not pull away from him. With a sigh, Erejzan let go and returned to Tyrus.

"Observe! I fold it once, and again, and again, and yet again!" Erejzan demonstrated each action with a grand flourish. He handed the gauzy bandage around the crowd, encouraging people to peer through the folded sash and be certain that it masked all the sun's rays. Then he tied the blindfold over Tyrus' eyes. Tyrus listened patiently as Erejzan went on. "Now we must turn him about several times. He must be confused and unsure where he is. Battle maiden, temple dancer? Do so! Let there be no trickery! Addle his wits, if you can!"

Tyrus' remaining senses sharpened. He heard the soft jangling of the dancer's bracelets and anklets. There were the scents of fur and leather, but also the sweeter aromas of pomanders and precious oils, the sort nobly-born ladies were likely to wear. Erejzan's strong grip was at his elbow. Tyrus also felt two smaller pairs of hands taking hold of him and forcing him to spin about.

Slowly at first, then ever more rapidly, they turned him, the women joining Erejzan in the game and laughing. When they let go of Tyrus at last, he swayed, feigning dizziness. The largest pair of those women's hands pressed tightly against his chest, supporting him, and he heard the battle maiden say in alarm, "We have been too thorough! Hetanya!"

Tyrus suppressed a grin and stammered, "Is . . . is it done? Where have I come to land? I pray you tell me. Is this Tor-Nali? Atei? Sersa-Ornail? What island of Clarique is this?"

"By gods of sea and sky, his wits *are* addled!"

"Now there will be no more show!" another specta-
tor lamented.

Tyrus did not prolong the suspense. He took a deep
breath, then knew the full success of his magic when
a babble of surprise and admiration erupted all around
him. Erejzan was making teasing comments to his left.
To his right the two women were chattering to each
other. "Look!" the dancer said with a gasp. "The funny
little dolls! And the feathers! Oh, Ja—"

"Shh! Do not call me that. Remember, you promised," came back softly.

What name had the temple dancer been about to say?
Tyrus envisioned the fur-clad woman pinching her
"cousin" as she warned her to silence. He used his
arts, unhindered by the cloth over his eyes, probing
their tempers and the outer portions of their thoughts.
The battle maiden was as caught up in Tyrus' spellcasting as her companion was. "How cunning! He cannot
see or move his hands and yet he works these wonders.
Such magic I have never witnessed before."

Heedless of the earlier warning, the temple dancer
blurted, "It must be true wizardry, Jathelle."

Tyrus expanded his senses, finding that no one had
heard that last save himself and Erejzan and the woman
called Jathelle. He treasured the information and went
on to complete his performance. When he had spun
the special trick to its limits, he murmured an incantation and the blindfold dropped from his eyes and the
thong fell off his wrists. The knots had opened mysteriously, freeing him.

Blinking, Tyrus adjusted to the bright northern sunlight, enjoying the scene in front of him. The gauzy
blindfold and the thong lay at his feet. A tiny army of
feathered puppets danced in and out between his legs
and those of the spectators. These pretty marionettes
jogged gaily, manipulated by invisible strings. Music

made by unseen instruments played them a merry tune. Coppery coins reflecting the sun danced and weaved around the dolls.

He did not allow the crowd to become bored. While their fascination still ran high, Tyrus said, "That is enough, my pets. Return whence you came." With a puff of smoke, the charming puppets disappeared and the music stopped. For a heartbeat, the audience stared in disbelief. Then they burst into cheers. Tyrus shammed dismay. "Alas! I did not mean for the little fellows to take the copper along with them. Those I meant to keep!"

The onlookers laughed at this appeal for reward. They began tossing coins and Erejzan finished his part of the entertainment by jumping and tumbling athletically, scooping up the money or leaping to pluck it from the air before it landed. Tyrus favored them with one of his gracious bows and told the spectators, "We thank you, good folk. The generosity of Couredh is well proved."

"Honest pay for good amusement," a gentleman said, his lady nodding and trading similar comments with her neighbors. "Let me know when next you put on a show. I would like to see more."

Tyrus bowed again and repeated his thanks. But he touched his forehead and said with apparent fatigue, "Conjury is tiring work. I must rest and marshal my energies against the future."

Erejzan tossed the harvest of coins between his palms. "He shall be quickly restored to strength, thanks to you. This will slake a goodly thirst and fill our bellies. Then indeed we will be ready to perform anew."

After a bit more applause, the crowd began to drift away. The young women, though, did not leave with the others. Tyrus picked up the thong and the scarf and handed them to the curious "cousins" and gave them particular thanks for their contribution to the show.

That done, he and Erejzan put their heads together, pretending to count their earnings and pointedly ignoring the women. The tactic served well. Piqued, the hoyden demanded, "I want to know how you worked that last trick, charm-weaver."

Tyrus peered around at her in seeming astonishment. "Why, battle maiden, a magician never reveals his arcane lore."

"I have seen many an amuser, but none your equal. The coin behind the ear, the pebble from a thumbnail—these illusions have I watched often. Yet you do much more, past explaining, unless you tell me."

As she spoke to Tyrus, Erejzan sauntered toward the temple dancer and eyed her closely. Like their pretended disinterest in the women, this too was a tactic. Erejzan had the easier task, for the dancer's defenses were quite inadequate. She could not match his intense stare; blushing and glancing away, she was compelled to turn back again and again. The battle maiden had spirit, however, and Tyrus knew she might shift from curiosity to anger if he handled this ill.

"I am but a simple charm-weaver," Tyrus protested. "My friend and I make our way in the world with our humble skills, hoping our audiences will be kind."

The battle maiden prowled in a circle around him, her stride long and assured. She surveyed Tyrus from head to toe. "You do not look at all simple. Nor were your conjurings of a common sort. Who are you? And where do you come from?"

Once more her rustic accent did not conceal an imperious and well-bred voice. Tyrus kept his own voice calm and level. "Your favor. This is Erejzan and I am Tyrus. We come from . . . Qamat."

"Qamat? Where is that?" She brushed back one of her loose tresses toward her hood. As she did, she disarranged the mask, not aware of this, engrossed in questioning Tyrus.

Remembered pain constricted his throat. "Qamat is far to the south beyond the Hurnbul Sea."

"One of the Arniob islands, then?" she said, brightening. "I have heard of those. That is a long journey, charm-weaver, from there to Couredh."

"A very long journey indeed."

Her eyes narrowed as she asked, "Do you flee from misadventure? Is that why you have roamed this distance?"

"We have broken no laws," Tyrus said hastily.

The temple dancer was still pinned by Erejzan's penetrating gaze. In a dreamlike tone she said, "Perhaps they are on a quest."

With a sigh, her companion chided her. "Do not be foolish. You pay too much heed to . . . to the storytellers. Quests are found in fables only. They do not concern us."

"I . . . I only meant . . ."

"We *are* on a quest," Tyrus said. Erejzan looked at him anxiously but relaxed as his friend went on, "A quest throughout Clarique, to see what can be seen and meet whom we may meet. Sometimes, however, one need not travel far at all to learn a great deal." He held out his hand and a tiny point of light appeared, hovering on his fingertips. Both women watched the glowing dot as Tyrus lulled them. "Traveling, traveling . . . far, far, and ever farther northward, meeting so many people, common folk and gentry and Sirai and their ladies, kings and queens. Can you see us as we travel and do these things? Look closely at the light . . ."

The four of them were alone in this small corner of the bazaar, lost amid the noise and bustle. No one else noticed the magical light cradled in Tyrus' fingers, because he willed it to be so. He worked this spell for a very private audience. The woman in leather was trying to resist but the dancer was as delighted as a child. "Oh, I *do* see images within the light. Islands and ships on the sea and smoking mountains and a city with flags and . . . why, now it is Couredh! It is Couredh's harbor and it is as if we were coming into the quay!"

Tyrus continued the account, his words soft and soothing. "See the bazaar and see a poor charm-weaver and an acrobat? And see two women—young and fair? One clad in frontier garb, the other veiled? The dancer hides her beauty, for truly she is so lovely all who have seen her must ever after adore her, unable to forget. She is well known and if she would go among the people and not be recognized, she must be thoroughly disguised in this way. And this battle maiden, her cousin . . . her sister . . . ?"

"Stop!" The battle maiden ground her knuckles across her eyes and jerked away, refusing to look at the light. She seized the dancer and pulled her away, too. "Release her! I command you. Release us both! You are bewitching us!"

Tyrus shut his hand into a fist, enclosing the dot of light. "Do not be alarmed, LaSirai. I never intended to affright you. These are merely ruses and illusions—a game. Forgive me, LaSirai, if I have offended."

Taken aback, less angry now, the taller woman said, "Why . . . why do you call me lady?" She tried, none too successfully, to regain her composure and assume once more that barbarian accent.

"Is the title improper? Surely you are gently reared. Your soft hands, your speech—all these betray you, LaSirai," Tyrus said with a wide smile. Behind his courtly phrases, his mind was racing, collecting scraps of rumors and information. All the bits he had learned on nearby islands and on the ship and coming through the bazaar—the puzzle nearly solved.

Still attempting to play the barbarian, she said, "If . . . if you are saying that I am nobly born . . ."

"Royally born," Tyrus corrected her. "Indeed. LaRenya. Is this not so?"

The battle maiden chuckled nervously. "You parry
and dodge well. But I think you are bluffing, charm-
weaver. You . . . you cannot know such things. If you
are a true conjurer, reveal . . . one of my secrets. I will
not tell it to you—nor will she," she admonished the
dancer. "Not a word! Not even if he brings back the
magic light. LaRenya! Bah! Such nonsense!"

"The light is not necessary," Tyrus said. He squinted
and pressed a hand to his brow. "I see the royal daughters of a king, the late king of Couredh. One lady is tall,
a princess of great courage. The other is exquisitely fair,
her mother's Irico blood giving her matchless beauty.
Within their court, these sisters are pent by rules of their
rank. And at times those rules chafe, like a prisoner's
chains, especially to the eldest sister. Would not a brief
escape lighten their burdens? I see them devising some
scheme between them, eluding lackeys and maids, dis-
guising themselves, undertaking a bold adventure. Fearing their masquerade will not be sufficient. Ah! But they
have succeeded most well, and more. A day of freedom,
unhampered by rules, enjoying the anonymity of their
pretense, mingling with the people . . ."

Tyrus abandoned his pose of foretelling, looking
directly at the battle maiden. "I see, writ in the records
of Couredh, the names of the new ruler of the realm,
LaRenya Jathelle, and her beloved sister the LaSirin
Ilissa."

Erejzan was as amazed as the women. The dancer
let out a great sigh of relief. "He knows, Jathelle. It is
at an end. I warned you we could not carry off such a
trick for very long. Oh, I am glad to be done before
something awful could happen." The princess lifted all
but the thinnest of her face veils. Tyrus had borrowed
from the tales he and Erejzan had heard. Now he saw
those few phrases had done little justice to LaSirin
Ilissa. "Beautiful" was an inadequate word. The face

seen through the diaphanous net was one to honor a goddess.

Another face, however, interested Tyrus more. LaRenya Jathelle drew aside her half-mask, impatiently dragging it down to her throat. Though not so perfect of feature as Ilissa, she was a most attractive woman. Like her sister, the inheritance of Irico mixed with Clarique, making her skin delicate, running white through her yellow hair, adding to her height. She accepted her defeat with a smile. "I think the game might have gone on a while longer if . . . How did you discover me, conjurer? I admit it. You have won fairly. I would know where my plan went amiss, though."

Tyrus and Erejzan would have knelt to the royal sisters, but LaRenya Jathelle did not permit it. She bade them continue standing and insisted on hearing how she had been identified. With mock horror, Tyrus repeated his protest. "I cannot reveal my secrets, LaRenya."

"Then am I never to know? My hands gave me away, you say?" Jathelle flexed her long, slim fingers and grimaced. "And I put off all my rings ere I left the palace, too. In vain! Next time I will besmear myself with dirt. Then we will see if any master conjurer can see past my disguise!" Ilissa took alarm at her sister's mention of a next time. Jathelle patted the younger woman's shoulder, calming her. Then she said, "You are a charming fellow, Tyrus of Qamat. You put the matter accurately: I *am* much constrained by my royal duties. I yearned for at least one day without titles and rank and responsibilities. But how did you know?"

Tyrus hesitated, buffeted by memories. Mastering these, he said again, "A magician's tricks, LaRenya."

"So much came so quickly upon me this winter, since our father went to Keth's portals," the young queen said wistfully. "When Hetanya smiled on the earth and festival began, I could not resist. I remember times when I rode on frontier campaigns beside my father—free!

On the frontier, the women wear such redolent garments as these," Jathelle said with a laugh, indicating her soiled leather tunic and breeches.

Ilissa laughed with her and Jathelle tugged playfully at one of Ilissa's white curls which had fallen below her veil. "You are shameless," Ilissa cried.

"But it was fun, was it not, little one? I promised you it would be. You have been too long locked behind walls, growing pale. Fresh air becomes you. As if you needed enhancement of your beauty!" Jathelle said, her expression doting.

Suddenly, Erejzan thrust Jathelle to one side and dived toward Ilissa. Belatedly, Tyrus saw the cause— a cutpurse was sidling near Ilissa, his knife out to sever the bindings of her small coin purse. "Your favor, La-Sirin!" Erejzan panted and vaulted past Ilissa, his hands out to seize the thief.

He had taken space to dodge aside, lest he run the startled woman down. That gave the thief warning, and the cutpurse quickly ran back into the crowd. Erejzan loped in pursuit until Tyrus hailed him back. But the disturbance inevitably drew attention. People began staring at them, and someone set up a cry for the thief-takers, pointing after the disappearing cutpurse. Others focussed on the woman in veils, shock rippling over their expressions. Men bowed and women spread their slashed, paneled skirts.

"LaSirin! It is our LaRenya and the LaSirin Ilissa! Hetanya bless them! They have come to the festival!"

Jathelle's countenance was at war with itself. She honestly enjoyed the people's adulation and responded warmly. But she was sorry to be so completely unmasked, her game now fully ended. Ilissa was shivering and holding tightly onto her purse.

Erejzan asked with concern, "Did he harm you, La-Sirin? If he did, I will find that clenru and strangle him."

Then he murmured with an embarrassed blush, "I . . . I am sorry, LaSirin. I should not have said that."

"Clenru?" Jathelle chuckled. "She has heard that blunt name before, even in the palace. Her father and I are . . . were accustomed to ride with the troops. Do not apologize. He *was* a clenru—and a whoreson, no doubt." She seemed touched by Erejzan's chagrin and his eagerness to avenge the attempted theft.

Her sister nodded, gulping. "I . . . I am all right. He did not get close enough to hurt me. Thank you, Erejzan of Qamat. I . . . you saved me from danger." Ilissa smiled, a smile that made onlookers sigh and Erejzan gape in dumbfounded awe.

Jathelle shook her head, used to this phenomenon of her sister's spellbinding beauty. It was a spectacle she obviously relished. There was no trace of jealousy in her manner. She glanced fondly at Ilissa, then turned back to Tyrus, peering up at him intently. "You amuse us and you save us from thieves. I suspect we have learned but a small part of your talents."

"Jathelle?" Ilissa hurried to her sister, clinging to Jathelle's cloak. Her smile had vanished and she looked like a child discovered in some naughtiness and dreading punishment.

"What is the matter, little one?" Jathelle took the smaller woman into the crook of her arm, trying to comfort her.

"LaRenya! My treasure . . . Ilissa! Thank the gods of Couredh we have found you at last!" Courtiers and well-armed soldiers shoved their way through the horde of spectators surrounding the queen and her sister. The nobleman leading the entourage commanded the others, snapping out the words. The soldiers formed a cordon, pushing back the people, shaping a large circle that imprisoned Tyrus and Erejzan and the two women. The nobleman who had ordered this was expensively dressed and very comely, almost effeminately so, his face clean-shaven and soft, his fair hair glistening with perfumed oils. He knelt to the royal sisters, grinding his highly polished boots in the dirt. Fervently, he kissed Ilissa's hands, like a man recovering from panic. "When . . . when we found you had left the palace alone, without any maids or attendants, we feared some terrible plot. Then the mistress of wardrobes said those clothes were missing and . . ."

"You worry too much, Aubage." Jathelle was irritable, fussing with the ties of her fur cloak and the hilts of her dagger and sword. "We were at no risk. I am armed and I know how to use a blade."

"LaRenya, I beg your favor. Hear me. Couredh has its enemies, and there are always brigands who might seek to capture you for ransom, you and my betrothed." He continued to clutch Ilissa's hands and stroke her fingers possessively.

Jathelle exclaimed hotly, "I tell you there was no danger."

Instantly, Aubage agreed, anxious to praise her, extravagantly, in fact. "No danger, surely. Omaytatle witness how everyone loves you. None would knowingly harm you. But . . . some accident might have occurred."

"Nonsense!"

Tyrus reserved judgment. He did not much care for the looks and manners of the foppish nobleman, but perhaps Aubage had spoken with wisdom. Jathelle's disguise had not been so secure as she believed. Tyrus had his arts to look past her mask, but Rof, he suspected, had also known who they were the moment he saw Jathelle and Ilissa. It would explain why the Krantin had left so precipitously. Most likely he feared that where LaRenya and LaSirin would go, soldiers and thief-takers could not be far away. A cutpurse had tried to take Ilissa's coin, not knowing her for royalty. If still rougher men had wanted to harm them, what might have happened?

Jathelle was carrying on a half-hearted debate with Aubage. It was a quarrel with only one side, for if she countered him, the Sirai changed his opinion to suit hers, yielding everything. Tyrus was glad that Jathelle did not appear fooled by such compliments and acquiescence. Ilissa, however, doted on each word and nodded at everything Aubage said.

"And what have we here?" Sirai Aubage asked, finding a target he could aim at with less caution. "Who are these vagabonds? Why are they staring? Have they shown you some insolence, my treasure? We should have them flogged to teach them respect and manners."

"The only manners wanting here are yours," Jathelle cut in. Her tone made Aubage pause and bite his lip thoughtfully.

"Do not be angry," Ilissa pleaded, interceding for the courtier. He caressed her hand as she said, "Aubage is concerned for our safety, Jathelle."

Unmollified, Jathelle retorted, "I thank him for his concern, little one. But in Couredh *I* am the judge of who offends the house of Fer-Sro and who shall be flogged to answer an insult to you or me." Her sweet-faced sister clung to Aubage, begging for peace between the queen and the nobleman. Seeing this, Jathelle relented and dismissed Aubage's interference with a shrug. "What matter, though? The game is done because of that wag-tongue of a maid. It was already done, despite my disguise, was it not, Tyrus of Qamat?"

"Your secret would have been safe with us, La-Renya . . ." he started to say.

Aubage cleared his throat loudly and talked over Tyrus' reply. "May we escort you back to the palace, LaRenya? We have brought horses and a carriage for your pleasure."

"In a while, Sirai."

Ilissa mutely warned Aubage to be patient, but he did not heed her. "Surely there is no further need to linger in this dirty bazaar, LaRenya. In your absence, messages have arrived from the outlands and Ulinia. These require your opinion, LaRenya. There are also the caravans arriving from—"

Her blue eyes sharp as ice, Jathelle snapped, "I will return to the palace when I am ready, not before. I have a conversation I will finish. You will give me leave for that, I trust, Sirai?"

The sarcasm was wasted on Aubage. He gaped at Tyrus and Erejzan. Nonplussed, he exclaimed, "With . . . with these amusers, LaRenya? But how can that be? Amusers have nothing to do with us."

"With you, no. I make my own decisions, as my father did before me." For a moment, Tyrus thought Jathelle would strike the courtier for his stubbornness. But once more she smothered her rage and fondly patted Ilissa's cheek, succumbing to the worry in those lovely eyes. In a calmer voice, she said, "Sirai Aubage, take my sister and your men some distance apart while I speak to the conjurer and his friend. I will join you soon. Leave us, now."

Mumbling under his breath, Aubage obeyed. Ilissa laid her hand on his arm and he led her a few lengths away, under the shade of the canopy. The soldiers widened their circle about the LaRenya, keeping the growing crowd at bay. The courtiers whispered together, now and then glancing wonderingly at Tyrus and Erejzan and Jathelle.

When Aubage was out of earshot, Jathelle said, "I must confess he may be right, at least for Ilissa's sake. She is poorer at games of life than I realized. It is a lack I will correct, though, with love and time. Mayhap I *did* endanger her with this wild scheme." She looked down at her stained clothes.

Tyrus read her thoughts and said, "It was a very good disguise, LaRenya. I do not think the LaSirin was in peril. I believe you do know how to handle a blade as well as Sirai Aubage. That cutpurse was fortunate Erejzan chased him off, ere you skewered him."

"Hetanya, how you jest!" Jathelle had detected the glimmer in Tyrus' gaze. But she enjoyed the sly praise. "I *could* have skewered him, whether you quite accept that or not. Some day I will prove it to you. I like you, Tyrus of Qamat. You have some wit in your compliments." She included the acrobat in her accolade. "Erejzan, your skills and bravery please me, too. You were as swift as my best bodyguards in chasing off that thief. The game was too short, but the day was enjoyable, thanks in part to you both." Jathelle took out a money pouch and tossed it to Tyrus. "It is my wish you come to the palace tonight and amuse my court. That coin will seal the bargain. There will be more after your performance."

Tyrus knew by the pouch's weight that the young queen had been very generous. Caught off guard by her sudden demand, he searched for an answer. "We . . . we had not anticipated such . . . such an honor as this, LaRenya."

To his relief, Erejzan rushed into the gap. "Your pardon and favor, but you see we have just arrived in Couredh. Tyrus fears we have little to wear that would be seemly at court."

Jathelle would not be denied. "There is enough in the purse to clothe you handsomely and more. Besides, it is not posturing and foppery I desire. I have more than enough of that from . . . certain of my courtiers. I would see further of your conjury and acrobatics. I am convinced you *have* more. You will come?"

Tyrus bowed and said, "It will be as you command, LaRenya."

"Good! Come at the sunset hour and the steward will conduct you to my hall."

The order had been given and acknowledged. The coin that would hire their talents rested in Tyrus' hand.

But Jathelle remained, gazing at the magician. Tyrus returned that gaze, wondering at the meaning of this scrutiny. His tools were magic, but LaRenya Jathelle owned a magic of her own. It was a guileless femininity. She was not coy nor did she turn her head or flutter her lashes in the manner of some women. Her interest was open and as direct as a sword thrust. She looked at him a long while and Tyrus grew disconcerted, troubled by emotions he had never known before. That enigmatic smile held him as surely as one of his enchantments could blind a helpless victim of his sorcery.

At last Jathelle turned away, saying no more. Her leather fringes flowing, she went briskly to the canopy where Ilissa waited. The pace was a regal one, proud, that of a barbarian woman—or of one confident in her rule. The soldiers and courtiers clustered about the sisters and Sirai Aubage. With Jathelle at their head, the retinue moved off, hurrying through the bazaar. Tyrus and Erejzan watched them until the women were out of sight, lost in the bustle and confusion and the bright colors of festival time.

III

"The Glass Speaks of Peril, LaRenya"

❈❈❈❈❈❈❈❈❈❈❈❈❈❈❈❈❈❈❈❈❈

SHADOWS WERE BEGINNING TO LENGTHEN AS TYRUS and Erejzan walked along streets and alleyways, always climbing, heading for the highest area of the city. It was not yet dark enough to need a torch, though honest citizens were retiring to their houses, leaving the streets to those who could afford protection or defend themselves. It was so in all the petty realms of Clarique and the friends were not surprised to find this custom true in Couredh as well.

"Are you certain this tunic fits properly?" Erejzan mumbled, fidgeting with the yarn-trimmed cuffs and collarless neck of his new garment. "It is not too gaudy? I do not want to imitate Sirai Aubage. And red is a Krantin color; perhaps I should have . . ."

"For the last time, the tunic is quite suitable. Cease your fretting." Tyrus rolled his eyes toward the darkening sky. "You look like what you are."

Erejzan froze, then galloped to catch up with Tyrus. "What do you mean? You said we dare not reveal our true purpose yet."

Sorry to have alarmed him, Tyrus gave Erejzan's shoulder a comradely squeeze. "I meant that you look

44

like a most skilled acrobat. The red tunic will please LaRenya *and* the LaSirin, I promise you."

The shorter man eyed Tyrus' new fawn-colored blouse and breeches enviously. "Do you think so? I wish I could wear garb with *your* princely air."

"I must not look like a Sirin," Tyrus muttered, uneasy. Then pride nudged him. "Still, I suppose there is no harm in dressing well when need be."

They emerged from a long patch of shadow and made a last-moment check of each other's apparel. Satisfied, they looked around to see how far they had climbed from the city's main quarter. During the hours since LaRenya and her sister had left them, the friends had wasted little time. They had explored much of the city and memorized locations of things they might need to find in less savory and shadowy areas. They had made tentative arrangements to spend the night at a clean lodging near the bazaar, once their performance was done. Tyrus had reserved the room with some of the gold Jathelle gave him, being generous. He had also been lavish in purchasing the clothes he and Erejzan now wore. He spent with a frivolous air, like an amuser with little thought of the future.

Tyrus nodded toward the end of the alleyway. "It must be . . ."

"The way to the palace," a sharp voice said. The tone was silky. Rof was lurking in a shadowy niche in a nearby wall. Several ruffians were with him. In the fading light, there was a dim shine of much metal—weapons. Rof gestured carelessly to his companions and came forward. "Have no heed of them. I have told them you are poor fare, since you have spent what LaRenya gave you. How wasteful. But then I suppose coin does not mean all that much to a sorkra."

Tyrus and Erejzan kept close watch on the bandits in the shadows. But so far the other men seemed bored by the conversation. Tyrus stared at Rof and said coldly, "I am not a sorkra, merely a charm-weaver."

"Mm. So you say."

Taking the offensive, Tyrus said in accusation, "You recognized LaRenya and the LaSirin in the bazaar this afternoon. That is why you left us so suddenly. You could have warned us."

"Bogotana! I have enough to do to guard my own skin. LaRenya Jathelle is a spirited young queen, too spirited for her own good or to forgive a bandit lord too readily. Ai, I saw through her little disguise. That *is* my calling. I have that skill and many another." Rof's men constantly peered up the alleyway and down again, plainly fearful of being caught so near to the royal residence. There were no thief-takers patrolling this lane, yet they never abandoned their guard. Rof said affably, "But I knew you would have no trouble coping with LaRenya, a clever pair of amusers like you. Nor did you!"

"You left us, but you did not go far away," Tyrus guessed.

Erejzan took up the conjecture smoothly. "You hid and watched us while we performed. Else how did you know about the purse LaRenya gave us, or that we spent it on new clothes? You have been following us."

"That is how you knew where to accost us on our way to the palace," Tyrus finished.

Rof's head swiveled back and forth as first one and then the other spoke. His men were puzzled, unable to follow the quick exchange. Rof grinned and said, "By Bogotana! I was not wrong. You *are* my sort, exactly what I need, measures above these dull-brained throat-slitters!"

"Indeed?" Tyrus was cool, very disdainful and haughty. "Perhaps, and perhaps not. You spied on us. Why? Are you here to avenge that foolish cutpurse who tried to rob LaSirin Ilissa?"

"Bogotana shrivel him. Another lackwit. Not worth the blade to end his miserable life. He is not one of mine. You should have killed him, friend handri," Rof said, taunting Erejzan for his red hair.

"I am not your friend. Nor am I a handri. That fire-hair of legend was a slave of Traecheus. No slave I," Erejzan retorted with some heat.

Rof leaned toward him, acting as if he would touch the new tunic and admire it. He laughed when Erejzan irritably fended him off. "You have a temper, handri, and the strength to go with it, eh? I can use that. And I can use you, charm-weaver. I wanted to be sure you obeyed my . . . invitation. There is no place for you at the palace. LaRenya may hire a night's amusement, but she keeps no jesters or such in her train."

"We had not intended—" Tyrus began.

"Nor will that ass Aubage employ you. M'lord has his hangers-on, but he picks them carefully. You will not suit his taste at all. Your tongues are too sharp." Rof waited for a reaction. Getting none, he went on in a cocky manner, "I might find work for you, though. When you are done conjuring and capering for the La-Renya, seek me at the Inn. It is on the street of—"

"We know where it is."

"How do you know?" Rof asked, suddenly suspicious. "You just arrived in Couredh."

"As you yourself noted, we are clever fellows. Spies," Tyrus said waggishly, laying a finger along his nose and looking sly. "We are not without our resources, as you should know, if you have been following us these past candle-marks."

In unison, without need of saying what they were going to do, Tyrus and Erejzan stepped back and away from Rof and his men. Clear of their weapons, they moved out of reach and up the alleyway. "Enough of this, lord of brigands. It is unwise to keep a queen waiting, when she is a queen with too much spirit for her own good, as you claim."

"The Inn of the Cutpurses!" Rof shouted, startled and annoyed by their deft maneuver. His men grumbled and Tyrus heard knives drawn. But no one came after them. "Be there," Rof said, his words bouncing between the damp wallstones.

Tyrus and Erejzan climbed over huddled beggars, street dwellers, and slinking curs. These walkers-of-the-night were napping amid the slops and dirt, complaining when the friends disturbed their uncomfortable rest. Only when they rounded the corner at the far end of the alley did Tyrus and Erejzan peer back at the niche in the wall below. In the fire of a freshly-lit torch from an upper storey tavern, they could see the brigands clustering around Rof. The men were talking uneasily, now and then glancing in the direction the amusers had gone. However, they made no move to pursue Rof's acquaintances.

A trifle reassured, Tyrus and Erejzan went up a snaking line of steps and out onto a cobblestoned plaza. Ahead stood the whitewashed walls and outer gates of the palace. Walking more slowly now, they approached the barricade. The palace abutted—or was part of—a fort, where army aides and messengers came and went upon the realm's business. The palace did not bristle with barred gates and crenellations and steep walls, but it was still an imposing structure. Soldiers patrolled the walls and gates. They did not seem hostile, though, to the men nearing their post.

Erejzan looked over his shoulder, once more checking to see if they were followed. "I do not trust that scar-faced clenru."

"Rof? Nor do I."

"I should have lessoned him, when he called me a handri," the acrobat grumbled. Then he bit his lip. "Is it possible he can help us? If he has journeyed as far as Couredh's outcountry and the legendary Ice Forest . . ."

"Has he? Or does he copy the gossip of other outlaws? His mind is difficult to probe, as muddy as a silt-clogged stream. Such a masterful liar can deceive himself—and *me*—when I search his thoughts." Tyrus added grimly, "He might also be one of Vraduir's tools, knowingly or not. His order for us to come to the Inn could be a ruse to lure us to death.

"He may already have found powers beyond most wizards' arts. That is why he undertook this blasphemous path. There is something else, mai fiyel. Some . . . force. I cannot describe it. We must take care." They were close to the gates then, and Tyrus donned his amuser's guise. "Ah! Good even! We have come to serve the royal pleasure. Pray let us in, bold troopmen!"

The guards were young and green at their duties. Nervously, they looked behind them and sighed as the sergeant of the post walked out of his watch house. Happy to turn inspection of strangers over to him, the recruits stood to attention, eyeing Tyrus and Erejzan sidelong. The veteran sergeant said, "So you are the amusers I was told to watch for, eh? You, troopman, go fetch the steward and be quick. Come inside, amusers. It gets damp early this soon in the festival season."

While his underling ran to get the steward, the sergeant led Tyrus and Erejzan through the gates. The plaza had been twilit but the palace halls were quite dark. Menials were setting torches to illuminate the corridors and courtyards. The sergeant limped around the obstructions, cuffing servants who got in his way, muttering, "Amusers. Frippery. None of this in my day. We ate stale bread and glad to get it, and no amusements for us, out on the frontiers. By Soronos and his moon mares. Waste of LeRenya's good coin to hire 'em." Tyrus and Erejzan tolerated his mumbling in silence and winked at each other behind his back.

The steward met them at the far side of an entry yard. He was a little man much filled with his own importance. He wore a robe far too long for him, the sleeves turned back to the elbows lest they cover his hands. He sniffed at Tyrus and Erejzan, then crooked a finger.

"Mind your manners now," the sergeant cautioned them as they followed the steward into a series of shadowed passageways. They noticed that the steward's hem dragged by a hand's width. Erejzan teased at the temptation of stepping on that hem and Tyrus shook his head, grinning.

The palace had been constructed some generations earlier with a good thought to defense. Tyrus approved the sharp turns and narrow doorways along the passage and idly mused how he would position troops to bar the way. Once Tyrus and the soldiers of his island had blocked access to a Qamat bastion by just such methods, fighting off an invading band of pirates. He knew those tactics, as he knew how to steer a ship, arts he had been taught since he was a boy—those arts, and deeper ones. Past rulers of Couredh had known battle, too, and had sheathed wall timbers of hard Irico wood in iron and native stone and stepped and staggered the corridors for better defense. Tyrus imagined Jathelle, the battle maiden, daring any challenger to intrude upon her palace. He smiled, sure none who had wisdom would accept that dare.

The passageway split, and the steward took the right fork. A group of soldiers passed the other way along the main branch. Their leader was an older man, strong-looking, the queen's warlord, from appearances and the way the steward and his aides gave him room and respect. As he went on by, Tyrus whispered to Erejzan, "That hall for those of rank. We amusers take the menials' route."

True to his guess, the narrower hall led through the

kitchens. A walkway spanned the pit where ovens and open fires produced much heat. Aromas of roast wool-back and motge haunch and fish stew and cobbled fruit rose from where the cooks and scullions were working. Erejzan sniffed and looked longingly at the food as they hurried to the ready rooms beyond. These chambers all interconnected, with steps leading up from one to the next. Each successive room was cooler and tidier than the one below. The lowliest kitchen helpers gave way to liveried waiters. Food moved up from the kitchens, and emptied platters and salvers were carried down to be washed. In the last room, a low archway gave onto a royal chamber just beyond. A hum of busy conversation filled the ready room. Stacks of dirty plates and empty wine bottles sat on the side tables. A stout matron oversaw all, preventing collisions and making sense of the scene.

"Wait here," the steward said. He glanced at the heaps of half-eaten food, apparently having seen Erejzan's greedy stares when they passed the kitchens. "I charge you—I will not tolerate pilfering or gluttony."

"The farthest thing from our hearts," Tyrus said.

"An oath written in Rorsa's rain," the steward retorted with a scornful glare. "When your services are required, I will summon you." He swept on through the archway, plucking up his robe and mincing to avoid tripping himself.

The matron supervising the servants aped him and whined, "When your services are required . . ." Then she shifted to a far earthier manner. "Services! Be certain no real woman would require *yours,* you mewling lap dog. Sirai Aubage's toadying lap dog, that is what you are. Fah!"

The servitors chuckled and urged her to more mimicry. But she had lost enthusiasm for that, turning to Tyrus and Erejzan and brightening. "Amusers, ai? I am Ceshti, and I am mistress here. Pay no attention to the steward. Are you hungry? Help yourselves from any of these trays, good lads."

There was not that much difference in their ages, but she appeared to enjoy that term for them. Tyrus bowed and made her giggle and blush when he kissed her hand as if she were a lady. "Our thanks, Mistress Ceshti. You are as generous as you are wise." He took a piece of coarse bread as a sop and collected fish broth and steamed grain swimming about in a platter of leftover mutton sauce. Erejzan had already selected a meaty motge rib from another plate. The acrobat perched on a stone shelf near the archway. He sat crosslegged and gnawed at the bone, taking care not to drip fat on his new tunic.

Through the archway, Tyrus and Erejzan saw the court dining in far more elegant surroundings. Two smoky candle lanterns were the only lights in the ready room. But the large chamber beyond glowed in the radiance of tens of costly tapers. The area around the royal dais was particularly well lit. Three people sat there— Jathelle and her sister and Sirai Aubage. The nobleman was to the queen's right and Ilissa to her favored side. Ilissa's exquisite face was no longer veiled and her snow-cloud hair was spread free over her bare shoulders. She laughed shyly as Aubage plied her and Jathelle with compliments. Aubage rivaled the women in the splendor of his garb. Gems covered his hands and earlobes; his tunic glittered with more jewels; and his cloak was trimmed in Couredh's fabled grir fur.

Tyrus' gaze locked on the third figure at that table— Jathelle. Was this the same battle maiden who had gibed and questioned him in the bazaar? Gone were the leathers and wolves' teeth. Jathelle now wore a gown of Clarique green; her hair was elaborately braided and curled and a golden tiara rested on her fair head. Gracious and regal, she reigned over her ladies and courtiers, drawing them into her conversations. That courage

Tyrus admired when he first met her he now saw tempered charmingly with lovely manners.

Mistress Ceshti reigned over a smaller and cozier realm. One of the waiters had eyed Tyrus and Erejzan and had whispered to the matron. She perked up and said, "Is it so? You are the charm-weaver and the acrobat who found the sisters in that fanciful disguise?" Tyrus and Erejzan acknowledged this and Ceshti flapped her apron, chuckling. "Then it really *did* happen. Hai! Such a bold she-wolfing, our LaRenya. But the poor princess! The LaSirin must have been frightened. She is such a delicate little thing..."

An old butler was leaning against a wall, half dozing. He came awake and said, "Why, never so. Born in a tent, the LaSirin was, and rode before she could walk. I remember it very well. I served the Renya when he conquered the frontiers, I did, with the LaSirin fighting by his side. What glorious days those were."

"She is no longer LaSirin but LaRenya, you dotard," Ceshti scolded him. "You are living in your memories."

He did not hear her, continuing to reminisce, his eyes moist. "Saw it all. When I was in my prime, a few years past. The Renya himself, on the line of blood in those terrible battles with the barbarians and woods-dwellers, driving the Skull Breakers themselves back into their cruel forest. And the pretty little princess, as brave as any lad, there with him, while LaRenya ruled the city..."

"And she was rearing a *second* pretty LaSirin," Ceshti cut in. She looked pityingly at the butler, then explained to Tyrus and Erejzan, "He does not realize. The Renya and his lady have gone to Keth's gates. He thinks he sees our late queen reborn in LaRenya Jathelle."

"Perhaps the gods give him the farseeing," Tyrus said piously. "Indeed. The daughter may well re-create the courage and beauty of her noble mother."

"Just so! How well you have told it, charm-weaver!"

The steward rushed in and began pushing roughly at the waiters. "More wine for my Sirai Aubage and his lady. Quickly!"

When he had gone out again, trailed by the annoyed waiters, Ceshti grimaced and said, " 'My Sirai Aubage and his lady'! How dare he speak so familiarly of La-Sirin Ilissa? She is betrothed to Aubage but not yet wived."

Erejzan lost interest in his food, tossing the still-meaty bone back onto a platter. "Her betrothed," he said morosely. "I thought perhaps he merely boasted that, when he said so in the bazaar. Is he . . . is he one of these Rasil-yan who keep many wives?"

Ceshti nodded, confirming the acrobat's suspicion. He was not happy at any of this news. Nor was Ceshti. She pouted and said contemptuously, "He is a border-man, and the least of his household at that. Bah! To hear the steward talk of him, Aubage is near being a Renya himself. But do not be fooled, amusers. Aubage is none of that."

"A youngest son," Tyrus said tonelessly. He gazed through the archway at Jathelle and those at her royal table, speculating.

"Ai!" Mistress Ceshti seemed amazed that he had fathomed that about the foppish courtier. She lowered her voice like a conspirator. "If you ask his kin-brothers as to his worth, they will make no hesitation. A youngest son indeed! And the kin-brothers of Huil-Couredh on the border keep numerous wives and have no land left to give a last son such as Sirai Aubage. He makes up with strutting and pretty clothes and speech what he lacks in land. I think that is why his kin-brothers sent him to LaRenya's court, to make his fortune away from their estates." Ceshti heaved a heartfelt sigh. "And now we must put up with him and his pack of toadying servants, like that milk-lapper of a steward!"

"But the steward is LaRenya's hireman, is he not?" Tyrus wondered. He lifted a fair eyebrow, curious at this arrangement. "LaRenya does not seem the sort to be gulled by such a simpering dolt."

"She is not!"

"Then why . . . ?" Erejzan said.

"Why?" Ceshti exclaimed. "Iesor-Peluva always shine warmly upon you, my firehair! Because of LaSirin Ilissa, of course." When Tyrus and Erejzan looked at her without understanding, the matron went on impatiently, "LaSirin adores Aubage. He won her heart the first ten-day he was here, during LaRenya's coronation. Oh, Aubage wasted no time pressing his suit, you may be sure! Spun LaSirin's head with his pretty words. He is good with words, always telling her fanciful tales of heroes and quests and talking as if *he* were as brave as the men in the stories. Bah!"

"And LaRenya dotes on Ilissa," Tyrus said, again studying the three people seated at the royal dais.

Chuckling bitterly, Ceshti said, "As Ilissa dotes on M'Lord Aubage." The kitchen supervisor used the same scathing inflection of "M'Lord" that Rof the bandit had, in referring to Aubage. Apparently that was a familiar epithet in Couredh for the courtier from the border lands, one that said much about Aubage's reputation among the common folk. "LaRenya can deny her little sister nothing. How could anyone with a soul, eh? Ilissa was so sickly throughout her childhood, you know. We never hoped she would come into her courses or live to woman's time. But now she is well, a flower blooming all the sweeter for those seasons when she was so weak. Hetanya be praised! And LaRenya is so happy at this that she would give LaSirin the world, if she could. Ah! Thanks to Aubage's soft manners, our princess wants *him*, though! Willing to be that border-man's first wife . . ."

"To be but one of several, the greedy man," Erejzan muttered.

Troubled by his friend's mood, Tyrus said quickly, "And the steward is one of Aubage's people. Aubage found a sinecure for him."

"Just so, amuser. When the late Renya's steward died, Aubage promptly wheedled the position for that fool," Ceshti agreed.

"It is a common practice at many a court," Tyrus remarked.

"Ai! But if not for Aubage and his flattering tongue, it would never have happened at Couredh," Ceshti insisted.

Artfully, Tyrus and Erejzan steered the gossip to other waters. They continued to seek out stories about missing peasants or trouble in the north or tales of the stolen treasures of Clarique's isles. The servitors told them little more than they had learned elsewhere, though. Inevitably, the talk drifted back to subjects dear to the servants' minds—the festival which had brought the lords and ladies of LaRenya's court here from their many scattered estates, the plans for further events in the on-going celebration, and the annual ritual at Summer's Height, a moon's time distant.

Waiters staggered in from the dining chamber, setting down picked-over plates and bowls. One man sighed and said, "We will have more work on the morrow. Mark me, *I* will be one of those chosen to load the wagons and serve the meal when they go hawking at Drita Meadows."

A chill of apprehension snaked along Tyrus' belly. "Hawking? Where do LaRenya and her court go to hunt?"

"To her royal lands, north of here," a kitchen wench said. "How I wish I could go instead of staying here and scouring kettles. LaRenya and LaSirin will look so

pretty in their festival clothes. All the grand Sirai and
LaSirai and the fine horses and the falcons . . . ah!"

Tyrus hoped his deep, growing concern was not obvious. He could not help asking, "Is it safe for LaRenya
to travel that far north? Are not her royal lands some
five measures out of the city? We heard dark rumors in
the marketplace."

Ceshti reached up and gave his beard a maternal,
teasing yank. "No fear. You were thinking of the butler's talk of barbarians and Skull Breakers, ai? They are
many measures distant from LaRenya's meadows. Besides, her bodyguards will accompany the court. It is
just an outing, part of Hetanya's spring greeting."

The steward ran back into the ready room. He fluttered his hands and squeaked in his excitement. "Hurry,
amusers! It is time. Come, come!"

Tyrus and Erejzan straightened their attire, preparing
to follow him, when a waiter grumbled to no one in particular, "All this fuss because of Aubage. The Sirai
wants to show off his new brace of hawks . . ."

"Hush!" Ceshti warned. Yet she went on to say, "It's
not the hawks he wants to show off, but himself. And
not for the sake of LaSirin Ilissa, either, I vow. By
Hetanya's sweet earth, I swear it is LaRenya he *really*
covets, and her title."

"Hurry!" the steward cried. He waited beyond the
arch, jittering with impatience. Tyrus and Erejzan dared
not linger. Nursing the final bits of gossip they had
heard, they ducked under the stone arch and went out
into the royal dining chamber, marching past several
smartly-dressed bodyguards.

By now the queen and her entourage had finished
eating. They had left the tables and were sitting in a
half-circle of chairs, listening to a troupe of musicians.
These tunes of northern Clarique were alien but pleasing
to Tyrus. The soft jingling of bells and a themshang's

glimmering took hold of his mind, however, carrying him into time past, to an ugly memory.

Atei. A green and fruitful island, the gem on the western edge of the Qlitos Sea. Autumn, two seasons ago, a landfall after a rough crossing from Tor-Nali. Searching, tracking Vraduir's scent and the tales of a strange, enchanted ship that sailed Clarique's oceans and inlets, doing Vraduir's evil work. Atei. The island was in an uproar when Tyrus and Erejzan landed, so much so they had been forced to play the amusers most carefully, for soldiery and merchants' guards, questioned everyone, merciless in their panic. The people mourned and begged their priests for some omen or explanation. The minstrel, the fabled harper of Atei was gone! Mysteriously vanished, nowhere to be found. He was the realm's delight and Atei's pride. No one could imagine how he had been taken. His servants were found the next morning, their wits forever shattered. There were no signs of struggle, only the wild stories of that alien ship and its silent crew in some hidden cove along Atei's coast. The harper, like many another treasure of Clarique, had disappeared, it seemed, from the world.

Yet Tyrus had found a trail the soldiers could not, for he walked paths unknown to most mortals. Amid Atei's lamenting and uproar, he and Erejzan followed their quarry and took ship north again toward Sersa-Ornail, risking a winter trapped in the ice of that cold region. The trail of the harper, like all the other trails they had followed, aimed for the edge of the unknown. To Couredh, eventually, and beyond.

Where was the harper? And where was the great red stallion of Tor-Nali island, the pet of the warlord, the divine beast who dwelled in Gros-Donaq's own sacred grove? And where was the priceless silver net of the man-fish, the ages-old heritage worshipped by the people of Bendine? Maitu's tapestries? The Hetanya

crown famed ŏn Sersa-Ornail's mountain temple? Each
was beyond value, and each one had been stolen during the past year. Gone!

The music had become an eerie twinkling sound
as Tyrus' mind carried him backwards. Then, all at
once, he felt a terrible, arcane pressure. He missed a
step, his senses reeling. Hastily, he tightened a spell
about himself and Erejzan, reaching into places filled
with unearthly colors and peopled with beings of smoke
and air. Tyrus borrowed rapidly from that sorcerous
fount, blurring his identity and Erejzan's, wrapping
them in obscurity lest the hunters become the hunted.
The hostile wizardry thrusting at Tyrus was tricked,
turning away . . .

Vraduir! To be so powerful, his magic so strong,
he must be very near, as sorkra counted space. The
trail was hot and fresh at last!

There was something else, though, something new
and terrifying, a force Tyrus had felt earlier, now renewed and intensified. A coldness, past his ability to
describe, cold and dark and awful. He shivered at the
icy contact, his marrow shrinking.

Erejzan pressed his arm, calling him back to the
world of light and humankind. It took considerable
effort for Tyrus to put away his numbing fear of that
cold presence. What was it? And there was Vraduir to
contend with as well! He must not forget that, ever!
Tyrus tied final knots of a protective spell about himself and his friend, then nodded reassuringly at Erejzan.

The musicians had finished their performance and
were leaving the ring of candlelight as polite applause
praised their tune-making. The steward led Tyrus and
Erejzan into the vacant circle and began a rambling in-
troduction with many asides to flatter his patron,
Aubage, and the royal sisters. As the little man prated,
Tyrus took the leisure to look around the chamber.

Cunningly-wrought hangings covered the stone and timber walls, and fixtures set with many candles dangled from the ceiling beams. Gilt was everywhere, the harvest of Couredh's gold-rich streams. Many furnishings were imported from other realms and provinces of Tyta'an, some at considerable cost. Though Couredh was a petty kingdom compared to the larger islands or the holdings of Krantin's lords of the Interior, LaRenya Jathelle and her forebears had made a handsome palace here and ruled a prosperous people. There was even a thick carpet to cushion Tyrus' feet, a creation of Couredh's skilled fleece artisans and their best dye masters. Tyrus smiled inwardly at the thought of what such a springy surface would do to help Erejzan's acrobatics.

Jathelle squirmed in her chair, tiring of the steward's flat-toned fawning. "That is enough," she said, dismissing him with a curt wave. Like a fish cast on shore, the steward opened and closed his mouth pathetically. He glanced pleadingly at Sirai Aubage, but the courtier was busy whispering to LaSirin Ilissa, ignoring his toady. Abandoned by his sponsor, the steward withdrew with poor grace, slinking toward the ready room.

"Sirai and LaSirai," Jathelle said, and those who had continued to talk during the steward's speech now fell quiet and attended the queen most respectfully. "I present a special delight to you: Tyrus and Erejzan, from Qamat, a realm beyond the Arniob isles. They perform marvels. I can attest to that, and now you shall, too."

"I am sure we will, LaRenya," Aubage put in. "No monarch has such an eye for cleverness nor beauty of manner."

She raised a pale, winged eyebrow, smiling wryly. Then she preceded to describe briefly her encounter with Tyrus and Erejzan in the bazaar. Slashing to the gist of the adventure, she hid nothing, unabashed when her

ladies and noblemen gasped at such things. "And now,
you will see why Ilissa and I were so impressed with
these amusers. Confound us, men of Qamat, as you
promised you would!"

Aubage had placed his armchair so that he was
upon Ilissa's left and now he leaned close and whispered
amorously to her. Jathelle frowned and stopped this
intimate discussion, lightly touching her sister's hand
to draw her mind back to the performance. Ilissa
reacted with a blushing apology, looking expectantly toward Tyrus and Erejzan. Aubage too adopted an interested manner, though much less convincingly than
his betrothed.

Tyrus and Erejzan began by repeating many of the
tricks they had demonstrated that afternoon. As Tyrus
anticipated, the plush carpet gave impetus to Erejzan's
feats and softened his dangerous landings. The candle
glow lent a helpful, flattering light to Tyrus' simplest
illusions. The court was as pleased and mystified by
Erejzan's death-defying leaps and Tyrus' magicks as the
gentry and commoners had been. Since Jathelle and
Ilissa had seen these things before, they enjoyed a
certain superiority and could predict what astonishment
would happen next. In fact, Tyrus and Erejzan had
planned matters so, a way of pleasing those who had
hired them, a familiar business with street entertainers.
They played the roles of amusers with sly skill. Like the
common folk, a few of Jathelle's courtiers feigned
boredom at first, then succumbed to the fascination of
conjury and wild acrobatics. Pretended disinterest disappeared. The audience was theirs.

After each trick or stunt, Tyrus and Erejzan solicited
approval, though more politely than they would have
in a street performance. As the ladies and noblemen
clapped, they listened to their comments and decided
which way to turn the next part of the show. They
especially strove to entertain the royal sisters. When-

ever Jathelle's sharp features brightened, Tyrus found himself working to outdo previous deceptions. And he noticed Erejzan reserving his most spectacular leaps for those times when he was directly in front of Ilissa.

"A fine pair of amusers!" courtiers were shouting.

"Did not LaRenya say they would be something to see?"

"I have never seen that trick before, that one with the rope."

Subtly, the two friends shifted the thrust of their performance. Erejzan's incredible strength and agility enabled him to essay ever more risky feats when most tumblers would long since have dropped in exhaustion. Tyrus aided his friend, giving Erejzan brief chances to rest and incorporating him into his magic simultaneously. His body rigid and seemingly without feeling, Erejzan hovered between two benches as Tyrus enchanted him, then climbed onto the acrobat, standing his full weight upon him. A while later, he made the acrobat float in mid-air and wove meshes of illusionary gold and silver and gems completely around Erejzan. His energies renewed by these bits of leisure, Erejzan resumed his perilous stunts, jumping ever higher and farther, taking great risk.

Tyrus should have cautioned him, but he sensed part of what drove Erejzan to such bravado. His own feelings were tangled. He himself had used many magicks that invited suspicion—true sorkra conjury, not mere charm-weaving. Erejzan strutted and dared his life to catch Ilissa's eye. And whenever Aubage bent his flattery in Jathelle's direction, Tyrus wanted to attract her away and put the lord in darkness. This was a new sensation for him, a troubling one. Since his quest had begun, he had not let lures of the flesh distract him. Now LaRenya Jathelle, without any apparent guile, was captivating him when jades and harlots and even flirtatious well-born women had not. He was irked by this weakness in himself, but relished the experience also.

He could *not* let this go on! His head must be clear, his will free from any bondage but the hunt for Vraduir!

"I have never seen their like," courtiers were saying. From the archway, Ceshti and the waiters were watching and enjoying the show, too. Why could Tyrus not be content with so much success, he asked himself.

Then one of Jathelle's noble ladies said, "This will give us something to talk about when we ride up to the Meadows on the morrow."

His heart thundered, blood surging up his throat like a fever within him. Tyrus extended his powers, again touching that evil presence he had felt earlier. Vraduir was still somewhere close. Northward! The rumors of peasants, the stories about hidden coves— too much danger and much too near to Couredh's city and to Jathelle! This hawking expedition would take Jathelle and her sister out of the city walls and north, into the open. Somehow, he had to stop them. No place was safe while Vraduir was alive, but Jathelle must not court his attention in this way.

"More magic," Jathelle begged. "Erejzan, more of your gifts, please!"

"Qlitos' keen winds and Wyolak's holy lightnings are in my limbs and veins to delight you, LaRenya," Erejzan boasted, grinning at his own words to show he did not take them too seriously. His smile was aimed mostly at Ilissa.

"More magic there shall be," Tyrus said suddenly. Perhaps there *was* a way to warn the sisters, to frighten Jathelle into giving up the hawking expedition! Yet he must work this gingerly, or his true calling might be learned.

He reached inside his tunic to that small packet he wore always bound close to his heart. He drew it forth and carefully unwrapped the strip of Bendine silk from a diamond-shaped object. Its black surface caught the tapers' light and reflected it blindingly for a moment.

Erejzan's matchless balance failed him for once. He saw what Tyrus was holding and stiffened with shock. Too tense, he landed badly from one of his leaps, almost sprawling his length on the carpet. Women shrieked and noblemen reached out with an instinctive urge to catch him, though they were seated too far from him to help. Erejzan took several running steps and flailed wildly, awkwardly regaining his feet. After a gulp or two, he struck a prideful pose and acted as if the mishap were but a ruse to create suspense. Nervous laughter filled the royal chamber, then loud applause.

Amid the clamor, Erejzan spoke from the corner of his mouth. "What are you doing? Have you gone mad, Tyrus?"

"My wits are my own, mai fiyel."

"But if Vraduir is using *his* vision-glass . . ."

"I must do this. Trust me, and follow where I lead." Erejzan's eyes were green circles shining with fear. But he nodded and Tyrus raised his voice and announced, "Most Gracious LaRenya, Most Beauteous LaSirin, lords and ladies of Couredh—a new wonderment now! I show you here a magic glass, a tool of conjury, rare and most costly . . ."

"Worth your very life," Erejzan muttered unhappily.

No one heard him. Jathelle leaned forward, her breath quickening. "Tell us of the magic glass, charmweaver. More marvels!"

Tyrus lifted the vision-glass above his head. "Here is a glass which can give me the farseeing, LaRenya." Erejzan frowned but held his tongue. He was as curious as the nobility, wondering where Tyrus was taking them all. Using that sonorous, theatrical tone he had practiced so often this past year, Tyrus said, "I shall bring forth the denizens of the magic glass and they will reveal to us what may come to pass. Behold!"

Dipping into his storehouse of illusions, Tyrus created a fiery nimbus and framed himself and Erejzan. This dramatic effect added to the crowd's babbling excitement. Women shivered and clung to their lords, as Ilissa did to Aubage. Only Jathelle scorned such protection, eager to see the magic.

Reaching still deeper, Tyrus wandered shaded groves of alien trees and moved into echoing cells, selecting what he must have. He concentrated and held his breath, focussing the will in his mind. Three shriveled hags popped from the surface of the vision-glass, miniature beings who grew in an instant to full human forms. They writhed like smoke for a bit, their shapes distorted, then alighted on the carpet directly before Jathelle. They pranced and curtsied and began to sing shrilly.

"A darkness gathers in the north, where tales of vanished peoples run!"

A second beldame howled, "In ancient times, 'twas ever said, the Death God's icy kingdom shun!"

They stabbed their bony fingers at the courtiers and ladies. "Bide fast and live here long and well, far from the Death God's frozen breath!" In harsh-voiced unison they swung upon Jathelle and cackled, "Dwell safe within your subjects' love. The north, O Queen, the north is death!"

They joined hands and scampered in a ragged circle. The wavering red glow Tyrus had made cast an eerie power over the scene, enthralling Jathelle and her entourage. A few of the noblemen murmured uncertainly, "The north? It is so! But far beyond Couredh's realm. What can this portent mean?"

Jathelle silenced them, her eyes bright. "It is a cunning show. Heed them! They are ready to make us quake and tremble again!"

The hags finished their strange dance and chanted, "Couredh is strong in her Queen's love and shall her loyal province be. Abide here in Couredh, good Queen, abide in peace and in safety."

Tyrus saw his own creations through a hazy film. Sweat trickled down his face and beard and made his tunic stick fast to his back. Holding the vision-glass so tightly that his fingers hurt against the sharp edges, he braced himself to feel Vraduir's descending wrath at any pulsebeat. With his most skillful art, he willed the hags back into regions of darkness and occult things.

As they melted, he brought forth in their place giggling imps and an elfin being that looked to have stepped from a storyteller's fables. These pretty illusions sang more sweetly to Jathelle, but their message was the same. In dulcet notes, they warned the queen of Couredh, promising that she would only be secure if she remained within the city. This time Tyrus bade his puppets tell more, speaking of the hawking expedition and advising the LaRenya, through these imps, to abandon the outing. Tyrus cloaked this in verse and song, dressing the sharp words with poetic references. He chose Summer's Height, yet several ten-days distant, as a time when most likely it would be safe for Jathelle to venture forth from the city. Safe then, or it never would be.

He returned the elf and imps to the vision-glass. Erejzan was watching him narrowly, the only person who realized how very much Tyrus was gambling. Yet Tyrus could not let matters go. He felt compelled to give one final warning.

"The glass speaks of peril, LaRenya," he said. "We must hear now from another, a most venerable sage, a man gifted with the farseeing."

Tyrus gave existence to a rheumy-eyed elder in

golden robes, carrying a staff. How well Tyrus remembered this gentle being who once had kept a holy vigil upon the slope of Qamat's smoking mountain. He remembered, too, the old man's prophecy, foretelling his own terrible death and the disaster that would soon befall his people. He had seen true, promising a tragedy that would make his small world Vraduir's victim.

Silently, Tyrus begged forgiveness for using him so. He did not think the holy man would begrudge his image and voice in this good cause. The illusion addressed Jathelle and Ilissa. "Long years to you and your realm Couredh, northernmost jewel in Clarique's crown." So real was he that the court heard his staff creak when he propped his chin upon it. The sage went on, "Hear me, LaRenya. There are omens writ in sky and frozen wastelands. I counsel patience. Await a better moment to travel from Couredh, till restless fortune be at peace. By Summer's Height, all will be well, danger fled. Till then, beware the dark clouds in the north . . . beware . . . beware . . . beware . . ." His words echoed, fading, as the figure itself melted into nothing.

Tyrus hastily wrapped the vision-glass in the silk and returned it to its secret pocket against his breast. To his great relief, he had detected no intrusion of evil wizardry while he worked the spell, no indication that another sorkra knew he had conjured with the glass. He had won, for now!

The red glow dissipated and he and Erejzan stood in candlelight again. Tyrus had not realized he was unsteady on his feet till Erejzan's arm closed around him, keeping him from swaying. He licked his dry lips and said weakly, "It . . . it is all right, mai fiyel. I am done, and we are still safely hidden."

"This time."

A stunned silence had held the court a long moment. Then there was a collective gasp and a swelling tumult of applause. Ladies waved fans of whantola feathers and noblemen tipped their caps to the magician and the acrobat. While the illusions had been before them, they had been genuinely afraid. When those were whisked out of sight and sound, merriment ruled. To Tyrus' dismay, Jathelle and her court regarded the frightful apparitions as part of the evening's entertainment, no more.

"That gave us a delicious shiver!" Jathelle exclaimed, to a chorus of assent. "A masterful show, men of Qamat!"

Tyrus wanted desperately to contradict her and say that the illusions warned of real danger. But he could not. His ruse had been too successful, as was his chosen disguise. He was trapped, with no easy way out. The only hope remained that he had planted a seed of doubt in Jathelle's thoughts. More he dared not try.

LaRenya Jathelle rose and came toward him. Her smile was warm and again she would not permit them to make an obeisance to her. "I am very content and the bargain was fairly made," she said. Jathelle summoned a page, who brought her a purse stitched with silver thread. The purse was worth much in itself and plainly it was weighted with considerable coin. She held out the reward to Tyrus. "To show our thanks, here is my part of the bargain, and willingly given."

Dejected by his failure to convince her, Tyrus made no move, his limbs numb. Erejzan hesitated, then took the purse in his stead, murmuring his gratitude for them both.

Jathelle was a trifle puzzled. She mistook the reason for Tyrus' lethargy. "Be of good cheer. Truly, it was a fine performance. The best conjury ever seen in Couredh."

Tyrus cleared his throat and managed to say, "Perhaps . . . perhaps not all of it was performance, La-

Renya." Erejzan sucked in his breath, but his worries were allayed when Tyrus added, "But we have done our best. We can do no more. If the gods will it, may we serve you as well another time, LaRenya."

"If the gods will it," Jathelle agreed with a pious gesture. She was anxious to assure Tyrus he had been very well received, still fretting over his somber countenance. "Couredh is a tiny realm, I know. You must have journeyed to many a finer palace and grander dominion. Yet I would make of my little land a haven of beauty and peace that welcomes the people of all provinces, all riches of the earth and the mind. I hope you will stay in Couredh and adorn us with your skills. With such amusers, we are become equals to the sophisticated courts of Laril-Quil or Walis, or may even match the silver-clad castles of Krantin."

"You are most kind to ask us, LaRenya. We will consider it, indeed."

Social custom had been satisfied. The promised payment was made and received with thanks. Politenesses had been traded. This was also part of the role of an amuser, one Tyrus and Erejzan had enacted in other cities. They were hirelings, and their services were no longer needed. Inclining their heads courteously to LaRenya and her court, they retreated from the ring of candlelight. Jathelle honored them by continuing to face them as they left her presence, rather than turning back to her companions. Ilissa was also watching Tyrus and Erejzan depart, her expression wistful.

The steward was sulking in the archway to the ready room. With a sniff, he said that Tyrus and Erejzan could find their own way out of the palace, shook his finger, and bade them not steal any plate or tapestry along the way. That unnecessary admonishment made Tyrus smile, and Erejzan deftly tossed the fat purse and jangled the coins triumphantly, annoying the little steward further.

Most of the waiters and other servitors had gone back to the kitchens and their own quarters. Ceshti and a few wenches and boys were sweeping up scraps. As Tyrus and Erejzan retraced their steps through the descending halls to the kitchens, Ceshti and her subordinates praised their performance—more compliments they gave back with thanks.

Tyrus suspected the steward had hoped they would be confused by the twisting passageways and get into trouble or lost. But he and Erejzan were no strangers to palaces and bastions. They moved unerringly out through the corridors and courtyards, aware of scrutiny from bodyguards and sentinels along the way. At the gates, the sentinels gave them a cursory inspection. The old sergeant of the post identified them as the amusers and grumpily asked if they were done for the night. He barely heard their reply, jerking a thumb and sending them on out into the cobblestoned plaza beyond the gates. In a few paces, they were under the stars, enveloped by the cool, misty night of a northern summer.

IV

Rof of the Brigands

⊰⊱⊰⊱⊰⊱⊰⊱⊰⊱⊰⊱⊰⊱⊰⊱⊰⊱⊰⊱⊰⊱⊰⊱

NOT UNTIL THEY ENTERED A DARK STREET AT THE FAR side of the plaza did Erejzan growl, "What were you hoping to accomplish with the vision-glass?"

"Not yet. Be still. Someone might overhear us." Tyrus groped his way along a slime-wet wall to his left. He could have conjured a light to show the way but feared this would attract undue attention.

"There is no one here." Tyrus stared into the blackness toward Erejzan's voice. "Vraduir's curse is sometimes a help. You know I can see perfectly in this darkness, and I tell you we are alone. I ask again, why did you take out the vision-glass? If Vraduir had——"

"But he did not!" Then, less fiercely, Tyrus said, "I am not such a fool. We were protected." He fumbled for the wall again; with an exasperated snort, Erejzan took his hand and led him forward without any hesitation. After a few steps, Tyrus said in his defense, "I . . . I know it was dangerous. But I had to warn them about Vraduir and the things I have felt lurking northward."

"Yet you did not . . . warn them." They had come to one of the numerous crooked stairs that cluttered

71

Couredh's lanes. Erejzan guided Tyrus down the flight. At the bottom, he paused and said, "If only you would enchain them to your will, as Vraduir imprisoned us . . ."

Tyrus yanked free of his grasp, shocked. "A forgetfulness or a skimming of the outer thoughts or a suggestion. But binding them? No!"

"Forgive me." Erejzan spoke so softly Tyrus had to strain to catch the words. "It is . . . Vraduir has no scruples at all. That is why I fear so for LaSirin and her sister. LaSirin reminds me . . . reminds me so of my lost Dalaen," Erejzan said sadly.

Tyrus knew by sound and scent that his friend had turned to face him, with head hanging in grief. His irritation cooled, understanding and sympathy taking its place. He himself saw scant resemblance between LaSirin Ilissa and the woman Erejzan mourned, save that both women were fair and sweet and dear to the acrobat. But he was careful with the other man's hurt. "I *did* try to put the suggestion in LaRenya's thoughts, mai fiyel. She is very strong, not easily swayed. More I could not do, without risking our cause and her honor. Let us not quarrel. That would please Vraduir, if he knew we still lived and were hunting him."

He reached out, and Erejzan clasped his hands. The brief disagreement had never been, and the bond between them was as firm as always. Erejzan said huskily, "You were right. It was worth all to try to warn the innocent sisters. A pity they took it for mere show."

"Indeed." Jathelle was in Tyrus' mind's eye. "Innocent, but bold."

"Not bold. She is gentle natured, a goddess-faced being who needs sheltering from the world's rough ways," Erejzan corrected him.

Tyrus knew Erejzan could read his expression, as he could read the surge of Erejzan's feelings, a tangible emanation requiring little arcane art to touch. "We have the same concern, my friend, but for different sisters. Rasven! What folly is this? We cannot indulge such dreams."

Out of the darkness came a heartfelt sigh. "Ai! Yet she is so beautiful, Tyrus."

"And she is the betrothed of Sirai Aubage," Tyrus reminded him gently. "Such women are not for us, Erejzan. We must be wanderers without a land, our only purpose the defeat of the enemy."

The acrobat grunted assent. "Where, then? To the lodgings near the bazaar? Or should we start north and look for that cove where Vraduir's ship may have put in?"

"I think not. There is perhaps something here in the city. Vraduir and another presence, one I cannot quite fathom. I do not want either of those at our backs while we take up his trail," Tyrus said.

"You have the link with him. What shall we do?"

Tyrus held out his hand, waiting to be led. "We have listened to many an honest folk and the gossip at the palace. There is a sector of Couredh we have not yet explored, mai fiyel, a sector where evil rumors would be first repeated, among evildoers."

"Rof's sector." Erejzan did not argue, for they had journeyed through forbidden sectors elsewhere in Clarique. Their courage did not flinch at this, not after what they had endured.

The keen-sighted acrobat guided Tyrus to the end of a lane, where they came out into a torchlit street. Their explorations earlier in the day served them well, for now they oriented themselves with little delay and headed down toward Couredh's river backwaters—a place where poorly favored clans and thieves would dwell.

Some streets and squares were bright with torchlight or the glow of communal fires. Others were left in blackness, and Erejzan had to lead Tyrus through those. For a while, they traveled through ways that were patrolled by the merchants' police and the queen's guards. Sometimes these would question the two friends. Always, Tyrus and Erejzan explained they were merely looking for a tavern, without naming the Inn of the Cutpurses. Their easy manner lulled suspicions. Yet the patrols warned them to seek a better section of the city. It was plain soldiers and police rarely would venture into the river sector, not unless they went in considerable force. Tyrus and Erejzan would take care to thank the patrols for the advice. When the guards left them, however, they would resume their former course.

Eventually, they descended into twisting alleys the police shunned. The atmosphere was heavy and even Erejzan's abnormal senses could not probe all the darkness. Tyrus muttered, "No patrolmen here, to wonder why I wear a weapon. I think it is time to put on a more warlike guise, mai fiyel."

Erejzan nodded and began hunting. He finally located a dead end lane where no windows or doors opened, prowling its short length to be certain it was empty. As he did, Tyrus selected a broken canopy pole from the litter underfoot and took a few coins from the purse Jathelle had given them, pressing the gold against the splintery wood. Assuring Tyrus there was no citizen or traveler or guardsman about, Erejzan stood between the young sorkra and the outlet of the street while Tyrus drew within his mind. He was falling swiftly, then running, for time in the real world was sharp. He could fly or swim through the air in that place of sorcery, rifling stores of magical objects, pouncing on what he needed. Climbing, swimming back to the surface, and entering the dark little pocket of a street once more. The broken pole shimmered with light, a green and silver twinkling up and down its length.

"A cloth," Tyrus said absently. "Some scrap . . ."

Erejzan scooped up something from the puddle-filled street, touched it to the shining pieces of canopy pole. The rag shone too. Then the light was dying to a faint reflection, metal and polished leather dimly visible in natural torchlight from the street beyond the alley.

Tyrus held a sword and a leather scabbard and baldric. He had made the weapon plain but sturdy, shaped the rag into a baldric to suit the custom in this region. He took off his cloak and donned the baldric and slid the blade into its sheath, then refastened the mantle over it.

"A precaution, mai fiyel. They will see I am armed and may stay their hands. I do not want to spend my magic against them unless I must. Conjuring a sword is far simpler . . ."

Erejzan's eyes had a strange inner fire. It did not startle Tyrus, for it was very familiar to him. He sensed that his friend was laughing, making no sound, however. Then Erejzan said, "Simple? What would Rof or some general pay you for such a simple trick? You could arm whole bands of thieves or soldiers."

"That would *not* be so simple," Tyrus said, amused. He did not ask Erejzan if the acrobat wished him to conjure another weapon for his use. There was no need.

They went on down toward the river and, one by one, prowled taverns and noisy inns. Most of these were cluttered with stuporous beggars, brawling cutpurses, and robbers. Whenever they entered such dens, Tyrus and Erejzan spent a coin or two, shamming drunkenness, encouraging their companions in carousing to talk. Again and again they heard tales of mysterious happenings to the north or stories about the enchanted ship that sailed Clarique's seas, but nothing new. Discouraged, they went deeper into Couredh city.

In finer sectors, the streets were reasonably clean

and wide. Here they were little more than offal-strewn runs. Whores and thieves huddled in the rubble of ruined buildings. Sometimes they ran out and wheedled at Tyrus and Erejzan, seeking alms. Bodies lay in the dirt, so closely packed in places the friends had to tread over them. Now and then someone would curse them or aim a feeble blow. But often there would not even be a groan or protest. In a more civilized area, Tyrus might have offered his help to these wretches. Here prudence made him hurry on without stopping.

Paving stones and bricks had given way to muddy paths and sodden planks. Erejzan pointed through the gloom to a low portal at the juncture of two crumbling walls. Lewd laughter and firelight came up from the cellar. "That is the place," the acrobat said. "That cloth merchant spoke of collapsed stairs, there, and . . ."

" 'Tis the Inn of the Cutpurses, ai." Erejzan had been conscious of the presence before the man spoke. But he was tense now, fearing there were accomplices he could not see. A one-eared man stepped out of the shadows and held up his empty hands to prove his friendliness. "Take no ill of me, amusers. Rof sent me to fetch you. I have been following you through the sector. He knew you would come. He is waiting."

Suddenly, three men came yelling and pummeling up the cellar steps. Tyrus put a hand on his sword hilt, then hesitated, comprehending that the bandits had no interest in him or Erejzan. Snarling like beasts, they fell across the topmost step. People crowded to the smoky entrance below and howled at the combatants.

"Kick him! Teach him respect!"

"Ai! And never to do that again, the dust-licker!"

Bronze and steel flashed and one man screamed, the sound bubbling away into the foggy night. His attackers were not satisfied, striking and stabbing again and again, slaughtering their victim.

From the Inn rose sounds of disgust and disappoint-
ment. No one wailed in lament for the dead man. Nor
was there much praise for the victors. The onlookers
went back inside, leaving the murderers to gloat. The
pair dragged the gory body off near one of the walls.
It was plain they intended to strip the corpse.

The one-eared brigand waved Tyrus and Erejzan
down the steps. One of the killers glanced up from his
ruthless plundering, baring his teeth. When no one
threatened him, he turned back to squabbling with his
fellow conspirator, fighting over the spoils.

The Inn's steps were slippery with blood and excre-
ment. His stomach churning, Tyrus swallowed his
nausea and walked through the stinking clutter. He
ducked to miss the lintel, entering the cellar tavern.
Erejzan moved to his right, clear of the sword, should
Tyrus need to draw the blade. Together they surveyed
the frenzied scene.

A motge carcass, probably stolen from some local
butcher, roasted on a great spit over an open hearth.
Smoke snaked across the cobwebbed ceiling and the
splintery walls, sifting through the numerous cracks.
Not all the fumes could escape, however, and the
room was thick with haze and the odor of seared meat.
Pots of burning fish-oil provided extra illumination—
and smoke. The customers were eating with their knives
and fingers, scorning such pretty manners as Tyrus and
Erejzan had seen at the palace. Wenches hacked off
chunks of the half-raw motge and took it to their patrons. The lurid light and haze changed all the people
into red-limned demons, creatures out of the Evil God's
domains. In a brief glance, Tyrus saw every race of
Tyta'an represented here and many a rogue as well
whose heritage he could not guess at. Hair ranged from
Irico white to deepest Krantin-Y black, skin from a
Clarique paleness to a Sarli's dark brown flesh. In
only one thing were these men and women alike—

they all defied Couredh's law and the laws of most other realms. Tens of eyes turned toward Tyrus and Erejzan, taking their measure.

From beyond the roasting pit, a hoarse voice hailed them. "Well and at that! They *did* come! Hai! By Bogotana, to me, sorkra and tumbler!" Rof emphasized his invitation by upending one of his ruffians, throwing the man off a bench at the side of his table. The brigand chief raised his whip, challenging the unseated thief with the butt end. The man scuttled out of reach as Rof roared, "Make room for them, you louse-ridden golhi whelp! Breg, Slit-Nose, Oaur . . . move!" Grumbling, the bandits obeyed.

The one-eared bandit conducted Tyrus and Erejzan through a corridor of hostile stares. As they passed the roasting pit, they saw why Rof had selected this particular table; there was a draft coming through a large chink in the wallstones nearby, and the breeze blew smoke and stink away from Rof's makeshift throne. Attended there by his brutish followers, he held court.

"Wench! More wine here and be quick, or I will toss you to my men!" The threat was cheerily said, but the serving jade eyed the surly thieves in terror and ran to fetch the wine Rof demanded. The brigands laughed and pounded the table and called ribald suggestions after her.

Tyrus and Erejzan did not sit beside Rof. Instead they dragged an empty bench around at right angles to the long table and Erejzan carefully sat clear enough still to free Tyrus' sword arm. Rof noticed the weapon and frowned in puzzlement. "Where did you get that blade? No one told me of this. I need better spies, I think." One-Ear and some of the other bandits cringed at this. Tyrus did not reply, his hand on the sword hilt as he smiled enigmatically. Rof shifted his scrutiny to Erejzan and said, "But you go unarmed."

"Do I?" Erejzan's smile was less cryptic than frightening and Rof uneasily turned away from him.

The serving wench returned. She was nervous, spilling some of the wine as she poured. She handed chipped and battered cups to Rof, Tyrus, and Erejzan. Like the other women in the Inn of the Cutpurses, she was aged well beyond her young years. If she had been bathed and perfumed and dressed in fine clothes, she might have been almost comely. But cruelty and hardship hardened her features and saddened her eyes. Rof grinned and pinched her painted cheeks. "Treat these outlanders well. They are my guests. If you please them, you shall be theirs for the night. Would you like that, girl? I thought you would. A rare man for you who is not missing a nose or ear or marked by disease, eh? Off with you now, and bring us salt and spice roast. We have much to discuss, and talk makes a man hungry."

As the jade left, Rof added, "Happily would she join flesh with you two. Any of these whores would, in truth. Our women do not see your like often at all." He stroked his pock-marked face, laughing at his ugliness. His men were far less prepossessing. As Rof had described, they bore many a sign of past punishments, mutilations that proved they had not always been successful in evading thief-takers and the queen's justice.

The Inn was loud with false gaiety. There was music, harshly played and jarring. A steady round of quarrels, often leading to knives and blood, was one other entertainment. The most common, though, was watching the women ply their arts. These made no coy game of selling their favors. Skillful at dodging a man who had no coin, they were shameless when one paid them. Like rutting animals, they lay upon the tables or the earthen floor while spectators cheered and commented on the show. Tyrus refused to watch and Erejzan expressed his contempt with a pithy curse.

"No taste for such shopworn women of ease?" Rof asked. The phrase was a Krantin one, but Tyrus and Erejzan had heard it in other ports and knew what he meant. Rof shrugged amiably. "How went your amusements for LaRenya? Did she pay you well?"

They met the brigand lord's gaze levelly, seeing the avarice in his black eyes. "Well enough," Tyrus answered. He had no real hope that such an offhanded tone would fool the greedy man.

" 'Well enough'! Hai! How delicately you put it, sorkra!"

"Charm-weaver," Tyrus corrected him.

Smirking, Rof said, "Very well—charm-weaver."

One of the thieves roused as from a dream. "They has been to the palace and has been paid for it? And we never robbed them?"

"How is this?" Rof cried in mock outrage. "They are my guests, I told you, you bejit. Being an outlaw is no excuse for such stupidity. I did not leave *my* wits behind when I was driven from Ve-Nya and cast out of the Brotherhood of the Zseds. Stand up! Seek pardon from them at once, or by Bogotana I will have your impertinent tongue as sauce for my roast!"

"I . . . I meant no insult, Rof," the hapless thief muttered. He staggered to his feet and, under Rof's angry prodding, managed a lame apology. Tyrus and Erejzan were uncertain how to react. As the besotted bandit continued to mumble at them, Rof abruptly yanked his minion's breeches loose from his belt and poured his cup of wine into the man's groin. Rudely shaken out of his drunkenness, the thief gasped and clutched himself while his companions yowled in laughter.

"That will lesson you, stander," Rof said, cuffing the wine-drenched thief. All the other brigands struck him in turn. Rof seized the sot's hair and hurled him bodily toward Tyrus and Erejzan. "Take your vengeance."

Had the man been a harmless dupe, they might have refused. But they remembered the killing on the steps outside and knew what sort of men all these were. Tyrus grabbed the babbling thief by the collar and spun him around roughly. Thus tempted, Erejzan landed a solid kick on the proffered buttocks. Together they picked him up and heaved him over the table toward Rof. The bandit lord evaded him and let the drunk slither off onto the bench and thence onto the floor, where he lay vomiting.

Rof hammered the table with his mug, adding to the general clamor of the Inn. "Artfully done! You are my men! I knew it when I met you!" He was still laughing, wiping tears from his eyes. Then he saw the serving wench approaching and swept bones and other garbage from previous meals off the table, clearing a space for the wench to set down a heaping tray of motge haunch. Like ravenous beasts, the thieves fought over the food, burying their filthy hands to the wrists in the cooling fat and threatening each other with their knives and axes. Rof saw the revulsion of his guests and smiled, edging away from the bickering. He had selected a prime piece of meat for himself before the chaos began. Now he laid the steaming chunk on the moldy table top and scooted to the end of the bench where he could converse with Tyrus and Erejzan.

"No appetite, eh? Too dainty, you are." Rof bit off a morsel of his meat and washed it down with wine. "But you have the right sort of touch to chastise a drunk. Bogotana shrivel me if you do not."

Erejzan slammed his hand down hard on the table. "Do not say that! Never say that!"

Tyrus, a trifle to his surprise, had been pleasantly exhilarated by the action of buffeting the drunk and throwing him back at Rof. But now he grew alarmed and gripped Erejzan's arm, worried by the fierce look in his friend's eyes.

Taken aback, Rof asked, "What did I say, Quick One? Calm you, friend handri. I was not aware—"

"Do not call me friend. And never call on the Evil God to strike you. He may oblige you!" Erejzan said angrily.

Rof choked on his wine. "Piety! You astonish me. Well and at that: *I* am not so persuaded that the gods have any care for me. I will make what oaths I wish to what gods I wish."

"You defy Bogotana at your peril. The Evil God can shatter a smoking mountain in a moment and lay waste to an island and its people ere they can draw breath." Tyrus pinned Erejzan's arm more tightly, shaking him.

Leaning chin on palm, Rof regarded them thoughtfully. The wavering light from the fish-oil lamps and the pit gave him the look of one of Bogotana's own demons. "There are no smoking mountains here, nor is Couredh an island." He paused and mulled Erejzan's words. "You have seen a mountain explode like that? Bogotana's wrath indeed! La ben da! That would be something to watch!"

Tyrus decided to reveal part of the truth. "We have seen its aftermath, bandit lord. You could not witness it while it was happening and live to tell of it. Take heed what curses you call down on yourself, I say. The gods may answer you."

"Well and at that, I will take what Bogotana deals me," Rof countered irrepressibly.

One of his tipsy thieves raised a brimming cup. "Ai! Here is a toast to Bogotana. We will all meet him whenever the Death God takes us and sends us to Keth's gate. For certain, *we* shall never enter the realms of the good gods and the heroes!" That defiant boast made the brigands laugh. They were men with no prayer of the future, no hopes of knowing another existence or the divine ones' favor.

"Hold your bragging, whoreson," Rof grumbled. "I am talking here, not you." He waved his whip at them and they were cowed, going back to arguing over the meat and wine. Rof glowered at them a moment longer, then turned to Tyrus and Erejzan. "They are like wolf cubs, dull wits but clever hunters when I put them on the proper scent."

"And who do you track?" Tyrus said casually.

Rof toyed with his mustaches, not dealing with that, probing at a former topic. "This wrath of Bogotana you saw—where? When?"

Erejzan sank in sadness, staring into nothing. "It was a long time ago, it seems. Far away. Many died, nearly all who dwelled on the island. They were suffocated, then burned, turned to smoldering ash before they could flee or protect themselves . . ."

Tyrus did not interrupt him, but the lament faded away of Erejzan's own will. For a while, there was silence in their small corner of the Inn of the Cutpurses. Rof appeared much impressed, considering what he had been told, a bit chastened. Then he preened his mustache again and said, "If it is my time to die, I will. I will still serve Bogotana. What better master for a brigand?"

"Perhaps one who promised him power and gold in this life," Tyrus ventured, watching Rof closely as he spoke.

Rof rose to that bait, but not in the way Tyrus had hoped. "A master? Or a mistress? You did not find a permanent hire place at the palace, did you? But you saw the court, ai? Bright, much gold, much power? Our royal sisters of Couredh inherited that gold and power and the leisure to enjoy it, now that the barbarians are driven back to their holes. Ah! It must be a fine thing to be so rich! Rich enough to play at disguises or go abroad on a hawking trip. An outing to make a brigand's mouth water, that. LaRenya and her escort will go in their finery. Such a temptation!"

Tyrus and Erejzan could not hide their consternation. Was Rof spinning a bandit lord's greedy dreams? Or did he actually speak of a plot he and his men might undertake? The picture he drew troubled them greatly. Logic said Rof and these unkempt throatslitters would never dare attack a royal party. Not within Couredh's walls, perhaps. But what if LaRenya and her retinue were far from the city, guarded by a small soldiery, unaware of their danger?

Searching his mind, Tyrus remembered Ceshti's bitter remark, that the plan to go hawking was the idea of Sirai Aubage. The pretext was a chance to show off a new brace of hawks. Or was there a more devious reason? Did Sirai Aubage traffic with Rof, hiring brigands to . . . to do what? Frighten Jathelle and bend her more to the nobleman's own way? It would not have been the first time an ambitious young lord sought for circuitous means to achieve a crown he could not win honestly. *Had* Aubage hired Rof? Or did Rof sell his loyalty to someone far more powerful and dangerous than a foppish courtier? A wizard? Rof seemed to know entirely too much about sorkra and the ways of magic.

Rof was smiling at him, his gaze unreadable. "A temptation, ai. But no brigand would risk dealing with her bodyguard. No menace to her at Drita Meadows at all. LaRenya is quite safe. No brigands, no barbarians . . ."

"No barbarians?" Erejzan repeated with a note of doubt.

"Oh, now you will query me about barbarians, eh? Or about missing peasants north on that same frontier? Next you will ask about every wild legend and tale the gullible prate. Ask about Krantin's myth of Andaru and uniting her divided peoples. Ask about fables that there are aliens far beyond Clarique's Eastern Sea, aliens who will come with the sun and bring us grief, some time in the dim future. Ask about—"

Tyrus cut in on him. "Since you mentioned it, we *will* ask—about the peasants, at least. The other myths you may keep. Many of the citizens believe these tales of missing peasants were begun by Couredh's barbarian enemies to cause unrest in the uplands and barren country. They think it is a trick to keep patrols away from the frontier and ready it for invasion by Irico barons or other warlords on the borders."

Rof pursed his lips skeptically. "No ruse, and no invasion that I have heard. The peasants *are* gone, though. I have seen it in some places I have been."

"You have been north recently? How far?" Tyrus wondered.

"Far enough. I have traveled the region, even to the Ice Forest at the edge of the Death God's forbidden realm. Take my advice. Shun that place. There is nothing there but danger and cold and things mortals should not see." Rof banged his cup loudly on the table, summoning the wench to refill it. As she did, he said slyly, "You are not drinking much tonight, amusers. You still distrust me and fear to become drunk here in this charming nest I rule? Well and at that, you are wise. You should be wiser and give up all these questions. And why did you ask me whom I serve? I am my own master. There is none other."

Tyrus rolled his cup idly back and forth between his palms. "We might wish to hire a guide to lead us through certain . . . alien regions."

"Hire me? La! To travel to the Ice Forest and the forbidden lands? Why would you want to go there?" Rof asked with a chuckle. He was too light with the request, arousing again their suspicions that he might be in Vraduir's power. "No, the Ice Forest is inhabited by a gruesome tribe of creatures called the Skull

Breakers. Well named they are! They would gnaw your flesh and eat your entrails and make bowls of your foolish heads if you went there. I will make you a better offer. Come work for *me*, amusers."

"What?" Tyrus gaped and Erejzan spilled his wine in his astonishment.

Rof spread his scarred hands wide, his broken teeth looking like bloody fangs in the smoky firelight. "I can use men like you, and you will find me a strong leader."

"Take no insult, bandit lord, but I think the wine has confused you," Tyrus said. "We are amusers, not thieves. How could we serve you?"

Rof's countenance darkened ominously. "I tire of this game. Tell others what you will. I saw you at work. Both of you. You are no ordinary acrobat. No mortal could do what you can. And you, who call yourself a charm-weaver, I know a sorkra when I see one. You are one of the wizard kind. I have been everywhere. I know true sorkra. Oh, you wear no brown robe like those people in Krantin and Sarlos who have started to name themselves web walkers. But you have real sorcery at your command. Let us finish with pretense. I offer you protection. Make no mistake, I *can* protect you. And with my knowledge of Couredh and the surrounding territories and your combined skills, we can all become very rich."

Tyrus and Erejzan did not reply at once. They gazed around the shadowy room and gauged their situation. While they had been talking with Rof, more men had arrived at the Inn of the Cutpurses. Not all of these were drunk and a number looked particularly vicious, bristling with weapons. Most of the customers seemed to pay no heed to the well-dressed strangers sitting with Rof. But Tyrus and Erejzan knew they were being closely watched. Rof's dominance here was plain, fortunately. No one challenged them, honoring Rof's corner and his rule.

"We will give you an answer, if we have your oath first," Tyrus said finally.

"Oath?" Rof's rude laughter rattled in his throat. "What oath can bind me?"

"In a moment. First say that whatever the answer, you give us leave to depart when we wish and you will not stop us." Tyrus held the swarthy brigand captive with his stare. It was against his principles to use his skills to harm the innocent. But Rof was certainly no innocent, though he had not hurt them yet, nor drawn weapon. Tyrus brushed the fringes of Rof's mind and drew back, disliking the feel of that contact greatly. He did not detect Vraduir's imprint there, but had he probed deeply enough to be sure?

A bit unnerved, Rof set aside his cup. "What oath?"

Erejzan took control now, employing his own peculiar unwavering stare. It had great effect, and without any hint of sorcery. "An oath you will make on your own Evil God. Swear that if you break this oath Bogotana will bring upon you now that same agony we described—striking you with fire, searing your lungs and guts, boiling your blood and marrow!"

Though Rof was accustomed to fierce vows and sudden death, this oath Erejzan demanded made him pale. He tried to shrug it off and said with feigned unconcern, "Well, so be it . . ."

"Swear it!" Erejzan growled. "You need no talisman or holy things to swear upon. Bogotana will hear and will bind you fast. Be warned!"

Involuntarily, Rof looked down at the earthen floor. His thoughts were fully apparent. The Evil God, Bogotana, ruler of the realm below and the fires of the depths. Bogotana—bursting through the very ground and birthing a smoking mountain in the heart of Couredh! Destroying everything. And Rof would be the first to die if he was forsworn! His voice noticeably unsteady, Rof repeated the oath, prompted by Erejzan.

" . . . and you will not stop us."

"And I will not stop you," Rof concluded. He wiped sweat from his brow and began to be annoyed. "The oath is made—"

"And will be kept," Erejzan said, stabbing a finger toward the floor to remind the bandit lord.

"Now, our answer: no!" Tyrus said, and he and Erejzan got to their feet. "We decline your tempting invitation, Rof. You promise much, but we have made our own promises. We will not join your band of thieves and murderers."

Rof's scarred jaw dropped. He did not know whether to rage at them or applaud their audacity. In the end, he laughed. "By Bog—I mean, by my beard! Well played, sorkra! A most skillful game! The tumbler seizes me by the throat while you deliver the death blow! Ha!"

Walking close together, the two friends edged away from Rof and his men. Rof got up and followed them, shoving underlings, serving wenches, and other customers of the Inn out of his way. "You have tongues to equal your wits. Sorry I am you will not hire with me," Rof said, a menace under his pleasant words.

A woman of ease blocked the path. It was the jade who had served the wine. Seductively, she wriggled against Tyrus and Erejzan and indicated she would lie with them both, wherever they chose. Erejzan caught her about the waist and lifted her effortlessly, putting her down to one side. Quickly they hurried on toward the door, leaving the woman pouting.

"Not even she can persuade you to remain?" Rof asked. He went on in a taunting manner, "Then perhaps you are not men after all but mewling fops like LaRenya's courtiers." Several brutish throatslitters rose out of the shadows near Tyrus and Erejzan and drew their weapons, moving to bar the exit. Rof cracked his whip, driving them back. "Let them go. I have given Bogotana my oath."

His minions did not have an answer to that. Bewildered that any oath would stay their chieftain's hand, they muttered among themselves. Rof smiled and bowed, a host bidding his guests a good night. "Go well with whatever gods you honor. But there is something you should know before you depart, amusers."

Tyrus was already on the cellar's steps, Erejzan about to climb them. They hesitated, wondering what caution the brigand meant to give. Rof's smile widened into a leer. "I have taken oath, as you bade. I *would* have been your lord and kept you safe. But once you leave this Inn, you belong to no one. I have sworn to let you depart unharmed. Bogotana witness I will! Since you refuse my protection, I charge you to guard your backs beyond that door. Couredh hides many a danger for the unwary. Oh, *I* will not be your enemy," Rof protested, raising his hand in a sham oath. "I vow I hold no hatred for you. In fact, I rather like you. But there are others who may not be so kind. I am not the only one in Couredh who knows you have been asking questions—and questions disturb *some* people very much."

They waited to hear no more. Tyrus climbed the steps in two long strides, Erejzan at his heels. The acrobat rushed ahead of him into the darkness, leading the way. He made for a passageway opposite the Inn of the Cutpurses. A naked, glazed-eyed corpse sprawled in the path and they leaped over the body. Once hidden in the shadows beyond, they paused to look back at the Inn. No one was chasing them. No one came to the low door and peered out. After a profound, momentary silence when they had left, the noise and discordant music started up once more. It was as if Tyrus and Erejzan had never entered the den of thieves. The lewd revelry resumed full force.

But a dead man lay almost on the steps, and Tyrus and Erejzan knew he would not be the only victim of those predators within. Rof's final words seemed to echo in their minds. Somewhere in this realm or close by, Vraduir was working his wizardry. Enemies near at hand and enemies waiting to pounce . . .

Thinking of this, the sorkra and his friend moved off into the night, swallowed up in the black streets of Couredh.

V

Assassins Cloaked in Darkness

❄❄❄❄❄❄❄❄❄❄❄❄❄❄❄❄❄❄❄❄

TYRUS HAD NOT THOUGHT THE STREETS OF COUREDH could be any darker than when they had descended into the river sector. Now the night was so black he felt as if he were walking through a cave. Soronos had driven his moon mares to the far pastures of that heavenly orb and it gave no light. The stars were obscured by low clouds. Even had that not been so, the rickety buildings loomed so close overhead they blocked out even reflections of torchlights and communal fires coming off the clouds. Without Erejzan's preternatural sight to guide him, Tyrus would have been utterly lost.

"This way," Erejzan was saying. "To the right and up. There are some steps."

Sometimes he took Tyrus' arm and led him. At others he walked behind him and kept a hand on his back, steering Tyrus along, urging him to walk more quickly. "Caution may be wiser than haste, mai fiyel," Tyrus said, complaining mildly as he stumbled through water and over dirt-smeared cobblestones.

"Not until we are safely out of the brigand's territory." Erejzan's voice was broken by whistles of exertion—or tension. "I am taking us back to the bazaar, to that lodging near the cloth merchant's."

"Well enough, until we have time to make plans." Tyrus tripped upon an obstacle, perhaps a body. His hands scraped painfully along a rough wall. "Iesor-Peluva! Is there no light at all in this pit? Where are the torches? Was not this street better lit when we came the other way? I will make a light of my own."

Suddenly, Erejzan's hand closed tightly over his mouth, muffling further speech. Tyrus held his breath, waiting in the black silence. He heard nothing. But he trusted Erejzan's acute senses. After what seemed a very long time, Erejzan let him go and exhaled loudly.

"What was it?" Tyrus whispered.

"I am not sure. If it was someone stalking us, he stopped and retreated back down the steps at the end of this alley. Let us hurry. I do not like this at all."

Tyrus tried to match the acrobat's sure-footed pace. His palms felt raw and wet and burned. He knew he had opened the skin when he ran into the wall earlier. When Erejzan stopped a moment to get his directions, Tyrus swabbed his hands on his cloak, wondering if he were leaving bloodstains. No matter. When there was leisure to rest, he would tend his hurts and cleanse the garment anew. Many of his cloaks had seen blood before, and so had Tyrus—blood and death, the death of an entire island, the people of Tyrus and Erejzan.

Hindered by Tyrus' inability to see in this darkness, unwilling to risk conjuring a light, they were forced to progress slowly. Once they heard feet tramping along an adjoining lane and Tyrus probed, then assured his friend it was only one of the merchants' patrols. If that were so, they must be close to the more civilized sectors of Couredh. Heartened by that likelihood, they went on more confidently, feeling themselves almost out of danger.

There were noises in the night, an assault on one of

the senses remaining to Tyrus. Groans and snores and whimperings came from the beggars and street urchins sleeping on the stones; yelps and snarls from curs who fed on the offal and garbage. Clatters sounded from behind shuttered windows and barred doors. And now and then came the ugly sounds of scuffling and mortal fear as the deadly fight outside the Inn of the Cutpurses was re-enacted with similar results. Tyrus wondered if all these distractions did not confuse Erejzan, who must be the eyes of two men and deal with his honest fear as well.

When Erejzan made him stop and hold his breath again, to no obvious purpose, Tyrus chided him gently, saying his friend was too nervous. It was good, indeed, that Erejzan was so alert. But his wariness might exaggerate any possible threat, making menaces out of dozing beggars or quarreling whores. Perhaps his friend's imagination was overstretched by the long seasons of their quest.

Without any warning, two men hurtled into Tyrus, knocking him off balance. Somewhere very close, Erejzan was shouting in surprise, the voice changing sharply, deepening.

A heavy object swished past Tyrus' head. A cudgel! A bit to the left, his brains would have been scattered over the filthy street.

"Assassins! We are no easy prey!" he roared, mastering his shock and turning it to fury. Tyrus flung his arms high. The assassins apparently believed he meant to fend off their blows. He felt them coming at him again, unprepared, scenting victory.

A strange, noiseless explosion filled the crooked alley. A miniature sun popped into being directly above Tyrus' fair head. Forewarned by his own intentions, he lidded his eyes and braced for the startling brilliance.

"Aaa . . . !"

"A torch!"

"Wh—where . . . how?"

"No torch! A . . . a god . . . come to earth to slay us!"

Fear abruptly shifted sides in this murderous encounter. Terror gripped the would-be assassins who had cloaked themselves in the darkness. For a precious heartbeat, their attack was arrested, their eyes were wide and stunned by the arcane light. Like living statues, they cowered, unmoving.

Tyrus took in as much as possible at a glance. Three men confronted him, carrying cudgels, knives, and slender Irico swords. Held at bay by the light, their hands were cupped over their brows, their eyes nearly squinted shut.

He could not see Erejzan, though he peered frantically into the shadowy corners beyond the circle of his magic little sun. There were awful sounds in the darkness—thrashings and snarlings and teeth snapping. Time was measured in the beat of his pulse, which throbbed through his ears. Fearing for his friend, Tyrus abandoned any further magic, his anger a blood fever. He drew his sword. The blade made a whispering as it slid from the scabbard; exposed to the air the transformed metal glimmered with an eerie green inner radiance.

"You do not like it when your victims can see you, ai? The battle is even!" Tyrus exclaimed.

It had been a long while since he had used a sword —too long! He had practiced, hoping his skills would serve him against Vraduir. But until now in his quest, there had been no opportunity to strike back at his foe. With keen delight, Tyrus rushed at the assassins.

The astonishment of Tyrus' wizardry was beginning to wear off even though the floating light continued to shine over them. The assassins rallied and lunged. Tyrus leaped aside, adroitly parrying and chopping a cudgel from one murderer's hand. As that man fell back, fumbling for a weapon to replace the one he had lost, another tried to strike.

Tyrus fended off the blow, letting it slide harmlessly by, thrusting for the bandit's throat. His new-made sword tasted blood. Tyrus pulled free and jumped aside to avoid another vicious slash of a blade.

Once this had been a game, an exciting game his tutor employed to train a prince. Heir to a throne, commander of the little fleet, and scourge of pirates, he must own these physical arts as well as those his sire taught him. Tyrus had learned well and quickly, swordplay as well as letters and wizardry and manners. Now the deadly art of the blade served him well.

He slashed and dodged a stab aimed at his belly, then severed the arm that held the knife. This man's throat was untouched, and his scream rent the blackness beyond the dancing light.

Tyrus used the magic light as a second weapon, moving it, hunting, playing the deadly foes as he would trapped golhi-wolves. "Erejzan?" he cried hopefully. "Erejzan?" Then he had to dive to the wet pavement as two black-clad men grabbed for him. They closed on air, and Tyrus lashed at their legs, biting into one and producing howls of agony.

In the darkness, another scream rang out, one of stark terror. There was horrible growling, as of some predatory beast clawing and fanging its prey.

"Help me!" an assassin yelped in desperation. Tyrus could hear him scrabbling about at the edge of the light's range. "Omaytatle! Ecar . . . an ecar kills me!"

The wail faded into a strangling death rattle. Tyrus knew what was happening, his spirits soaring. He rolled over and jabbed his sword hilt into a boot close beside his face. Then he turned and made a stake of the blade, impaling the assassin who loomed over him, intending to crush his skull. Tyrus' old tutor would have scorned such ruffian tactics, but Tyrus did not. This was not a practice room in a palace, where student and mentor bowed politely before and after they had at each other with their blades. Survival was the only thing that mattered, here.

Tyrus scrambled to his feet and dashed back under the magic light. Its brilliance was waning but the magic glow still gave him sufficient illumination, and befuddled his foes.

"Run, while you can!" he yelled. "Before it is too late, you curs!"

"He . . . he is no charm-weaver! He is a sorkra! A true sorkra!" someone cried in shocked realization. "Magic!"

"Atara? Rithai?" they called for their fellow assassins, receiving no replies.

"Try again!" Tyrus taunted them. "They will answer you from out the Death God's frozen land!"

Then a great furry shape dove past him and pounced on the foremost of the frightened murderers facing Tyrus. Men panicked, climbing over one another in their haste to flee. One went down with a crash under the flying, bestial body, and Tyrus heard the snap of bones.

The light flickered, almost winking back to the occult regions from which he had brought it. Tyrus waded into the fray, wasting no conjury to strengthen the little sun. Another assassin fell to his sword and the furry creature brought down yet another with much animal growling and slavering.

Footsteps pattered, fading into the distance, the last two assassins taking to their heels, abandoning any of their companions who might still live. Tyrus slumped, his sword loose in his sweaty hand. He stared at the scene of carnage and negligently drew on his arts, bringing the light back to its former brightness. A dying murderer lay at his feet, moaning his last, his life's blood pooling in the cracks of the pavement. Others sprawled everywhere about, dying or already dead. Tyrus blotted the few whimpering sounds of those pathetic men out of his mind, listening intently for a different sort of noise. Finally he heard what he had searched for—a soft coughing. He stepped over the bodies, his light moving with him. "Erejzan? Mai fiyel? Where are you?" Another weak cough guided him to its source and he knelt beside the acrobat. He sheathed his sword and looked over his friend anxiously.

Erejzan was naked. His tunic and mantle and breech-clout had been ripped off when the change began, as Tyrus knew must happen. The change had not been of Erejzan's choice this time. The murderous attack had stimulated his friend's alteration, and when this was so, recovery was always slow. Painfully, with much coughing and groaning, Erejzan was regaining his humanity. As Tyrus supported him, Erejzan bowed his head against Tyrus' breast. He gulped and pawed feebly and Tyrus held him tightly by the shoulders lest he topple into the blood and dirt. He could feel Erejzan shuddering violently.

"Are you hurt?" Tyrus asked softly, insistently. "They may come back for us."

"Not . . . not hurt. Not much. Help . . . me up . . ."

Tyrus did so, propping the acrobat against a wall, worrying that Erejzan would slither back down the stones, so shaky was he. But the smaller man continued to stand, gasping, while Tyrus looked in the shadows and hastily gathered his friend's discarded clothing. "I am afraid the tunic is badly torn. But it will do. Can you hold up your arms a moment?"

Moving like one of Tyrus' sorcerous puppets, Erejzan obeyed. He wriggled into his garments. Despite his denials, Tyrus saw a gleam of red far too brilliant to be the acrobat's hair, streaking across his ear and down the side of his neck. Tyrus traced the flow to the scalp. Erejzan did not react when he examined the wound.

Still dull-witted from his abrupt shape-change, the acrobat drew the back of his hand across his mouth. His hands and his mouth were dabbled with blood, but Tyrus knew the gore was not Erejzan's.

Far in the distance, there was a ululation. And behind the shutters on either side of the street people were recovering their courage after the fearsome uproar outside their dwellings. Tyrus sifted the confusion and said, "Merchants' police. Someone has hailed them. They are coming to see what the disturbance is."

"M—more assassins," Erejzan mumbled.

"Perhaps. We cannot tell, faithful one. The police may intend to restore order. Or they may mean to finish what the throatslitters bungled." Tyrus wrapped the cloak about the staggering acrobat. "We dare not stay here. No place in Couredh may be safe. Can you walk?"

Erejzan coughed again. This time, the sound was thoroughly human and growing steadily stronger. "Ai." Then he said with less assurance, "I . . . I think so."

Tyrus made a quick decision. "A moment. We will go slowly." He touched his forehead, reaching within, drawing forth a fragment of his being. As he did, the miniature sun found new life. It was a cheery, supernatural presence that chased back the darkness.

"They . . . they will see that and find us by it," Erejzan protested.

"No." Tyrus frowned, completing the spellcasting. A peculiar glow filtered down from the small sun, a veil of light that enclosed him and Erejzan. "Now they cannot see us, though we will be able to see *them*, dimly."

"Taxes . . . it taxes your strength," Erejzan said, blinking and shaking his head. He groaned and clutched at the bleeding cut, and Tyrus dragged his hand away from the wound.

"In good cause. Come now. We must make for the

gates. Remember that area beyond the cloth merchant's lodgings? We saw a postern door past there. With the help of the gods we will leave our pursuers far behind." He put an arm around Erejzan and led the tottering acrobat up the street.

With the magic light, Tyrus could find the route easily. But he was forced to move carefully because of Erejzan's weakness. At times Erejzan shambled, almost fainting, leaning heavily upon Tyrus. Little by little his steps grew more assured and he stood up a trifle straighter. When they met a merchants' patrol at a corner, Erejzan was able to move nearly as swiftly as Tyrus, shrinking into the shelter of the glamour and out of the guards' way. One of the police brushed the surface of that veil of light and recoiled. The man peered at his hand in confusion and shuddered uncertainly. But he saw nothing to explain the phenomenon. For a moment, he stared directly at Tyrus and Erejzan, in fact looking through them to the wall at their backs. Puzzling over this strange sensation, he hurried after his fellow patrolmen.

When the two friends reached the bazaar, they found it was lit by torches and well guarded, for the merchants paid for this protection. Taking advantage of the torches, Tyrus abandoned his magic sun and freed more of his powers to weave the glamour still more securely. Erejzan remained unsteady and Tyrus did not press him. At a careful pace, they wended their way through the marketplace. Peddlers camped in their wagons or slept on their blankets under the sky. A few cook fires had been built on the stones, and people gathered about these to relax and gossip after the day's haggling. Guards marched their rounds, kicking beggars out of privileged areas and checking with other sentinels. Once a dog bumped into the glamour and scuttled away, yapping in terror. Tyrus feared someone would be curious to know what had frightened the animal. But its barking only earned the poor cur a hail of rocks as angry citizens tried to shut off its noise. Tyrus and Erejzan passed close to two of the merchants' police, close enough to overhear the men talking about an event elsewhere in Couredh.

". . . is there more to report?"

"Not yet. Only what Litas said a short while ago. Something about bodies all over the Street of the Butchers. And citizens hysterical and claiming they heard an ecar attacking someone right under their windows."

The first patrolman guffawed. "An ecar?"

"Ai! They said it sounded exactly like a wild ecar."

"That peasant who exhibited an ecar—it must be his cat escaped."

"I already saw to that, and it is not. This ecar is another. The citizens said it spat and coughed most awfully. And Litas described several of the corpses ripped and bitten, just as one of the killer cats would rend them."

At Tyrus' side, Erejzan buried his face in his hands and stumbled along blindly for a few steps. Tyrus led him until his shame and anguish eased, still listening to the patrolmen.

Skeptical, the older man said, "An ecar, bah! Who cares what happens down in the river sector anyway? Those clenru kill each other all the time."

"The Street of the Butchers," the other reminded him. "That is too close to the quarters of honest folk for me."

"And there is your answer as well. Some butcher's apprentices must have played a prank, throwing out carcasses to make it look like an ecar is roaming Couredh."

"It was *men* it killed, not woolbacks or motge," the second man retorted.

Tyrus could hear no more, being too far away. For

Erejzan's sake, he was grateful, hoping that the acrobat, too, was out of range of that conversation. There should be no wrong in what Erejzan had done, but he knew Erejzan would not share that opinion.

Walking closely side by side, they crossed the bazaar. The streets to the north were better ones, lined with the dwellings of prosperous citizens. Here there were more torches and more patrols that must be avoided. But Tyrus could see well enough that he did not re-create the light, continuing to rely on the torches. He found the Lane of the Clothmakers, a street they had explored that afternoon while they made plans to sleep in one of the pleasant hostels. When they arrived at that inn, however, Tyrus saw several merchants' police lounging in the door, talking to the proprietor. It was as he had feared, and he went on by. The thought of a soft pallet and a place to rest was very inviting. But how could he explain his own bloodsplattered clothes and Erejzan's state of wild disarray? He could enchant away the signs of struggle, cast spells over the merchants' police to forestall their questions. But there were so many of them. Such a large use of magic might attract Vraduir's interest anew. It was not worth the risk. There were easier, safer ways. Reluctantly, Tyrus steered Erejzan away from the hostel.

"Not much farther," he encouraged his friend. The glamour cloaked noise as well as sight, but the less he spoke the less the possibility of someone detecting them.

"I . . . I am stronger. I think I can stand alone now."

Erejzan was still very shaky, but he did not fall when Tyrus let go of him. They left the Lane of the Clothmakers and went along several twisting streets beyond, heading always for the walls. Only when they were under the protecting shadows of a watchtower did Tyrus abandon the glamour, taking its power back into his store of sorkra resources. The veil could trick the eye and ear of those inside it as well as those they were hiding from, and henceforth he would need his senses free of encumbrance. Tyrus peered into the night, discerning a few dim masses and objects. There were watch fires and shore beacons atop the walls, but these only served to make the shadows below deeper. "Can you see?" he asked Erejzan hopefully.

"Very well. There is a wooden gate ahead of us—there."

Gradually, Tyrus' eyes were adjusting. Now he too could see more of what lay before them. The cloud-filled sky mirrored the torchlight and showed him that they stood between the inner walls and the bastion line.

Erejzan pressed his ear against the gate, listening for sounds on the other side. "No one," the acrobat said, nodding. He stepped aside and Tyrus pointed at the damp planking. They could hear the bolt sliding back; then the gate swung open noiselessly. Tyrus gathered the hood of his cloak over his fair hair to mask himself against lookouts on the walls above. They sidled through the little door, peering around warily.

Tyrus searched his memory for what he had learned that afternoon, turning to the right. Erejzan was slow to follow, not yet fully himself. Tyrus supported him for a few paces until the acrobat irritably shrugged him off.

From what they had been told, this section of the city wall was seated along the northern shore and the anchor of the promontory rocks. The shore was barren and guarded by cliffs, so the defenses need not be heavily manned. A postern gate was the only obvious exit here, and would suit their purposes.

They crept through a series of earthen hummocks studded with horse traps and other impalement devices. High above them, sentinels marched from tower to tower and back again. But their attention was aimed outward, not down and within the walls. Tyrus and

Erejzan hid in the barricades, watching until the soldiers turned their backs before making a dash to the next in the line of defenses. At last they were able to run under the hulking shadow of the outer wall itself.

A short distance away, a sleepy guard kept watch over the strongly barred postern. It was not critical duty. His head drooped and he braced his shoulder on his spear. Here so close to the cliffs and deadly reefs, Couredh's walls were very secure and the men assigned to watch these sections could not be blamed if they dozed at their posts. Yet the guard might rouse if he heard an unusual sound, such as that made by fugitives approaching his gate.

Erejzan breathed in Tyrus' ear. "I am strong enough now. I can knock him senseless."

"There is a safer way, and a kinder one."

"You have spent your powers lavishly, already," Erejzan said, but Tyrus quieted him.

"Just a bit more." He closed his eyes and willed his being toward the drowsy sentinel. Tyrus spoke, but there were no words to hear, the arcane chant filling his mind. Then he woke from his magic making and said, "He will not challenge us."

Trusting him, Erejzan followed Tyrus without hesitation. They slunk through the shadows at the base of the wall, heading for the postern gate. As they came to the small barrier, the sentinel lifted his head and looked directly at them. But he said nothing. His eyes were vacant and his jaw slack.

"No one was here," Tyrus said in an odd, crooning voice.

"No one was here," the sentry repeated, his lips scarcely moving.

"You saw nothing out of the ordinary."

"Nothing . . ."

"You have been alert all night, guarding LaRenya's wall, and no one came to your post. All was quiet."

". . . all was quiet."

Tyrus went to the sentry and gently shoved him to one side. A massive bar and a lock sealed the gate. Tyrus saw this and sighed, then steeled himself to fresh effort. He concentrated on the lock first, then shifted his force to the bar. He nodded to Erejzan and together they took hold of it and lifted it back. Thanks to Tyrus' conjury, it made no sound whatsoever and felt feather light in their hands. Tyrus cast a final glance at the entranced sentry, then he and Erejzan eased the postern gate open just far enough to let them slip through. They pushed it back into place and Tyrus bent to his conjury arts once more, returning the bar and the lock to their former positions.

Irony struck him hard. Rof had offered to hire him. How well the bandit lord had judged Tyrus' abilities. What thief would not give much plundered treasure to own the sorkra skills Tyrus had employed this night? Tyrus did not revel in his powers, though, particularly not in such furtive situations as this. These were necessities, things he must do to accomplish a far more important task of wizardry—the overthrow of Vraduir!

Erejzan hunkered down, his back against the wall. He breathed through his mouth, plainly still much weakened by the violent change that had taken him unprepared. At last, he levered himself up to his feet and they surveyed the terrain below the walls. The land had been burned off and cleared of trees and brush to deny any hiding place to possible invaders. Tyrus approved these wise military precautions, but it worked a burden upon him and Erejzan.

There was no choice. Tyrus gazed toward the sea. The fog was mounting the cliffs, rolling in over the scoured barrens past the walls. He waited till the mist helped conceal him, then once more formed the glamour. To conserve his power, he made the veil thinner and constructed no light.

Moving as quickly as their flagging energies would permit, wrapped in magic, they made their way down the long slope to the north. Weeds and pebbles crunched wetly underfoot, the sounds swallowed up within the glamour. The guards could not hear Tyrus and Erejzan gulping for breath as they ran away from Couredh.

It seemed a very long time until they reached the far side of the barrens and hid behind a brushy hill. Tyrus stared back toward Couredh. The sentries still prowled their posts methodically, their shapes silhouetted against the watch fires occasionally. To the seaward side of the walls, beacons chased the fog back a trifle, warning any ships to steer clear of the reefs beneath the cliffs. The torches within the city cast a soft glow up to the low clouds and this was suffused down over the walls and the area beyond, a pale, natural luminescence enhanced by the fog. The scene was a quiet one, a city and a people at peace.

Qamat had been at peace, once. But it had been devastated despite that.

Erejzan was stretched his length, using the grassy hill as a bed. Tyrus smiled at him sympathetically, then urged his friend back to his feet. "Not yet, mai fiyel, not yet. We must find shelter. Those clouds are thickening. Gros-Donaq will most likely send down his rain upon us ere morning. And we still have a long way to go if we are going to run Vraduir to ground."

VI

The Sorcerer's Victims

❧❦❧❦❧❦❧❦❧❦❧❦❧❦❧❦❧❦❧❦❧❦❧❦

TYRUS NURSED THE FIRE TO HARDIER LIFE, BLOWING gently on crumpled leaves and dry twigs. As he did, Erejzan crawled back inside their crude shelter of broken boughs and heaped brush. The acrobat had excused himself on the pretext of wanting to check the makeshift protection they had reared and see if it was proof against the rain. But Tyrus knew Erejzan had been emptying his belly as he often did when a shape-change came upon him shockingly and unbidden.

Erejzan lay down, leaning on one elbow, watching as Tyrus fed the flames. A few raindrops fell through the roof of thick leaves, but not so many as to trouble them or put out the fire. That steady drizzle had lulled the nightbirds and insects. Close to the overhang where they had thrown up the shelter, a rivulet trickled over rocks, making another constant, reassuring sound of nature.

During their flight upcountry from the city, they had seen a number of peasant villages and clan gatherings dotting the low, rolling hills. They avoided all such habitations. After the battle in the streets, neither of them was in a mood to trust strangers. Night was at its darkest and rain falling when their weariness made them halt. With axes Tyrus conjured out of branches, they hacked down saplings and brush and threw up a rain shelter on the protected side of a small hill. It would keep them dry enough and hide their fire from any peasants or herdsmen, at least until morning.

Tyrus glanced at Erejzan thoughtfully. His conjury could do much, but their wounds had been given by true weapons, not magic, and his sorcery had less effect against those. Fortunately, none of their hurts was serious. Of more concern to Tyrus was Erejzan's weakness and morose mood. He carried a remedy, an herb that would have better effect than any of his charms or enchantments. Tyrus rummaged in the tiny pack and took out a bit of the root, offering it to Erejzan. "Take it. Do not be stubborn. I have no power against this, you know. The laidil root will settle your stomach and help heal your cuts."

"But not yours," Erejzan muttered. "The laidil works on me because I am . . ." He broke off, looking at the proffered root with loathing. With obvious reluctance, he accepted it and chewed on the bitter, pungent medicine. After a moment, he said, "Have I ever told you my father's mother was a Destre?"

He had, but Tyrus forebore to say so. If this reminiscence would ease his friend's sadness, he would listen with patience. Erejzan looked into the fire and said, "Ai. She left Deki on the River forever when she wed my grandsire. They sailed the South Clarique Sea most of their lives, ere they made their home on Qamat. But in all those years, she never ceased to call herself a Destre-Y, an Azsed, one of the worshippers of Argan, the devil goddess. Laidil root! By Wyolak's mighty lightnings! She would spit on me if she saw her grandchild eating laidil. Laidil is accursed by the Destre." He chuckled, a harsh sound, full of hatred. "It is fitting that I must eat laidil to heal myself, ai? A cursed root for an accursed man-beast."

Tyrus bade Erejzan cant his head so that he could examine the clotting cut on his scalp by the firelight. He washed away some of the dried blood carefully and said, "You are no Destre, my friend. Your parents were Clarique born, as mine were. That is our heritage alike."

"But I *am* accursed, an animal thing, no more a true human, no more Shiija of Deki's grandson. Not even *you* can break this enchantment that makes me tear flesh and drink blood like a . . . a . . ." Erejzan hammered his fist into the rain-soaked earth.

"Stop it. You are Erejzan of Qamat, a man, and by rights you are now chieftain. That honored title lives through you."

Erejzan's eyes glistened at that reminder. "Rights of a survivor. Sole survival of all Qamat's clans. Dead, lost in the ruined mountain's gray ashes . . ."

Tyrus shook him hard and exclaimed, "You open our wounds anew with this."

"Wounds that cannot heal—not till Vraduir is dead!"

At Tyrus' urging, Erejzan lay back. But he continued to talk. "Dead, as he left *us* for dead, rotting."

"He could have killed us outright, my friend," Tyrus said, blood urging him to defend their enemy, even now. "The enchantments let us live."

"Why? So that he could gloat over us, taunt us, as a brutal master taunts a chained beast." Erejzan would not be convinced that Vraduir had showed them mercy, even for a cruel reason. "No, it was fate that spared us, no design of his. He will not be so careless with our lives, if he gets another chance to kill us."

"He will not. The gods had a purpose in rescuing us from Qamat. It must be we are their instruments, to be sure Vraduir never defies the holy ones again. To do that, though, we must be strong. You must recover."

"From being an animal," Erejzan finished, then moaned in shame.

"You are *not* an animal," Tyrus said with exasperation. "A shape-changer is not a true beast. You are a man. Eat the laidil. Do not let Vraduir best you."

Resigned, Erejzan chewed the root. Between bites, he said, "We must hide while Vraduir is free to work his black wizardry. Do you think those assassins were his minions, like the crew of the bewitched ship? The men who tried to kill us seemed human enough when I . . ." He wiped his hand across his mouth.

Tyrus waited until the other man's revulsion had passed. Then he drew up his long legs and crossed his arms on his knees. "I have been thinking about that. It seems more likely they were simply Rof's men. He knew about the reward the queen gave us. He knew where we had come from and how to follow us. He seems to have watchers posted everywhere in Couredh."

"Could he himself be Vraduir's spy?"

"Perhaps." Tyrus voiced a worry that was on both their minds. "Rof also knew about LaRenya's hawking party tomorrow. He spoke of robbing them, saying how small the escort would be. By the gods, that bandit lord knows far too much."

"Spies in the palace?" Erejzan speculated. He winced and probed at his ribs as if they had been sorely bruised in the deadly fight. "Aubage might be his spy, his ears within the palace."

A smile tugged at Tyrus' mouth. "Aubage is a fawner and a fop, but a very unlikely ally for Rof." His amusement faded and he said, "But they both could be Vraduir's tools, in some evil scheme aimed at the palace."

Alarmed, Erejzan sat up and stared at him. "What? LaSirin Ilissa and the queen? You think Vraduir means to harm them?"

"I felt a strange, ominous force when we were at the

palace, mai fiyel. It was new to me—Vraduir's touch and something more, far more. I did not sense it before we entered the palace or after we left. But in the royal dining chamber it was incredibly strong, awesome. It struck me dumb for a moment."

"So I saw. Could it be another sorcerer, one stronger than Vraduir? Has he found someone as evil as he is?" Erejzan wondered.

"I pray not, and I do not think a wizard lives who can match him—except me." Tyrus weighed the possibilities while Erejzan waited silently. The shape-changer honored Tyrus' experience in these matters of sorkra. Now and then he chewed on the root and color slowly returned to his face.

After much thought, Tyrus reached into his tunic and drew forth the vision-glass. Erejzan was aghast and Tyrus hurried to answer his objections. "I must! And I am sure I can protect us."

"But your magic is already so much in play!" Erejzan protested. "The way you have blurred our identities so that he will not recognize us even if we meet his spies. The way you repair our clothes." He gestured to his cleverly rewoven tunic. "The weapons you conjure . . ."

"I have done this without strain. And we must find out where he is and what he plans, mai fiyel. I will form a special glamour to guard us while I use the glass."

"The vision-glass is your one best weapon. How often have you told me that? Vraduir has its mate! You said we must save this advantage for when we are upon him, ready to strike. Now you will look for him blindly? Why?" Erejzan exclaimed.

Very slowly, with reverence and some apprehension, Tyrus laid open the delicate silk and bared the black vision-glass. He cradled the instrument in his abraded palms. "Because I think we *are* almost upon Vraduir, nearly to his lair. And because the royal sisters are in great danger, my friend. When we were on Atei and Sersa-Ornail, I tried to find him with the glass and could only touch faint reflections. The distance was too far to aim its power well. Now—after what I sensed in the palace, I know I can meet his vision-glass with mine. It is time to use that advantage, Erejzan."

The shape-changer bravely laid hands upon the wizard glass. He was shivering. "And if he is so near, how much stronger will the contact be. If you touch him, he can touch *you* . . . kill you!" He did not mention his own peril. Erejzan accepted that, a man willing to give his share of vengeance with his life, if only he knew Tyrus would go on to finish the quest and stop Vraduir.

"They are in danger," Tyrus repeated, with heavy emphasis. Erejzan turned this way and that, tortured by anxiety. Tyrus knew he had acted unfairly, but his own dread was great. "LaRenya and Ilissa can be his intended prey, as was the harper of Atei."

"No!"

"To save them, we must be sure." Tyrus owned the gift and the sorkra art. He could have proceeded without Erejzan's consent. But they had been bound by friendship and ordeal throughout their quest. He would not go ahead now unless Erejzan agreed. The mention of Ilissa had won his argument, as Tyrus guessed it might. Erejzan was defeated, mutely signing for Tyrus to begin.

Tyrus did not pose with the glass nor display it boldly as he had during the performance at the palace. Then he had employed it as a prop, no more than a focus point to concentrate his creations of hags and imps and the venerable sage. Here in the privacy of their rain-drenched shelter, he held the gleaming mirror before him, making no grand gestures at all as he peered into its fathomless depths. Erejzan squirmed

around to sit by his side, sharing the danger, wanting
to see what the vision-glass would reveal.

Speaking with studied care, Tyrus murmured the
potent incantation. He had learned it long ago, faithfully copying Vraduir's lessoning. An eager pupil,
admiring his sire, Tyrus had worked to emulate the
master sorkra of Qamat and become in all ways Vraduir's equal.

"Spirit of Rasven, you who first touched the world
within and beyond, guide me in this. Send the dancers
of Rab to tighten the magic about us. Protect us against
countering evil. In sorkra must we rule, for the good,
for the will of the gods . . ."

Tyrus was dimly conscious of the crackling of the
fire, of the rain, of his bruises and hurts, of Erejzan's
close presence. He was one with the vision-glass, his
being strangely elongated and shining, a part of the
black surface. Two vision-glasses, birthlings of the same
sorcery-laden piece of obsidian. Vraduir had lured the
magic creation from the bowels of Qamat's smoking
mountain, gifting his son with one half of the precious
instrument. The glasses were linked, as father and
son were in their blood and in their talents.

"What is he doing at this instant? I will know, glass
of magic. I will see what Vraduir sees and hear what
Vraduir hears. If he is near, in his sanctuary, treating
with demons or his enchanted, enslaved minions, I
will be with him. Reveal him to me. Let me be invisible
but beside him, wherever he is. Reach out for me, take
me with you, take me to him . . ."

The black surface rippled like a pool formed out
of a night sky. Countless stars in colors impossible to
name streamed past Tyrus' mind. There was his reflection, and Erejzan's, in the vision-glass. And then their
images disappeared and Tyrus was entering the glass
itself and going past it, into another place. The window
was open, and he was floating as swiftly as a star-streak

across the heavens. He was going through the obsidian, through the fire that made it, yet feeling none of the smoking mountain's terrible heat.

Layers of black shimmered and parted, one after another, doors upon doors, opening . . . opening . . .

Tyrus narrowed his probing and the unsteady movements abated but did not entirely cease. One particular layer of blackness coalesced. A vivid picture leapt into being. Tyrus' viscera roiled; faintly, he heard Erejzan breathing a most awful oath.

Vraduir!

For more than a year, they had not seen him. Sometimes, amid their wandering, Tyrus had painted his sire's image out of memories, keeping their yearning for vengeance hot. In the past, when he had consulted the vision-glass, he had been able to conjure only a few murky shadows, nothing he could grasp and lock solidly into place. Now, after so long, Vraduir's face and form were so strong he seemed to be within the humble shelter, in front of them, defying them.

As Erejzan had said, that face was no longer so much like Tyrus' own. The fair hair had thinned a bit at the temples and crown. Vraduir's jaw was clean-shaven, for unlike Tyrus he had no need to grow a beard to disguise his identity. Indeed, he thought his only serious rival was dead. It was the eyes that revealed the change and altered the face and the man so terribly; once those eyes had been mirrors of the eyes of Tyrus, wise and filled with a desire to learn and to help their people. The keen intelligence still shone in that face, but a lust for power ruled the eyes, a coldness that made Tyrus tremble. Greed—a different and far worse greed than Rof's. Too well, Tyrus recalled when that change began, the day he had mastered one of Vraduir's most potent sorkra skills, the season Vraduir had realized his son was no longer a child but a man, with arts and abilities equal to his own. The guilt of that moment, of seeing the change begin because of his achievement, was Tyrus' most aching and unhealing wound.

A part of Tyrus' being sensed that Erejzan was quaking with rage and saying, "If only . . . so close! If only I had him by the throat, I would repay his curse ten-tens of times and over again!"

Tyrus barely heard. He was busy chanting and sealing the image tightly in the vision-glass. That done, he allowed himself to breathe, coming to the top of his consciousness as he would swim to ride atop waves. "I have found him at last. Oh, my friend, how I have longed for this. Carefully, carefully! I must make no mistakes. The glamour is bound fast about us. Warn me if you see him turning toward us and I do not, Erejzan."

The acrobat nodded, leaning forward, fascinated by the moving picture in the black glass. "He is doing something, Tyrus. Holding something." In the background of that image they saw imps and devils scampering about and a few hideous forms that might have been spellbound men and women—Vraduir's slaves, shuffling to and fro and doing the evil wizard's bidding. Erejzan strained to make out what Vraduir was holding, then grunted as if he had been struck a fair blow in the belly. "Tyrus, it is . . . it is his own vision-glass!"

"Then we will see what *he* sees," Tyrus said with a cold confidence he did not actually feel. He spoke a charm to make it so. "These glasses are twins, Rasven, twins of the same fiery rock. Let this twin see what the other does."

The black surface shimmered again, the layers separating. One remained—Vraduir's moving image. But Vraduir's face dimmed and the shapes in his own vision-glass were those in the upper layer seen from Tyrus' point of view. For a heartbeat, the conflict between the two images was very confusing. Tyrus worked to separate them and finally the uppermost one—the thing Vraduir himself was studying—was sharp and clearly visible.

"A room!" Erejzan said excitedly, even as that thought came to Tyrus past his network of magic making. "A fine room, with carpets and tapestries . . . a palace chamber!" In his agitation, Erejzan started to clutch at Tyrus' arm. Then he remembered how dangerous this endeavor was and hastily drew back. "Tyrus, you were right to worry about LaRenya and the La-Sirin Ilissa. Vraduir is looking into the very palace of Couredh. See the markings on that chair? It is the royal symbol. We saw it over the gates and in the dining hall."

"Ai!" Tyrus divided his mind, using a small portion to express himself to the shape-changer. "His vision-glass is hampered by distance, just as mine is. He could hardly see so clearly as this unless he was near to Couredh—which means he is quite close to us, Erejzan. If he were in Irico or Sersa-Ornail or an outer island, the image would be so blurred he could not be sure, nor could we, that it *was* a room!"

"Rooms," Erejzan corrected him, pointing without touching the surface of the vision-glass. "Adjoining chambers, with a portal between them."

"Your eyes have always been quicker than mine. Now, we must see what he is doing, looking into these chambers." Tyrus gripped the obsidian gently, examining the scene in the rooms and Vraduir's leering face beneath that picture. He dared to reach through the layers, masking himself in his most potent protection, skimming the surface of Vraduir's thoughts, gathering words and emotions while he and Erejzan looked into the black layers.

Vraduir's vision-glass was a weapon, roving, searching those two rooms within Couredh city. Unknown observers, Tyrus and Erejzan watched and searched with him. They beheld dainty objects and feminine garments laid over racks, awaiting their mistresses' pleasure. There were pallets behind screens where personal maids slept near to their ladies, ready to wake should they be needed. Two rooms. Two sets of garments and jewels and accompanying finery. With a fraction of his attention, Tyrus assessed these things, seeing the tight breeches and slashed panels and closely-cut bodices of the garments, identifying these as stylish costumes such as noblewomen would wear on an outing. A hawking expedition! What they were seeing was now, and the clothes had been thus put out by the maids so that LaRenya and her sister could dress early in the morning and be about their enjoyment at Drita Meadows!

Vraduir's glance, too, swept over the jewels and garments, bored and disinterested. Then his probing sorcery rushed across one room and hovered by the bed standing there.

With a soft gasp of pain, Erejzan expressed Tyrus' horror as well as his own, though Erejzan's was the greater. Vraduir's vision-glass was spying on LaSirin Ilissa.

She was asleep, poignantly lovely, a child-woman, exquisitely innocent. A smile curved her pink lips and her moon-cloud hair was flowing loosely over silken pillows. No veil hid her perfect face now. And here within her own private chambers she had no need for other veils or maidenly modesty. No one could see her but her sister and her servants. No one but Vraduir —and Tyrus and Erejzan! Tyrus was embarrassed as Vraduir's glass roamed over that womanly form, exploring the places where the sheer nightdress did not cover breasts and thighs completely. Her very innocence seemed to lure Vraduir, inviting him to linger in his spying. Tyrus felt the emotions behind the search and exclaimed in outrage, "Lascivious brute! How dare you defile her and shame my mother's memory!"

"Wh—what is it?" Erejzan pleaded, frightened for Ilissa's sake. "What does he want?" But he knew the answer. Erejzan covered his eyes, his face reddening. Like Vraduir, he had enjoyed seeing Ilissa's flawless beauty so openly revealed. But unlike Vraduir, he and Tyrus knew guilt and wished they could beg the young woman's forgiveness for this cruel intrusion.

Tyrus held his breath, driving out his fury, putting his focus back strongly on the vision-glass once more. It was far too obvious what motivated Vraduir. Though the contact had been necessary, Tyrus was almost sorry he had restored the link between the vision-glasses. He longed to remember Vraduir as he had been, in days before power had consumed all else in his nature and made him more and less than human.

Mercilessly, the evil sorkra's vision-glass pored over Ilissa's body and face. The magic instrument was an invisible and lewd hand, groping over slender limbs, crawling across her breasts, caressing her goddess features. Eventually, Vraduir withdrew, a lecherous and reluctant retreat from his vicarious carnal pleasures. He was leaving Ilissa safe in her chastity, moving through the portal into the adjoining bedchamber and rushing toward the bed there.

It was Tyrus' turn to feel a deep personal loathing and resentment on a woman's behalf, even more than he had suffered for Ilissa. Jathelle, like her delicate sister, lay asleep and unaware of Vraduir's prying. Though not so astonishingly lovely as the LaSirin, to Tyrus she was most beautiful. And that spirit which so attracted him was apparent in her sharp face even as she was dreaming.

Her body was stronger, her breasts fuller and not so ideally formed as Ilissa's, her skin rosier from tanning in wind and sun. Erejzan was smitten by Ilissa's fragility, but Tyrus found more appeal in Jathelle's pride and assertiveness. He was man enough to be drawn by what

Vraduir revealed. Yet he wanted to protect Jathelle, too, particularly from the rude view of all other men.

Vraduir, however, was not looking upon Jathelle with lust. Tyrus extended his tendrils of thought a trifle further and could hear Vraduir's comments as the wizard-king of Qamat observed Jathelle.

". . . send patrols to guard your frontier, eh? You do not know of me, my little queen, but you would actually defend your realm against me. Worrying over tales of a few worthless peasants! What are they to you, meddling female? Bogotana take you . . ."

"As he took Qamat because of your wickedness," Erejzan cried. Anger had overridden his fear of detection. Realizing he might have risked all by that outburst, he clapped his hands tightly across his mouth to shut off his own rage.

Vraduir had not heard the accusation. He continued to watch Jathelle and speak of his plans. "You dote on her as if she were your pet. But it will do you no good. No mortal can defy me! I will slay you if you try, La-Renya of Couredh! What are you to me? If you oppose me, I will leave your bones for the scavengers or my imps to gnaw. She will be mine! I have use for her, that goddess-creature you protect so tenderly. She is no longer frail and sickly as she was those long years. She is a woman and ready for a woman's usage, a goddess-woman, fit for a god's own bed!"

Abruptly, Vraduir was leaving the palace, leaving the city, his shameless spying done. The second layer of the image rippled and dissolved and only Vraduir's face remained before Tyrus and Erejzan. Though Vraduir seemed to have laid his own vision-glass aside, it was still linked to the one in Tyrus' hands and with that they still could watch him. Tyrus enlarged his scope, increasing the danger, following the sorcerous thread from his glass to its twin.

In the black depths, he saw field and forest and

peasant villages and rocky hills. These sailed back beneath him, for Tyrus seemed to be aloft, invisible and soaring, high above Couredh's realm. He was approaching the frontier, moving far faster than any hawk, sorkra his wings, carrying him like Wyolak's holy lightning streaks. He was crossing rough lands, rugged upcountry regions where human habitations were widely scattered. Then, beyond the barrens loomed a solid line of giant trees, an unnatural forest marking the outer boundaries of the known world. Within the forest Tyrus sensed creatures more animal than man and some powerful, lingering magic that might have given him pause had he been afoot. But he was aloft, able to cross that barrier unhindered, his mind going where his body could not without strong weapons and charms to shield him. Beyond the forest, snow and ice dominated the land and the sky lowered darkly, no matter what the season. It was a place the Death God owned, and beasts long vanished in other provinces here clung to life and haunted the dismal rocks. Tyrus' sorcery carried him over that blasted, wind-swept iciness and a frozen plain beyond, toward a looming citadel. The immense fortress was framed in blackness, for it sat within the curtain of the dreaded region of Eternal Night. Following the beacon of the vision-glass, Tyrus' mind plunged through thick walls and past terrible monsters who guarded the citadel, into a sanctuary at the very heart of that structure.

"I can see him!" Tyrus exulted. "I have him! I know where he is and how to get there, mai fiyel! Northward! Toward the coves where his ship must have berthed, and where that cloud lurks. Past the Ice Forest and the forbidden lands and . . ."

Erejzan gulped audibly. "Ice Forest? Forbidden lands? Tyrus, that is Nidil's holy territory, the Death God's realm."

Tyrus was bending nearly all his will toward the

vision-glass. "Ai! There is a citadel there, a palace or a fortress. It is the creation of mortals, not the god. How did Vraduir achieve it? Slaves! That is the only explanation! Rasven! How cold it is there! I can feel it even this far away, through the glass."

He suddenly fell silent and a panic engulfed him. Tyrus saw Vraduir, walking slowly across a marble-floored hall. His proud head was erect, his eyes as bright as a clear winter sky, his luxurious grir fur cloak sweeping grandly over the priceless floor. His footfalls echoed startlingly. The sound was . . . cold. Tyrus had no other description for the sensation. Everything about the room was cold, save Vraduir. He alone was warm with blood and life, there in that hidden sanctuary. Things gibbered in the icy corners of the vast chamber. Tyrus could not look directly upon them, dreading them, horrified, knowing he might break the spell if he were not diligent. Erejzan regained his courage to peer over Tyrus' shoulder, and he was taken by the same awful fear that gripped his friend.

"What is *that*?" the shape-changer asked, his voice cracking.

Stunned, they stared at a shape which was rising to fill the entire center of that citadel's chamber. Was it beast, bird, human? It was all of those and none of them. Vraduir was addressing the shifting, smoky form, bowing to it, his manner far different from when he gloated over Jathelle and Ilissa. He was familiar with this . . . thing, yet he was groveling, all his pride put by in worshipful respect.

It was never still. And always, cold emanated from it, reaching across space, through the vision-glass, wrapping its icy fingers around Tyrus and Erejzan. It was omnipotent, past human fathoming on such abrupt meeting.

Tyrus' soul shivered, his mind dizzy with awe. He could not cope with that terrible presence. Without comprehension, he saw Vraduir turning, looking directly at him, as if he were following that deadly cold across many Couredh measures, tracking it to the place where Tyrus used the vision-glass.

"He senses we are hunting him!" Erejzan yelped. "Now he is going to hunt us!"

The sharp warning woke Tyrus from his enchantment. Reflexively, he abandoned the link, throwing up a powerful shield and many confusing hints that would shunt Vraduir far off the path. The scene in the vision-glass melted away and left the black surface flat and blank.

Erejzan doubled over, flinging his hands about his head, braced for a mortal blow of wizardry, expecting death. Tyrus remained where he was, rigid, acting with frantic speed. He continued to throw out false trails and ruses and interlaced an impenetrable—he hoped! —barrier all around the crude shelter, strengthening the one he had established earlier. It took nearly all of his reserves; when it was done he waited and held his breath, ready for Vraduir's attack.

Moments crawled. Tyrus tested the inner power of the glamour he had cast, wary for any countering thrust against his sorkra arts. There was none. Distrustful, he kept up the illusion at its strongest until at least a quarter period had crept by. Finally, weak and dripping with sweat, he let the heavier part of the glamour fade, leaving only the core to shield them. Outside, the rain had almost stopped. Birds and insects were resuming their calls. Tyrus heard nothing else. More importantly, he felt nothing, no touch of sorcery at all.

"We . . . are safe," he said, sagging.

Erejzan was apologetic. "I should have done something to help."

"There was nothing you could do. This was all sorkra dealing. Your part was played well earlier and will be again." Tyrus exhaled and admitted, "Rasven! But that was very sharp."

Now that the danger was over, Erejzan tried to be cheerful. "As you say, the gods have a purpose for us, and will not let us die till it is done."

"Do not become overbold, my friend. If that presence is Vraduir's ally . . ."

"Nidil, the Death God," Erejzan murmured. Tyrus' own fear was matched in Erejzan's expression. The acrobat's dread turned to sickness. "Does he intend to blaspheme with his sorcery? Again?"

"I fear so." Unwillingly, Tyrus confronted squarely that lurking suspicion he had nursed throughout their quest, a suspicion that intensified each time they discovered some precious person or object stolen by Vraduir's minions. "Like the beasts and people he enchanted on Qamat, to earn Bogotana's favor, now he plans to bargain with an even more terrible force. We must stop him now, before he can put his unspeakable scheme into play, before it is too late."

"LaSirin Ilissa and LaRenya," Erejzan said, putting their mutual apprehension into words. "Have you no skill that can protect them?"

"Not from here. I have no god to lend *me* power across such a distance." Tyrus was frustrated by the limitations. Indeed, he had pride in his sorkra arts, a wizardry as strong as Vraduir's—if Vraduir could not tap reserves forbidden to all other mortals. "I could only feel the urgency of his plan, aimed against Jathelle and her sister. He means to strike, but I do not know how or precisely when. Nor dare I use the vision-glass again to seek that from him. This time, he would be on guard and he would turn on us, perhaps slaying us."

"Soon? You could touch that in his evil mind?"

"Very soon, as early as sunrise," Tyrus said, not wanting to say this but knowing it for the truth.

Almost soundlessly, Erejzan said, "The . . . the hawking party."

"Erejzan, I fear you have hit upon it. His spying on the sisters, the feeling of impatience—everything points that way. I have to prevent it! But how? It is hopeless," Tyrus cried, his exhaustion battering at him.

The shape-changer caught his arm and made him look up. Tyrus was held by his friend's unwavering gaze as Erejzan said, "We will never give up. Not even if Vraduir traffics with the Death God! We must try and we will succeed. Gros-Donaq will give us the strength of his storms, and we will win!"

Encouragement and fresh spirit flowed between them. Gradually, Tyrus was heartened and forced a weak smile. "Ai! You are right. We will win."

"So! You told me I was wearied from shape-changing, but you are worn from making sorcery. It makes your mind thick as with wine. In the morning, you will see things better. Is it not always so? We will find a way. After all, after so long a search, we know where he is, where he keeps his lair. We can track him down now."

His friend's enthusiasm was infectious. In the back of Tyrus' mind were images of those icy lands and the terrible presence within the citadel. But he shoved the thoughts aside. Worry would avail nothing. "In the morning . . . in the morning, mai fiyel, we must return to Couredh city. I will reveal my identity to LaRenya and convince her to use me as her private sorkra— anything! If I am close to her, I can protect her and LaSirin against Vraduir the better. We got to the islands too late. Vraduir's enchanted ship outraced us. This time, I can put my sorcery between him and his victims. Here it will stop, Erejzan."

Their decisions made, they lay down to sleep. Erejzan wrapped himself in his cloak and curled up, quickly dropping into that state of deep, regular breathing. Tyrus knew that Erejzan was proof against mortal intrusion, for the shape-changer's keen senses would waken him at any threatening noise or scent, just as an ecar's would. Tyrus probed for other dangers but touched only the quiet countryside and sleeping peasants. Thus reassured, he closed his eyes.

At first, sleep would not come. A parade of ominous speculations crowded his head. Only when Tyrus gave up conscious striving did sleep take him. He was pulled down, a swimmer drifting in warm ocean currents.

Drifting . . . waves rocking him, bearing him toward a tree-lined green shore. The water was always soft and gentle, here within the royal cove. Tyrus floated, looking up at the palace perched high above the white sandy beach. The castle was built of black stone, the congealed molten rock of the smoking mountain. In Tyrus' dream-colored vision, a feather of glowing cloud trailed from the peak of that cone, high above the island, tracing across the south Clarique sky.

. . . he was walking up the sands, a manservant bringing him his princely garments, drying his wet skin. Fisherfolk and boatmen and other subjects greeted him along the way. Tyrus saw fear in their eyes, fear which washed away his serene mood. Fear . . . fear he had caused, by besting Vraduir's magic in the pride of his young manhood and newly-perfected sorkra arts . . .

. . . climbing . . . climbing carved lava steps. Tyrus did not wonder how he had arrived so quickly at the palace grounds. In his dream, a man accosted him at the gates and fell to his knees, supplicating. Tyrus relived his shock, recognizing Erejzan's father, horrified that the spreading unrest among the people had come to crisis so quickly. Erejzan, keeper of Vraduir's forest preserves and beast pens, and Tyrus' hunting companion through many a boyhood jaunt and mischief. Erejzan, chieftain's son, too hot-tempered and rebellious to hold his tongue when Vraduir's latest experimentations had mingled demons and creatures from Bogotana's depths with the harmless beasts in Erejzan's keeping, when that magic turned evil and menaced even humankind.

As wrenchingly as when he first heard it, Tyrus endured the chieftain's heartbroken plea: "Sorkra-prince! Sirin! Save my son, I beg you. Save him from the anger of Renya Vraduir! My son is accursed, made a beast, imprisoned!"

Rebellion! Rebellion that should have been Tyrus' own! How he had refused to see the truth, refused to admit the changes in Vraduir, not wanting to believe his beloved sire and mentor could do these things. And now—he could no longer turn away . . .

Belatedly, ashamed by his cowardice, Tyrus stood in the palace sanctuary and confronted Vraduir. Again he did not wonder how the scene had changed. He had lived this before, many times, and must live it again and suffer again. Knowledge. Blasphemy. Bargains struck between wizardry and evil in exchange for power. Power Vraduir must have . . .

Knowledge, coming too late. Tyrus was hearing Vraduir's malicious triumph again: "You think you have bested me, my son, my would-be usurper! Know that Bogotana himself has given my arts new privileges, new force, beyond that of any wizard—even you!" And again Tyrus relived the terror and shame of betrayal, Vraduir ending all argument with wicked magic before Tyrus realized what he intended or could move to defend himself. Striking, with Bogotana's own fiery strength . . .

. . . Tyrus was suffocating, cramped into a black, stifling hole of a cell. He was trapped on a prison rock, a craggy, uninhabited island off Qamat's lee shore. The only light came from an air shaft bored to the barren surface high above. There were two prisoners in the cell—himself and Erejzan. They had been condemned to rot there, now and then taunted by Vraduir. Tyrus could not break the enchantment that bound him. Nor could he alleviate the curse Vraduir had put upon Erejzan, with Bogotana's power; the beast keeper changed to a beast, helpless, battered by abrupt shiftings from man-ecar to man and back again as Erejzan slowly and painfully learned some measure of control over his dreadful affliction. Locked together, sharing agony, the casual boyhood friendship had ripened into a firm bond. They had only each other's companionship and the encouragement of Erejzan's woman Dalaen, who eluded Vraduir's guards as often as she could and let down food and water to the enchanted prisoners. Dalaen was their sole contact with the outside world, with Vraduir's worsening madness. She called down to them, telling them of the strange magicks ruling from the palace, how all the people save Captain Drie's crew of the king's ship and a few guards had turned against Qamat's lord, of fear that shook with the smoking mountain itself . . .

Then Dalaen came no more, and the island heaved, the prison rock tossing like a ship on stormy waves. It was a feeble imitation of the cataclysm befalling the mother island and tearing it to pieces. Molten rock and boiling seas vomited as Bogotana set free his demons in a mind-shattering roar. In their earthen and rocky tomb, Tyrus and Erejzan heard screams and suffered from some of the hot water and ash and noxious fumes. And as this happened, Tyrus discovered that the enchantment binding his sorkra arts was loosening. Vraduir fled the scene of his unsuccessful bargain with the god of the depths, and Tyrus was finally able to break through to freedom. He could not lift Erejzan's curse, but he could open the bars of their cell and conjure a ladder from the rocks lining the air shaft. Together they climbed to the surface of the isolated prison island, emerging after uncounted days of darkness and hurt.

They found Qamat a smoldering ruin. All life had vanished. A bay occupied the place where villages, pastures, fields, beast pens, and palace had been. In the warm waters of the new-made bay, a tiny plume of smoke rose from a spawn of the old mountain. This miniature cone was all that was left of what Qamat had been—this and two men who had been saved because they were imprisoned on a distant prison rock.

In helpless grief and rage, Tyrus and Erejzan had searched through the ashes, mourning, finding in horror that the ashes were bones and flesh reduced to the very earth. Amid the debris, drawn by his sorkra calling, Tyrus came upon his vision-glass, magically unharmed, the only object to survive the holocaust. With the glass, the friends searched and found Vraduir and the crew of Captain Drie's ship, fleeing Bogotana's fury. Vraduir, who had brought down this disaster—alive and free to work his magic elsewhere!

Tyrus was clutching his vision-glass, vowing fierce oaths, swearing to take revenge for his poor slaughtered people. His fault, that he had not acted sooner! Now he must find Vraduir and punish him, and Erejzan would be repaid for the curse he must bear. The cost did not matter. They would venture blood and life to conquer Vraduir . . .

"Tyrus?"

He came to himself wildly, lashing out. Then Tyrus wakened fully and saw he had hold of Erejzan's tunic and was shaking his friend. Erejzan bore the abuse without complaint. Tyrus released him, groaning, and oriented himself. Couredh. The shelter of saplings and brush. Jathelle! And Vraduir leering menacingly at her and her fragile sister! Tyrus' throat was raw, as if he had been screaming defiance at Vraduir while he slept. "Is it morning?" he asked huskily.

"Very near." The fire was almost dead, but it gave enough light to show Tyrus the shape-changer's understanding expression. "You were dreaming of Qamat. I did, too."

Tyrus grimaced. "It will not happen again. Never happen again."

Erejzan had been busy. He had collected berries from bushes near the creek and dug a few edible roots and tidied Tyrus' pack. He divided the food and gave half to Tyrus. "We can eat on the way. It is light enough for me to retrace our steps to the city without trouble."

He was unquestioning, eager to travel and counter Vraduir, no matter the danger. Tyrus had grown used to that trust, to Erejzan's faith in Tyrus' skills and information. Yet it never ceased to touch his emotions, as it did now. "You are right, my friend," he said softly. "It is morning, and things *do* seem better. I think we will win."

"Of course we will." Erejzan's hungry grin would have been frightening, had he been an enemy. He kicked dirt over the dying embers. "We will win. And we will save LaSirin and LaRenya. But not if we linger here. Come. The hunt is on, Tyrus, and our quarry is running out of places to hide from us."

They hurried out into the late night fog and headed southeast, back toward the city, to Couredh and to Jathelle and Ilissa.

VII

The Price of a Sorkra

❊❊❊❊❊❊❊❊❊❊❊❊❊❊❊❊❊❊❊❊❊❊❊❊

TYRUS AND EREJZAN HUNKERED AT THE EDGE OF THE
thicket and peered through the scrubs and young trees.
Irritably, Tyrus shifted his baldric and set the sword it
held at a more comfortable angle, then returned his
attention to the scene ahead. Twenty lengths beyond
their hiding place, the road led straight on to Couredh's
gate. They had made good time, reaching the royal
highway at dawn. The road had already been busy with
peasants and drovers. Tyrus and Erejzan had paralleled
the traffic for two candle-marks, scurrying from copse
to copse alongside the dirt trail, keeping out of sight.
A few times military patrols had ridden past. When
they did, the sorkra and his friend waited quietly until
the soldiers were well in the distance before they resumed their trek.

Now they had come to the end of easy concealment.
The area between the thicket and the walls, like the
one to the east, along the shore, was scorched and
cleared, offering no cover at all. Yet they could clearly
see the guards patrolling the towers and gateways.
Merchants' policemen were keeping tally of incoming
traffic, and now and then these private soldiers rode

forth to settle a commercial dispute or demand payment from some outlying clan village.

Erejzan turned his back on this sight and sat down heavily on the still damp grass. He winced as a thorn stabbed his bare leg and plucked it out. Then he said, "Look at that. They are checking everyone who comes and goes, Tyrus. We will never get into the city past them, not without too many questions we dare not answer."

Tyrus frowned, continuing to watch the gates. "They questioned us last night and yesterday afternoon while we roamed Couredh's streets, with no harm done."

"Since then, much has happened—mysterious murders in the Street of the Butchers, swordplay and magic lights and bloodletting by a wild ecar. Little wonder they are now suspicious of everyone newly come to this realm. Especially of a man who can work magic." Erejzan peered over his shoulder and went on, "Perhaps . . . can we travel east to the rocks and get to the postern gate again?"

Mulling the dangers of conjury, weighing how much magic he could use, Tyrus hesitated. Before he could answer, Erejzan cocked his head and exclaimed, "Listen! Heralds! LaRenya and Ilissa are leaving the city. Already! Tyrus, we are too late!"

Soldiers and merchants' police snapped to attention. People on the road, eager to see a spectacle, stepped aside, herding their flocks to clear the path, then looked toward the gates. Cheers rose as LaRenya and her retinue came into view. The sun had burned off most of the fog and Tyrus saw everything with great clarity. No standard bearer preceded the royal party, and the heralds who had cried the announcement were those regularly posted at the gates. They went no farther, nor did any accompany LaRenya. With remarkably little pomp, smiling graciously, the queen of Couredh led forth her court from under the shadow of the city walls.

Jathelle rode astride, the custom in these outlying realms of Clarique. Her mount was frisky, but she handled the animal well. It was a dredis stallion, its red coat gleaming, in striking contrast to the LaRenya's bright blue and white costume.

Ilissa followed her, riding a more tractable mare. LaSirin's hair was a fair cloud, drawing the eye. Sirai Aubage attended her closely, as would be expected. Everyone else in LaRenya's party rode the dredis breed horses but Aubage favored an Irico gray, perhaps the better to stand out among so many copper-colored beasts. He touched spurs to his mount and made it prance and rear. Ilissa's hand flew to her throat and Tyrus could imagine her cries of concern and pleas for her betrothed to use more care. Such boastful displays seemed typical of Aubage, as if he enjoyed affrighting his gentle lady, or were trying to impress Jathelle. If he hoped for the latter, he failed. She did not deign to look back at him. Her head up, a jaunty plume waving from her cap, she put her stallion at the canter, leaving Aubage in her wake.

By ones and twos, her ladies and courtiers trotted along the road. Two wagons rumbled at the rear, accompanied by outriders on shaggy ponies. Erejzan narrowed his eyes, studying the carts. "The hawks are in the first, ready to be unhooded and set on their prey. But what is in the second wagon?"

"Most likely the luncheon Mistress Ceshti arranged." Tyrus glanced toward the sun and then at Jathelle. Her horse at a lope, her honey gold hair flying, she rode past, twelve lengths from where he hid. But she was as far from him as the fabled unknown lands across the Great Eastern Sea. "How many measures to Drita Meadows? Do you remember what those gossipers in the bazaar said?"

"Five," Erejzan answered in an absent tone. He was

gazing adoringly at Ilissa as she galloped to catch up with Jathelle.

Both sisters wore the habits Tyrus and Erejzan had seen in Vraduir's vision-glass. The panels were slashed to the waist, the skirts thrown back to free the snug-fitting trousers for easier riding. They had bound their cloaks in bundles behind the cantles, baring their faces and arms to the warm spring air. Jathelle in blue, Ilissa in silver, they were living gems, talking gaily with one another, their expressions animated and happy. If Ilissa had known a sickly girlhood, such weakness seemed lost in her new strength. She was trying to match Jathelle's bold manner and nearly succeeding.

An array of nobility passed then, the gaudy colors of their habits showing the mood of this merry party. Hawkmaster and his assistants bounced on the seats of the first wagon. Within, their feathered charges fastened talons about their perches and swayed back and forth in their cages, unalarmed by the motion because their eyes were veiled. Aromas wafted out of the second wagon, smells of rich food and warm bread.

Abruptly Erejzan gasped and exclaimed, "Tyrus, is that to be the escort? Why, they are whantola birds, not soldiers!"

The queen's elite bodyguard was handsomely garbed for the occasion. Their tabards sported broidered trim and their boots shone with spit and polish. Ribbons fluttered from the shafts of their pikes. Smartly, they divided their column and took up positions to either side of the noblemen and their ladies. Onlookers applauded this drill-field maneuver.

Tyrus counted softly. "Ten and six, and a young officer to command them. No doubt he considers to-day's work pleasant duty."

"It is too few! Even if they know how to use those pikes," Erejzan moaned. "Aubage and the other courtiers are wearing swords, but what help will such toadies as that be, if real trouble comes?"

"Why should they fear any trouble?" Tyrus said bitterly. "Couredh has been at peace for five turns of the seasons. Did not everyone in the city tell us so, and proudly, as they should. Their frontiers are secure, the barbarians quiet. What is there for the bodyguard to do but put on a pretty show and display their handsome uniforms?"

"Too few," Erejzan repeated. "A ten-ten of armed men were not enough against Vraduir. And what of bandits?"

"Rof is no fool, mai fiyel. And I do not think those soldiers would be easy targets, for all their gaudiness." Tyrus tried to sound encouraging, but added, "If Rof is Vraduir's man, he *might* try to distract the soldiery while Vraduir readies to strike."

Laughing, delighting in the rain-freshened morning, Jathelle and her people disappeared around a curve in the road. The travelers who had made room for them to pass returned to the path and set forth for Couredh city again, talking about the nice clothes and blooded horses they had seen.

Tyrus and Erejzan retreated into the thicket and back into the line of woods to the north. Once more they paralleled the road, heedless of raking brambles and slippery footing. Desperate in their haste, they skidded over heaps of wet leaves and leaped across deadfalls and bushes. Now and then they went to the edge of the woods and looked out, examining their progress along the road, each time hoping they would see the highway empty. Once they saw a small unit of merchants' police halted on the highway. A fight had broken out between peddlers, and someone had fetched the police from Couredh to settle the quarrel. With muffled curses, the two friends fled back into the trees and continued their race northward.

For a while, much against their wishes, they were forced to turn away from the road the queen's party had taken. The line of trees went straight, although a western fork of the highway angled off sharply from the main road. "Tyrus they are . . . getting too far ahead," Erejzan panted. "We . . . we have to leave the trees . . . and follow them."

"We will be further delayed," Tyrus said, pausing to gulp for breath and stare out of the woods again. "You yourself warned that they would be on guard for us. Ah! There is no one in sight. Hurry!"

They ran like hunted outlaws, fearing at any moment they would hear the approach of soldiers or city patrols. Loping up the fork of the road, they rounded a curve and found shelter in another line of brush and young trees. There they stopped and collected more energy, staring down the narrowing track of cleared highway. "It . . . it goes into nothing," Erejzan said with dismayed surprise.

Tyrus surveyed the land ahead. As Erejzan had noted, the road was dwindling into a grassy trail, which was swallowed up in the valley beyond. The only concealment henceforth was on the low hills far to either side of the valley, well off the direct path. LaRenya and her party were already far along the valley. Tyrus could barely see the dots of color and the fluttering of the beribboned pikes and bright costumes. He could not hear even the rumbling of the wagons or the horses' hoofbeats.

Leaning over, hands on his knees as he sucked in air to extend his strength for the next part of their chase, Erejzan said, "At this rate . . . we will never catch up with them."

Refusing to be discouraged, Tyrus said, "They will not keep up that pace."

"Can . . . you slow them down with conjury? Or . . . make us run faster?"

Tyrus smiled wanly. "One or the other? Not both? I am a sorkra, not a god, mai fiyel, as well you know. Come. The wagons hinder them, and they are not making speedy time. Five measures is not so far, and Drita Meadows is no further, we were told. We have traveled that much many times."

"Not at a steady run. And we will need to do so if we hope to succeed." Erejzan stood up, flexing his hands, swinging his arms in an arc, and stamping his feet, as if about to perform some of his wild acrobatics.

Acknowledging that possibility, Tyrus pulled back into himself, one hand to his brow. It was not an easy thing, this. He sought the dark, twinkling caves and strange groves for no tangible object at first. Then he created an alien charm out of nothing, an essence of a root, like the laidil that countered Erejzan's shape-changing. Laidil, however, was a natural growth of the provinces. The herb Tyrus seized upon was never known upon land or sea, only in that eerie region where sorcery roamed. He did not bring the strange herb back with him, extracting its power and returning to himself in that slow, uncomfortable sensation of rising out of water while his lungs and brain threatened to burst.

"Give me your hands, Erejzan," he commanded. Bewildered, the acrobat did so and a green incandescence leaped from the sorkra's hands to his. There was no pain or heat, but the firehair started with apprehension all the same. Tyrus sighed and nodded, feeling new and supernatural energy flowing into his limbs, as he knew it was nourishing Erejzan. "Now we can run the distance with less difficulty. And safer than trying to conjure ponies or horses out of woolbacks or deer we meet along the way, my friend."

Erejzan looked guilty. "I . . . I did not mean for you to use *more* sorkra. You are using so much already."

"I will be spendthrift now and recuperate when the quest is done," Tyrus said curtly. He did not like to consider the risk he was taking. When the quest was done, what would there be left of Tyrus of Qamat? Would he have taken so much of that power from his depths that he would be wasted and like one dead? How deep did his resources go? He had never plumbed their absolute limits. Few sorkra had. Had Vraduir? But Vraduir owned borrowings of the god's own gifts, help for his wizardry. Tyrus would not hesitate in draining his own powers, if it would enable him to match Vraduir and defeat him. That triumph was worth anything.

Side by side, he and Erejzan followed the track through the grassland. They now made as straightway after Jathelle's course as they could. If the patrol sought them out, they were far from any copses or thick brush that could offer a hiding place. Casting worry aside, they continued in the open, running, Tyrus' magic giving them breath and blood to endure the punishment they put upon their bodies.

As everyone at the festival had proclaimed, it was the time of greenery come back to Couredh, lifting the white blankets of winter. Though Couredh was more blessed than neighboring Irico, thanks to the southern currents, yet the realm rejoiced in the blossoming earth. And it *was* blossoming. The countryside was bright with flowers and young grass and trees leafing forth. Soft winds carried the pleasant aromas of blooms and earth fresh-turned from the plows. Wildlife scampered through the meadow grasses, avoiding the men's pounding feet. Last night's rain enhanced nature, washing the air clean of dirt and dust.

The sun was well above the horizon now and beating down hotly. The breeze could not pluck the sweat from Tyrus' brow fast enough and his boots were sopping from the wet grass. He paid little heed to these things. If he and Erejzan could progress leisurely, as La-Renya's party was doing, they too could enjoy the scenery and the sweet warmth and growing things. The

Mother of Earth smiled on Couredh, Hetanya extending her gifts bountifully on the land. Tyrus longed to bask in the sun and be at peace. No more searching. No more relentless questing. He threw that dream aside, running, stretching his long legs in a pumping stride.

Little farms and pasturages nestled along the valley and wooded hillsides. At one point, an arm of Couredh's river made a lazy curve past the edge of a slope before it went on its way toward the city, and trees clustered thickly about the banks, making a pleasant, shadowy glade. Peasants tended their young crops or herded their flocks. Women worked near the huts and children played nearby. One woman was spreading her laundry over some rocks to dry. She cupped her hands over her eyes and stared at Tyrus and Erejzan curiously as they ran by. Though Erejzan often worried that Tyrus would exhaust his sorkra powers in conjuring, he glanced wistfully at the browsing woolbacks and motge in the pastures, and Tyrus could read his thought; if they could spare the time, Tyrus could enchant two of the brutes and make them into ponies or horses, long enough to serve the men, as they had occasionally done in the past. Here, under the gaze of the peasants, it would cost great effort to mask them while he conjured—and time they dared not waste. The herb Tyrus had used came at a price, but it would have to do.

Another valley lay beyond the first, past a low pass between wooded crests. They ran on into the next vale, not slackening their gait. How far had they come? Tyrus had run many a footrace against Erejzan and other youths of Qamat in other days. These northern meadows were far away from Qamat, but Tyrus cannily estimated his home island's system of measures against those used in Couredh. They must have traveled three measures and a half from the city, perhaps a bit more. The gossipers had said Drita Meadows and the queen's private preserve lay five measures away. Five. Then the hawking party must be very close ahead of them now. Tyrus longed to hear horses nickering or hawks wheeling and stooping in the sky. If only he could hear Jathelle's voice and know she was safe, that Vraduir—whatever his devious plan against her and Ilissa—had not yet struck.

The ruts left by the wagons and broken grass trampled by the horses angled off more to the northwest. Tyrus and Erejzan swerved to follow it. The track led over a knoll. As they topped the rise, they came upon a thick line of woods and thorny hedge, forming a natural boundary. Two stone markers framed the pass. Tyrus saw the crossed pikes of Couredh's royal house and exulted, "We are close now."

They hurried past the markers and into the queen's lands. An outcropping of boulders lay on the far side of the hill, and they circled around this. Tyrus and Erejzan scanned the valley ahead, hoping for some sign of LaRenya's people. But there were rolling hills and many depressions and curves in the track; as yet they could not see the hawkers and their attendants.

Suddenly horsemen rode out of a hiding place amid the boulders and surrounded the sorkra and the acrobat. No royal bodyguards, these! Mounted on a motley collection of stolen ponies and horses, the riders shouted threats in rough language and waved their swords, axes, and cudgels.

Tyrus and Erejzan swung around back to back and swiveled to confront an attack, whichever way it might come. Tyrus drew his transformed sword and Erejzan crouched, ready to leap toward an assailant as man or shape-changer. Tyrus prepared to counter danger with spells and charms.

After a moment's noisy confusion, one horseman left the others and rode boldly forward. Rof pinched his mustaches and grinned down at them. "Is that any way to greet your future hirekeeper?"

The other brigands encircled Tyrus and Erejzan but showed no eagerness to rush them, despite their greater numbers. There were more than ten of them, yet they kept their distance. Tyrus began to have some confidence that this meeting could be turned to his own favor, if he were not rash.

" 'Ware!" Rof taunted his men disdainfully. "Did you not brag that you would rob LaRenya's purse from them and leave them for the wolves? Bejit shore sweepings! Where is your courage now?" However, Rof did not threaten Tyrus and Erejzan with his whip or his sword, and he too stayed well back, perhaps thinking this would protect him from their sorcerous weapons.

The unkempt ruffians shifted in their saddles and grumbled. The horses scented their fear and were restless. "You had best beware yourself, Rof!" the bravest throatslitter cried. It was the one-eared bandit who had met Tyrus and Erejzan outside the Inn of the Cutpurses. "*You* did not have to deal with them in the Street of the Butchers!"

Tyrus stared hard at One-Ear, trying to sift his ugly face from among other recent memories. One-Ear could indeed be one of those two surviving assassins who had fled the carnage wrought during that murderous attack in the darkness. Tyrus slyly added his own gibes to Rof's. "You know what we can do, then. I advise you to ride away—fast! Or you might not be quick enough to escape us this time!"

At that, several brigands yanked on their reins and edged their mounts back out of the encircling line. They made no effort to disguise their apprehension. Rof had led them here, but his band was loosely controlled and anxious to find easier victims. Seeing their brewing rebellion, Rof took out his whip and snapped it above their heads, cowing them. In his calling, he dared not show fear and he must bully and be strongest to hold the outlaws under his rule. "Do you run from mere words?" he challenged them in loud scorn. "Spawn of Bogotana! Get back here!"

Another took up One-Ear's whining complaint. "Easy enough for *you* to boast and play the leader! You did not tell us that one was a true sorkra, or that a wild ecar would be waiting to rip Atara and the others like woolbacks ready for the pot!"

"Puling children! You need wet nursing!" Rof struck with the whip and men bent low over their saddles and wailed. None turned and ran, perhaps dreading a knife thrown into his back if he did. Satisfied his men were chastened for the moment, Rof turned his attenion to Tyrus and Erejzan again and smiled roguishly. "No fear from them. I have lessoned them to a bit of respect."

Not relaxing, Tyrus met Rof's gaze squarely. "You sent them to kill us last night."

Rof was charmingly honest. "There *was* that fat purse. I had no wish for your blood, sorkra. In fact, I would have regretted your deaths. I told them to rob you without blood, if possible. But you *would* make a battle of it. Hai! And the robbers were the slain! It is a good jest. No rancor between us, sorkra. You have your craft and I must pursue mine. I had to try, at least, to own that gold LaRenya gave you, eh?"

Such amiable greed was appalling. But the man himself won grudging amusement from Tyrus and his friend. Erejzan growled, "And now you bring men enough, you hope, to take the purse at last?" As he spoke he swung his burning stare across the line of bandits, now and then transfixing one with that awful look, forcing the thief to glance away nervously.

Rof reassured them. "Not at all! By my beard, you are a suspicious pair! I mean you no harm at all, I swear. By Bogotana, if you wish. You really should have trusted me there at the Inn. Then you would not have had this long walk. I would have helped you, if you were my men."

"On stolen horses? How did you get out of the city, riding these purloined brutes?" Tyrus demanded, still calculating their chances, one part of his mind roaming sorcery's ways, debating methods to elude Rof and his men. Curiosity made him wait upon choosing—curiosity, and the strength granted by the magic herb he and Erejzan were sharing.

"Oh, there are secret gates to the city, which you will learn if you come to my colors. I am no lord of the Interior nor am I a Sirin of the Destre tribes, but I can lead my underlings."

"And these mannerly curs will help us on our way, no doubt?" Erejzan snarled.

The brigand chief laughed. "They will do as I say. And I say that they will not strike, for now." Rof swung a leg over his horse's neck and dropped from the saddle. He coiled the whip at his belt and spread his hands wide to show he was not holding a hidden axe, sword, or knife. He walked toward the friends and stopped a length from them. "I renew my offer. I was not sure, ere last night's encounter in the Street of the Butchers, if you were worth your hire. But the Death God took my assassins from your hands. And by the survivors' tales, there was true magic in it. I say again, I can use you. Together we can become wealthy."

The promise Rof made held. The throatslitters and thieves hefted their weapons, but they made no other hostile moves and gave no sign of advancing. They seemed quite content, in fact, to keep their distance from the sorkra and his companion. At Tyrus' back, Erejzan was fidgeting with impatience and muttering, "This Bog' imp is a dog at our heels, snapping at our cloaks even this far from the city."

Tyrus played for time, saying thoughtfully, "You truly want to hire us?"

"Ai!" Rof said. "As good faith, I have decided you may keep the queen's purse. I make you a gift of it."

"Generous indeed to let us keep what is ours," Tyrus said with heavy sarcasm. "But we can earn coins anywhere. Talents such as ours require something more than gold and silver. We do not work cheap."

A shocked whisper ran around the circle of thieves and murderers. They could not guess where their lord's bargaining would lead. Rof himself was taken aback. "So? Well and at that, I have never hired a sorkra before. Or one of *your* kind, whatever you are," he added, glancing uneasily at Erejzan. "What is the price of a magician?"

Erejzan twisted around, peering over his shoulder, eyeing Tyrus sidelong. Like the brigands, but with better success, he was speculating where Tyrus would take them. The young sorkra said, "We have our purposes, things of wizardry that cannot be revealed to ordinary mortals." He put pointed emphasis on every mention of magic or arcane arts, with good effect.

Rof's dark brows drew together as he considered this. He tried to hide his misgivings, but a shadow of fear lurked in his eyes. Matters had turned very devious, in ways he was not braced for. "If not coin, what?"

Tyrus did not answer him directly. "Before a sorkra shares his powers, he must be sure of his allies. How far are you willing to venture in this hirekeeping?" Rof hemmed and hawed and then shrugged mutely. Tyrus dared to lower his sword, shamming unconcern of the threat around them. He swirled his mantle and said, "I am even now using my sorkra skills. I may not weigh any further magic until the present conjury is done. But I might be grateful for your help in my work . . ."

"Help? What sort of help?" Rof wondered, still more uncertain at the shift in matters.

"Help that might profit you handsomely," Erejzan

said, grasping Tyrus' intent. "You may earn a far greater reward than that paltry purse you thought to steal from us."

"Reward? What magic is this that you work?" Rof was held by wonderment and greed. He overcame his doubts, leaning forward curiously.

"Wizardry that will win you a queen's favor, bandit lord," Tyrus said in a haughty tone. "By sorkra methods, I have learned of a menace aimed at Couredh's sisters. We are on our way to warn them. But the bodyguard might prevent us from reaching LaRenya. It would serve us if you and your men would create a diversion and draw them off a space, long enough for me to speak to LaRenya Jathelle. Once she hears my news, I am sure she will be very grateful. For her sake and that of her sister, she will thank her rescuers most lavishly."

The mention of the armed escort had alarmed the brigands. But Tyrus' hint about a rich reward made them forget possible danger. They licked their lips like hungry predators. Erejzan sneered at their single-minded avarice, then hammered home Tyrus' persuasion. "Think, bandit lord. You could win gold and perhaps even amnesty from LaRenya. No further need to run from thief-takers and the merchants' police." Erejzan gestured and painted images in the air. "You could ride and walk abroad without any need to guard your skin. You might even be honored with title or rank," he finished, tongue in cheek. Tyrus elbowed him sharply, afraid this last was so outrageous it would surely bring Rof back to earth and spoil the lure.

But Rof was a plundering killer, snapping at the bait, fairly taken. Hand upon his breast, his beard tilted up proudly, he styled himself as Erejzan had described. "Sirai Rof, eh? I like the sound of it. How would that suit those whey-faced shopkeepers who call me king of cutpurses? Hai! By Bogotana . . . !" He looked from Tyrus to Erejzan. "Wizardry? And what reward will *you* gain from this?"

"The queen's smile," Tyrus said quickly. The brigands did not know what to make of that sort of reply. Jathelle's smile would hold no attraction for them, it was plain. Tyrus added in a darker voice, "And an accomplishment important solely to us sorkra. I cannot tell you more."

They did not care for that last and asked no questions on it. The hope of riches was ensnarement enough. As they had brushed aside thoughts of the well-armed bodyguards, they now would not listen too closely to any talk of sorcery. Only Rof appeared to have any reservations. His men began setting up a vulgar clamor, eager to be on their way and earn the royal reward Tyrus had dangled before them. The bandit lord cocked his head and peered intently at Tyrus and his friend. "We are alike, my quick-tongued warlock and you, shape-changer." Erejzan tensed angrily at this shrewd remark. But Rof went on, smiling. "We will all tell a lie and chuckle up our sleeves at him who trusts us completely. I do not trust you, not completely. But there is enough truth in your words to work the way. Ever since the peasants started disappearing up north, I have wondered if it promised some trouble aimed at LaRenya. If you have news of such, as I suspect, and mean to tell her—then we have no quarrel. I will help you warn her, sorkra. And then you shall speak prettily and gain her favor for us. Agreed?"

"Agreed." Tyrus expected some oath to be made, some seal put upon the bargain. But Rof had no concern for such things—as well he had proved the night before! Not even an oath sworn to the Evil God had bound him from sending assassins in the wake of the sorkra and the acrobat. Abruptly, he turned away from his new allies, his decisions made and no further guarantee asked.

"You and you—off!" Rof ordered, indicating two of his men riding sturdy mounts. The thieves were bewildered and slow to obey. This angered Rof and he swung up on his stolen horse, then spurred toward the two brigands and began flogging them mercilessly. He battered them with the butt of the whip, knocking them from their saddles. The pair ran for their lives while One-Ear and another bandit seized the loose reins of their mounts and kept the animals from fleeing, too.

As soon as the thieves had run into the sanctuary of the boulders, Rof gave up the chase, his purpose accomplished. Grinning and cheerful once more, he put his whip back on his belt and said, "They are the least of my men, not worth taking in shares of what the queen may reward us. But their horses are good ones. You can have them. Let those bejits walk back to Couredh. Mount up, sorkra, and you, handri-hair. Let us warn LaRenya and win our gold, eh?"

Recovering quickly from their surprise at all this, Tyrus and Erejzan hurried toward the proffered horses. The former riders were shouting curses at them and Rof and the other bandits, but they were cowardly and dared not come out of the rocks to try to reclaim the animals. Tyrus swung up on a big Irico gray and Erejzan mounted a nervous dredis. The sorkra took control of his new mount with reins and heels while Erejzan, as was his gift as beastmaster, quieted the red-coated dredis with a soft word. In an instant, they galloped down the valley, after the hawking party. Rof and his men were temporarily left behind but hastily came riding after, shouting reminders about the bargain.

A lifetime ago, before his world died in fire, Tyrus had ridden every day, relishing such a spirited brute as this at his command. Now he did not chase hurnbul or deer. He was grateful for years of experience, since the Irico gray had a jolting gait. Tyrus rose in the stirrups and urged the horse on, snapping the reins back and forth over the dappled neck and shoulder, wishing he had spurs.

How much time had they lost dickering and wheedling with Rof? Tyrus looked back and saw Erejzan a length behind his own mount's tail, Rof and the bandits much farther to his rear. Tyrus did not mean to outrun the bandits, for they indeed could prove useful if danger struck from ambush. Yet he did not draw rein. He jammed his heels in the gray's ribs and called for more speed.

The morning was wearing toward Iesor-Peluva's center stand. Could Vraduir's evil, dark sorcery be a-walk on such a brilliant, sunlit day? It had been so on Qamat. And many an island visited by the enchanted ship of the master wizard had suffered terrible theft, even by open light. Vraduir's arts would not shrink from attack by day, as Tyrus well knew. He thought again of the image in the vision-glass, of Vraduir bargaining with a god, perhaps. Once Vraduir had bargained with Bogotana. And now . . .

"Tyrus!" Erejzan was roaring, overcoming the steady drum of hoofbeats. Other voices were raised, too, the bandits calling to one another, terror in their words.

There was no need to turn to see what frightened them and so raked Erejzan with sudden panic. It was coming directly for Tyrus himself.

A slight rise ahead marked the end of the southern valley. Beyond must surely lie Drita Meadows. Five measures were done. And ahead, above, filling the sky, a wall of ominous black cloud boiled. It had erupted into existence in scant heartbeats, unnatural and looming.

Ripped by enormous lightnings, the darkness lifted

endlessly, towering to the very zenith. Like that awesome presence in Vraduir's citadel, the cloud was ever changing, vast, shrinking men into insects by its size and power. It was an inexorable force of nature—or of wizardry as black as the cloud itself!

VIII

The Demon Hordes of Vraduir

※-※-※-※-※-※-※-※-※-※-※-※-※-※-※-※-※-※-※-※

THE GRAY SNORTED AND SLAMMED TO AN ABRUPT stop, nearly flinging Tyrus over its head. Only years of experience kept him from being dumped off onto the lush meadow grass. The frantic horse fought the bit and plunged in a wild circle as Tyrus fought it.

The bandits' horses were also panicky, and several of the throatslitters lost their seats. As they went sailing into air, the animals galloped every which way, bucking and kicking. Their riders swore and chased them. Rof and his toughest thieves managed to hold onto their saddles, as Tyrus and Erejzan did, though with great difficulty.

As the cloud climbed heavenward, the wind rose sharply. Tyrus forced the gray to chase its tail and expend its terror in those futile gyrations. The air turned winter cold; skin prickling and shivering seizing them all. Tyrus felt a biting sensation in his nostrils as he breathed, the shock of the cold wind staggering him. He yelled above the icy howling at Rof. "Drita Meadows—how far?"

Some of the bandit lord's words were torn away in the gusts. But he was pointing, mouthing exaggeratedly,

148

and Tyrus caught enough of the reply to understand. "Y—yon . . . next . . . slope . . ."

Tyrus sought to suppress his own terror, one far greater than the gray's or that of the confused bandits. The sorkra feared for himself and Erejzan. But he feared much more for Jathelle and her goddess-faced sister. The women must be at Drita Meadows—beyond the next slope—in the shadow of those lightning-shattered clouds!

Cold! A cold that penetrated garments and blood and numbed the brain. It was swooping ahead of the furious darkness, stinging Tyrus and the others in a vicious assault of daggery ice. Keen blades of sleet tore their garments and blood weltered on faces and hands.

"Bogotana!" the brigands cried, half in prayer and half a curse. "He comes to take us!"

Erejzan alone among them controlled his horse well. He bellowed against the wind and sleet as he rode toward the oncoming cloud. "You fools! Bogotana kills with fire and brimstone! This is ice! And another god!"

Realizing the truth, the bandits set up a still louder howl. "It is Nidil! Nidil! The Death God! He Who Steals All Breath!"

Tyrus still wrestled with his horse, trying to see into the black clouds. The lightnings and the billowing expanse dominated fully half the sky. The darkness reached greedy streamers up toward Iesor-Peluva's burden and threatened to blot out the very sun.

Then, as if reminded of their true quarry, the terrible clouds condensed and folded—lightnings and thunder battering Tyrus. The cloud was falling. The entire boiling mass of evil night and roaring wind and sleet was descending like a curtain woven by a demon. His worst dreamings rushed upon him and assaulted the day. An arrow shape was forming from the thickest part of the mass, a dart hurtling out of the northern dark, stabbing toward the earth. Tyrus beat ice from his eyebrows and mustaches, knowing what was going to happen, helpless to prevent it. No charm could counter this!

The arrow of blackness vanished behind the slope ahead of him, plunging itself into the vitals of Drita Meadows! Were those screams Tyrus heard only the wind? Or did he now hear the agony of stricken men, women, and beasts, blasted by arcane forces beyond mortal comprehension? And one of the screams was his own—a horrified protest at what Vraduir had done.

The point of the cloud arrow landed past the slope. However, like an immense object thrown into a small pool, it created a tremendous, rolling series of waves, washing outward. A moving wall, the black cloud surged over the grassy rise, escaping from Drita Meadows, sweeping rapidly toward Tyrus and the others.

"Rof! It is . . . it is full of . . . things!" One-Ear was shrieking, his voice cracking like a beardless boy's.

A heartbeat later, they all saw the phenomenon and recoiled in new fear. If Rof's men had been shaken before, they now were witless as dumb brutes. They jumped off their horses, giving up all hope of subduing the beasts, and started to run blindly.

They had no chance. The cloud was upon them, covering them with its icy blackness. Out of it came gibbering demons, creatures never known on land or sea. They materialized from the cloud and leaped onto men and horses at random.

Tyrus drew his enchanted sword and slashed at a slavering snakeling coming at his face. Decaying flesh and splintered bone parted and gobbets of ichor splashed him, stinging like bits of fire. He had struck cleanly, and with a sorkra blade. Yet Tyrus was not surprised that his blow did not kill the thing. The writhing, many-limbed snake being was critically hurt but still flailed the air, flying, still seeking to drink his blood.

Another hideous demon was coming at him. Tyrus had a glimpse of glittering and faceted insect eyes and squirming tentacles dripping slime. He lashed out again with the sword and conjured desperately as he did.

Death could not be dealt, not in any terms men knew. These things were already dead, yet moved and clawed and bit with most terrible effect. The sword bit again, slowing the charge but a trifle. Where limbs were hacked, there was no maiming, nor could the demons feel pain.

Tyrus wiped his mind clean of encroaching terror. He reached for a calm discipline, amazing himself as he closed upon it. "Minions of the upper places enchain you. Bogotana's demons, I wrap you in links of wizardry," he chanted in the sorkra language. Skillfully, he formed the bands that must hold them and toss them back whence they came. He matched Vraduir's pets with his own white magic.

The insect-eyed demon was arrested in the cold air. It clutched for him but never quite touched him. Tentacles rippled obscenely and the thing made disgusting sounds in its murderous frustration, unable to break the enchantment. "Begone! Back to Vraduir! Back to the pits of Bogotana!" Tyrus commanded.

His spells wrought what even the magic blade could not. The demon hovered, a hand span from him. A noxious reek rushed from its slobbering mouth, making Tyrus' stomach roil. But it was melting, receding like water dragged back into the ocean, as Tyrus fastened the countercharm securely. Snapping, mandibles working futilely, its tentacles limp, it dissolved back into the black cloud.

All around Tyrus, other men were waging battles with similar horrible beings. Lacking Tyrus' gifts, they were stricken despite their weapons and struggling. Pleading for mercy, calling on whatever god might hear them, they crawled through the darkness, sobbing, bedeviled on every side. Hunks of rotting flesh came off the things as the bandits lashed at them. Sea monsters and imps of smoking mountains rode men as men rode horses, gnawing and biting and raking with talons. Men were half covered with bloated and maggot-riddled corpses of abominations that should have been aeons dead and rotted. Other huge beings followed the terrified thieves and tried to swallow them whole.

The wind, too, was an enemy, slashing them constantly with sleet and cold. Tyrus' horse fell with him and thrashed and whinnied, refusing to endure his weight amid this unnatural blast.

Close at Tyrus' right hand, Erejzan was being borne down by one massive demon. The acrobat had begun a shape-change, deliberately, abandoning any caution in an attempt to guard himself. But he had been taken before he could complete the form of a man-ecar. His hands were cloaked in fur and his beard wild, his face darkening with an ecar's dusky coloring. But in all other ways he was still a man and trapped by the magic brute at his throat. A three-toed thing, part wolf and part rapacious bird, stabbed its needle-sharp beak at the shape-changer's eyes, held off only by those powerful hands. But Erejzan's strength was faltering, as even his must under such pressure.

"Back to Vraduir!" Tyrus chanted, flinging his arms up against the ice storm. "Creatures of his making, slaves bought from Bogotana's bargain with Vraduir— back to the pits of the mountains and the evil realms!"

His belly shook and heaved with nausea. Stench engulfed him. His clothes were sodden and heavy with sheets of ice. His hair and beard were flattened against his scalp and face, giving him no warmth or protection. He could not rest, not until Vraduir's demons were vanquished and thrust into their holes once again.

"Return! Return to your demon master! You have lost! Lost! The spirit of Rasven and all good sorkra en-

chain you forevermore! Come no more to the world of
men! Begone . . . !"

No sham with a vision-glass, this! No pretty delusion
to amuse noblemen and their ladies. Jathelle would not
smile and delight in what he did here . . .

Jathelle! And her helpless younger sister! They were
Vraduir's true victims, Tyrus knew. And they were
there—within the black heart of the cloud, no doubt
beset by demons far more terrible than these!

Like the first sorcerer's creature he had bested, the
others yielded to Tyrus' countercharms. Some were
god's breedings and he could only trick them, not enchant them. But slowly they all began to retreat within
the spillings of the cloud. Tyrus felt no elation, sensing
that his powers were only in small part the cause. The
demon hordes created an awful cacophony as they went
away. Now the cloud, too, was withdrawing, folding
back toward that parent blackness, leaving Tyrus and
the other men under the open sky once more.

The brigands stared about in bewilderment. Tyrus
saw two lying dead, and several others had taken hurts.
It was possible such wounds would respond to spellcasting, for the only balm for such injuries would be a
healing magic.

Erejzan was nearby, staggering to his feet, and
Tyrus was heartened to see that his friend had escaped
his attacker with only minor gashes and bruisings. Hurriedly, lest the bandits see him half-changed, Erejzan
was reverting fully to his man form. He shivered and
swiped at the filthy excrescences on his garments, left
by the demon who had tried to kill him.

Belatedly coming to themselves, the brigands cheered
in relief and yelped, "Hai! Sorkra! The sorkra turned
them with his magic!" They closed around Tyrus and
Erejzan, including the acrobat in their praise. "Hai!
Fihar! Handri! Whatever you are, you are our man!"
They shouted and slapped Erejzan heartily on the back.

Erejzan shrugged them off, his thoughts one with Tyrus'. They were running, catching up the reins of riderless horses that looked fit enough to carry them. The bandits chased them, trying to lift Tyrus up to their shoulders and parade him in triumph.

"Put me down," he yelled. "It is not done! Those demons were but outriders of Vraduir's magic storm. Worse is taking place beyond the hill! If you want to thank me, help me get to LaRenya before it is too late!"

Tyrus wriggled away from the bandits and clambered onto the horse he had in hand. The animal was still panic-stricken, but he abused it mercilessly in his fear for Jathelle. "Move, move!" he demanded and beat on its flanks with the flat of his enchanted blade as well as with his heels.

He drove the wild-eyed brute headlong up the slope where the demon cloud was shrinking. He wished he had the art to give the hapless horse wings. But at this length, its own terror was as strong as any supernatural impetus Tyrus could create. Pitiless, he goaded it up the slope and over into Drita Meadows beyond.

Catastrophe awaited him just over the rise. Drita Meadows had been a lovely place of rolling hills and pleasant little woods. Now all the grass was dead and black and coated with rimes of ice. The flowering trees were uprooted and broken in the wind of evil wizardry.

The planned day of joyous festival had turned to tragedy. Men and women lay on the blasted meadow, bleeding, their fine clothes in icy rags. Many appeared dead or dying. Horses had been disemboweled or hamstrung and lay bleating pathetically or past all complaint. Nobility and hawkmasters, servants and pages, the royal bodyguard—not one had escaped some hurt. Wagons were smashed. The array of food and wines was scattered among the blood and horses' entrails. The waiter who had suspected he would be assigned to

attend the lords and ladies at this outing lay dead beside the noblest of Jathelle's court. A few of the hawks
had fluttered from their broken cages and loosed
tethers, flying about in hopeless confusion. But most
of the hunting birds were mere lumps of bloody
feathers.

Yet not everyone had fallen. The officer of the bodyguard and four of his men were fighting boldly against
their adversaries, as were several of the nobles. They
strove to protect the wounded, who were trying to
crawl away from the catastrophe. In the midst of it all,
Jathelle stood, shouting defiance. She had taken up a
dead soldier's pike; with it she stabbed and struck
valiantly at the seething black clouds and their terrible denizens. The pike's once-gay ribbons were limp
and stained with ichor, as Jathelle's pretty costume was.
With her fair hair about her breast and bare shoulders
she was now truly a battle maiden, awful in her wrath.

Tyrus raced onto Drita Meadows, hurrying to reach
Jathelle's side. The lesser demons he had banished were
beginning to gather into the cloud ahead of him, as
were those who had ravaged the hawking party. The
darkness whirled above Tyrus like night's blood coagu-
lating. That arrow of wizardry was drawing itself out
of the mortal wound it had made in the earth—the
destroyed Meadows.

The lords of the clouds were readying to leave with
the imps and demons. Tyrus gazed at them in shock.
Skeletons in armor! Their horses' caparisons and the
warriors' tabards were moldy and rotting with the touch
of extreme age. Their armor was fashioned in styles
common to empires long vanished. The double-headed
axes of Traecheus and the fabled red dragon of lost
Ryerdon adorned their garments and cloaks. These
badges were famous—no, notorious! A pantheon of
legendary traitors, these! They were Riir-shai who sold

his people to the barbarians, Prendrae who betrayed Traecheus and nearly brought the entire world to ruin . . . they were men dead countless generations ago!

Their eye sockets were empty. Faces were grinning skulls. Bones rattled within the rusting armor. Their chargers, too, were naught but skeletons strung together with rotting tendons, their noisome entrails dragging below the once-brilliant trappings. The stench accompanying this horde of mythic villains was nearly overwhelming, far beyond that of the imps and demons who had attacked Tyrus and Erejzan and the bandits.

Dead! Men and horses—dead! Years past numbering—dead!

Dead men who had found no rest. Traitors, they had been turned from Keth's portals, forever damned, condemned to roam the land below and never find life again! Wanderers between death and life, these lost souls of every Tyta'an province here entered the sight of humankind again to do Vraduir's bidding.

Some bore symbols and brands of realms unknown. With the fabled betrayers of Traecheus and Ryerdon, they rode, aiming for the cloud, climbing into the air. The ghastly army had come from the swirling blackness and now it was being recalled.

Darkness and wind were weapons, battering at Tyrus. Squinting through knives of ice, he saw the foremost of the skull-headed warriors riding toward him. The dead chieftain had taken a hostage—Ilissa!

The princess was held, in gauntleted, bony hands, before the skeleton warrior in the saddle. She was fighting desperately, struggling to get free, even though his horse was flying half a length above the ground.

Jathelle ran in the abductor's wake. She raised the pike above her head, preparing to throw it, then hesitating, fearing to harm Ilissa. She continued to run after

Ilissa and her cruel captor, her expression contorted with anger and hatred.

"Fight me! Turn and fight me! *I* will be your hostage, you filthy clenru! Fight *me!* Come back and fight me! Let her go . . . !"

She was near enough now to strike and Jathelle thrust the pike savagely into what should have been the hamstring of the warrior's horse. To her horror, the bones parted and the entire leg of the horse's skeleton tore free of the rest of the animated carcass. Bones and strewings of decayed tendons rained down on Jathelle. But the damage hindered horse and rider not at all

"Bring her back!" Jathelle shrilled.

Tyrus leaned against the buffeting gale and drew conjury up from his inner being. Time was hurrying too swiftly. And he felt Vraduir's sorcery mixed with a far more deadly power, one past any countering magic to prevent. The Death God's minions! As Vraduir had once bargained and stolen, seizing the lesser demons and imps from Bogotana, now he must have won the Death God's favor. The skeletons were not illusions nor a sorkra's creations. Tyrus probed their surfaces and shrank in momentary terror at the icy contact. They went on Vraduir's mission, but the skeletons belonged to Nidil Who Steals All Breath. Could Tyrus find any enchantment that could defeat them?

Erejzan was veering to Tyrus' right, lunging directly into the path of the oncoming skeleton chieftain. No ordinary human could have moved so quickly. But thanks to the curse Vraduir had laid upon Erejzan, he had special arts and skills. Erejzan scrambled up until he was balanced atop his saddle while the horse rushed along maddeningly, its course about to cross below that of the ascending skeleton warrior.

The skeleton horse and rider were a length above him when Erejzan made an incredible leap, calling on all his acrobat's strength. He found purchase about the dead horse's neck and clung to it and the tattered caparison.

Tyrus abandoned attempts to break through the spell Vraduir had thrown around Nidil's skeleton warriors. He bent all his efforts to help Erejzan. The shape-changer's daring attack could be nothing Vraduir had protected against. Maybe there would be a chink in the evil sorcerer's wall of magic!

Erejzan had broken through! He hung on frantically, the caparison tearing as he transferred his hold to the ancient saddle. Jathelle was running along beneath him, yelling encouragement, thrusting at the horse's remaining hindleg with her pike.

Tyrus, too, was running, hurling spells to guard Erejzan, hoping they could penetrate the charm woven about the skeleton warrior and Ilissa.

"Help me!" Ilissa screamed, her arms stretched down to Erejzan and Jathelle. The acrobat was sorely bedeviled by the skeleton rider, for that traitor from the past was swatting at Erejzan, trying to slay him with a bloodstained sword. Barely maintaining his grip, Erejzan dodged and swung wildly in mid-air, still attempting to reach Ilissa.

"A bit more, LaSirin," Tyrus heard Erejzan roaring. "I will save you! A bit more . . ."

Ilissa's beautiful hair was a flag against the black sky, her silvery habit streaked with ice. The evil cloud and the riders were a stark contrast to her pale loveliness and innocence.

Time ended, and Erejzan lost.

The skeleton chieftain crashed an age-encrusted boot into the acrobat's belly precisely at the moment leather trappings and cloth ripped asunder. Erejzan had touched Ilissa's hands in his final desperate effort. But she could not bear his weight for even the slightest instant. With a wail of grief and defeat, Erejzan dropped, tumbling toward the Meadows, now two lengths down. He was turning reflexively and curving his lithe body to absorb the inevitable impact.

"You cannot have her!" Jathelle exclaimed, tears streaming down her cheeks.

The cloud enclosed Ilissa and the riders. Ilissa twisted helplessly in the skeleton warrior's arms, looking back at her sister and Erejzan and Tyrus.

"Help me! *Help me . . . !*"

It was the terrified plea of a child, cutting into their hearts.

Jathelle raised her pike again, intending to risk hurling it, if nothing else would serve. The skeleton chieftain looked down and pointed at LaRenya. Tyrus sensed a crackling pressure, new and malevolent sorcery building. He seemed to see Vraduir in the clouds with the Death God's warriors and felt Vraduir's murderous anger as he had when they beheld him in the vision-glass. Anger—aimed at Jathelle!

The skeleton warriors were Nidil's property, but Vraduir was going to use them to strike his foes. Vraduir had promised that if Jathelle got in his way, he would slay her!

Tyrus sucked in air so violently his lungs were afire with pain. And from his hand flew green lightnings. At the same crack in the fabric of the real world, black flame left the skeleton chieftain's gauntlet—but it was Vraduir who was flinging the deadly fire!

The two tremendous forces, the magic of son and sire, met in an explosion of wizardry. The roar filled Drita Meadows and resounded from the wall of forest bounding the grassland. Tyrus and the others were knocked to the ground and he sprawled awkwardly. Supine, he frantically wove more conjury, an illusion, knowing what must be.

Ilissa was lost. Captive in the clouds, she was beyond his reach and secure in Vraduir's powerful spell. But Jathelle—*she* could be saved!

Tyrus gestured, and Vraduir saw falsely, seeing what Tyrus willed the skeleton warriors to see. Their eyeless sockets were Vraduir's window on the Meadows, and Tyrus showed them utter destruction—Jathelle and all her people slain, to the last. He concentrated intently, forcing that gory image toward Vraduir, making his enemy believe the lie.

The ruse worked. Satisfied, Vraduir bade his skeletons turn away, thinking their attack complete. The warriors and demons thronged in the black cloud, Ilissa with them. The cloud was lifting, drawing back toward the northern horizon with incalculable speed. The retreat left the sky clear and blue, the sun shining over a scene of bloody disaster.

Jathelle was sitting up, tracking the cloud, anguished. Her last glimpse of Ilissa was that perfect face and cloud of Irico white hair caressed by bone and blackness. Then the rattling armor, the weapons, the skeleton warriors and their ghostly steeds were swallowed in churning darkness.

In the time a candle might sputter twice, the cloud was gone, and Ilissa with it. Nothing remained save a distant line of ominous gray all across the lip of the forbidden lands to the far north.

Groans and sobs filled the now-sunny air. Animals whimpered and the surviving hawks keened. Tyrus crept over the blackened grass toward Erejzan. The acrobat lay on his side, gasping and stunned. Exhaustion and defeat racked him; but to Tyrus' relief, his friend was alive and did not seem seriously hurt from his terrible fight and fall.

As Erejzan's wits returned, his eyes grew haunted. He slammed his fists into the frozen earth and cried breathlessly, "Too . . . late! Could . . . not hang on! Too . . . too . . . late !"

"There was more than Vraduir's magic in this, mai fiyel," Tyrus comforted him. "Those warriors were borrowed from Nidil."

Erejzan rocked back and forth, massaging his belly. "G—gods! He traffics with . . . with gods. LaSirin! Oh, LaSirin! If . . . if only I could have . . ."

Tyrus clasped his shoulder, soothing the dejected acrobat as well as he could. He glanced around at Jathelle. His illusion for Vraduir had shown her broken and dead. But LaRenya was alive, on her knees, weeping heartbrokenly. Tears ran over her cheeks and fell upon her heaving breast. "Ilissa! What have they done with you, Little One? Forgive me! Forgive me! I could not keep you safe! Hetanya, save her! Save her!"

Like the bereaved young queen, Tyrus stared northward. The cloud lurked all along the horizon. Only he and Erejzan had looked into the vision-glass, and only Tyrus had flown—in his mind—across the great expanse into the Death God's realm. To the others, the cloud masked specific direction. But though Tyrus had not tracked every march of the way, he could narrow the place to a particular section of the cloud—there! To Vraduir and that citadel of his vision was where the skeleton warriors had taken Ilissa. There, to the citadel, and to Vraduir.

All across Drita Meadows, people were stirring. A few managed to get to their feet. They weaved dizzily, too hurt and desolated to move further. Others moved on their hands and knees, seeking their loved ones.

The officer, his bodyguards, and three of the nobles had fought with Jathelle, striking at the lesser warriors and trying to get to her side as she closed with the skeleton chieftain. Now the officer helped Jathelle to rise, fussing over her, anxious for her.

A few candle-marks earlier, the soldier and his men had ridden proudly forth from Couredh. Only he and four of the escort were still on their feet, and each had taken a wound. The officer was flushed with fury and shame at his failure to protect his royal charges. "La-Renya," he began, "I . . . we could not . . . oh, mai LaSirin Ilissa!" He sank down before Jathelle and bowed his head submissively, expecting death at her hands.

Swallowing hard, Jathelle scrubbed away her tears with her knuckles. There was a bright, hot gleam in her blue eyes. Watching her, Tyrus relived his own emotions. He had known such wrath when he saw the ruins of Qamat. How would Jathelle deal with *her* anger? Some rulers would vent their fury on a hapless subordinate, and the officer had bent his neck to her, ready for the sword or other punishment.

The soldiers' pikes were shattered and their blades blunt from the violence of their fight. The officer's face was cut and he was besmeared with his own blood as he numbly awaited Jathelle's judgment.

"Lieutenant?" Jathelle was a woman attempting to wake from a terrible dream. But this dream was true. She shook herself, staring down at the officer. "Lieutenant Utaigh, you . . . you and your men fought gallantly. There is no fault. The enemy . . . the enemy was too powerful."

A pitiful chorus of sobs and moans underlined her words, the plaint of the wounded and suffering. Jathelle exclaimed, "Oh, Hetanya, Mother of Earth, help us!"

The soldiers had grieved for their fallen comrades. But grim resolve took them now, their countenances burning with battle fever. "We will go after the skeleton warriors, LaRenya," Lieutenant Utaigh vowed. "We will bring LaSirin Ilissa back."

That brought Jathelle out of her anguish. Hastily, she said, "No, not yet. We must not go against this enemy like unprepared children. And . . . and our people must be helped. So much . . . so many afflicted." She clasped her arms tightly about herself, grimacing, plainly trying to collect her wits. The panels of her skirt had been torn away and her costly riding breeches were frayed and bloody. Her bodice was cut, nearly exposing her full breasts. Her hair was tangled and dabbled with remains of the ice storm, leavings that were slowly melting in the sun. She stared dully at Tyrus and Erejzan. She did not seem to comprehend their presence here, still struggling to cope with all that had happened.

As Tyrus helped Erejzan to his feet, Aubage lurched toward Jathelle. The nobleman's gaudy clothes, like Jathelle's, were covered with dirt and gore. Two other courtiers had survived the debacle relatively unhurt and they were as anxious as Aubage to win Jathelle's favor.

"LaRenya . . ."

Aubage hardly got his mouth open when Jathelle abruptly rounded on him, her pent-up fear and anger loosed. Apparently his voice had touched a raw place in her wounded heart. "You!" Jathelle cried. "You were riding beside her when the skeleton warriors swept down upon us! How could they have taken her when you were so close? You are her betrothed! Sworn to guard her against all harm! If *I* had been as near as you when they seized Ilissa . . ."

"LaRenya, they . . . they came so suddenly, with no warning," Aubage protested weakly.

"You let her be taken, you posturing fool!"

Tyrus had no fondness for Aubage, but he suspected Jathelle would rue these words when she had time to think on them. Carefully, he interrupted her, saying, "LaRenya Jathelle?" She turned toward him, blinking, and Tyrus went on, "Neither Sirai Aubage nor anyone else could have withstood the skeleton warriors and the demons and imps. No ordinary weapons could slay them."

His defense was poorly rewarded. Aubage shifted from whining in his own behalf to attack, pouncing on Tyrus' explanation. "Wizardry! It was wizardry! And he is a wizard! We saw him work magic past fathoming. LaRenya, *he* is responsible for all this! *He* took Ilissa— with magic!"

IX

LaRenya, Sorkra, and Bandit Lord

❉❋❉❋❉❋❉❋❉❋❉❋❉❋❉❋❉❋❉❋❉❋❉❋❉❋❉❋❉❋❉❋

TYRUS WAS STUNNED BY SUCH INGRATITUDE. HE AND
Erejzan were both badly rattled by their ordeal and
Aubage took advantage of their silence. "I knew at
once your tricks were *too* clever, amuser," he said,
moving as if he would put his sword at Tyrus' throat.
"No common entertainer could perform such marvels.
You planned all of this from the beginning, to beguile
us and work your scheme to capture my Ilissa . . ."

Erejzan was weaving drunkenly and breathless. But
he moved barehanded against the courtier and would
have closed with him had not Tyrus come between
them. The other courtiers restrained Aubage, while
Tyrus did the same with his friend. Erejzan wriggled
to be free and yelped, "Tyrus made your excuses to
LaRenya and you repay him thus?"

"Hold your tongue, tumbler, or I will cut it out."
Aubage beat at the hands holding him, roaring at his
fellow noblemen, "Let go of me and help me lesson
this whoreson acrobat!"

Despite his hurts, Erejzan's face split in a nasty grin.
"Try me, Sirai Aubage, and we will see how blooded
you can be in *real* fight . . . !"

165

"Enough!" Jathelle's voice sliced through the squabble like a warlord's axe. "Can you do nothing but quarrel? People are hurt and Ilissa has been abducted!"

Chastened, the men drew back a pace, still glowering.

Tyrus said, "If you will allow me, LaRenya, I have some skills to heal the wounds given by the imps . . ."

"Magic?" Aubage demanded, refusing to let go of the matter. "It must be magic. He admits it. He can heal it because he created this villainous sorcery. Look at them. Why are they here, these two? Why? If not to lead those skeleton warriors?"

Jathelle was disturbed by these accusations, staring at Tyrus and Erejzan. After a long moment, her countenance softened and she said, "If you meant us ill, you did not act the part. Never have I seen such courage as when you leapt upon the skeleton, acrobat. And you, Tyrus of Qamat, I think you saved me from death, matching that thunderbolt with your own magic lightning. Yet there *were* unnatural things. Why *are* you here? Is what Aubage says true?"

Aubage pressed her, exclaiming, "It *is* true, LaRenya. He conjured with that mirror, remember? Bringing forth hags and imps and a seer to prophesy."

"And if you had heeded Tyrus' warnings, LaSirin Ilissa would be safe and back in the city," Erejzan blurted.

That shocked Aubage to silence. Jathelle nodded and said, "You *did* try to warn us. I see it. But Ilissa and I thought it was merely amusement."

With much regret, Tyrus replied, "I veiled truth in illusions, for I believed I should not speak openly, then. But now—ai. I am a sorkra. But I am not your enemy, and the skeleton warriors were not my creations."

Though Aubage had been bold with his accusations, the moment Tyrus confirmed he was indeed one of the wizard kind, the nobleman edged away from him. Fear chased over his soft face. The other men, too, grew wary. But Jathelle continued to meet Tyrus' gaze levelly. He felt a renewal of that attraction that began when he first met her. Something new had entered the sensation, though. It was a strange familiarity, as if he had known Jathelle before, for many seasons, through other lives. The holy ones said such things were true, such relationships kindled in other times reborn if the gods wished it. Was it so? He stared at her, shaken.

"A sorkra," Jathelle said finally. "And the enemy who commands those skeletons is a sorkra, too, is he not?"

Pleased by her quick intelligence, Tyrus said, "He is, but rather call him a wizard, for sorkra do not deal in blasphemy and abduction, as he does."

"Wizard, then. And you know him." It was not a question. Jathelle's focus was pinning him. "You have known him a long time."

Other seasons, other lives ... Tyrus was spellbound. How often had he worked his will upon others with his arcane gifts. Yet Jathelle owned no sorkra arts. His will was ruled, nevertheless. "We know him, and he is our enemy, as he is yours."

"Tell me," Jathelle insisted. Tyrus imagined her riding to war, stirrup by stirrup with her royal sire. Learning how to cut away unessentials in times of crisis and go to the core.

Tyrus glanced at Erejzan. Helped by the magic herb, the acrobat could stand unaided now and he nodded, trusting the sorkra. Tyrus took a deep breath. "Your enemy was king of our island," he said with a calm that surprised him. "He ruled wisely and well for many years. But then dangerous fancies and ambitions took him and he turned his wizard's skills to paths none should walk, not even sorkra. He . . . experimented, working magic that was an offense to humankind and gods. His magic aroused Bogotana's wrath, and . . ."

When he hesitated, wondering how much he dared reveal, Jathelle prodded him with that spear of her gaze. "Yet he escaped this destruction, and so did you and the acrobat." Again, it was not a question. She was racing astutely with him, guessing ahead, astonishing Tyrus by her ready grasp of a situation entirely new to her.

"Indeed. He escaped, with the help of a ship's captain and crew which betrayed their kindred and followed their murderous ruler's standard. And Erejzan and I were prisoners on another island rock, out of the path of the smoking mountain," Tyrus said. He closed his eyes for a moment, conquering the horror. "We have pursued him a full turn of the seasons and more."

"Disguised." Jathelle was nodding, approving the ruse. "It must take great skill to hide yourselves from a wizard. That is why you played the amusers. It is a darker game than the one Ilissa and I played in the bazaar." She trembled violently when she spoke Ilissa's name. Then she said, "And he is here—was here?"

"Not exactly." Tyrus took another deep breath. "The demons and imps were his creatures. The skeleton warriors are . . . properties of Nidil."

The courtiers and soldiers gulped, and Lieutenant Utaigh whispered in pious awe, "He Who Steals All Breath, the Death God? We . . . LaSirin was taken by . . . by Nidil?"

"No. The warriors act upon the wizard's bidding, for the wizard has won the use of them, for a while, from Nidil. Once he trafficked with the Evil God, Bogotana, but overreached and nearly died. That is why our island was laid waste. Now he is trying to treat with Nidil."

Jathelle broke in on the explanation. "What does this wizard want with my sister?"

Tyrus hesitated. Erejzan, too, was watching him narrowly, his fear as keen as Jathelle's. With a sigh, Tyrus said, "He is gathering tokens as part of his sorcery, intending to use them to bargain with Nidil Who Steals All Breath."

"Tokens? What do you mean?"

"Your enemy seeks to rule all other wizards, and all mankind." Faces already pale whitened and turned bloodless as Tyrus spoke. His tone was very solemn. They sensed he was not performing or spinning tales to frighten them. Against their wishes, Aubage and the others were beginning to accept, terror gripping them. "If our enemy succeeds, the world will be his, LaRenya, all the provinces at his feet, all peoples his slaves."

"And Ilissa . . . she . . . she is part of this?"

"She is one of several precious tokens he has stolen and abducted." Curtly, Tyrus described the trail of thefts leading from Arniob in the southern seas, to the islands of Bendine and Tor-Nali and Atei and Sersa-Ornail to Couredh itself. Ilissa, he said sorrowfully, was merely the latest treasure to be taken by his minions.

Jathelle's hands were at her breast, trying to still the pounding of her heart. "What . . . what will he do with her? With all these treasures?"

Tyrus read the agony in Erejzan's eyes and knew his friend was thinking of what they had learned through the vision-glass. The truth could not and should not be kept from Jathelle. Tyrus would have preferred to speak only for Jathelle's ears and Erejzan's, disliking the audience of soldiers and courtiers. But there was nothing to be done. They must be convinced as well as the young queen. "He plans to use LaSirin Ilissa and the other stolen prizes as evil sacrifices to buy the Death God's powers."

"He will kill her," Aubage wailed dramatically. "Omaytatle! My beloved! In the Death God's clutches!" The other men said little, but their stricken expressions showed their feelings. Ilissa was betrothed to Aubage, but all Couredh loved the gentle princess, and they were horrified to think she was already slain.

"No!" Jathelle denied the idea fiercely. "She is not dead! Our souls are entwined. I would know at once if she were slain, for my own life would be as nothing then. Ilissa is alive. And we must rescue her, take her away from this enemy wizard before he can complete his blasphemous trade with the Death God!"

Tyrus straightened his shoulders, drawing himself to his full height. Erejzan was mirroring that same determination, putting aside weariness and hurts. Tyrus said, "That is our intent, LaRenya. Stopping him. We will return LaSirin Ilissa to your love, if the gods help us."

"His name! What is my enemy's name?" Jathelle cried. "I must know! I will curse him to Keth's portals and beyond, this stealer of my sister!"

Tyrus and Erejzan conferred mutely for a moment. That bond formed in the rocky prison opened to accept a third member—their spirits joining with Jathelle's. Tyrus spoke for them. "Vraduir. His name is Vraduir."

Jathelle soundlessly repeated the name, memorizing it, the glitter in her eyes frightening. "Your enemy, Vraduir. And mine! Your quest is mine. Hetanya guide me. Gros-Donaq lend me his fury—"

Alarmed, Tyrus tried to break in on her vow-making. "We will bring her back to you."

"No!" Jathelle was looking in frustration at the solid line of cloud across the far northern horizon. She whirled, stabbing a question at Tyrus. "You know where amid that cloud he is lurking, our enemy? You know how to find him?" Reluctantly, compelled by that fire in her spirit and the new-made link binding them, Tyrus nodded. "We will go together, sorkra. If you try to leave without me, I will have vengeance on you as well."

"LaRenya . . ." Aubage was plucking at Jathelle's

ice-flecked cloak. She tried to jerk away from him, irritably. But Tyrus tensed, seeing Erejzan on the alert
against some unexpected danger. The soldiers, too,
were clustering about their young queen, ready to defend her. Jathelle woke out of her dreams of rescuing
Ilissa, at last understanding what so worried the men.
"I see them, Lieutenant," she said with forced calm.
"Who are they?"

Rof and his brigands, those who had survived the
fight with the demons with only minor hurts, had entered Drita Meadows. They had replaced their lost
horses with those of the slain courtiers and ladies and
bodyguards. Now, like scavengers, the mounted men
skulked about the fringes of the hawking party, looking
for prey and prizes.

The officer pointed. "That one with the whip—I have
heard the thief-takers call him Rof. They say he is
Couredh's master of bandits."

Tyrus added, "It is so. We have clashed with him
before. He delayed us when Erejzan and I were on
our way here. I made him an ally for a while, hoping
he would aid us against our mutual enemy."

"Aid us?" a courtier cried, outraged. "They are
thieves."

"And they outnumber those of us still able to fight,"
Jathelle said. "Use your wits. In the city, they would
not dare attack. Out here they are carrion seekers, and
we are little better than carrion. If we do not find a
way to hold them off, they will finish what the skeleton
warriors began. Tyrus, you say you know their leader?
Can he be trusted?"

"Not far, LaRenya. He is a devious man."

Jathelle winced and managed a weak smile. "Yet
you persuaded him. How? And why?"

"Like you, we were outnumbered. And we need him
to guide us for part of the journey; he claims to know

the lands to the north, where Erejzan and I must go hunting for Vraduir."

"You bought his friendship? With what? I do not think that purse I gave you would satisfy such greedy men," Jathelle speculated.

Delighted at her sharpness, Tyrus said, "It did not, LaRenya. He was more interested in my sorkra arts, thinking to use them for thievery. I implied those *might* be at his disposal, if he let us go and helped me to help you and LaSirin. I planned to fret later over how I would win free of that not-quite promise to him."

Jathelle's amusement was tinged with bitterness. "You are rather devious yourself, Tyrus of Qamat. So shall I be. I think this Rof will be more taken with treasure in hand than the possibility of owning your sorkra skills. I will buy his loyalty."

"LaRenya!" Her courtiers and bodyguards were aghast and Lieutenant Utaigh warned, "Have a care, LaRenya. If we turn our backs for a moment on such brigands, they will kill us."

"Not if they think we are worth more alive than dead," Tyrus said cynically.

"I advise against this, most strongly, LaRenya," the eldest courtier said, and Aubage and the other nobleman seconded him. "Even the sorkra says these thieves cannot be trusted."

"We have little choice. Listen to our people, Sirai Miquit. Can you be deaf to their pain? You and Dorche and Aubage stand close. I must offer the brigands more than our ransom or plundering our bodies would yield. Summon him, Tyrus. The rest of you, make no challenging moves, unless they do so first. Do not look so troubled, Lieutenant. We have a sorkra as our ally. You will guard me, will you not, Tyrus?" Jathelle asked with an almost teasing lilt despite their desperate situation.

"With all my wizardry," Tyrus promised fervently.

"A few units of the army would serve us far better," Aubage said.

"The army is stationed in the city and on the frontier. We are here, and so are the brigands," Jathelle countered drily. "They would cut down any messenger I tried to send to Lord General Zlan. Our poor wounded friends and servants need our cunning, not foolish bravery. My way is better. I will haggle like a fishwife, if need be."

Rof did not respond immediately to Tyrus' beckoning wave. His men had encircled the hawking party, just as they had surrounded Tyrus and Erejzan earlier. The brigands had suffered far less in their encounter with the lesser demons than had the nobles and their servants. They had left behind their dead and worst wounded; in any struggle, the brigands would have an easy victory. After visibly arguing with himself for a while, Rof finally rode toward Tyrus and Jathelle, looking very suspicious.

Rof halted a length away from the queen and the sorkra. Jathelle greeted him with courtesy. "I give you welcome to my hunting preserve. I am Jathelle of the house of Fer-Sro, LaRenya of Couredh."

A leer spread over Rof's scarred features. "As well I know! I am Rof, bandit lord. What would you, La-Renya?"

"For you to stay your hand," she said with blunt simplicity.

"By Bogotana, you are honest," Rof complimented her. "I thought you would pretend that you had a column of soldiers hidden over the next hill. Wise you are, not to lie, LaRenya. We both know there are no troops nearby."

"That is why I am going to hire your men and you to act as my auxiliaries until I can summon help." Briskly Jathelle stripped off her rings and her pearl necklace. She walked directly to Rof and handed the jewels up to him. "This is first payment. Lieutenant Utaigh, you and the others collect gems and purses and bring them here. Aubage, help him. You too, Miquit, Dorche . . ." The men were dumbfounded, unmoving, and Jathelle said loudly, "Quickly! Jewels! Coins! Everything of hard value! Leave nothing, not even to the dead, if we are to save the living!"

Tyrus seconded her, speaking as he would to bewildered children. "Money and jewels will not help the wounded. The brigands will let us live if we give them enough shining metal and gems. LaRenya is buying us time."

"The sorkra sees what must be. Why do you not? Fetch what we require. Now!" Jathelle nagged them out of their stupefaction, and at last her followers rushed to do as she bade. Jathelle swung back toward Rof and repeated, "A first payment. There will be much more, when you guide us through the lands north to rescue my sister."

Rof was taken aback. He looked from Jathelle to Tyrus and muttered uneasily, "You said a sorkra's hire was not paid in coin. Do you call upon us, or does she?"

Jathelle wrung her hands, imploring Tyrus' support. He smiled to reassure her. "LaRenya and I are as one in this, Rof. The enemy who abducted LaSirin Ilissa is my enemy and Erejzan's too. Serve LaRenya and you serve me."

"Name your price, bandit lord," Jathelle said eagerly. "For you to guide me and your men to be my hirelings and find Ilissa."

Rof did not reply. He was staring across Drita Meadows, his thoughts transparent. This rich array of nobility had come to the capital for the festival, clad in finery and wearing their best gems. What wealthy estates they must own! And what loyal kindred who would pay handsomely for their release if they were taken prisoners!

Tyrus stabbed through that greed to a greater one. "Much ransom, Rof. But LaRenya is offering to pay you LaSirin's ransom *now,* with no need of taking prisoners or risking the wrath of her kindred."

Aubage was returning from his errand of collecting ransom. Overhearing Tyrus, he said testily, "I will pay to ransom Ilissa. LaRenya has no need to bribe these thieves. We kin-brothers of Huil-Couredh care for our own."

"Do not spend what is not yours, Sirai," Jathelle snapped. "Your lands and livings come from me. Your branch of Couredh's second family gambled away most of your wealth, *and* your claim to the throne. You have already borrowed against Ilissa's marriage portion. Do not meddle in matters when you cannot afford to pay the fee." She scowled at the embarrassed courtier, then turned again to haggling with Rof. "My sister is dear to me, past any reckoning, bandit lord. Tyrus says it aright. You may have her ransom. When Ilissa is safe, I will be so generous your head will spin. You will have to buy pack animals to carry your reward, Rof."

"Safe? Safe from what? And where?" Rof asked, very much on guard. He looked at Tyrus and his countenance fell, his suspicions confirmed. "You have persuaded her, eh? La! The Forbidden Lands?"

"You said you had been there," Erejzan cut in. "You bragged you were afraid of nothing."

"I am not!" Yet it was plain Rof held back, resisting the plan. The soldiers and courtiers had been spreading accumulated coins and jewels on a tattered cloak and Erejzan knelt by the treasure, running it enticingly through his hands, watching Rof as he did so. Seduced by the glitter, Rof licked his lips greedily. "Well and at that, I suppose if you will have it, I can guide you at least as far as the Ice Forest. And my men will go where I command. But I must know—who is this enemy? If those creatures that beset us were his . . ."

"He is a wizard," Tyrus repeated tiredly. "Are you afraid of him, after you have boasted so loudly? Or do you want the ransom LaRenya offers you?" Again Erejzan trickled gold and silver and gems through his fingers, making the riches jangle and clink, music that soothed away Rof's hesitation.

Frowning, Rof built his courage with words. "If he is a mortal man he can be dealt with, wizard or no."

"He is a man," Tyrus assured him, his tone flat.

"By Bog', then I am your ally. Give me your hand on it, LaRenya, and we will be sworn," Rof said with a laugh that sounded somewhat forced. "I fear no man or god, if I am paid well enough! That is my calling!"

"And how shall you be sworn?" Jathelle wondered, doubting his sincerity. "What promise have I that you will not take the first payment and kill us and run away?"

"Promise? Pay me, LaRenya, and I am promised. I trust your honor, even if you do not trust mine. Waste no breath on oaths. Words are lost in the wind. Ask the sorkra." And Rof winked, incorrigible. "But gold? Gold and silver are too heavy to fly!" he finished with a grin that showed his broken and snagged teeth.

Jathelle held her hand up to him, demanding that much sealing of the pact. Shrugging, Rof took her slender fingers into his dirty palm. Then Jathelle gripped his hand firmly, startling him. "No promise kept—no gold. *I* will swear on this, if you will not. Be my ally, and I will make you rich. Agreed? We are one —LaRenya, sorkra, and bandit lord. Your quest must be ours, Rof, until Ilissa is safe."

At length he nodded, and she let go his hand. Rof wriggled his fingers, amazed at her strength. He covered his lingering uncertainty with a chuckle. "So it shall be. At least we have our own wizard to match the enemy's magic. Hai! Never thought I to see the like! Me, Rof, allied with royalty and sorkra. I wish I could tell this around a Zsed fire. Ah! But no more the Destre brotherhood for me . . ."

Jathelle did not hear him. Her bargain struck with Rof, she quickly set about other matters. "Tyrus, you say you have skills to mend my people's wounds?"

"Some of the wounds," he said sadly. "I will do what I can, for your lords and ladies and the servants and bodyguards . . . and for Rof's wounded as well."

Rof did not hide his surprise. "You would minister to my ruffians?"

"Do you object?" Tyrus asked. "Perhaps you think they might feel some gratitude to me."

"Make no mistake, sorkra. They are loyal to me and to gold—me out of fear and gold out of greed. They know no other masters, not even a sorkra who heals them," Rof said. There was no rancor in his words, just an amiable statement of reality.

"Nevertheless, I will try to cure the bites and cuts the imps have left," Tyrus said. He turned to Jathelle and warned, "But the wounds given by the skeleton warriors, those were dealt by the god's minions, and I have no power to counteract such hurts."

"I understand. It is the way of it, and I thank you for what magic you offer us, sorkra Tyrus," Jathelle said earnestly, nodding. Then she lifted her head and looked around at her men. "Who is our best rider?"

There was some muttered discussion, but in the end the courtiers' pride gave way to honesty. A young body-guard stepped forward and saluted Jathelle. She had picked up her battered plumed cap from the frozen grass and gave this to the soldier, saying, "This will be my pledge, since I have surrendered my royal signet to Rof. Ride as fast as you can to Lord General Zlan in Couredh. Bid him bring troops and surgeons and wagons. He must keep the city safe against pirates and invaders, but send all else to me."

"Ai, LaRenya." The messenger hesitated, mulling his orders, anticipating his general's questions. "What . . . what shall I tell him is the cause?"

Jathelle seemed abashed that she had not thought of this, distracted as she had been by Ilissa's kidnapping and her people's distress. She started to answer when Tyrus held up his hand, courteously begging her favor. When she granted it, he said, "Tell the general that La-Sirin has been abducted by unknown invaders, possibly barbarians from the western borders."

Confused, the men whispered together. The messenger awaited Jathelle's approval and the young queen stared at Tyrus. Again that new-formed link between them, as of former acquaintance, worked its special spell. Without argument, she accepted, repeating his orders to the bodyguard. As the soldier promised to relay her words exactly, Jathelle demanded the return of one of her horses—her own stallion—from Rof, for his brigands had commandeered many of the loose stock running about the fringes of the Meadows. Rof blinked at her imperious manner, then submitted. Even at a distance, he could cow the man riding the queen's stallion, One-Ear. The messenger ran toward the thief and for a moment the men, natural enemies, glared fiercely at each other. Then, with ill grace, One-Ear got off the horse he had just claimed and the bodyguard leaped onto its back, mounting at a gallop and racing off toward Couredh.

Jathelle did not watch him leave. She was looking to the north, studying that ominous line of cloud. "Until he returns, we will care for our hurt and shroud our dead. But when the general arrives with my army, I will fling Couredh's might against you, Vraduir! Be brave, little Ilissa! I am coming to rescue you!"

Tyrus had feared this the moment he heard her send

for the general. Now he said softly, "LaRenya, I must talk to you. It is very important."

She eyed him curiously. "About this tale of barbarians stealing my sister?" Tyrus nodded and gestured to a more secluded spot near one of the broken wagons. Jathelle followed him a few paces away from the others.

"I plead with you, LaRenya—heed me. I am devoted to LaSirin, even though I have met her but yesterday. Trust me and Erejzan to bring her back to you." Tyrus used all his polished manners, his voice silken. Yet his concern was genuine. Always in his mind's eye was an image of Ilissa gripped brutally in the dead warrior's hands. Before they came to Couredh, he had worried over the fate of the harper of Atei and cared about the other prizes Vraduir's slaves had taken. But he and Erejzan knew the harper only through the people's grief. Ilissa they had met. Her sweet nature and lovely soul had captured their hearts. The pain of seeing her stolen raked at Tyrus, made worse when he beheld Jathelle's anguish.

"She is my sister. I will rescue her," Jathelle said stubbornly.

"If you send your army directly against him, it will cost the lives of many brave men, slaughtered by the skeleton warriors. Vraduir will laugh at such futility—and Ilissa will still be his prisoner," Tyrus said, forced to be blunt.

"Then how?" Jathelle wailed. "We must crush him!"

"Not that way. Believe me, Vraduir is too powerful, too canny. He cannot be bested by such force of arms."

Aubage was sidling furtively toward Tyrus and Jathelle, though Erejzan was trying to block his way. Rof, too, was interested in the conversation. He nudged his horse, feigning inability to control the brute tightly, edging closer to the queen and the sorkra. The courtiers, bodyguards, and brigands were starting to tend to the injured, but they cocked their heads and patently strained to overhear. All this was an audience Tyrus did not want, but he went on despite the eavesdroppers.

"We are puny, inconsequential enemies to Vraduir. I have dealt with him. I know how he thinks," Tyrus said, swallowing hard, trying to stand apart from his scarred memories. "If you listen to my plan, there is a way to defeat him and bring LaSirin home safe."

Jathelle's eyes glistened with tears. The beauty and color reminded Tyrus of soft waters of a Clarique inlet, bright in the sun. He had to shove away that human, desiring element of his will, resisting her spell with difficulty. "Very well. I will listen," Jathelle said at last.

"You must use the army for a feint," Tyrus said, talking rapidly. "Are there not always barbarians who need taming? Erejzan and I heard such tales in the bazaar. Well and good. Make Vraduir believe you have been fooled. It is likely you *would* think some evil shaman among the border tribes abducted the princess, to hold her for ransom or hostage. Send your army chasing the barbarians. While Vraduir watches them, with his magic, Rof will guide me and Erejzan to his heart and we will take him unawares."

Rof shivered. He had overheard enough and did not like this scheme at all. Other men had also overheard. Aubage gasped and exclaimed, "Three into the Ice Forest and the Death God's realm? If you mean to do that, alone and without the army, you are mad!"

"Or very brave," Jathelle said. She looked from Erejzan to Rof to Tyrus. The tears were overcome in a growing battle fever that made her eyes glint brilliantly. "So am I. Not three—four. I will go with you."

Chill snaked along Tyrus' spine. Erejzan shared his anxiety and said hastily, "Your favor, LaRenya, but the fewer who go, the less the risk and the better our chances of—"

"No. Ilissa is LaSirin of Couredh, my *sister!* This is

my quest, now, as well as yours. It is done." Tyrus
sensed that her firm resolve was on the edge of becoming anger, anger aimed at him, if he continued to oppose her in this.

They had been raising their voices, unaware. The
private conversation was no longer at all private. To
Tyrus' exasperation, the bodyguards now came forward,
insisting they would ride with LaRenya, even unto death.

Aubage was aghast. "How can you abet her, Lieutenant? And you, Sergeant Neir? You other men, soldiers
of Couredh, has the lash of Kida driven away your
sanity? If you let LaRenya go to the Ice Forest, the
Skull Breakers will dine on her bones, and on yours!"

"But no matter to you if Skull Breakers dine on *my*
bones, and the sorkra's and the acrobat's, eh?" Rof
said sarcastically. He looked at Jathelle with frank
admiration. "By Bogotana, you are a warrior woman,
LaRenya! I have not seen the like since . . . la ben da!
Who would believe a Clarique could have so much
courage?" He lapsed into a thicker Krantin accent than
was usual for him.

Aubage shook his hands at the heavens in a dramatic
way, crying, "In the name of Omaytatle's blizzards!
This is a mad jest. Say that it is, LaRenya!"

Jathelle smiled. "You are the one who told so many
tales of brave quests by heroes, Aubage. This is no
tale. Here is legend in the making. It is different from
your fanciful stories, ai?"

"You would go? On the word of such as . . . him?"

Tyrus endured Aubage's scorn, willing to take this
if it might dissuade Jathelle from the dangerous trek.
What imp had made him reveal so much to her? Yet . . .
the plan *would* have better chance of success with her
army's help—and Jathelle would not contribute that
army in a feint unless she went with Tyrus and Erejzan.
She read his mood and said, "I have no sorcery, but
I am not without skills. I can wield pike, sword, or

knife—or even an axe. I am not squeamish, nor will I shrink from shedding blood and killing. I am what Rof calls a warrior woman—the battle maiden you called me. I will prove it to you!"

"Not alone, LaRenya," the courtier Miquit said sternly. He was a man of perhaps thirty years, seeming steadier and more wise than Aubage and the other young nobleman, Dorche. "Fer-Sro is insulted by this attack and abduction. My blood is allied with yours, LaRenya. My kindred lie on this Meadow, crying for justice and vengeance. They shall have it, at your hands and at mine."

The instant Sirai Miquit made that declaration, Dorche seconded him and vowed to go on the quest, too. Aubage was left in a ticklish position, forced to make up his mind hastily. With loud bravado, he drew his sword and added fervent oaths to Miquit's and Dorche's, shouting that he would go forth and save his Ilissa.

"You must leave frippery and comfort behind," Jathelle warned them. "I will don the rough garb I wore during my father's frontier campaigns. You must do likewise. The journey will be dangerous and hard—and some of you might not return to lands and kindred."

The soldiers were not at all daunted; for pride the courtiers could not show doubt, either. Rof's men were equally intent on going, though for far different reasons. United by rash courage, loyalty, and greed, the men forgot, for a moment, divisions of rank and law, yelling defiance at an enemy none of them had met.

Appalled, Tyrus and Erejzan strolled some paces away from the noisy demonstration. "What are we going to do?" Erejzan said. "Look at that boasting rabble. If they all go, we will have nearly twenty trailing us."

Tyrus' head throbbed. Despite the influence of the magic herb, physical effort and conjury were taking a toll. Wearily, he gazed at the circle of men around

Jathelle as they repeated their promises to follow her
to the end of the world. Their names washed over
Tyrus' mind, barely heeded. They were Miquit and
Aubage and Dorche, the bodyguards Lieutenant Utaigh
and Sergeant Neir and troopmen Halom and Ris, and
a growling tangle of brigands, names few would believe
—Rof, One-Ear, Slit-Nose, Branded Hand, Bloody
Axe, and other titles they hid behind, outlaws with no
true identities.

"I . . . I will weave a glamour around us as we
journey," Tyrus said.

"Around all that braying herd?" Erejzan spat on the
frozen grass. "You will wear out your talents even
before we find Vraduir."

With calculation, Tyrus reached into his being,
touching the webs and gathering new sorcery. A trifle
heartened to discover he could do this readily, he said,
"I think not. In any event, we shall see. If my powers
are not equal to such a task as this, they will not pre-
vail against Vraduir, either. If I am not his peer in my
magic, there is no hope."

"But so many of them . . ."

Tyrus smiled. "In days to come, it may be we shall
need such allies as these. Remember, they are Couredh-
yan, my friend, people of this northern country. You
and I are unused to Omaytatle's snow and ice. Their
knowledge will help us survive."

Erejzan looked as if he thought they would be better
served by Tyrus' magic alone. Tyrus watched Jathelle
as she accepted the pledges of her motley little army.
Unlike the men, she was setting upon this quest not
for pride or gold, but for love of her sister and her people. In many ways, her motives were Tyrus' own.

But this army of gnats! Speaking so boastfully of
conquering Vraduir! Vraduir! Tyrus alone knew the
might of that wizard. Aware of it or not, all of Jathelle's
people would depend upon Tyrus' magic to protect

them while they were within Vraduir's deadly sphere. He should have staggered under the burden of that knowledge. Yet Tyrus, too, held up his head, as Jathelle did. This challenge from the gods would prove if he was truly worthy to defeat Vraduir.

"It must be, mai fiyel," he said with a bleak smile. "She is LaRenya. And Ilissa is her sister. She has this right, for Ilissa, and for her realm. Couredh will be the first land to fall to Vraduir's evil power if he gains what he seeks from Nidil."

"Mmm. It is not LaRenya who worries me. She is a fighter. It is Aubage who will get in our way." The acrobat's sullen jealousy was poorly concealed.

"Ah! But we must take him, too. He had to volunteer with the other courtiers, or lose all hope of Jathelle's favor henceforth. Rof concerns me far more than Aubage does." Tyrus eyed the bandit lord warily. "I admit it is better to have him and those outlaws with us rather than lying in ambush or tracking us. I want Rof where I can see him, at least until I determine whether or no he is Vraduir's minion. Out of sight, he could do us much mischief."

Erejzan turned, and Tyrus suspected his friend was hearing something not yet apparent to ordinary ears. Erejzan confirmed this, saying, "Horsemen, and chariots, and wagons. They are still some distance away, but approaching rapidly. A candle-mark or two and they will be at Drita Meadows. This must be Lord General Zlan and the surgeons LaRenya sent for."

For the next few candle-periods, all thoughts of a gallant quest and revenge and glory were put by. Soldier and courtier, queen and sorkra, bandit and acrobat labored side by side to help the injured. Tyrus countered the evil magic of Vraduir wherever he could. Sometimes the wounded nobility and servants resisted him, fearing more pain from his spells and incantations. But gradually they came to trust him.

Some he could not help, nor could the surgeons. Prayers and fresh vows to seek vengeance mingled with the moans and sobs. When the general and his aides and the van of his army came onto the Meadows, they were shocked by the extent of the disaster. Though the messenger's description had been strong, it had not fully prepared them for the terrible scene. Battle plans waited until the wounded had been tendered all the help anyone could give.

Jathelle longed to attend personally to each of her people, lords and ladies and bodyguards and servants. Once Tyrus paused amid the carnage and saw Jathelle cradling her slaughtered hawk to her breast, weeping, as if the pitiful corpse somehow gathered all her grief. She laid the bloody hawk down gently and turned again to the wounded. With her own hands, she staunched blood and she helped carry litters to the wagons. Even then, she would not leave her followers. Jathelle trotted alongside the surgeons' wagons as they rumbled back toward the city, talking encouragingly to the patients within. Only when the sad caravan topped the ridge exiting Drita Meadows did Jathelle stop and gaze after them sorrowfully.

The army was gathering, a vast camp spreading over the Meadows and beyond, linked by messengers hurrying to and fro. The bodyguard who had ridden to the city learned of the plan to infiltrate and insisted on joining his fellow soldiers, with Jathelle's approval. All those sworn to the quest—or bought with LaRenya's treasure—kept apart from the main forces, maintaining the secret. For the bulk of the army, the news was that LaSirin had been kidnapped by barbarians who took her northwest, and pursuit was about to begin.

The general, though, had to be admitted to the truth. He was the warlord Tyrus and Erejzan had seen in the palace, and his nature bore out his hard face and stiff posture. The man had been the late king's blood friend and was bound to Jathelle's family by oaths that would take him beyond death. Yet this scheme horrified him and he argued furiously against it, especially when he learned LaRenya intended to undertake the quest on the information of a mere amuser like Tyrus.

At one point, it looked as if the general might over-power Jathelle and take her back to the city by force, protecting her against her will. One part of Tyrus' mind wished that would happen. But another did not. He sympathized with Jathelle's feelings, knowing how she must yearn to ride after Ilissa. In the end, as Tyrus had been, the general was bested. Shrewdly Jathelle kept the thieves out of his sight, fearing not even loyalty would restrain the veteran if he knew of that element of Jathelle's band of infiltrators.

"On the morrow, at dawn, begin the feint," Jathelle instructed. She had conferred with Tyrus on how to delude Vraduir. "Light large campfires tonight and every night after, to trick the enemy wizard. Let him see you assembled and moving to the northwest."

The general looked suspiciously at Tyrus. "Wizards! And this enemy wizard, will he not attack us, using our campfires against us?"

"No, my Lord General." Tyrus took care to give the older man all his proper titles, conscious of his touchy pride. "He will be spellcasting and conjuring. Do not be offended, my Lord General, but he will probably think your army is beneath his notice."

"Beneath notice, are we? Then we shall give him cause to pay attention to us! Ai!" After many seasons of peace, the warlord and his troopmen were restless and welcomed this chance for action. If chastising the barbarians would help save LaSirin Ilissa, so much the better.

Like uncle and niece, both adept at campaigns, the general and Jathelle decided on tactics and supplies.

Wise to the dangers of northern climate beyond the reach of the warm current, they arranged for extra horses and provender for both humans and animals, for forage would be sparse or nonexistent in the lands they must dare. Surreptitiously, the supplies were sent to the place where the infiltrators waited, hidden in the forest at the edge of Drita Meadows. Jathelle followed them shortly. She had changed her ruined hawking costume for frontier garb, as had the men, and she came to join them, leading not her finely bred stallion but a sturdy brute more suited to the arduous trek.

Tyrus watched her coming into the woods, relishing the sight. She wore the same stained fur and leather garments she had when he first met her. She had no maids or servitors then, when she had escaped her royal duties for a while. None attended her now, either. Her companion of that game, Ilissa, was captive. The game was ugly and real, and Jathelle's expression was set. The necklace of wolves' teeth was her only adornment and seemed to warn of her grim determination in this quest. To Tyrus, she was more stunning than she had been in her finest gowns. Her hair was plaited and her boots plain, tough hide, well worn. The sword she was fitting into her baldric looked to be of finest Krantin steel. With a long stride, she entered the grove.

"We are ready," she said simply, gathering her reins, preparing to mount.

"There is not much time left to the day," Lieutenant Utaigh warned politely. He was an earnest young soldier but regarded the sky in a canny way, proving he had some experience in upcountry fighting.

Jathelle did not pause, swinging up on her horse and taking the lead line of some of the animals packed with food and extra arms and clothing. "Then we should not delay. I intend to make campsite at Three Forks by nightfall."

The Lieutenant saluted. He darted a calculating

glance at the courtiers and Tyrus and Erejzan, as if doubting their stamina. "Ai, LaRenya. It is ten measures, and easy riding."

"Eleven," Jathelle corrected him. "And I want to make twenty each day henceforth, at least. That should bring us to Couredh's border within a Five-Day. You see, bandit lord, you do not lead us where we know not the land," she said, raising her eyebrows at Rof.

He scowled fiercely. "You do not know it as well as I, LaRenya. If you travel as you would, there is no going boldly and marching with flags flying. I will teach you how to hide your colors. As you say, no delay. Have at it! Harshaa . . ." and he slapped his mount with his coiled whip, sending the beast lunging down the thicketed trail. Jathelle rode hard in his wake and the other men scrambled onto the horses, hurrying after them. In less than a candle-mark, they had left the tragedy-marked Meadows far behind and were moving deep into the heavily-forested uplands of the queen's preserves, aiming north steadily, toward their goal—the Death God's realm.

X

Into the Barren Country

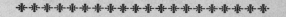

JATHELLE HAD SET A PUNISHING PACE, SOON OVER-
taking Rof and leading the infiltrators. As she had said,
she knew this land and as yet had no need of the brig-
and's guidance.

A fraction of Tyrus' attention was on his horse and
the path that wound through woods and glades. The
greater part of his consciousness floated above them
all, unseen and without substance, a net of magic. When
they were under trees, he kept the net a flimsy one,
skirting through the leaves. When they traveled across
open country he wove the veil far more closely. No one
but Erejzan realized why the fading daylight seemed so
unusually hazy as a result. Jathelle and the men thought
it a natural phenomenon, paying it little heed.

As evening fell, they had turned somewhat away from
the coast but were close enough to be touched by sea
fog. By the time this mist made travel too risky, they
had arrived at the three forks, led straight and true by
LaRenya.

They loosened cinches and unpacked food, and
Jathelle consulted Tyrus. "Dare we light a fire?"

"It is safe, since there are much larger fires on Drita

Meadows," he said. "And we are further shielded," he added cryptically, negligently flexing his hands.

Jathelle peered around, uneasy. "What are you doing?"

"Building barriers to trick the enemy. It is called a glamour."

The soldiers, noblemen, and bandits watched Tyrus apprehensively and Erejzan grinned at their discomfort. "When you sleep, though, the enemy will find us," Aubage said, as if wanting to find some weakness in Tyrus' skills.

"No, he will not," Tyrus retorted coldly. "Such a glamour can be made to last many candle-marks. This one will serve adequately until I wake. Light a fire to warm us and keep back animals, if you wish."

"There are no dangerous beasts in this area," Jathelle assured him, as the soldiers and brigands worked kindling brush and leaves.

"Not even the wild ecar?" Rof asked, very arch, looking sidelong at Erejzan. The acrobat's smile faded. There was menace in his green eyes, which caught the new-made firelight eerily. One-Ear elbowed Rof and whispered a warning. Several other brigands scooted well away from the sorkra and Erejzan, disliking these hints of sorcery. Jathelle seemed to wonder what had caused such sudden hostility, but no one enlightened her. Soon they forgot these petty frictions, warming their hands and gnawing on the plain food the general had provided for them.

The bandits grumbled that they had hoped for better than hard grain cakes and common dried motge, dining at the queen's table. But they were accustomed to taking what they could and made the best of it, as did the soldiers and Miquit. The two younger courtiers, though, complained about the food and the rough and scratchy clothes they must wear. Finally Jathelle quieted

them with a withering reminder that they were fortunate
to be alive, after what had happened on the Meadows.

The bodyguards did not quite accept Tyrus' words
that they were shielded from the enemy, and Lieutenant Utaigh posted sentinels, assigning turns. Tyrus conceded this was wise, if only to prevent the bandits from
causing trouble or trying to sneak away if their courage
started to flag. Aubage and the noblemen still mumbled
complaints, sleeping badly, turning and shifting and
quarreling softly with one another as they roused at
irregular intervals. The soldiers and bandits not standing watch seized the chance for rest and drowsed as
soon as they lay down. Jathelle was used to an easy life
at court but was adapting quickly to her former existence on the frontier, wrapping herself in her furry
cloak.

Tyrus knew he must sleep, though he dreaded dreams.
Erejzan, too, was wakeful, though much wearied. Jathelle noticed their extreme fatigue and commented on
it softly as they sat together beside the fire. Her own
eyes were red-rimmed from weeping and she had fought
and ridden hard. Yet she knew there was a special hurt
and tiredness afflicting the sorkra and his friend. Tyrus
decided to risk sorcery, even though Jathelle was a
witness.

He closed his eyes, sinking into a place of arcane
webs. Tyrus walked upon the webs, delicately, balanc-
ing, moving over alien chasms and darknesses where
immense, crimson eyes shone. He was hunting a particular portion of the spidery network, a particular key to
unlock a device. Often before, he had come here. But
the nature of his search this time threw obstacles before
him and made resistance strong. The charm must be
won through difficulties.

At last he found the nexus of webs he sought. It was
inhabited by supernatural dancing lights. Tyrus bor-

rowed two of these and rose up slowly to awareness, evading numerous traps of challenging sorcery.

He was beside Erejzan and Jathelle, by the camp-fire. The copper lights lay in his hand. Jathelle stared at them in amazement. As she started to touch them curiously, the lights changed and became odd-shaped flowers with curling orange petals and black stems. Tyrus smiled and said, "Do not think me impolite, LaRenya, but these are not for you." He thrust one of the flowers at Erejzan, forcing the acrobat's limp fingers around the stem.

Listlessly, Erejzan sniffed at the flower, as Tyrus was doing with the one he had kept. A peculiar expression crossed the acrobat's face, an imitation of Tyrus' own relieved reaction. Pain and fatigue melted, strength and relaxation racing through their veins and sinews.

"An unworldly fragrance, this," Jathelle murmured. She seemed to know this was something Tyrus did not want to share with the others. "Magic?"

"Magic to heal magic. My own magic, in this case," Tyrus explained.

"As you healed my people and the bandits who had been wounded by demons. But you did that with strange words and gestures. This was . . . those were the same copper lights that played among the puppets during your amusements in the bazaar," Jathelle said.

Tyrus took the flower from Erejzan, and that and his own converted again into coppery lights. He closed his hand; when he opened it, the lights were gone, sent to the world of webs till they should be needed once more. Jathelle gasped, then looked thoughtfully at Tyrus and Erejzan. "You are refreshed, and so quickly!"

"At some cost," Erejzan chided Tyrus.

"It was necessary, my friend." Tyrus kept his voice low so that only the acrobat and Jathelle could hear him. "This was to cure sorcery I cast upon us earlier." He described the frantic race he and Erejzan had run to Drita Meadows. Jathelle was much moved that they had punished themselves so brutally in an attempt to save her from Vraduir. At the conclusion, Tyrus said, "This is a different sort of healing, true, from that I used to heal your nobles and servants. Then I was countering Vraduir's charms, which were mixed with the powers of Bogotana and Nidil."

"Gods of evil and death," Jathelle said, shivering.

Tyrus crossed his arms atop his drawn-up knees and said somberly, "It is so. The smaller imps were Vraduir's slaves, bought from Bogotana. My people died to purchase those slaves. The wounds they gave will heal slowly under your surgeons' care—but they *will* heal, now that I have treated them. As for the skeleton warriors' dealings, I do not know if my incantations can cure those hurts. I have never dealt with true Death God's creatures before."

There was a long silence. Tyrus did not enter Jathelle's mind, but he sensed she was following him, making startling leaps in understanding for one who had never encountered genuine sorkra before yesterday. After a time she said, "Now I begin to see why you did not want us to come. You *could* have stopped us, with your wizardry."

"Perhaps," Tyrus said offhandedly.

Erejzan's eyelids were drooping. "That is not Tyrus' way," he muttered.

Jathelle nodded, grateful. "I see that, too. Whatever happens, you must save your strongest skills for yourself, Tyrus."

"As often I tell him," Erejzan agreed, muffling a yawn.

"Wisely! Tyrus must leave us all to our fate, if doing so will save Ilissa and bring down this Vraduir," Jathelle said tensely.

Erejzan had sunk down, curling up in his cloak, already asleep. That same sleep lapped at the edges of Tyrus' will, but he would not yield. Jathelle had captured him with her emotions and eyes, holding him fast. Firelight flowed over her face and golden braids. She laid her hands over his and the touch sent a languid, soothing wave up Tyrus' arms to his heart. "Rest now," she urged him. "Conserve your powers to fight our enemy."

Reluctantly, he obeyed. Jathelle remained close by his side, still wakeful, peering north into the fog. Tyrus brushed at the surface of her mind and felt a powerful longing and fear—Ilissa. The same frozen image that haunted Tyrus. Ilissa—arms held out, pleading for Jathelle to save her, terror ravaging her flawless countenance. And Tyrus' pain at that sight, he knew, was the merest fraction of what Jathelle was suffering. Her soul was bound to Ilissa's, the agony of loss giving her no peace. Troubled, Tyrus withdrew, leaving her to her grief, helpless to counter it. He sighed and gave himself up to sleep.

Mercifully, there was no recurrence of that dream. And because of the healing light-flower, he woke restored in body and in sorkra strength. He oriented himself quickly. Dawn was heavy with fog, but already he could make out ghostly shapes of trees and rocks and other landmarks that would guide Jathelle and Rof along the trail north. Stillness ruled the brushy glen. All around him, men were stirring, some groaning and sore from the fight and the hard ride of yesterday and evening.

Tyrus reached out over the hills and valleys, lifting himself out of mind and flesh. He could not use the vision-glass, but now he knew where to hunt. Carefully, he traced the path the glass had shown. Details were blurred. He would indeed need Rof's help for part of the way. But once within the Death God's realm, focus sharpened. Tyrus entered the citadel and grazed that awful, divine aura in the smoke of the altar. Hastily, he veered away, seeking the source of Vraduir's magic.

He could not pinpoint precise words and actions. He was unseen, moving with Vraduir's body, unfelt, unable to influence. The body—so much his own! The strong, long-fingered hands held out before his vision seemed Tyrus' own, the confident stride, the manner of moving —his.

He did not risk entering Vraduir's conscious mind. That would presume too much on any sorkra's awareness, and Vraduir was no ordinary wizard! Instead, Tyrus listened, hearing what Vraduir heard. He saw what Vraduir saw. Impish slaves and demons scurried about in the stony citadel. There was one skeleton warrior, just leaving that altar room. These arcane servants might have been reporting. Vraduir's voice appeared to issue from Tyrus' own throat as the master wizard gave the demons their orders. Some of them did not respond. Perhaps they would answer only to a greater master—the Death God himself. Apparently Nidil Who Steals All Breath was not in a mood to approve all of Vraduir's design, and the evil wizard must be patient.

The army. Vraduir was interested in Couredh's army, wanting to know where it was and what it was doing at that moment. Tyrus watched him searching, then realized most of the demonic servants had left. Alone, Vraduir would be more likely to detect a rival sorkra's spying. Frustrated to learn so little, Tyrus dissolved the focus. That done, he was coming back instantly to his mind, a momentary shock making him shudder.

"Tyrus?" Jathelle had been binding her pack behind her saddle. But she had come to the sorkra, leaning over him anxiously. Aubage and the other men were equally puzzled.

As Tyrus emerged from his self-enchantment, Erejzan said hastily, "It is . . . a kind of farseeing."

"Prophesiers and charm-weavers, they always give us pretty names for their illusions," Rof said. But he spoke with too much swagger, revealing his disquiet.

"For a thief, you show some wit," Aubage said. "If you want my opinion, he puts on a show for us, no more."

Jathelle ignored them both, asking softly, "The enemy? You were spying on Vraduir?"

Erejzan was startled by that definition, offended for Tyrus' sake. But Tyrus answered without resentment, "In a way, I suppose it *is* spying."

"Good! Never did my father and his warlord have such a spy as you, Tyrus of Qamat. What have you found out? Does he know where we are?" Jathelle wondered.

"No, not yet. He is more occupied with your army. I shall hide us from him as long as I can."

"Hide us?" Rof exclaimed with a rude laugh. "You will find few hiding places in the barren country."

Tyrus smiled and said, "A wizard knows how to hide from a wizard."

Rof's guffaw caught in his mouth, choking him. Aubage and the other men suddenly busied themselves with their horses and the pack animals. They lost all further interest in sorcery. Jathelle, however, was a wide-eyed girl, fascinated with this thing. "Is this the glamour you mentioned last night? Can it move with us as we travel?" Tyrus nodded, pleased by her quickness and that she did not shrink from him and his arts.

Erejzan brought his mount to his side with a soft whistle. The beast responded like a trained pet, for this was a talent Erejzan had always owned and which had made him Vraduir's beast master, a lifetime ago, on Qamat. "Best make the disguise a thin one, Tyrus," the shape-changer warned. "His pride will be our protection, too. He will keep no guard against such a small party. He thinks himself invulnerable."

"Do not worry, mai fiyel. I remember his pride."

For a moment, Jathelle was petulant, sulking. The reason eluded Tyrus until he realized she envied Erejzan's familiarity with Tyrus' sorcery. In time, he suspected, she would demand to know more, learning, as Erejzan had learned, how to recognize the different aspects of Tyrus' skills. Tyrus decided he would answer her questions when he could. He found he actually anticipated sharing that part of his being with Jathelle, bridging the gap that separated him from the rest of humankind.

"We are ready to continue the hunt," Jathelle said abruptly. "Ilissa must not be kept waiting, or she will think I have abandoned her."

"If she still lives," Rof muttered. Jathelle was indignant at this, refusing to accept the possibility of death at all. With a grimace, Rof swung up on his horse and said, "We will come to rougher country by tonight. And we must cross the Rock Hills tomorrow if we are to get to the warm springs and the only good pasture for our animals. I do not intend to risk *my* blood while you stand here gibbering of witchcraft!"

Jathelle had not yet smothered her anger over Rof's cruel remark. Aubage was more than ready to second Rof, though, sniffing and saying, "Your counsel is well taken, bandit lord. Steel and manly courage are far better than any posturings of a charm-weaver. As you have said, we must make all speed."

"The counsel were better taken," Tyrus said, "if Rof and his throatslitters were not burdening their horses with the first payment LaRenya gave them." Everyone looked toward the heavy, bulging sacks of treasure each brigand had tied behind his saddle. They had not been willing to leave Drita Meadows until they had argued hotly over division of that first payment, in fact.

There was no more discussion. The three factions were stiff with one another, saying little as they rode northward on the next leg of their journey. The fog had not burned off, but Rof had traveled here through bad weather and good and made his way unerringly. The farther they rode, the less Jathelle's experience and that of the bodyguards served them. Now Rof was following trails the armies of Couredh did not, nor did honest folk use these. Queen and sorkra and the others adopted the habits of Rof's outlaws, slinking under trees and through steep gullies, hiding from most haunts of men.

Tyrus' glamour went with them. It was part of the foggy haze clinging to them, but thin enough to let Rof find his brigand's landmarks and guide them without hindrance.

Even when the sun was fully up, dense patches of fog lingered in shadows and hollows that never knew steady light. And the air was much cooler, as they rode beyond the blanket formed by Couredh's warm current. The ice-free coast was well behind them and they entered the fringes of the barren country. Despite their exertions, they were forced to wear their cloaks even through midday. Their skins were clammy with their own sweat, raked by a sharp wind that made them uncomfortable but did not dry their flesh.

Jathelle had brought maps, but these helped less and less. It soon became apparent Rof had not boasted idly, at least so far as this. He led them around rock slides and sinks of deadly marsh and sand where men and beasts could be dragged down to unknown pits and never seen again. Always he sought sheltered trails.

Grassland and leafy copses gave way to scrubbier forests and wind-swept plains of weeds and poor grazing. Here and there great heaps of rocks burst through the thin soil, jagged upliftings of the very earth, scoured clean by some long-vanished ocean or god's terrible wind.

They saw few villages. Jathelle might be known here,

even in her barbarian disguise. And Rof and his thieves
could not raid and plunder so long as they were
watched by their new-made allies. A few of the greedier
bandits grumbled at this, wishing to steal a woolback
or a motge or to frighten peasants out of their property. But Jathelle kept them in hand, promising them
good reward if they would forget their thievery during
the quest to save Ilissa.

Tyrus let this discussion work its will without him.
He had a deeper reason for not wishing to enter any
of the peasant villages. Most likely, the simple herdsmen and farmers could be trusted. Yet knowledge of
Jathelle and the others might make them prey to Vraduir's wary probing for any rival to his power. If
Vraduir acted alone, Tyrus would not have worried on
this. The leavening of the Death God's might with
Vraduir's wizardry made him wish them well away
from any not gathered under the veil of his glamour.
Unfortunate enough that Jathelle and all these men
were coming with them and Erejzan! They must bring
no more into that fragile alliance.

Herds and wildlife were less common here. They saw
chusa, that large rodent native to the north country. A
few birds fluttered about in the gnarled trees and low
bushes. Rof's men and the soldiers clubbed or speared
some of the chusa, planning to dine on fresh meat
when they made camp. Aubage and the courtiers turned
up their noses, for chusa was peasant fare, not the sort
of food they were accustomed to. Jathelle chuckled and
assured them they would find the taste to their liking,
if they were hungry enough. She had eaten chusa during her father's campaigns and slyly claimed it was
succulent and very good.

Traveling grew much harder. The bandits and bodyguards stood it best, though even they were not used to
such rough riding every day. Jathelle had once been
seasoned. Now she cursed her recent life in the city that

had made her soft. She would not call an early halt, however, nor ask favored considerations. The courtiers Aubage, Dorche, and Miquit had played at horsemanship on their estates or acted out warriors' roles at festivals. Such exercises were poor preparation for this venture. They swallowed their groans, trying to match Jathelle's endurance. Aubage, particularly, drove himself to keep up the pace at Jathelle's side.

Swathed in cold fog and buffeted by an ever-rising wind, they leaned low over their horses' necks to shelter from the elements. Garments gave little warmth. Doggedly, they rode through the afternoon's candle-marks, pausing only to rest their mounts and pack animals and to eat a few hasty bites.

Shortly before sunset, they came over a rocky hill and saw an isolated peasant community. Huts straggled along the shore of an ancient inlet of the sea. Countless ages ago, the inlet had been cut off from the ocean. This small pocket of water stole warmth from Couredh's southern breezes, though. A remnant of the inlet was a lake. Its waters were thawed in the spring and wavelets jumped. A quarter measure away, a ship was locked fast in the ice-bound inlet. It was an unnatural thing, for her seamen had not lowered sail nor made fast her lines. She looked as if she had sailed straight over the perpetual sea ice and the land between, coming to rest here beside the little lake. There was no sign of life aboard, the sails beginning to fray after days of inattention.

Along the lakeside lay many salt deposits. It was plain that peasants had settled in this place at the edge of forbidden lands to harvest the precious mineral. They must have earned much profit, trading the salt to caravans or sellers journeying south toward Couredh's more populous regions. The salt made life in this grim area worth the peril.

Jathelle drew rein, staring at the huts. Aubage hinted

that perhaps they no longer need to hide and might sleep under roofs for the night.

"They would ask too many questions," Rof said curtly. He wiped dust from his mustaches and made as if to ride around the little lake. "They will want to know how such a strange army as this came here."

"No one will ask us any questions," Tyrus said tonelessly. "There is no one living here."

"Magic, again?" Rof sneered.

"Look at it," Erejzan cut in. "No magic is needed. The village is empty. No men harvest the salt. No women wash clothes or tend children or cook pots. There *are* no children. Or dogs. Or flocks. It is dusk, yet they have lit no fires."

Aubage pulled his cloak tighter and said unhappily, "I think the acrobat is right, LaRenya. It is too quiet. Perhaps the enemy wizard is waiting there to ambush us."

"No." They all looked at Tyrus. "Vraduir is not here. Sorcery *was* here. But it is old magic. It came with the ship and now it is gone."

"How . . . how do you know?" Jathelle asked, gazing toward the vessel.

"Because the marking on those sails is the royal crest of Qamat," Tyrus said with taut anger. "Once that ship carried Vraduir to safety out of a holocaust made by his own evil magic. And the ship has sailed on his orders since this past year, plying the Clarique seas, stealing and kidnapping. Now, it seems, he has found other slaves than her crewmen to do his villainous errands."

He did not mention the skeleton warriors and Ilissa's abduction. There was no need. Unwilling to be out-argued, Aubage said, "But the ship is frozen fast in the ice, measures from the ocean."

"Vraduir enchanted the ship," Erejzan said, growling. "And the crew were traitors. I hope they have earned death and betrayal at his hands. He made a path through the ice with his wizardry, much further north than Tyrus and I expected."

Puzzling over these words, the band of ill-assorted allies made their way down toward the village. On guard, swords, pikes, and cudgels in hand, they entered the lonely streets. Everyone soon saw that Tyrus and Erejzan had judged correctly. Wall stones were unrepaired after the winter's gales. Doors hung open, letting in the weather. Salt carts and cooking pots stood where their owners had left them. Chusa and mice nibbled at ropes and at the villager's salt machines on the shore.

"Look inside, Lieutenant Utaigh," Jathelle ordered. He and his bodyguards peered into the huts. The brigands made their own search, running in and out of dwellings, carrying a few utensils and rodent-gnawed blankets. A soldier tried to stop the looting and he and the thieves fell to arguing loudly. Rof and Tyrus separated them, yelling over the noise until the quarrelers forgot their purpose. Jathelle dismounted and adjusted her saddle girth as Lieutenant Utaigh came to report. "It . . . it is as if they might come back at any moment, LaRenya. Things are covered with dust and melted snow from winter storms. Nothing has been stolen, until now," he finished, glowering at a thief who was clutching plunder.

"Where are the people?" Jathelle asked of no one.

"Taken as slaves," Rof said bluntly. He pointed to a strip of dried mud near the lake. The weather had erased part of the evidence, but enough remained to show many footprints and signs of people being dragged away by force. The graphic trail led along the eastern shore and vanished in the harder soil and rocks beyond.

Badly shaken, Jathelle said, "I thought those rumors of peasants disappearing were . . . just wild tales. It has really happened!"

"Every realm hears its fantastic stories," Tyrus comforted her, not wanting her to blame herself for the peasants' tragedy. "This time, sorcery was involved, and for once the stories were true. I think there were probably other villages along this barren country which have suffered the same, and from the same cause."

The soldiers and the courtiers went from hut to hut, seeking survivors. Skulking out of their reach, the brigands searched, too, but found little to appeal to them. "How could this be done?" Aubage wondered.

The lieutenant added, "It is strange, ai! There is no sign of raiders. No blood or broken weapons."

"They did not want to injure the peasants," Tyrus said soberly. "They needed them whole and able to labor for Vraduir."

"How dare he enslave my people?" Jathelle paced back and forth in helpless rage. "How dare he? We will rescue them, too, as well as Ilissa!"

"Worry about rescuing ourselves, queen," Rof muttered. "Anyone who could do this is a powerful wizard indeed."

The setting sun was turning the lake into a red ocean. Fog seemed to boil above the little waves, a scene from Bogotana's fiery depths. Tyrus said, "He had help, demons to affright them and put them in magic chains. And perhaps Captain Drie and his men aided, ere they knew they would be Vraduir's slaves as well. He knew where the inlet and the villages were. But Vraduir does not know we are here. I suggest we make use of blankets and other basic supplies we find. Lieutenant, bid your men gather those."

Jathelle whirled, her eyes as bright and angry as the sun-washed water. Belatedly, Tyrus sensed he had forgotten his role. Absorbed in thoughts of Vraduir and how to reach him, he had fallen back on old customs and spoken as a prince ordering his subordinates. "My apologies, LaRenya. I did not mean to assume your prerogative," Tyrus said in what he hoped was a contrite manner.

Her irritation faded and she replied, "No matter. The suggestion is a good one. Carry it out, Lieutenant. How cold it grows!"

"And we are only entering the barren lands," Rof warned her, his countenance grim.

There was a brief but heated squabble over what would be taken from the village. To Tyrus' surprise, Rof cooperated with Jathelle's men and used his whip to beat the thieves into submission. He made them leave trinkets and petty baubles, scorning them as fools for trying to steal such worthless things and further burden their mounts. The confiscated blankets and a bit of grain the chusa had not fouled were loaded onto the animals.

Jathelle watched this and lamented, "My poor peasants. We are robbing them."

"We will rescue them, as you say, LaRenya," Aubage put in airily. It was plain he cared little for the peasants' fate but was babbling what Jathelle might like to hear. "That will be recompense, will it not?"

Jathelle was not cheered, staring at the deserted huts. Tyrus and Erejzan privately feared the peasants were far beyond any concern about theft, but they did not tell Jathelle.

The horses were restless, pawing the salty earth, wanting to be away from the empty cottages and the scent of dark magic. Tyrus read the signs along the shore. "He took the peasants away last year, I think. But the bewitched ship came to berth more recently."

"From Atei," Erejzan muttered. "Bearing as captive the famous harper. Another sacrifice, as he sacrificed my pitiful enchanted beasts and my kindred on Qamat. Now he steals LaSirin. When is there ever enough pain to satisfy him?"

Frowning, Tyrus pressed a finger to his lips. He

glanced at Jathelle and prayed she had not overheard. She did not seem to notice what Erejzan had said. He raised his voice, addressing her and the others. "It is not wise to spend the night here. Where Vraduir's minions have been, they may return."

They needed little urging, even if Jathelle had not translated his comment into a royal order. Under descending darkness, they left the village. The horses were eager to gallop and they had to keep them in tight rein to prevent falls and stumbles, so anxious were the brutes.

Rof promised that there was a campsite five measures beyond the lake, and they found him true to his word. Travel had been hard and the unnerving encounter with the deserted village and enchanted ship had left the questers much spent. They were more than ready to stop when Rof pointed out the shelter. Again Tyrus wove a glamour to guard them while they slept. Again they posted watch, taking turns as sentinels.

The next day, they went more slowly, nearing the outer boundaries of known lands. Couredh claimed this territory, but it was so hostile even the barbarians disdained it. Only an occasional habitation broke the rocky hills and, like the lakeside village, these were abandoned, the people who had been there taken by force and wizardry.

They had left civilization, and they had left Hetanya's climates and were about to leave Iesor-Peluva's shining warmth. The air was frigid; when they reached an isolated spring at center stand, they had to break a skim of ice on the water to let the horses and themselves drink. Rof was amused by the courtiers' complaints and shivering. He advised them to enjoy the chill, for it would get much worse as they neared the Ice Forest.

Another day went by in still harder riding and still more bone-aching cold. They halted more frequently, careful with the horses, which were beginning to stagger. The further north they went, the more obvious it became why no one who had a choice would enter these forbidding lands.

Near sundown, the sky became overcast. The fog did not plague them any more, but now before them lay an unbroken gray wall of ominous cloud. It did not boil or speak with lightnings, like the one carrying the skeleton warriors and Ilissa. Yet its darkness filled their eyes and dashed their spirits. When night fell, they could see neither stars nor moon.

Even this far into this awful country, Rof knew a shelter, a collapsed cave still partially able to shield against the elements. It was more a jumble of immense boulders than a true cave, but there was water. It was warm from the bowels of the earth and stank of sulphur. The horses did not like it but they drank it. The courtiers, especially, did not trust the reeking water, fearing poison. But when none of the horses or soldiers died, they gave in to their thirst and gulped down the nasty liquid.

Quarrels were muted. Soldiers, noblemen, and brigands gathered around a scrubwood fire, huddling in cloaks and blankets. They were grateful for the warmth of other bodies, even those belonging to men they disliked.

Tyrus had chosen the first watch as sentry and was perched on the rocks two lengths above the cave. He saw Jathelle working her way up the slippery path toward him. Aubage followed her, shuddering with cold but still acting the part of an eager and attentive courtier. Jathelle stopped and looked back at him. "It is my turn to stand watch with the sorkra first, Sirai. Go seek your rest. You have earned it."

Earnestly Aubage protested, "I prefer to stay by your side, LaRenya, in case of attack."

"Your concern is appreciated, but I do not believe we are in imminent danger. Go. I insist."

"But, LaRenya, it will be colder still in the morning. I would rather finish my watch before that time," Aubage said, for once open in his reasons.

Jathelle hid a smile. "Then take the mid watch. It will be warmer than dawn. You have my permission to go back to the fire now, Sirai."

With great regret, Aubage climbed down. He shoved in close to the fire, butting aside Dorche and Miquit, rubbing his hands briskly and holding them over the flames. The other courtiers smirked at each other behind Aubage's back. They tolerated his rudeness, amused. Jathelle watched this and laughed softly. Then she continued climbing to the top of the rocks. She sat beside Tyrus and he joined her laughter. "Aubage is quick to make excuses."

"But he does not delude me."

"He could not be too obvious in speaking his true motive for wanting your company," Tyrus said cautiously, waiting with interest for Jathelle's reaction.

"I know his motive. He wants me to be his second wife. He thinks that would make him the Renya he fancies he should be. His kin-brothers sent him away from their estates for his pride. Even they deem him a foppish seeker after titles and properties, however he may get them. They are content to be second family. Aubage thinks it a stair to climb to my throne." Jathelle leaned her chin on her hand tiredly. "Ilissa was willing to wed a border-man. I do not think I could accept their custom of wiving several women, though." She turned to Tyrus expectantly, probing his expression.

"My island kept the custom of but one mate," Tyrus said at last. "One man, one woman . . ."

Did he imagine she was relieved to hear that? Jathelle nodded. "You would assume that Ilissa's love would be enough for a man, would you not? Love. I doubt he knows its meaning. I vow he will not come to Couredh's throne through wedding *me!* Errant fawner!"

"Perhaps I am too bold, but . . . why allow him to marry Ilissa?" Tyrus wondered. "He is not worthy."

"No, he is not, not if he were twice the man." Jathelle sighed. "But she loves him, and she will have him, no matter how often I tried to suggest how shallow he is. He has done it without deeds, merely glib tongue and pretty manners. He won her heart when he came to court this winter. In truth, I believe his kin-brothers sent him to the city to keep him from meddling in their affairs! Well, Ilissa loves him. And so he shall be her devoted consort—or will rue the day he came to Couredh! I swear! I . . . I cannot deny Ilissa anything, even to spare her from a fop like that."

Dim, wavering light sifted up through the rocks, showing Tyrus the young queen's sad expression. She was gazing into the moonless night—to the north.

"We will find her," Tyrus said gently.

Jathelle buried her face in her hands a moment, then lifted her head. "I have such ugly dreams every night. I see Ilissa, tortured, terrified! Reaching for me. I can never quite touch her hand. Her tears! They are daggers, stabbing my brain! It was painful to see her when she was a sickly child, so sweet in her suffering, so uncomplaining. Every day, every breath, might have been her last. And when she grew strong and we knew she would live, it was Hetanya's blessing. I rejoiced and thanked the Mother of Earth countless times that Ilissa was well and safe. And now . . ." Jathelle asked woefully, "Is she alive? Rof doubts that she is. Can you tell me, Tyrus? Can your sorkra arts tell me?"

He was tempted to lie, but Jathelle deserved an honest answer, and he suspected she would detect any evasion. "He is a seeker after treasures. LaSirin is a priceless treasure. I do not think Vraduir will squander such dearly-bought prizes. It is likely he will hoard them carefully as part of his great spellcasting."

"All those things he stole—the Hetanya crown and the man-fish's silver net and all—*what* magic? You said he wanted power," Jathelle whispered. "Sacrifices!" And she trembled.

"No." Tyrus put his arm about her. Her cloak had slipped off her shoulders and Jathelle was heedless of the cold. Tyrus replaced the cloak and added part of his own blanket to shield her from the bitter air. They sat close together, their body heat chasing away the night's chill. Jathelle pressed his hand in thanks. Her warmth matched his, even through their gloves.

Slowly Tyrus said, "Power consumes him, a lust for it. But he made a critical mistake the last time he matched his wizardry with a god. He will be wary, now. If he stole Ilissa so recently, it means his plan is not complete. That is in your favor, LaRenya. Search your heart. You said you felt LaSirin's presence there, that your lives were one. Is it still so?"

A ghost of a smile curved Jathelle's mouth. "It is so. You give me courage to go on. If I should doubt again, I beg you heal me with the same magic."

"No magic, LaRenya, save the magic of sisterly love."

She continued to hold Tyrus' hand, looking intently at him in the firelight from below. "I must tell you something. When you arrived at Drita Meadows so suddenly, I . . . I almost believed Aubage's accusations. I was suspicious of you for a pace, thinking *you* might have taken Ilissa with magic."

"I would never do that." Tyrus reveled in this closeness far more than he would have enjoyed the best spot by the campfire.

"I know that now. The skeleton warrior would have

killed me, if not for your sorcery. Does . . . does this Vraduir hate me so much as that?"

Tyrus recalled when he and Erejzan had spied, watching Vraduir invade the palace bedrooms, sensing Vraduir's murderous hate. Pained, he nodded. "You stood in his way."

"And he kills those who get in his way," Jathelle guessed, once more exploring Tyrus' soul. "What is he like? I hate Vraduir, yet I do not even know him. Yet he seems to know me, and he sent his warriors to capture Ilissa."

It seemed fitting to Tyrus that Jathelle should be repaid for Vraduir's evil invasion of her privacy. "I will show him to you," he said, and he gestured, forming an image in the frosty sky beyond the rocks.

Jathelle gasped and leaned upon Tyrus' chest, momentarily disturbing his magic making. The image started to dissolve before he could compose himself and quiet his thumping heart. Concentrating anew, he made the misty shape coalesce. It became a man, hovering in the night, limned as by unseen tapers' light.

Jathelle studied her enemy with loathing. Tyrus had concealed nothing. He had created as accurate a portrait as he was able. Vraduir was there in his kingly garments, the wizard-king of Qamat—handsome in the fullness of his years, his fair hair silver streaked, his brows pale and hooded, his mouth wide and smiling. A smile of unquenchable ambition wiped bare of mercy and humanity.

"How real he is!" Jathelle exclaimed. "As if I could touch him."

"Ai. It is his true appearance as I last saw him on Qamat. His soul is there, too, though it takes bravery to look full upon it," Tyrus said.

"I see it!" Jathelle cried softly. "How dark he is!" She referred not to Vraduir's blond coloring but to his nature. "Tyrus . . . he looks like you."

"Does he?" Without moving, Tyrus willed the image to disappear.

"Forgive me," Jathelle said. "The form is similar. That is all. There is no evil in you, such as fills his being."

Tyrus said in a constricted voice, "We come from the same heritage, the same . . . people." It was as much as he could bring himself to confess.

Jathelle's fingers curled about his and gradually Tyrus grew easier. "I saw other things in his image," she said, gauging Tyrus' mood by pressing his arm, apparently ready to stop if he became angry. "I felt a thread of respect, even of love, between the two of you. And I felt . . . fear. His fear. What does he fear, Tyrus?"

"Death. Age," Tyrus said tonelessly, knowledge long locked in his heart erupting like a smoking mountain's relentless molten rock. "He fears to be mortal, to be prey to life and time, as all humankind is."

"And . . . the thread of love?" Jathelle asked carefully. "It was as if you knew him as yourself. The thread broke. From treachery? As a king might betray his honored duty to protect his people? Losing their trust and the trust of their . . . prince?"

Startled, Tyrus murmured, "What makes you say that, LaRenya?"

"I think it is the truth. You need not speak it, if it gives you pain. But you have the gift of rule, a gift usually allied with blood and rank." Jathelle hesitated, then said, "You cannot resume your rank until Vraduir is repaid for your land's destruction. I understand. Vraduir betrayed you. And Erejzan? Erejzan hates him far more than you do, I suspect."

"Erejzan realized, far sooner than I did, what Vraduir was becoming. And for his courage, Erejzan suffered a terrible punishment. It was . . . a betrayal, ai. A betrayal of loyalty, as when Vraduir betrayed me. Thus ended relationships of many years," Tyrus concluded awkwardly.

"Not too many years. You are not much above my age, Tyrus, and I am not yet a shriveled crone." Jathelle lightly coaxed them both out of their gloominess. "We are young and we are strong, and you have magic. The gods will not let Vraduir succeed."

Tyrus looked at her intently and nodded. She owned a very different and more potent renewal than that in the copper lights. Cold and darkness and fatigue left him, left them both. They helped each other, Jathelle's resolve blending with Tyrus' own, their spirits soaring.

Side by side, under the shelter of the glamour, they winged a challenge into the night, northward. Then, for a while, Tyrus put his worries and his sorcery to another part of his mind. He was content to sit with Jathelle, gathering this respite so sorely needed. Like the soft waters of Qamat, Jathelle's warm presence carried him, sustained him, a tide of her will, bearing him up, on into the misty candle-marks.

XI

Ice Forest and Skull Breakers

❦❦❦❦❦❦❦❦❦❦❦❦❦❦❦❦❦❦❦❦

THE TRAVELERS GAZED APPREHENSIVELY AT THE LINE of trees. The dark barrier extended east and west as far as they could see. Rof had been to Irico and said that even there the Ice Forest was unbroken. It stretched across all the land and beyond into realms no one knew. To the east, where Couredh met the sea, the trees marched to the edge of the frozen ocean and joined where eternal ice blocked all ships.

It was an unnatural forest, black with shadows, thickly grown in a land beyond all other trees and brush. Nothing had grown here for ages, yet the forest was alive. It hulked beneath the constant gray overcast, a wall of twisted trunks and leafless branches. The stillness was profound, filled with a peculiar menace, as if something more unearthly than the brooding trees lurked within, waiting.

A new chill clawed the travelers with talons of ice. It was not the northern wind but fear. The frozen trees and oppressive silence gnawed at them. The horses scented their uneasiness and jerked at reins and tethers. Roughly, the riders quieted their mounts and the spare animals.

Rof pointed. "The end of your realm, LaRenya. Couredh is no more. This is the entrance to the Death God's domain."

Jathelle was afraid. But like Tyrus and Erejzan, dedication to her cause made her conquer fear of the unknown. She said boldly, "I have seen the Ice Forest, bandit lord. When my father bested the barbarians to the west, we came very near the line of the trees."

"But did not enter the Forest, I wager."

"Have you?" Aubage demanded testily.

Rof's answering grin was as cold as the wind. His thieves cowered in their mantles and muttered unhappily as if recalling a bleak enterprise sometime in the past. "I have ventured there, ai," Rof boasted. "You might say it was a matter of life or death—*my* life or death. Some seasons ago, my men and I had, ah, a disagreement about some furs with a nomad tribe. They cut off our escape to civilized regions. So we sought the one place even barbarians shun—the Ice Forest. We lost them readily, you may guess, and we followed the trees for some distance. No longer than we had to, be sure. We are not lackwits."

Tyrus listened to all this absently. He focused on the Forest and the darkness hiding within it. Suddenly he asked, "How deep is it? I am finding it difficult to measure it accurately."

Jathelle and all the men save Erejzan gaped at him and Aubage wondered aloud, "How can you measure it, amuser? We have not yet traveled into it."

"I have methods," Tyrus said, and Aubage asked no more questions. Like the rest of Jathelle's entourage and the brigands, he seemed of two minds; he hoped Tyrus had magic to help them, but he disliked dealing with things he could not see or believing arcane weapons could serve better than club and blade. Tyrus went on, "I have plumbed it and find sorcery. Like the sorcery at the abandoned village, this is old, some seasons past, but much stronger. And there are other things, things outside the enchantment which mean us no good."

"You have named the Skull Breakers," Rof said. He masked his own dread by turning to Erejzan and saying tauntingly, "Little wonder the sorkra knows how to detect a man-beast such as they."

Tyrus quickly stopped an angry outburst from his friend. "The Skull Breakers are not the enemy's tools. I am more concerned for this old magic he left in his wake. I can fight it, for a while. But it is best if we reach the opposite side before sunset. Do you agree?"

Rof squirmed in his saddle and said rather sharply, "I am no wizard. I cannot see where I have not been. I *told* you—we only went into the edges of the Ice Forest, that time past."

"As a guide, you do poorly," Tyrus remarked, returning the barb Rof had flung at Erejzan. "You shall have to trust my skills henceforth."

"We will all end up food for the Skull Breakers if we go in there," Rof said loudly. "You are mad!"

Jathelle countered him. "No. We must go through the Forest and on, if we are to find Ilissa."

The bandits howled and cried, "Not us! Let us have our reward now and we will go."

Others took up the shout. "We brought you here, as we promised! The bargain is done! Give us the reward!"

"Reward . . . !"

"Reward!"

Rof could have quieted them. But he did not. His scarred face reflected his feelings. He shared their greed and fear and had no confidence anyone could return from beyond the Ice Forest. If they did not receive their reward now, Jathelle would not be able to deliver it, they thought.

Furious, Jathelle drew her sword, and her bodyguards and courtiers quickly formed a defensive line to either side of the queen. "The bargain is not done, bandit lord! You swore to guide us till my sister was rescued. She is not yet free. And you will not be paid further until she is!"

The numbers were equal, and Rof saw that Erejzan and Tyrus would support LaRenya and her men. It was not the same situation as on Drita Meadows. There was no advantage on either side, and any clash would mean bloodshed for the bandits as well as Jathelle's people.

"Guide you?" Rof tried to sound exasperated. "I cannot guide you to territories where I have never been."

"One section of the Ice Forest must be much like another," Tyrus said drily. "Why do you hesitate? You bragged you braved it before. Lead us through. Is that so much to ask for such a rich prize?"

Jathelle abetted Tyrus' tactic. "A *very* rich prize, Rof."

"What will that serve if I am dead?" Rof sought a gap in the line of bodyguards and courtiers, finding none. "And if we do get to the other side, how do I get back to spend my reward?"

Tyrus winked at Jathelle and she laughed, enjoying his audacity, not at all offended. With a grin, he told Rof, "Why, then I suppose you will just have to go on with us into the Death God's lands, to make sure we survive and can help you back to civilized realms again."

Seizing his chance to gibe at Rof, Erejzan added, "Is this the bandit lord who said he did not even fear Bogotana's wrath? LaRenya, you have been cheated. He is nothing but wind. He merits no reward at all. The bandit lord is master of braggards, not of thieves."

Aubage, for his own confused motives, heaped his share of scorn on Rof. "Ai! The only prize he should get is a severe flogging for his impertinence. Let us be gone, LaRenya. Forget these worthless fellows. We are

ready to follow you. *We* are not afraid!" A chorus of
cheers went up from the courtiers and soldiers. They
chased away their fear with noise, finding bravery in
numbers and shouting.

Defeated on every side, Rof struggled to recoup his
losses. He sat up very straight and puffed up his chest
like a parading whantola cock. "By my beard, a bargain
is a bargain! I will make you eat those words, Sirai.
Rof is no liar or coward."

Erejzan took up his reins as if meaning to race the
brigand to the Ice Forest. "Prove it with deeds. I say
you can be blown away by Qlitos' gentlest breezes,
your courage no more than a puff of dust."

"I *shall* prove it!" Rof stabbed a finger at Tyrus and
went on in a less steady voice, "But . . . but I want the
wizard's promise that his sorcery will protect us, there
in the Forest."

"I do not desert my allies, Rof," Tyrus replied with
heavy emphasis.

Rof grunted, not quite convinced. One-Ear and the
other bandits were shifty-eyed with dread. However,
they could not easily get past the line of Jathelle's men.
As they had been pinned by the nomads some time
past, now they were again to be forced into the Ice
Forest. Rof decided to play the leader and act insolent,
lest he lose his brigands' respect. "Well and at that,
let us begin." He bowed from the saddle, mocking Jathelle. "With your royal permission, of course."

"I have been ready a long while, as you dallied,"
she retorted. Jathelle would have put heels to her
mount, but Tyrus stopped her.

"Wait. All of you. Remain where you are." Bewildered, they obeyed, and Tyrus loped in a wide circle
around them. He pointed and a sparkling silvery rope
seemed to flow from his fingertips as a spider might
spin out a web. It formed a slender boundary around
Jathelle and the men and the horses. As Tyrus rode

back to his starting point, he said, "That marks the limit of my glamour, in case we are sore beset within the trees. Stay inside, and it will guard you against evil magic. If you step beyond the rope, you leave my sphere and I will be hard pressed to aid you with countercharms. I am not certain how well this will serve against the Skull Breakers. If they are the Death God's creatures, perhaps only he can stop them. If they are not human, mortal magic may not affect them strongly. Be on guard if that happens. But against true magic, the ring will protect you. Remember—stay inside the ring!"

Now, at his mention of the Skull Breakers, an unknown threat, Tyrus pulled forth his transformed sword, its eerie green twinkling making the travelers stare in awe.

Much chastened, the bandits and the courtiers nodded. The bodyguards took his commands more readily, seeing LaRenya agreeing; her acquiescence was their own, even if Tyrus seemed too lordly in manner to suit them all. Carefully, they followed Tyrus and Jathelle down the slope toward the trees. Men glanced nervously at the twinkling line, hovering a half length off the bare ground, as it paralleled their progress. When it bobbed or dipped or seemed to come closer, they nudged their horses away from it. Tyrus assured them it would neither burn nor freeze them dead, but they did not entirely accept his comforting promises.

At the edge of the Forest, Tyrus said, "LaRenya, I think Rof should go first. The bandit lord must earn his fee."

"I would willingly lead," she replied, smiling wanly. "Do not think I am not the daughter of Fer-Sro . . ."

"No one does," Tyrus said, answering her smile. "But Rof has been here before and can indicate pitfalls, as he did in the barren country."

Jathelle skillfully reined her horse to one side, leaving the space open for Rof to precede her. "We await you, guide," she said with a significant stress on the final word.

Rof did not take the invitation immediately. He looked around at the motley group within the sparkling rope and said, "Put the spare horses and pack animals in the center. Knot the lead ropes tightly to your saddles. They will try to bolt if the Skull Breakers attack. The Skull Breakers will take them as quickly as they will a man. They are not very particular. Never stop moving." Jathelle began an order to keep weapons at the ready, but Rof rudely overruled her. "Blades and cudgels, ai. But not those pikes. Keep them in their scabbards. They are too unwieldy among trees."

Some took out the flasks of fish oil every Clarique carried when traveling and formed torches of worn clothes and pieces of firewood they had been toting on the pack horses. As they prepared these torches, Erejzan whispered furtively to Tyrus, "Would not magic lights serve better?"

"Not in there," Tyrus said grimly. "I need all my art to maintain the glamour, I suspect, and to fend off Vraduir. The magic within is his. When we enter the Forest, he is bound to know another wizard is intruding on his domain. The danger worsens badly from this point on, my friend."

Erejzan asked no more questions. He took one of the torches and with the others gathered himself to dare the unknown woods.

The way was too narrow to ride more than one abreast, for the most part. Tyrus elongated the sparkling rope, and the travelers moved single file. Jathelle took her place directly behind Rof. Aubage wanted to be her escort. But Tyrus overruled him, saying, "La-Renya may need my skills against sorcery." With all grace, Aubage gave way and dropped back to ride with the other courtiers.

The air inside the Forest was very short-breathed

and close, barely sufficient to feed the torches. As the trees closed behind them, the sky disappeared, blotted from view. Although there were no leaves, only bare limbs, the trees grew so compactly that they cut off all light from Iesor-Peluva. The shadows were particularly gray, as if the trees were giving off some supernatural light of their own, a threatening glow. The torches sputtered and their feeble flames sent little shimmers of heat up through the darkness. The trees began to drip icy water as the travelers rode under them.

There was no path, though here and there a snaking track wandered among the thick trunks. In Tyrus' estimation, Rof had a keen sense of direction, for he seemed to be leading them as straight as he could for the point opposite the place where they had entered. Driven by fear, trapped in his bargain, Rof hoped to make as fast a traverse of the Ice Forest as possible.

For a candle-period or more, they rode through the alien woods. Ice kept dripping stinging water on them. The horses' hoofbeats and their own voices were swallowed up by the gnarled boles and darkness. Yet now that they were inside the Forest, they heard sounds not apparent from outside. There were sometimes crashing noises, muffled by distance. Or the same crash would be quite near and boom so that the horses shied wildly.

Tyrus speculated that these were the deadfalls common to any woods. The reports were stunningly loud, however, as unnatural as everything else about the Ice Forest.

No birdsong or animal cry broke through the steady, thundering rain of falling limbs. So far, too, there had been no sign of Skull Breakers. Perhaps Rof and his men had spun tales of nothing, making that danger out of fantasies. Tyrus peered through the trees ahead, hoping to see some glimmer of light that might indicate they were nearing the far side of the Forest. From his skimming flight through the image in the vision-glass, he knew the Forest could not be too wide. But . . . how wide was wide? Judgments were often blurred by the vast regions he might span in the space of a wizard's mind-traveling. If there were not too many perils, they might still reach safety with no hurt.

Quite unexpectedly, one of the heavy limbs snapped off just above the place Tyrus had passed a moment earlier. The massive branch landed with stunning force on the glamour and a mind-wrenching shock raked through Tyrus. One of the spare horses had stretched its tether; as Tyrus reeled under the blow from above, the animal pulled outside the sparkling rope. As it did, the branch slid off the invisible barrier of the glamour, crushing the brute with its monstrous weight. Screaming, the horse went down. To the humans' astonishment, they saw that the branch was made of solid rock. It cracked and shattered into chunks of stone as it buried the hapless horse.

"What is happening?" someone yelped in panic.

Rof wrestled with his terrified mount, as surprised as the rest. He stammered, "It . . . it was not like this when we . . . . when we challenged the Ice Forest west of here. I swear . . . I swear . . . the trees . . . !"

"Wizardry!" Tyrus roared, recovering his senses. He shot extra power to the veil within the rope, trying to prevent further catastrophe. "The trees are enchanted. The Forest itself is our enemy. It will take our lives if it can!"

"Guard us, sorkra!" Rof pleaded. "Leave the horse. It is past saving. Run! Keep moving!"

"Cut its throat," Jathelle wailed. "Do not let the beast suffer . . ."

The bandit lord grabbed her reins, dragging Jathelle's horse close behind his. "No time! It will not suffer long.

The Skull Breakers will find it and finish it. Move, La-
Renya! Move!"

Jathelle flung her hands over her ears to shut out the
dying horse's shrieks. They rushed ahead, squeezing
between the trees, no one wanting to be left alone. Apprehensively they peered up, trying to stay within Tyrus' glamour, wondering which branch would fall next.

The frozen earth was already littered with many earlier deadfalls, giant remains of other immense branches
of stone. Ice rimed the trunks and limbs and the broken
rocks of the petrified wood strewn over the forest floor.
Beneath some branches and rocks there were bones,
skeletons that looked not quite human. A few skeletons were whole, but most were partial or torn apart.
At first Tyrus thought these had been rent by falling
limbs. Then he saw that many of the bones bore tooth
marks. Others had been forcibly splintered over the
rocks, the marrow cracked, damage done after the trees
had crushed their prey.

The others noticed these grisly remains, too, their
eyes drawn against their will. One particular skull rested
upon a gnarled root, seeming to laugh at them as they
rode by. The skull was a thick-browed relic of a brutish
being. It had been hacked raggedly just above that
heavy brow. The upper portion was gone.

Rof guessed their suspicions and confirmed them,
calling back to his followers, "Skull Breakers did that.
They make food of each other's tiny brains and eat
them from the containers the gods gave them."

Many men retched. Tyrus' stomach roiled and he
fought nausea and Jathelle exclaimed in shaken horror,
"They . . . they eat their own kind?"

"Ai! And anything else they find, LaRenya. There is
not much game in here." Rof guffawed at his gruesome
joke, then spurred his horse till blood flowed from its
ribs.

The candle-marks crept by. More stone limbs fell.

Tyrus divided his mind, on alert for Vraduir. Surely Vraduir would sense this disturbance in the Ice Forest. The trees were animated from very long ago, Tyrus guessed. But there was a new malevolence in them the Death God would not have made—a malevolence created by Vraduir. Vraduir had come this way, and so had Captain Drie and the crew of the ship and all the prisoners and stolen objects, save for those delivered to the warriors elsewhere, so perhaps they were confined to a short sky chase within reach of the Death God's frozen domain.

A greater part of Tyrus' will went into the glamour and the sparkling rope. It worked with his fear of Vraduir. So long as they stayed under the glamour and within the magic line, Vraduir would not touch them, not without tremendous effort. Impossible! Not this far from his sanctuary.

He would not need to, though, if the trees and the savage Skull Breakers did his work!

Sweat poured down Tyrus' face and spine. He braced the glamour and the rope with his arts, tightening places where it weakened as horses kicked it or limbs broke through. He could not protect the horses and have wizardry enough to shield every man and Jathelle against magic.

The limbs were falling more and more frequently, a malicious assault. They landed on the invisible veil, dragging at it, and as they dragged the veil, they battered Tyrus' strength. Each time a branch hit the glamour, Tyrus reeled under the blow as if the limb had struck him, not that extension of his mind.

He was not aware Erejzan was bellowing at him until his friend's arms fastened about Tyrus' chest. Erejzan was pulling him to one side of the saddle. As he was jerked aside, cold air rushed past Tyrus with shocking force. Dimly he realized an enormous club had swished through the space where his head had been.

Confused, distracted by the constant need to maintain the glamour, Tyrus glimpsed a figure from the tail of his eye. It was a man. No! It was a man-thing, a hideous, furred creature, its maw adrip with spittle. The brow was beetling, like that of the broken skull. Its wide, bestial nostrils flared and snorted.

"Defend yourselves!" One-Ear howled.

"They . . . they are getting through the sorkra's magic . . . !"

"All around us! Kill them!"

Over the din, Rof was yelling, "Keep moving! If we stop, we are dead!"

"Tighten the glamour," Erejzan shouted, almost in Tyrus' ear, making him wince. The Skull Breaker which had tried to brain Tyrus was rushing them again.

"Cannot. Not . . . not Vraduir's. Not the Death God's," Tyrus gasped. "Nothing . . . nothing there to counter! How are they finding us? They should not . . . should not be able to see us through the veil . . ."

"They smell us! They are beasts!" Erejzan guessed.

"Do not . . . do not change to fight them . . . too strong," Tyrus begged his friend.

"No need!"

Sirai Aubage was riding close to the rump of Erejzan's horse. Erejzan wrenched the torch out of the dumbfounded nobleman's hands and delivered a violent backhanded blow with it, striking the oncoming Skull Breaker across its furry face.

Gobbets of flames and wood and sparks exploded into the icy air. The Skull Breaker staggered back, gibbering in agony, clutching its eyes.

Aubage gaped in admiration at this maneuver, then stared at his suddenly empty hands, so abruptly bereft of the torch. Erejzan thundered at him, "Draw your sword, you clenru! They are mortal! They can be killed!"

Aubage had no breath to waste answering that crude

insult. He grabbed his blade and hastily fended off another Skull Breaker charging in from his right. He fought with more panic than art, but the sword brought blood and drove the man-thing away.

"So many of them . . ." Tyrus moaned through gritted teeth. Ripples of pain moved across his mind as a steady rain of broken limbs battered the glamour.

"Guard us from the trees," Erejzan cried. "We shall best the Skull Breakers with steel and fire!" He slapped the rump of Tyrus' mount and goaded the animal forward at a dangerous pace. Erejzan valiantly protected the sorkra's back again and again, killing or chasing off the murderous denizens of the Ice Forest.

The Skull Breakers apparently feared fire greatly, a thing others in the train quickly learned. Jathelle rode ahead of Tyrus, a sword in one hand and a torch in the other as she galloped after Rof. Tyrus lashed out reflexively with his own enchanted blade, now and then scoring a blow that brought animal screams from the darkness on either side. The Skull Breakers' wails mingled with those of frightened or dying horses. Deadly missiles poured down and now hurtled through the glamour as the Skull Breakers burst past the veil and heaved broken stone limbs at Jathelle and the men.

Tyrus knotted his fingers in his horse's mane. The glamour was a tangible thing, intimately connected with his mind. It was a contorted cup, giving and stretching this way and that; each time it did, the awful impact was an unseen, jagged barb thrusting through his brain and vitals.

"Come back here!" Lieutenant Utaigh's voice penetrated the confusion in Tyrus' thoughts. "Those brigands! They have taken three spare horses and are turning back south!"

"Let them!" Jathelle's command was broken, her breath forced from her as she rode at a gallop. "We dare not chase deserters. Stay together!"

"The magic rope," Tyrus said, hoping she could hear him. "Stay inside the rope."

"I will get them, LaRenya," someone was crying, refusing to obey either order.

"No! No! Dorche! Sirai, come back," many warned the nobleman.

On the heels of that plea came a scream. Several screams—of men and beasts. "LaRenya . . . help!" drifted faintly through the thick, cold woods. There was a crash as of living beings borne heavily to earth. Triumphant gibbers followed, and a horrifying wail that bubbled away into nothing.

"Do not stop!" Rof was Gros-Donaq's worshipper, the heaven's own raging storm in his words, dinning at them. *"Do not stop! Not for anyone!"*

Two Skull Breakers waddled out of the shadows in front of Rof and Jathelle. Tyrus saw them but was helpless. The demands of sorcery were vises shut tightly about his breast and head, pounding at him under the trees' steady rain. He could not even speak, his heart mutely crying for him, "Jathelle . . . !"

But she whirled to confront one inhuman thing, bracing her sword hilt on her saddle. She dodged the Skull Breaker's club, and in the next instant her attacker became her prey, impaled on the blade. She did not cringe from blood and death. Battle maiden, indeed! She drew the sword free and trampled the dying Skull Breaker under her horse's hooves. All who followed rode over the carcass, reducing it to gore, pulped flesh, and shattered bone.

Rof dealt summarily with the other Skull Breaker, blinding it with the butt of his whip and splitting its face with his sword. The maimed thing stumbled blindly into the woods and fell writhing, no obstacle to those in Rof's wake.

They could no longer gallop, for the way was too crooked. Heaps of stone logs and limbs often blocked the way, making them detour. Tyrus swayed dizzily and Erejzan took his reins, leading him. The glamour and the sparkling rope that kept them hidden from Vraduir and safe from the trees were an arcane fabric stretched past endurance, the strands beginning to fray dangerously.

Tyrus lost all sense of time. How many candle-periods were gone? Was it still day, or had night fallen? How could he tell, here in this supernatural gloom?

The glamour—he *must* keep it solid! His thoughts were spinning, in a whirlpool of sorcery and mortal dread. Bargains. The Ice Forest was a bargain, Vraduir's evil sorcery combined with the Death God's stone trees. A wall to guard the path so that none could trace Vraduir and his victims into the Death God's realm.

Bargains . . . bargains . . . how did one bargain with a god? Vraduir had bargained once with Bogotana, and . . .

Tyrus' belly ached, slashed by frost knives. His blood was congealed. He was being battered into blood and bone, like that slaughtered Skull Breaker. Soon there would be nothing left of Tyrus, Sirin-sorkra of lost Qamat, not even his mind, seeking out magic.

"Light! I see light! Hurry! We are almost there!"

Jathelle's voice was guiding him back to consciousness and life. It was a line, a brace, taut on the sails, slender, feminine, yet very strong. He clung to the voice, wrapping the golden sound about himself, his anchor in a gale of sorcery. It was pulling him, bringing him to safety, as he had so often drawn himself up out of worlds of darkness and webs.

An end to the Ice Forest? The candle that marked time had never burned so slowly! He yearned for light, clinging to Jathelle's words.

He and Jathelle were on a ship, laughing, together, side by side, as they had sat on the rocks last night. Thoughts and hearts one. The tiller was in Tyrus' hand

—or was that an enchanted sword he was grasping? Jathelle's honey-gold hair tossed in a sea breeze. Was it the warm wind of Qamat or a brisker air, the sharp and invigorating wind of Couredh? It did not seem to matter. They ruled the ship and the sea, walking the waves toward a beckoning shore. A safe harbor awaited them, the gates of the city open wide—as Couredh's had opened wide to welcome Tyrus when first he came to that land. Jathelle looked up at Tyrus, smiling, and he gazed at her, rapt. She pointed to the harbor, to the haven . . .

Not a ship. He was on horseback. And the deadly rain of limbs was decreasing. Gaining strength as the assault weakened, Tyrus searched desperately for the light Jathelle had promised. There! Ahead!

To the rear, the Skull Breakers' howls were fading as they were left behind. They lamented as their prey escaped. The horses sensed a way out of the Ice Forest and, like animals smelling water after a long thirst, set a reckless gait, scraping their riders' legs against tree trunks, abusing the sparkling rope that enclosed them all.

Then they were out under the gray sky, laughing wildly with relief. They rode twenty lengths beyond the outermost trees before anyone drew rein. Horses dropped their heads, foam and sweat dripping, tongues lolling. A few fell, dumping their riders.

Hysteria swept Jathelle and the men. Some got down from their staggering horses and danced drunkenly, clapping their hands. As yet, they were too delirious at their narrow victory to comprehend fully their losses or what had happened.

Eventually, laughter and giddy caperings stopped and they looked north. Winning through the Ice Forest was an ordeal no one but Vraduir and his slaves had accomplished, until now. Their victory, though, was as bitter as the wind off the tortuous peaks and ice-sheathed hills. Snow swept across a vast white expanse. Fog and wind here became a frigid suspension of ice crystals, thickening in clouds around the tors and frozen valleys. Unearthly bayings and keenings rose from the crags. The Skull Breakers, at least, had borne some remote kinship with humankind. The eerie cries echoing in this land of ice seemed to come from beasts which had never walked where light and warmth had been. It was a land of death and demons, endless, blending into one forbidden wall with the perpetual gray of the dark sky.

XII

Gateway to Death

❖❖❖❖❖❖❖❖❖❖❖❖❖❖❖❖❖❖❖❖❖❖❖❖

DAZED, THEY COUNTED THE PRICE OF WINNING THROUGH the Ice Forest. No one cared about the two bandits who had deserted, not even their fellow brigands. It was far worse that five spare horses had strayed outside the magic rope and had been struck by branches or killed by the Skull Breakers. Past measuring, though, was the death of Sirai Dorche, who had foolishly ridden in pursuit of the deserters. They mourned, and the bandits, too, added their prayers to this, perhaps fearing the nobleman's spirit would bedevil them otherwise.

Miraculously, they had suffered few serious hurts, none that needed Tyrus' magic—and he had no potion or charm to care for cuts or bruises the bestial Skull Breakers had dealt. Instead he moved apart from the others and replenished his strength, breathing deeply. Erejzan watched him anxiously until Tyrus said, "It is well."

An especially hideous series of screams resounded from the peaks ahead. Erejzan massaged the back of his neck, working kinks from too-tense muscles. "I thought the Skull Breakers were awful enough," he said. "Must we fight more monsters?"

"Many more, I fear."

"Vraduir?"

"Beyond those ridges," Tyrus said. "Very near. He is watching, and he is not watching. He senses that another sorkra is somewhere about. But he does not know who I am or precisely how far I have come into his territory. And he is still quite intent on Jathelle's army. They seem to be making a fine show to the westward. Vraduir is uncertain if that is a genuine threat or a mere nuisance he can ignore."

Erejzan addressed the distant warlord, "Keep his attention fast, Lord General Zlan. Hold him, and we will tear out his evil heart!"

Involuntarily Tyrus winced. Blood called to blood, even after all Vraduir had done. He had pondered this often the past year. Did he have the will to slay his own sire? Would not the gods curse him forever if he did? Tyrus forced his thoughts from that. "Before we confront Vraduir, we must try to rescue his victims. I hope Ilissa and the harper of Atei and the peasants are still alive."

"Ilissa . . ." Erejzan stared into nothing. "Tyrus, I . . . I have never felt so about a woman. I was no moon calf ere Vraduir enchanted me. I have known women. But Ilissa . . . it is as if our souls are bound, as if she owns the spirit of my poor, lost Dalaen. I did not think I would ever taste such sweetness again. We *will* save her! I vow it on my very life!"

Jathelle was walking toward them and she heard his final words. "Your resolve is companion to my own, Erejzan." Her face was ashen and tear-streaked, and much of her braids had come loose during the struggle in the Forest. With a tremble in her voice, she exclaimed, "But the cost . . . !"

Suddenly, she was swaying and would have fallen if

Tyrus had not hastily put his arms about her. Jathelle clung to him helplessly and he embraced her more tightly, pillowing her head on his shoulder. He had acted instinctively, out of kind concern. But as he held Jathelle close, much more personal sensations stirred, ones most pleasant.

Above Jathelle's fair head, Tyrus saw Aubage glaring at him jealously. Jathelle was not his betrothed and Aubage owned no claim or right to her affections at all. Yet it was obvious he bitterly resented any other man who won her favor. He seemed especially furious that it was Tyrus who was so honored and that Jathelle leaned upon him without any care for rank or birth. Tyrus answered Aubage's red-faced anger with a coldly superior smile, perversely enjoying the situation.

Erejzan had fetched a waterskin and steadied Jathelle's shaking hands as she drank. Gradually, color came back to her cheeks and she thanked him with a smile. Then she said in some embarrassment, "I . . . I did not mean to play the frail damsel." Tyrus sensed she wanted to prove her strength and stand alone. As she moved out of his arms, he felt bereft. Jathelle said earnestly, "I will not yield to such weakness again."

"There is no shame in it, and I did not mind. It was a harrowing experience for all of us, LaRenya."

The brigands had recuperated faster than the others in one way, for reasons of greed. They were squatting around an open saddle pack, snarling and arguing. One of the deserters' horses had eluded the Skull Breakers and escaped the Forest with the rest of the animals. Its dead owner's pack carried his share of the coins and gems Jathelle had given him. His heirs now bickered over the treasure. Tyrus shook his head in disgust and turned away from that ugly scene as Jathelle said, "Dorche came of one of Couredh's bravest tribes. This is such a cruel death for him to suffer."

"You are not blaming yourself?" Tyrus asked and

quickly added, "We are all at risk, LaRenya. You as much as the others. The gods will choose when we will die and who will live. Your grief is an adornment he will carry with him to Keth's gates."

"I will make sacrifices in his name when we return to Couredh."

"An honor and a proper lament for him who died in good cause."

"Did he?" Aubage cut in sharply. "Dorche died for this quest of yours, sorkra, not in any true war or fight with his peers. He was slaughtered by those filthy savages!"

Jathelle said with heat, "Tyrus did not set you upon this quest. You came of your own will, or so you said. If you have lost your heart for it, go back, and *we* will rescue your betrothed for you!"

"No, of course not, LaRenya. I did not mean . . . I am ever your devoted subject and I will go to the ends of the earth for Ilissa's sake. I vow!" Aubage shifted from his fawning then and pointed accusingly at Tyrus. "But you have been deceived by this man, LaRenya. He claimed to be a sorkra and said he would guard us with his magic. But I saw no magic, and Dorche is dead because he failed us."

The others gathered around them interestedly. Sirai Miquit and the bodyguards looked as if they might be persuaded to Aubage's point of view. The bandits had finished splitting up the plunder, and Rof said, "Best be careful, Sirai Aubage. He *is* a sorkra, I can assure you."

"Shut your mouth. I want none of your advice. The word of a bandit and a throatslitter! Bah! What is that worth? You see, LaRenya?" Aubage went on in a petulant tone. "Those who say he is a sorkra are no better than these amusers. We were the ones who fought and died in the Ice Forest, and his magic did nothing to help us. He lied."

Tyrus' smoldering temper erupted and he flung up his arms, his fingers spread wide. "Indeed? You saw no magic? I am a liar? Then I bid you tell me what manner of false sorkra can strike you dumb?"

Aubage gaped, his eyes bulging, his mouth open and his tongue waggling futilely. He could make only muffled, unintelligible sounds and soon choked on those. Clutching his throat, he twisted about, frantic to regain his voice.

Sirai Miquit politely hid a smile. The soldiers were less courteous, though they forebore to laugh out loud. The brigands whooped and slapped their thighs, relishing Aubage's plight. "I told you not to tempt him, Sirai," Rof said maliciously. "Next time, pay some heed to this whoreson of a throatslitter. I may know a thing or two you do not, eh?"

Tyrus closed his hands and drew his power back into himself. Aubage exhaled noisily and then tentatively licked his lips and felt his mouth. He behaved as if he feared most that the enchantment had disfigured him. Seeing this, Sirai Miquit grimaced disdainfully at his fellow courtier's vanity. As Aubage found he had taken no permanent hurt, he flushed bright red, his chagrin made worse by the bandits' raucous laughter.

"If you still doubt me," Tyrus said icily, "go back into the Ice Forest without me. Surely your sword will be enough to protect you from both the Skull Breakers and the enchanted trees. What need have you for any false sorkra?"

Slowly the laughter died away and the men eyed Tyrus with awe. Aubage gulped down his outrage, warier by far than he had been. Tyrus sighed in resignation. Such a little demonstration, and how sobered they were! The brief spellcasting which had so impressed them was a simple thing, one of the first sorkra arts he had learned. If this daunted them, how were they going to deal with the much greater magic which must come when they met Vraduir face to face?

Jathelle showed less fear than the men. With a sly glance at Aubage, she said, "I swear I have not doubted your gifts, Tyrus. Will you let me keep my tongue and breath?"

His good humor restored, Tyrus flourished his cloak and bowed. "I always give respect where respect is given, LaRenya."

Jathelle chuckled. But her amusement was short-lived and for Tyrus' sarcasm alone. She confronted the others. "I trust this is an end to divisions among us. Have done with it. If you cannot accept the sorkra's commands as well as mine, you must remain here or return to Couredh. If you come with us, you will obey us. Our enemy is a wizard, and Tyrus knows how to counter him—not you and not I. If he orders a thing, we must do it. Understood?"

She was a striking woman, her fur cloak billowing, her clothes spattered with Skull Breakers' blood, her loosened braids streaming in the wind. The snows of Omaytatle and Wyolak's lightnings seemed to march about her, the gods approving her right to her crown.

The bodyguards declared their unchanged intent to follow LaRenya. Aubage and Sirai Miquit could do no less. Once these men had made such declarations boldly, whipping themselves into fierce vows and challenges. Now they spoke simply, much of their earlier eagerness seared away in the Ice Forest.

The brigands were unsure what to do. They had been forced through the Ice Forest, lured by greed and Rof's bullying. Now they dared not go back without Tyrus' magic to protect them. In the end, greed won. Rof said sourly, "We will go with you, LaRenya. If we stay here, the evil wizard may strike. The sorkra owes us his guardianship. We demand it. And we do not follow you for loyalty of house or realm, only for the ransom."

"I welcome your numbers and weapons," Jathelle said sincerely. And she promised them once again, "When my sister is free, you shall be amply rewarded, past your wildest hopes."

Aubage tried to wipe out the ignominy of being chastised by Tyrus. He waved his sword at the sky and said, "I will go forth into the Death God's lands and slay any who oppose my queen—be he mortal, demon, or wizard."

"Or god," Tyrus added, gazing at the snow-swept peaks. "Before we are done, we may indeed meet all of those."

They agreed they should go as far as they could before the horses quit and while there was still light to make their way. Two horses had already foundered and had to be put out of their misery. There was no leisure to butcher them. The travelers consolidated the remaining supplies and grumbled that the brigands were burdening the train unnecessarily by toting along the gold and gems Jathelle had given them. Slowly, working against the wind, they headed up into the snowy mountains.

There was no certain method to gauge time. Thick clouds ruled the sky from the Ice Forest to the northern horizon. There was no sunlight, only a dismal, suffused grayness, stark against the white-capped rocks. As they made their way across the trackless ridges, strange cries bounced from one needle-sharp peak to another. No one voiced a guess as to what sort of beasts could make such sounds.

To guard their flanks, they ruthlessly led the spare horses along the outside of the train. They carried provender on their mounts and put on all the extra clothes they could, ready to sacrifice the pack animals if attack came.

The unmarked route was steep and slippery, winding up toward a pass between two peaks. Tyrus had become their guide. He followed the path in the vision-glass, and now he also had a new means of tracking their quarry. A pressure had begun, a thing he sensed ever more insistently as they left the Ice Forest. Vraduir! His force of magic, seeking out another wizard who was invading his realm. Tyrus' glamour confused him, turned him aside again and again. But the emanation remained in one place—the citadel in Tyrus' vision. Vraduir's pride was Tyrus' help, too, for the wizard-king of Qamat could not believe any other wizard could use his magic-making to trace him to his lair. Nor did he know that Tyrus and Erejzan had survived Qamat's destruction. His magic was a beacon, leading Tyrus through wind and driving snow and the keening of the Death God's pets.

The heaviest riders dismounted and led their horses. Snow squeaked under boots and hooves. Teeth chattered. Exposed flesh felt raw and burning as pellets of ice flew within the downy flakes.

On every side, alien shapes loomed from the frozen landscape. These grotesque rocks resembled strange animals. Their lifeless eyes were gleaming ice and their fur the frost rime. Sometimes the wind would sweep the snow aside abruptly, revealing one of these menacing statues, and men would reach for weapons before they realized it was only stone. Steady tension and cold took their tolls as they struggled up the ridge. Gloves tore and fingers bled when they sought handholds along the rocks or heaps of ice-encrusted snow. Beards and mustaches and eyebrows grew coated with accretions of their breath, frozen as quickly as it left their nostrils and mouths. Tendrils of Jathelle's hair, escaping her hood, suffered the same fate. The horses slipped and fell often, whinnying piteously, their cries nearly drowned in the keening from the peaks.

Tyrus tried to ignore the cold and his complaining body. He had to keep the glamour around them as they worked their way closer and closer to that citadel in his vision. Two ridges and then . . .

The curtain of howling snow tore asunder, and they saw an immense animal hunched athwart the path. Multiple fangs bared, countless eyes shining redly, it was a lizard out of some nightmare. Hastily Tyrus tightened the glamour into a shield, diverting his strength and weakening the fabric elsewhere.

Jathelle was beside him, her sword drawn. The lieutenant and his men rushed up on either side of the sorkra and their queen, their pikes aimed for the monster's head and breast. Those to the rear could not see what was happening, bumping into those ahead of them, cursing and shouting questions.

"Wait!" Tyrus ordered the bodyguards. Remembering Aubage's lessoning, they held their pikes ready but did not lunge. Tyrus studied the hulking thing as it roared and gnashed its many teeth and prodded at his glamour with its bulbous nose. "It can no longer see us," Tyrus assured Jathelle and the men. He had called forth much from his reserves to make the barrier solid against it, and a tremor through his belly warned Tyrus he could not maintain such powerful magic very long. Before he faltered, though, the awful creature lost interest in the riddle of the glamour and ambled away, soon swallowed up in the snow.

Men gasped in relief and the soldiers lowered their pikes, staring at one another. "What . . . what was it? Where has it gone?"

"More worry if it comes back!"

"Was it damp-breather or snake-wing . . . ?"

". . . never saw its like . . ."

"We did," Jathelle corrected the brigand who had said that. "A smaller one was on Drita Meadows, snapping at us while the skeleton warriors captured Ilissa."

Their words drifted past Tyrus as he reworked the glamour more evenly around them. He clenched his jaw to still the irritating chatter of his teeth. Reluctantly, he dipped down into the arcane world and drew more strength for his spellcasting. The time might have come at last when he would have to discover his limits. Yet he *must* save his greatest arts for the inevitable clash with Vraduir!

"There . . . there are likely to be more of them," Tyrus cautioned them. He shivered so badly his words seemed to rattle. But everyone was shuddering with cold and sounded the same. "Try . . . try to stay close together. If you . . . if you tear through the glamour, it . . . it diminishes my protection for the rest. And . . . and I cannot help you if you are outside."

"Will you weave the silver rope to show us where to stay, sorkra?" Rof asked.

Tyrus clamped his hands tightly over the saddle, stilling the racking shivers that assaulted him. "Dare . . . dare not. All I can do . . . to keep the glamour. Stay close . . . stay close . . ." he advised faintly. "The Death God's creatures. Not . . . not illusions. Real . . ."

"Can we kill them, if we must?" Jathelle wondered.

Frustrated that he could give her no sure answer, Tyrus murmured, "I do not know. I hope so."

They moved on up the slope, forced to work back and forth tediously in order to make the ascent. Despite their care, the slippery footing betrayed them. A horse and rider fell and started sliding out of control along the way they had climbed. The horse crashed against other horses and more went down, men spitting oaths and scrambling to get free and find footholds. The entire mass of four horses and men tore against the glamour, ripping at it, going through.

The shock of its shattering knocked Tyrus out of the

saddle. He hung off his mount's neck, barely conscious, while the frightened animal tried to sidle out from under him completely. Jathelle and Erejzan were grabbing at the reins and Tyrus, helping him.

The world was splintered with hurtful light and ice, the full fury of the storm hurtling at them, once the glamour broke. It was a fragile veil, unable to prevent entry, and entry was made.

From the twisted rocks shaped like beasts came true beasts, a two-headed golhi and a dragon-hatchling sheathed in shimmering blue scales. They leaped into the opening the accident had made, pouncing on the downed horses and men with murderous force.

There was no chance to consult Tyrus. Men fought for their lives, striking desperately with steel and bronze and cudgel. They hacked like butchers and used swords like cleavers, killing the things from the rocks, mingling their ichor with that of two dead horses and a badly hurt soldier. His comrades were dragging the man back toward Jathelle and Tyrus when another monster appeared.

It was a lesser version of the many-eyed creature that had accosted them earlier. Taking them off guard, it slew another horse before the brigands and Sirai Miquit brought it down and stabbed it to death. Though dead, it flopped and twitched horribly, the limbs and claws still dangerous during its throes. They shrank away, ripping packs off the slaughtered horses, hurrying to marshal their forces more closely together.

Erejzan and Jathelle had pulled Tyrus back onto his horse. Tears of pain streamed from his eyes and he bit his lip to keep back his groans. Shakily he raised his hands, enveloping them once more in the glamour. The snow lessened, beating against the invisible veil, the worst of it at bay, as he had forestalled the monster with multiple fangs.

"At least . . . at least we know they can be killed," Rof panted, mopping reeking ichor from his sword.

"So can we," Lieutenant Utaigh said angrily. He and the other soldiers were lifting their wounded comrade up onto one of the remaining horses. The man was too weak to ride alone and the sergeant got up behind him, bracing the other before he fell.

"Tyrus?" Jathelle bent over, peering worriedly at Tyrus' drooping eyes.

"Valley . . . beyond the ridge. Less wind . . ."

No one needed to tell them to hurry. Blood marked their tracks up to the pass and down the far slope. Descent was almost as difficult as the climb had been. It was just as slippery, but no monsters harassed them. In the bloody place just behind them, over the crest, they could hear stomach-churning noises—unknown beasts feeding on their own and on the dead horses. The sound drove them through the cold and their fear.

The gray sky was darkening, a creeping black pall spreading overhead. As this happened, an eerie new phenomenon of the Death God's realm was seen. The terrible snow possessed an inner light. A blue iridescence shone all about them, only partially blurred behind the veil of the glamour. Some of it got through Tyrus' magic and the coldly beautiful blue flakes clung to their garments and the horses, twinkling like numberless little stars.

As Tyrus' probings had found, there was a valley between the ridges. It offered scant shelter from the wind, but it was enough. None of them could go any farther for a space. They slogged to a stop, dull-eyed and almost too tired to shiver.

The wounded soldier had died during the descent. Solemnly, the other bodyguards wrapped him in his mantle and scooped out a shallow place in the ice, covering him and heaping stones over the corpse to bar scavengers.

There were tasks to perform for the living, as well. Though none of them had fully realized it until now, the remaining kindling had been lost with the pack horses, back on the ridge. They still had food for humans and beasts, but these northerners knew, too well, that without fuel, life would end quickly in these regions, limbs numbing and blood thickening into ice. With some desperation, they spoke of burning their extra clothes. That course, too, would lead to death, eventually.

Tyrus said, "Henceforth, I shall keep your fire. Give me a moment." He worked his ragged gloves together briskly, chasing chill and conjuring. He sensed ancient wood, under their feet, a substance some long-dead wizard must have touched once, leaving his scent of magic upon it. Under Tyrus' instructions, the questers dug loose the chunks, wood that had become stone. It was strange fuel, but it served as Tyrus focussed part of his will upon it, using an art Vraduir had perfected. At first there was only a glow. Then the stone-wood sparked and fed itself, producing an alien and smokeless heat, pulsating and wavering much as true fire might. The nature of this enabled Tyrus to maintain the glamour about them far more tightly than he could if he must allow for an ordinary fire with its stinging smoke and fumes.

They gobbled half-frozen grain cakes and leathery dried motge meat, all that was left of their stores. The horses ate their rations of meal and whinnied for more. Uncertain of the future, their masters kept the brutes on short supply. Water was running low, and the Couredh-yan warned Tyrus and Erejzan not to eat snow. They filled waterskins with the eerie flakes and laid the bottles beside the fire to melt the snow into drinking water. Outside the glamour, beyond Tyrus' power to control, the howling went on unendingly. They could not see the Death God's creatures, but the sound was a burden as terrible as the cold. Exhausted, the men slept poorly, jolted awake again and again by the bloodcurdling yowls in the darkness. Some men seemed half-crazed with futile anger. Jathelle sat stiffly, her eyes closed, as if she were trying to blot out the noise.

Within the glamour, there was warmth and life, but it had no power to keep out the sound of the Death God's creatures, beasts immune to such sorcery.

Erejzan squatted beside Tyrus and whispered, "Vraduir would laugh at our woe if he saw us thus. We cannot sleep while that clamor goes on. And you must marshal your skills and hoard your strength."

"I think I can keep them at bay," Tyrus said absently, distracted by the many demands on his magic.

"How long? There is no need." Erejzan flexed his hands and Tyrus began to sense what his friend intended to do. "I have a way to deal with them, and Vraduir will not know it is an invader, merely another beast."

"You should not . . ." Tyrus protested.

"Are they all true beasts?" Erejzan asked, his mind set and refusing to hear arguments.

"There is a monitor, at the end of the valley, an illusion left there when Vraduir came this way earlier," Tyrus said uneasily.

"Then you keep watch on that one. I will take care of the others."

"No!" Tyrus cried softly. "You do not even know how many there are."

Erejzan grinned slyly. "You underestimate me. There are four." He stared into the blackness beyond the glamour, scratching his ice-fringed red beard. Then he shrugged out of his cloak. He was eyeing Jathelle sidelong as he said, "I need only kill two, and the others will feed on them and be content. You . . . will make sure LaRenya does not . . ."

Nodding, Tyrus still pleaded against the scheme. "It is too cold. Do not go."

"Open the glamour for me." Without heeding Tyrus' last warning, Erejzan scuttled into the dark.

Picking up the discarded cloak, Tyrus held it tightly. Erejzan's body heat and the smell of his sweat permeated the rough wool, aiding Tyrus' sorcery. He felt Erejzan pressing lightly against the boundary of the glamour; with a little sigh Tyrus separated its fabric a crack to let the shape-changer through.

His will went with Erejzan, following his friend. Tyrus did not delve deeply into Erejzan's mind. Nevertheless, he was one with him, enduring as he had in their shared cell on the outer island. His own body tensed with shock as Erejzan took on another form, one far more powerful than any ordinary man. The acrobat had no knife or sword, but he was weaponed with deadly fangs and claws, his clothes replaced by thick fur. He had become a man-ecar, a killer animal dangerously endowed with human cunning.

Peculiar sensations twisted at Tyrus. He was Erejzan, running on all fours, now slowing, stalking. He could see incredibly well, helped by the strange, glowing snow. Ahead of him was a tusked abomination. The thing twisted to fend off attack . . .

Too late! Tyrus, with Erejzan, was leaping, pouncing! Teeth and claws rent scales and alien skin. Bones cracked between his jaws, and he was tasting . . .

Tyrus recoiled back into himself with a rush, shoving his knuckles against his mouth to keep down his vomit. Out in the snowy darkness, one source of the keening bubbled away in a death agony. For an instant, the other cries stopped also. Then, smelling blood or ichor, the other three creatures began yelping eagerly.

Bracing himself, Tyrus awaited another bestial collision beyond the fire. It came swiftly. This time, the terrible howls did not resume. Instead, after a while, there came awful muted slavering noises as predator ate predator. Fearful, Tyrus reached out with his mind and was greatly relieved to touch Erejzan's being. The shape-changer was alive and reverting to man form again, his gruesome task done.

Forcing his weary limbs to move, Tyrus walked away from the magic fire. A length and a half into the blackness he stumbled across the rest of Erejzan's discarded clothes. He waited by them for his friend's return. He fumbled in the pack he always carried under his arm, finding a piece of laidil root. The root was frozen, like everything else, but Tyrus methodically cut off a piece with his dagger, busying his hands to keep his thoughts from lingering over the killings.

Even with the snow light, he could barely see Erejzan approaching. But he felt the soft pressure on the glamour and opened it again until Erejzan was safely inside. He stood between Erejzan and the light, hiding him as the acrobat hastily donned his clothes. Erejzan laved his sticky hands and face in snow, scrubbing furiously until his skin glowed like flames. He brushed aside the proffered root irritably, saying the change had been his own wish and he had no need of such a remedy. Together they went back to the camp of arcane fire and Erejzan sat down heavily, shuddering.

The others seemed too tired to have noticed they had been gone. Glad to be freed of the noises from the darkness, men sank down into exhausted sleep. No one was wakeful enough to volunteer as sentry, and they all seemed to trust Tyrus' glamour, yielding completely to his protection. Though Erejzan had claimed he needed no laidil root and was unaffected by his venture outside the glamour, he succumbed quickly to weariness, asleep as soon as he laid his head against a saddle. Tyrus draped his friend in the cloak Erejzan had cast aside and sat back to spellcast more, ever alert for any sign that Vraduir had detected them.

He rubbed his chest, feeling the vision-glass in the silken wrapping close to his heart. The glass was pulsing, a counter rhythm to his heartbeat. There was no mistaking the sensation. It was very real, no longer the barely tangible fluttering Tyrus had followed so long these past seasons from far southern islands that had no such seasons as Couredh. Closer, closer—now close enough that his heart and Vraduir's throbbed back and forth, a subtle, tugging force and counter force of wizardry.

Tyrus followed the shimmering line of the glamour above his head, its sheen hazing the starless sky. Vraduir's picture was there, gleaned out of Tyrus' mind's eye—Vraduir, in his citadel, in the Death God's citadel. A citadel built with blood. Whose? The peasants'? That of Captain Drie and his crew? The harper's? Or . . . Ilissa's?

Tyrus wakened from that grim speculation. Jathelle was seated beside him, watching him narrowly. He cleared his throat, ill at ease and forcing a shaky smile. "Were you weaving the glamour again?" Jathelle asked. "That is what Erejzan calls it."

"Ai. It is . . . a sorkra term."

"Erejzan knows a great deal about your arts. You said you were prisoners together, bound by Vraduir's evil magic. Is that when Erejzan learned these things?" Jathelle wondered, once more amazing Tyrus by her swift grasp of things.

She had unbound her braids and her hair flowed from her hood and over her breasts. Cold brought bright color to her cheeks and lips. Tyrus caressed her with his eyes, his fatigue eased.

"Can you not trust me?" Jathelle said suddenly. "I have trusted you. What would have happened had I not accepted your tale there on Drita Meadows?"

"There would have been a clash," Tyrus said numbly, "a struggle between your men and me and Erejzan, with Rof's brigands reaping the spoils."

"You would not have used your sorkra powers to defeat us all?"

He looked away, uncomfortable, not liking to consider the question. "I have never worked hurtful power against the innocent. And casting an illusion over so many intent on my blood and Erejzan's . . . it would have been difficult."

"It did not come to that," Jathelle said, reminding him, "because I believed you." She hesitated, then added very softly, "Sirin Tyrus."

He accepted the title, admitting he was a prince. Delicately Tyrus encased himself and Jathelle in a glamour within the larger glamour, a shield that locked them away from other eyes and ears. They two were alone in the frozen valley, surrounded by slumbering men.

"Vraduir is your kinsman," Jathelle guessed. In her eyes there was more, the painful truth.

"My sire," Tyrus said, words spilling from him, long pent-up anguish only Erejzan had shared with him till now. "He taught me how to use my sorkra gifts. I wanted to emulate him, and two years ago I had matched his every art. That was when . . . when he turned to ways no wizard must tread. What has happened, my island, the deaths, the stolen treasures . . . my fault. If I had not become his rival . . ."

"The evil in his heart is Vraduir's own," Jathelle said gently. "He must answer to the gods for his own guilt. You are not to blame. You would not let me blame myself for Ilissa's capture or Dorche's death. I will not let you punish yourself for your father's wickedness and blasphemy."

Tyrus swallowed hard, clenching his fists. "Only I can stop him. Only I have the skills. And if I fail . . ."

"You will not. You have strong allies," she said, smiling encouragement. "We will get you to him and help you best him. You must not assume all the burden. Let your friends take some." Jathelle paused, glancing toward the sleeping acrobat. Tentatively, she said, "Why . . . why did Erejzan leave the campfire a while ago?"

Cornered, sighing, Tyrus said, "I cannot tell you. If he wishes to, he will."

"I think I already know. I hope he, too, will learn to trust me. Why does he hide this? Rof teases him, and I am no fool. I can guess. If Rof owns Erejzan's secret, why not me? Am I so much less than a brigand?"

Tyrus was bemused. Then he read the compassion in her face. "Not less. More. Far more. It is because he honors you, and he adores your sister. He is shamed by this thing. That is why he hides it from you."

"A curse Vraduir put upon him," Jathelle said, nodding soberly. "I have suspected that. But he misjudges me and Ilissa. Neither of us would scorn him for being the victim of Vraduir's cruelty. We are the sisters of Fer-Sro. It is not in our blood to be so unkind and unfeeling." Jathelle smiled fondly at the sleeping man. "This . . . this thing that hurts him—it cannot be countered by your magic?"

Tyrus hung his head. "No. I strove to break the evil enchantment many times, while we were pent in our prison, and since then. Vraduir had that power from Bogotana, and I am helpless to remove the curse. It is a wound that may never be healed. Erejzan lives to repay it and to rescue Ilissa. Since he met her, his

existence has taken on new purpose. He still wants
his vengeance. But now he yearns to help Ilissa, to be
her devoted warrior. You need never doubt his loyalty
and courage in this, Jathelle. He will go on despite all
dangers."

"I have sensed that often," Jathelle said. "It is
strange. He met her but three times, yet he has seemed
to worship her from the first, and he risked his life,
jumping onto that skeleton warrior's horse. Like a man
bereft of all concern for his own fate . . ."

"He is smitten," Tyrus explained, deeming this no
breech of his friendship with Erejzan. Then he understood the words told his own state as well. He could
not resist Jathelle's beauty and intelligence and will.
They, too, were one.

Jathelle leaned toward him, responding. Her voice
had led Tyrus out of the Ice Forest. Now her touch
was a fire that gave no hurt, racing through his veins,
the spell sweetly woven about them both. Her mouth
was under his and Tyrus yielded to that answering fire
within his soul, embracing her. Neither had been conscious of willing this, yet it had happened. Just as suddenly, they drew back, startled by the intensity of these
emotions.

Tyrus realized the glamour had weakened alarmingly
as he had given himself over to human desires. Quickly,
he reframed the veil and tested for any sign of Vraduir's attack. When he found they were safe and still
hidden from Vraduir's clear knowledge, he sagged in
relief.

Jathelle was stricken and apologetic. "I am sorry.
I . . . I did not mean to imperil us."

"No harm was done." Tyrus reached out, wanting
to kiss her again. But he held his urgings in check,
chastened and frustrated.

"It . . . we dare not," Jathelle said wistfully.

His voice was husky. "No. If it were lesser magic, I could separate my mind and heart. Against Vraduir, with what is at risk . . . no."

Jathelle nodded and bit her lip. "I understand. Not yet. We can have no peace, no . . . weakness. Not until the enemy is defeated and Ilissa is rescued."

As she said this, Erejzan stirred and murmured, dreamily repeating Ilissa's name. There was deep longing in the sleep-slurred word, a longing Tyrus and Jathelle knew too well. The acrobat had flung aside the cloak in his fretfulness, and Jathelle moved toward him. Tyrus conjured away the inner glamour, restoring himself and Jathelle to the larger circle of travelers. Jathelle knelt by Erejzan and carefully drew the cloak up over the acrobat once more, giving her sister's sworn rescuer the comfort she could not yet give to Ilissa. She looked again at Tyrus, a speaking gaze that told him what was in her mind and heart. Understanding, accepting, she lay down close by Erejzan, wrapped herself in her fur cloak, and soon was asleep, secure in Tyrus' guardianship.

Tyrus forced his eyes away from her sleeping form. He must not allow himself even that small human pleasure. He gazed up into the night but did not see the black clouds. He was walking the webs, finding reserves he had not tried to reach ere now. Now the limits must be explored to the last. Tomorrow would decide all—his life, and the lives of those he loved.

Jathelle . . . no! No temptation. No weakness. She and Erejzan were his limbs in this quest. Tyrus must be the brain, locked away from everything but sorkra arts. He had learned his lesson. The others could sleep. He could not. Tyrus became sorkra, concentrating, delving.

Tomorrow, after so long a search, he would meet Vraduir again. And he would meet Vraduir's new ally,

that god mortals feared most of all. Tomorrow Tyrus
of Qamat, wizard-prince, must conquer. There could
be no alternative. Vraduir was reaching too high, had
slain too many, and he must die, or Tyrus must die in
the attempt.

XIII

The Shattered Glass

❈-❈-❈-❈-❈-❈-❈-❈-❈-❈-❈-❈-❈-❈-❈-❈-❈-❈-❈-❈

FOR ALL THE VOWS THEY HAD MADE JUST BEYOND THE
Ice Forest, the men were slothful in the morning. No
one wanted to leave the warmth of the magic fire. Snow
had melted into puddles around their sleeping places
and under the horses' hooves, rendering the space
beneath the glamour into a dank quagmire. Yet they
stirred slowly, groaning and thumping stiff backs. Jathelle cursed them for laggards and did more than her
share of breaking camp and saddling the horses. Now
and then she cast Tyrus a knowing smile, seeming in-
spired by the things they had said in secret last night.

The brigands and soldiers noticed, at last, the ravaged carcasses of the Death God's beasts. They wondered on this and asked one another what had killed
the creatures. Tyrus and Jathelle shrugged noncommit-
tally, Erejzan refused to look at the frozen remains.
There was no stench, for what the alien predators had
left was now ice-hard, like the land around them. Yet
the travelers hurried to leave the scene behind, riding
wide of those places where the slaughters had occurred.

Then, to their puzzlement, Tyrus led them straight
toward a heap of frosted stones where another, living

creature awaited. A few mumbled protests but they were too wary to defy the sorkra openly. Slowly, they rode toward an immense dragon-thing. As they drew near, Tyrus gestured, smiling maliciously. At once, the dragon-thing began to melt—no, to shimmer and change. And when the air cleared, they saw it had not been a terrible beast at all but an illusion conjured from the rocks.

"I . . . I thought it was one of those monsters," Sirai Miquit said, marveling at this.

"No, it was a sentinel, posted here by our enemy," Tyrus explained. "I masked us from it last night, and now I have countercharmed and overcome Vraduir's magic. It told him nothing. Nor will it ever affright us again."

The men cheered his power and made missiles of the snow, pelting the now-frozen dragon like rowdy youths. "Hai! Niyah! Our wizard is greater than your wizard, Foul-Face!" they taunted. "Sit there and bite the wind!" Much heartened by the little victory, they rode on with less complaining.

There was no true day, merely a lightening of the gray overcast from black to a deep, gloomy sky cover. The air was colder still than it had been, as they penetrated farther and farther into the Death God's realm. More deadly creatures lay in ambush along the next ridge. But the way to the top was not so precipitous as in earlier ascents. No one fell, and the horses plodded steadily up to the crest without mishap. Though less perilous, the climb was very wearying. Tyrus longed to hurry them, but he did not, understanding. He bested more of Vraduir's monitors, hid them from more of the Death God's incredible creatures. The spells came easily, negligently cast, casual displays while the greater part of his will bent beyond the ridges to the enemy, now so close ahead. There was no longer any reason to stint with his arts, and he did not. All was gathered, all the power he could claim. It would serve, or the day yet to dawn would not matter.

Remembering the losses of the day before, the travelers were cautious. In steep areas and where they suspected monsters lurked, they blindfolded the horses and led them if necessary. The brutes could smell danger, but could not see it and were forced up the trail, kept within Tyrus' glamour.

Only Tyrus knew that yet another, far more deadly threat loomed. It did not hide in rocks or wait to pounce on horses or riders. But it was always there, frowning over the disappearance of its posted sentinels, mystified at who these journeyers were and why it could not strike through and kill them.

Vraduir prodded at Tyrus' veil again and again, increasingly angered and confused. Tyrus smiled thinly, countering each sorcerous blow with his own potent magic. Vraduir's hostile touch was a pair of invisible hands grown gigantic, constantly exploring the outer surface of the glamour, sensing life inside yet unable to reach it. Tyrus almost laughed at Vraduir's bafflement. But he did not grow cocky. He felt Vraduir turning more and more of his attention away from other matters—the feint by the army, his dealings with evil sorcery and gods—bearing it upon Tyrus and those he protected.

"Once you took me unawares, a lifetime ago in Qamat," Tyrus murmured. "That will not happen again. Not ever. I had an excellent mentor and I have learned much more since you cast me out to die."

"What did you say, sorkra?" Rof asked. His tone was friendly, that of one conspirator to another.

"Things of magic." At Tyrus' reply, Rof's grin vanished. He could be a merry enough companion, if unpredictable, so long as he was not reminded of Tyrus' wizardry. Any touch of those arts, though, dashed his enthusiasm and made him cautious.

Tyrus wondered what Rof would think if he knew another matter besides sorcery was now strongly involved. Behind Vraduir's probing, there was that terrible force he had first noticed when they landed from *Wave-Walker*. He and Erejzan had not known its source or meaning then. The vision-glass had shown them Vraduir, and Vraduir's awful ally. Nidil's presence was everywhere here, a blanket that covered the land like the perpetual clouds and snow—gray, omnipotent, immortal.

As they climbed to the final crest, a fresh wave of alien beasts and illusions came upon them. Perhaps this was to be the last and most dangerous barrier of all. Tyrus, however, drew upon a new confidence, banishing illusions, keeping the true beasts at bay. Erejzan's help last night had allowed him to nurse his power, storing it, and now he began to feel those nearly limitless resources he had saved for this confrontation. It would be now, soon, the quest at its end.

Tyrus bent his energies to holding back the bitter weather, easing their passage across the slope. It was still very difficult for the horses. They stopped in a sheltered area just beneath the top of the ridge, transferring and consolidating more packs, discarding much. Three more horses had to be put out of their suffering. The brigands, as usual, began whining as soon as they found breath. Rof had shrugged and accepted the trials better than his men. But he must be their spokesman and echo their complaints if he remained their leader. He shook his head over the carnage and their reduced horseflesh, for now there were no spares at all and some men rode double. "I am not sure any ransom is worth this trouble," he growled.

Jathelle answered him with a glare. "No more! I warned you at the Ice Forest. No reward unless the bargain is done and Ilissa saved."

Irritated, Rof sought another target, lighting on Erejzan. "Do you want the dead horses, acrobat? No way to make a fire and sear the meat, but that should not bother *you*."

Tyrus had been helping shift packs, most of his mind aimed toward any possible attack from Vraduir. Distracted, he heard Rof's taunt but did not respond immediately. Belatedly, he sensed Erejzan's rage, turning in time to see his friend leaping through the air and bowling Rof over into the ice and snow.

The sudden attack caught Rof off guard. He and Erejzan tumbled wildly about. Though Erejzan struck with fury, he had controlled his shape-changing, only his hands and face revealing that duskiness and a blur of encroaching animal fur. Rallying, Rof groped for a knife, trying to beat Erejzan's hands away from his throat as they kicked and punched one another.

Exasperated by this quarrel, Tyrus waded into the fray. He dragged Erejzan off the bandit lord, pinning the shorter man's arms. Some of Rof's men were eager to abet him, but Tyrus gestured with a free hand warningly and Rof held his men back, chastened by the threat of sorcery. Erejzan was still struggling and Tyrus thrust him back against a wall of snowbank. "Stop it! You help Vraduir by this!" he roared at the acrobat.

Erejzan squirmed, unwilling to give up the fight. "He has been too sly too long, ever hinting at . . ."

"Words! Wind! Vraduir is the enemy! Forget Rof's words. He is baiting you, and you strike at it like a lured fish!" Rof was bending down to pick up the knife he had dropped, and Tyrus paused to point at him and say ominously, "Remember, we are allies."

With elaborate motions, Rof flourished the wicked blade and returned it to its sheath in his belt. His smile was wolfish. "Of course, sorkra. Rein your magic. I meant no harm. The fihar is too touchy, that is all."

Other men clustered around them, asking what was going on and why. Tyrus pretended they were not there, concentrating on Rof. He narrowed his eyes and said, "Allies, do you hear me? If we survive, it must be as one. Dissension serves our common enemy. Remember, too, whoever slanders my friend is my prey."

Hastily Rof said, "No offense. I only meant . . ."

Erejzan shoved again Tyrus' restraining arm in a new surge of anger, and Tyrus growled, "We know what you meant. Say no more, if you value your skin."

Jathelle was watching all this silently, occasionally meeting Tyrus' eyes, her understanding and sympathy plain. The storm had begun to subside when Aubage demanded, "What is all this about?"

Tyrus glowered at Erejzan, ignoring the courtier. "He will hold his tongue. And you will hold your wrath. Agreed?" With ill grace, the acrobat nodded. Tyrus let him go and steered him away from Rof.

"I said, what is this all about?" Aubage insisted. "If we are all allies, I have a right to know . . ."

Erejzan whirled, his fists clenched. "Shall I show you what it is all about, Sirai?"

Tyrus sighed and stepped between Erejzan and the other man. "This is a private concern, Sirai Aubage. Whatever he and Rof quarreled about, it is done. Let it rest. All of you. We should move on." He prodded Erejzan, and his friend obeyed like the others, though grumpily.

As the men tightened cinches and soothed the weary and frightened mounts, Jathelle came to Tyrus and said softly, "Why did you not stop them with magic?"

"There was no need. I should not have chastened Aubage earlier. He may be a fool, but that is no excuse to manipulate him with my arts."

"Once more you prove you are not like him." He realized she had been comparing him to Vraduir again. "I do not think *he* would have cared if his friend's secret was revealed to others, or if that man died because of Rof's taunting."

"Vraduir has no friends," Tyrus said tonelessly. "He shed friends and kindred in a search for power. In some fashion, he killed all love he could give or receive."

"You gave him love once," Jathelle guessed. "That love, too, he rejected. But is your own completely shattered?"

The query made Tyrus acutely uncomfortable. "We . . . we must hurry. Day and night have no meaning in the Death God's realm, but time does, and time is on Vraduir's path."

To their surprise, the slope beyond the ridge's crest was not at all steep. Nor were there any more hills past those two dreadful ones they had crossed. Even the wind and snow abated and mist or fog replaced those elements. The fog was oddly beautiful, ice vapor, drifting in thick patches here and there, sending back ringing echoes of hoofbeats and voices. The character of the cold had altered, becoming very dry and still. It should have given them relief, but this quiet, frigid fog and the unmoving air disturbed the travelers far more than bitter wind and snow had.

The fog blocked their clear view and they judged the rate of their descent by their positions in the saddles. They sensed they were coming down gradually upon level ground. Tyrus gestured, using his sorkra arts as a knife to cut away the fog in front of them, clearing a road through the darkness of afternoon. They came to a halt, staring as the wizard's invisible blade trimmed back the ice mist. The fog hovered and swirled above them, though there was no wind. Beneath that ghostly canopy, they saw a frozen plain stretching before them and as far to the east and west as land and sea could run.

"Hetanya protect us!" Jathelle cried, her words amplified and returned to them, echoing many times.

The field of ice was studded with embedded bones

and ruins of man's works. Ages-old ships and carts and chariots lay broken. Warhorses' trappings and peasants' wagons lay tangled together. Stricken, the journeyers gazed out upon that dreadful icy arena of the end of human hopes and possessions.

A half measure distant, an immense structure crouched above the bones and relics, dominating the plain. Beyond this bastion, there was nothing at all but endless ice, at one with the eternal black of the northern sky. Fog walked the lofty battlements and towers. Larger than many cities, the citadel was a fortress at the end of the world, awesome as that presence in Tyrus' vision-glass.

Transparent shapes floated out of the fog toward the travelers. Some of these sad-faced specters were gray-fleshed. Others were but gape-jawed skulls and bones clad in rotting garments. The horses snorted and rolled their eyes as these apparitions approached, and the humans fought their own terror at the sight.

"They are . . . the dead," Rof exclaimed. The frosty air gave back to them, ". . . dead . . . dead . . . dead . . ."

The foremost of the specters said in a quavering voice, "We are the dead. Look for us no more among the places of the living, for we serve a different master here."

The ghastly forms that were once men and women hovered and spoke morosely. "We were king and harlot, peasant and seaman, thief and warlord, priestess and pirate. Now we belong to Nidil, He Who Steals All Breath."

Erejzan started, gripping Tyrus' arm and pointing to a group of the specters—men whose clothes were less tattered with age than some of the others. Their flesh had not yet decayed. The ritual scarrings on their brows marked them as seamen. The faces were distorted into death masks. But Tyrus and Erejzan recognized them very well.

"Captain Drie," Erejzan whispered. "My . . . my kinsman . . ."

Long had the friends wished for vengeance on these traitors who had fled Qamat, carrying Vraduir from the destruction he so richly deserved. On Vraduir's commands, they had plundered and stolen as pirates, their ship armed with Vraduir's enchantments as they prowled Clarique's seas and islands. The ship, though, had been abandoned near the village by the lake. And it was plain Captain Drie and his greedy crew had been abandoned by their master as well.

Tyrus and Erejzan gazed with pity on the sailors, thoughts of vengeance fading. The people of Qamat had died horribly, but they had gone to Keth's portals, to the gods of Clarique. Captain Drie and his men, however, were here—specters, trapped, dead yet not dead, roaming this frozen plain with countless other corpses, the damned of every province.

"My people," Jathelle said suddenly, pointing to the peasants among the hordes of ghosts. "My poor people!"

Deeply troubled, Tyrus shook his head. "The traitors and cursed are here through their own evil lives. The peasants are slaves. Even in death, they are Vraduir's slaves and cannot find rest."

Jathelle moaned, arms clasped about herself, suffering with the helpless country folk. Several held out their arms in the direction of the travelers and pleaded, "Dwelter-man, go ye back. 'Tis the Death God's realm. We are lost. Save ye if ye can, dwelter-man. Go back!"

"They do not see us," Tyrus guessed. "The glamour holds fast. They are Vraduir's eyes and tongue. They can see and say no more than he wills."

"My poor people," Jathelle said again, with tender

compassion, and she would have gone to the pathetic
ghosts.

Tyrus caught her in his arms, shaking her back to
sanity, as the specters continued their warning. They
spoke no specific names. The dialect was that they had
known in life, but the warning was Vraduir's, a usage
of ghostly puppets to scare away intruders. The travesty angered Tyrus. He tried to shut out the insistent
cries of "Dwelter-man," that term Couredh's peasant
folk applied to people from the city.

"I am your queen," Jathelle said hopefully. There
was no reaction. The wailing went on, unabated, and
she hung her head, admitting what Tyrus told her.
"They are lost, no longer my subjects but his."

"Dwelter-man, is there among ye the stranger who
defies our master?" That accusation gave Tyrus pause.
He felt Vraduir's attempts to pierce the glamour. Magic
and words, interwoven—all of it a form of attack. The
spokesman for the peasant ghosts turned languidly,
swiveling in the ice-fog, pointing toward the citadel.
"Go no farther, strange sorkra. Go back. 'Tis the Death
God's citadel. Our master builds it for the god. Aen
we has mortared it with our blood and bone. 'Tis not
done. Never will be done. Turn back, or *your* blood—
and your magic—will chink the wallstones, too."

Tyrus did turn, but toward Jathelle and her men and
the brigands, ignoring the ghosts. "There is some truth
in this. Stay here. I will weave you fast in a protective
veil. Erejzan and I will go to the citadel alone. It is us
Vraduir will follow, he and the ghosts."

"No." Jathelle had recovered from her shock. She
met Tyrus headlong with that fiery spirit which both
delighted and worried him. "Ilissa is in that citadel.
Do not seek to leave me behind."

"Nor me," Aubage said, startling Tyrus by his solemn
sincerity. Tyrus recalled the nobleman's boast that he
was a ruler, had he been so born. Now, for a rare mo-

ment, Aubage honored his house. "No one will deny you your revenge, sorkra. But LaRenya and I seek our own revenge. Ilissa awaits her kindred and her betrothed, and she shall not wait in vain. We will go to her and bring her to the light again. It is our right. And it is the way of Couredh and the Rasil-yan and the border tribes."

Jathelle favored Aubage with an approving smile. "We have chosen. We accept the risks. Let us go." Tyrus locked stares with her for several heartbeats, then conceded defeat. "Thank you," Jathelle said, and Aubage gaped at her in astonishment, his regal manner of an instant earlier wiped away. He paled as Jathelle explained, "I know you could have enchanted us against our will and bound us to stay here. You have courtesy as well as magic."

"More courtesy than cunning, at times," Erejzan muttered. The remark earned him a wry grin from Tyrus.

"Patience, mai fiyel. You underestimate me, too," Tyrus said. Then he went on briskly, "We must leave the horses. From this point on, they are likely to panic and be a hindrance. We can waste no effort fighting them. There will be much else to contend with."

Rof and his men were whispering, shifting about, the whites of their eyes showing as they surveyed the parade of ghosts. The soldiers had taken keen note of this. "They will steal the horses, LaRenya," Lieutenant Utaigh said unhappily, indicating the bandits. But he and his bodyguards obeyed Jathelle, using a broken wagon frozen fast in the ice as a hitching place for their horses and those of Jathelle and the others.

Tyrus sidled past bobbing spectral forms, leading the way. Jathelle said loudly, making certain Rof's men could hear, "If they have no part in Ilissa's rescue, they will get nothing."

The threat was effective. The thieves jostled one another comically in their eagerness to tie their own horses and run after Tyrus. Part of their motive was greed, but a greater reason was fear of being left alone in this land of death. Bumping together, sometimes walking on one another's heels, united in dread of the unknown, the ragged band of travelers headed across the icy plain.

The specters continued to wail at them. In the distance, ice cracked and boomed, a deep, alarming sound that sent shudders through the surface under the travelers' feet. The same surface squeaked with every step, a sound of terrible cold, sometimes mixed with suggestions of ancient bones breaking as they trod over them.

The ghosts clustered along their path, drifting through the eerie ice-fog, shrieking warnings. Occasionally, driven by the nerve-grating repetition of these voices, the men struck at the shades. Blade, club, or axe had no effect. Yet neither could the specters harm the living, it seemed. The bloodcurdling cries chilled the invaders, but the ghosts' touch was without substance. They began to move with more assurance. Unlike the Death God's pets, these ghosts could not rend flesh nor drink blood.

They passed ruined ships, chariots, and wagons beyond numbering. Like the regalia of the skeleton warriors, these relics bore many a mark of empires and kingdoms long vanished, and of fabled betrayers and villains of all history. Some leavings were nameless, and there was no way to know what sin their owners had done, what thing had so offended the gods that Nidil trapped both the dead and their property here, forever, on the endless plain.

Tyrus stretched forth his will toward the citadel, toward Vraduir. How desperate Vraduir was! The blows on the veil were tremendous with every step Tyrus took, each step taking him closer to Vraduir's sanctuary. The quarry—run to earth at last!

"Try again," Tyrus taunted him softly. "Surely there is a place you can fathom my sorcery."

Jathelle heard him, exulting for his sake. "You are his master."

"I *must* be. And I was well taught." Triumph mingled with Tyrus' long-nursed bitterness.

Then pockets of the fog separated and reshaped. The whining ghosts that had followed them like dogs begging scraps had been left behind. Now new specters appeared from the mist. They were not familiar. These were not skeleton warriors or traitors or any of Jathelle's peasants. Tyrus sensed Vraduir's hand strong upon the materializations, though, and braced himself for some trickery.

"Gold . . ." they chanted. "Much gold and silver and gems! More than anyone can count. Priceless treasure! Yours! Yours!" The sepulchral voices lured them. The hands of brittle bones and rotten flesh cradled riches, dripping these across the ice, a trail to seduce mortals. The frozen plain soon glittered with strewn jewels and bright metal. "Gold! Silver . . . !"

Rof, One-Ear, Slit-Nose, and the other brigands tripped over one another in their eagerness to collect the treasure. They stuffed coins and gems into their tunics and boot tops, squabbling over the biggest jewels and gems, only to forget those for fresh ones falling from the ghosts' hands.

"Who here is the better wizard?" the ghosts challenged, their hands overflowing with brightness. They could not come inside the glamour, but many of the thieves were reaching *outside,* tempted unbearably by the array spread before them. "Our master can make you rich. Rich! Serve him. Give over to him this strange sorkra—and our master will make you richer than any lord or sovereign has ever been."

Aubage, Miquit, and the bodyguards tried to pull the brigands back inside the veil. Rof and his thieves beat them away. "You only promise reward, LaRenya," Rof shouted. "Here is reward, and already in our hands! No need to enter that citadel. The treasure is here!"

"It is only an illusion," Tyrus roared at them. He risked weakening the glamour a moment, gesturing, turning the gold to dust as Rof held it.

"*Your* illusion, sorkra! You try to fool us!" Rof flung down the dust and stooped to grab more gold from the frozen plain. "They say true! Who is the better wizard? The one who pays us, like this!" And Rof raised a gleaming fistful of wealth, waving the ransom of a lord.

The hoard rained forth, inexhaustible, poured out by the specters. "More treasure! All you desire! Serve our master! Deliver to him the enemy sorkra and those with him, and we give you all you wish."

Tyrus gestured and countercharmed frantically, but as fast as he whisked the illusionary treasure away, Vraduir conjured still more. Tyrus could not get ahead of him and maintain the glamour to protect Jathelle and the others.

"Ai! We are your men, master wizard!" Rof whirled, his sword unsheathed. His predatory grin blossomed. "No ill will, sorkra. But he pays too well!"

Hastily, the courtiers and soldiers drew back as a bristling wall of weapons confronted them. Tyrus shifted, reshaping the glamour, excluding the bandits as quickly as he could. They had been too long within that same magic and followed it, eager to win their new lord's good will—and more of the gleaming reward his specters dangled!

"Guard LaRenya!" Aubage was ordering, though Jathelle's sword was out and she was quite able to guard herself. "Your magic, sorkra. Foil those specters!"

Tyrus did not reply, feeling a powerful surge of opposing wizardry. Even as Vraduir wove the temptation for Rof's men, he continued to batter at Tyrus and the glamour. Power—vast power! Was Vraduir drawing on Nidil's own divine strength? Tyrus prayed it was not so, or all was lost!

The leader of the specters pursued the glamour, showing the bandits where to attack, while Vraduir pounded again and again at Tyrus' will. It was as bad as the assault of the stone trees in the Ice Forest, and Rof's men had become the Skull Breakers, seeking their former allies' blood!

"Kill the enemies," the specters exhorted the throat-slitters. "Please your new master! Kill them!"

Tyrus reached through the veil, appealing directly to Rof's intelligence. "False treasure!" he warned, thrusting this into Rof's mind. The bandit lord's will was strong. It would take more magic than Tyrus could spare to enchant him and all his murderous band.

"It is real when you bite it, sorkra, and it *is* my calling," Rof answered, maddeningly cheerful. Then his expression turned hard and he yelled to his men, "At them, you bejits. Now."

"Rasven, to me, upon the webs, water in a circle, drawing into itself and gone . . ." Tyrus murmured. He stumbled back. "Bind them, hold them . . ."

There was another veil now, between him and the bandits, shutting off his efforts to touch them, as unpredictable as the magic net Tyrus had thrown about himself and those he guarded. He and Jathelle and the others saw the brigands through a milky fog, the glamours warring and clashing violently. Blades sang in the icy air.

Step by step, Tyrus retreated, countering but unable to defeat the enemy's magic. They were equal.

"The citadel," the specters commanded. "Drive them into the citadel! Our master will help you!"

Rocks, discarded spears, pieces of ancient war equipage—these became weapons, hurled back and forth between the desperate factions.

"The citadel! The citadel! Your reward awaits you —there!"

"But we *want* to go into the citadel!" Aubage exclaimed above the tumult of weapons and voices.

"Not on Vraduir's terms, you fop!" Erejzan answered him. He lunged toward the barrier of Tyrus' glamour, begging, "Let me through. I will draw them off!"

Tyrus restrained him. "No! Another way!" He spoke a most potent incantation, and the area about them was plunged into utter blackness for long moments, a curtain of magic descending. It was like a silent, dark ocean splashing outward, engulfing the brigands as well. Tyrus had endured invisible batterings as blades and cudgels—from within and without his glamour— had struck and met. Now he relaxed a trifle. Once the initial blackness eased, there was a tiny light, enough to show them the way.

"It is not so dark a night after all," Jathelle said, encouraged.

"Not if we are careful. Circle to the right. We will go to the citadel, but by a circuitous route, arriving where Rof and his men do not anticipate. Come," Tyrus said.

He was a human rope, greatly extended and tautly quivering, near the edge of danger. He hurried his companions along, fearing Vraduir would find new magic.

Even as he did, a brilliant light stabbed out of the darkness he had created. The thing had no source, no glow of tapers or torches. It sprang into being in mid-air, a wizard's light. It thrust at Tyrus' sorcery and swung to and fro, searching the frozen plain, sweeping above the brigands' heads like a great, malevolent demon's eye—Vraduir's eye!

"Rasven!" Tyrus breathed, less a prayer to that patron of sorkra than a curse at his sire's cleverness.

"How well he has bound his light with deep charms. I cannot break it." He stopped, maintaining the shroud of darkness as well as he could against this new assault. The light was strengthening. Time was drawing very short.

"Tyrus . . ." Jathelle dodged, crouching low as the light swung past her fair hair, missing discovering her by no more than the thickness of a dagger blade.

Tyrus continued to spellcast, cloaking them. Erejzan gripped his arm and panted desperately, "You *must* let me go!"

"Too late for that. The god. I cannot let him call on the god." Tyrus reached within his tunic, clutching the silken thread binding the vision-glass against his ribs, snapping it in his impatience. "Stay by me. Both of you. I need you."

Jathelle was bewildered, but she waited, looking apprehensively at the arcane device. Erejzan tugged at his beard, unaware he did so. He was like an ecar, coiled to spring aside out of a spear's deadly path. All around them, the soldiers and bodyguards crowded, wild-eyed and sweating despite the terrible cold. Each time the evil light swept toward them, they ducked behind heaps of ruined boat timbers and wagon rubble.

Out in the plain, Rof and his men were kicking their way through similar debris, searching with the light, heartening each other in their greed.

"Over there!"

"Omaytatle's snows! I already looked in that wagon! Try here!"

"We will find them!"

"How much will the wizard in the citadel pay for their heads?"

Tyrus filled his lungs, then exhaled slowly. He peered into the vision-glass, leaving a tiny fraction of his sorcery outside to keep the glamour tight. All the rest of his being burned through the vision-glass and sought its twin with fierce intent—its twin, and its master. Jathelle and Erejzan would have supported him, for he was trembling with exertion. Tyrus shrugged off their help violently. "Back! Give room!"

He was flowing into the black glass, a man become liquid, or smoke. He was one with the shining obsidian, its powers a part of him. The dark surface swirled, the depths opening, dividing . . .

And he was looking at Vraduir. Jathelle was there, and not there. It was the same with Erejzan. Tyrus was kneeling on the frozen plain, within the glamour he had built, hiding himself and his companions from the seeking light. Yet he also was within the Death God's citadel, confronting Vraduir at last.

No distance at all between them, as sorcery counted paces. The impact was stunning.

Vraduir leaned over a table spread with wizardly contrivances, the vision-glass among them. He bobbed and weaved, casting spells, directing the light upon the plain, speaking through those animated corpses, leading his quarry-takers, and luring Rof's brigands with promises of treasure.

Then . . . Vraduir blinked, drawing back, losing the thread of his magic. He stared disbelievingly into his vision-glass, taking it in his hands.

To Tyrus, those hands came toward his face, touching him. When he was a child, Vraduir had touched him so, gently, paternally fond. Now the touch was almost as delicate, but for far different reasons. Tyrus knew that in his father's vision-glass other layers and depths were separating and swirling, an image taking shape—*his* image.

He did not wait for the picture to be clear. He took his advantage. Tyrus could see Vraduir, but Vraduir had not quite completed the link in the opposite direction. "I am your long-sought enemy," Tyrus said quietly. Within the citadel his voice boomed, rattling between cold stone walls and shocking Vraduir with its intensity. "You cannot escape me. I am coming to repay you for what you have done."

Vraduir's handsome face split in a strange smile. "Who are you? You boasting fool! I will see you . . ."

"So you shall," Tyrus said, resisting the final contact a moment more, holding Vraduir at bay, enjoying the power. But there was fear in his action as well. He was committed. He could not step back—not now. This was the only hope of eluding the light and Vraduir's evil minions.

"You are either a dotard or a yapping puppy, to think you can challenge *me*," Vraduir ranted. He twisted his vision-glass savagely this way and that, striving to clear the muddled image. "How is it you speak to me thus?"

"My powers are as great as yours," Tyrus said, surprised by his calmness.

Vraduir laughed, a heavy, masculine guffaw Tyrus remembered well. It was his own laugh, whenever he was moved to amazement. Memories were knives in his vitals. Vraduir was crying, "No sorkra is my equal! I am supreme! I tamed the god of the depths . . ."

"You lie. Bogotana taught you none may master a god. Qamat died for your pride and vanity, Vraduir. And now you must render first payment for their agony."

Tyrus' hands tightened on the vision-glass till he threatened to cut his palms on the black edges. He opened a most inner part of his being and at last allowed Vraduir to penetrate the layers between them.

"T—Tyrus!" That came clear, in the lilting accent of Clarique's far southern islands. For a year, Tyrus had cloaked his name and Erejzan's in magic. Now Jathelle and the others thought they heard an altered form of those, frowning, not understanding. But the next words reached them all. "My . . . my son?" Vraduir asked in disbelief. Rarely had Tyrus heard Vraduir stammer so. About him, as from far away, he felt his companions reacting to this revelation of kinship. Their astonishment equaled Vraduir's, save for Jathelle and Erejzan, who were one with Tyrus in this knowledge.

For an instant, a precious instant, Vraduir was stunned past rational thought. Tyrus said, "I am your son, and I am not dead. Nor is Erejzan, the clan chief, your beastmaster you sought to kill. We are come to take our vengeance. You have hidden from us, and we from you. Now we are both exposed, and we both will be at the mercy of others, my father. We shall see who is the better served—you by your slaves, or I by those who accompany me out of hatred for you."

Vraduir was still amazed, unable to cope with this meeting with his fellow wizard—his son whom he had thought slain in Qamat's boiling catastrophe.

Tyrus did not hesitate. He threw his will upon the vision-glass and abandoned all his shields, focussing everything. His entire sorcery was put into this over-whelming burst, which ricocheted wildly between the two vision-glasses. Godlike forces had birthed these from the smoking mountain. The forces converted into other energies, ones beyond ordinary experience.

With a deafening roar, the vision-glasses shattered simultaneously. It was an explosion from Bogotana's depths and the web world of magic.

Tyrus saw and felt Vraduir's confusion melting, turn-ing into terror, his hands clawing at his face. The image of Vraduir was splitting into pieces, ever smaller and smaller—Vraduir dissolving, and screaming in pain.

Pain that was shared. Inevitable. Expected. Tyrus was braced for it, knowing it must come, the cost of such terrible wizardry. He was toppling, his arms flung up to cushion his brow.

Falling, falling, his eyes two seared pools, stricken by magic.

Jathelle was cradling his head and shoulders, her gentle fingers prying at his fists, which were clenched against his tear-filled eyes. "Tyrus, what is it? What has happened? Hetanya, help him!"

Pandemonium reigned around them. Through his torture, Tyrus heard men crying, "The light! The light is gone!"

"And the blackness!"

"The . . . the glamour that kept us safe! It is gone, too!"

In the distance, Rof's men were shouting, helpless, utterly lost. "Where are they? One-Ear?"

"Hai! Wizardry! We should have known!"

There was a cracking sound, as if Rof were summoning—or herding—his thieves with his whip, with poor success, apparently.

Tyrus managed to pull his hands away from his eyes, groping. He clutched the rough fabric of Erejzan's tunic, and Jathelle's slender hand wrapped itself around his.

"Vraduir did something to him," Erejzan said, hoarse with fury. "When I find that clenru . . ."

"No, mai fiyel." Tyrus tightened his grasp on them, fighting the fire in his face. "Vraduir is . . . is in the same state I am. We . . . we are both struck."

Aubage's voice cut in. "LaRenya, the bandits are in confusion. Now we can take them."

"No!" Tyrus gasped. Coughing, he struggled to sit up, leaning gratefully on Erejzan's support. "The citadel. Our only chance. Now while . . . while Vraduir is helpless." He sucked in air, trying to control his bounding pulse.

Jathelle and Erejzan were refastening his cloak about him. Perhaps it had come unbound in the battle of sorcery. Tyrus had no recollection of that. He breathed through his mouth, forcing the torment to a manageable level. "No magic . . . Vraduir will have no magic to oppose us," he told them. "It will be sword against sword. No more. For a space. The odds are . . . almost fair. But you must count without me, I fear. I will be a burden, for a candle-mark or several."

Fingers tenderly explored his brow. Jathelle. "The glass," she said. "It was some magic thing, in truth, not a conjurer's pretty game."

He nodded and immediately rued the action. Red flashes speared through his eyes and brain. Tyrus had to sit motionless for several moments till these lessened. Then he said, "*Both* glasses—Vraduir had one also. His shattered when mine did. We are together once more, united in pain. You must lead me, Erejzan. I am blind."

XIV

Citadel of Sacrifice

❃❃❃❃❃❃❃❃❃❃❃❃❃❃❃❃❃❃❃❃

TYRUS' OTHER SENSES FILLED THE CHASM LEFT BY HIS
wounded sight. He felt and heard Jathelle's dismay and
Erejzan's. Tyrus forced a faint smile despite protests
from his facial muscles. "Do . . . do not fear for me.
The blindness is temporary." Was he certain of that
last? He could not be, for such a gamble had never
been taken by a sorkra ere this. Yet he must have hope,
and give hope to his friends.

Jathelle examined his face, her touch a caress. "There
is no blood, only tears."

"And pain," Erejzan said, his voice shaking with
fury. His bracing arm tightened comfortingly about
Tyrus' shoulders.

"There . . . is pain," Tyrus confessed, gulping. "I
did not realize how much there would be. But . . . but
it was the only way. As my sight returns, so will my
powers. It is the same with Vraduir. My . . . my sorkra
skills are much linked with my pain. Until that eases . . .
when it does, we must . . . we must be within the citadel
and have Vraduir at bay."

"How can you treat this with such measured calm?"
Jathelle cried in horror.

Aubage cut in. Apparently he had been listening, puzzled by Tyrus' tactics. "But when you conjured for us in the palace, you were blindfolded and it did not hamper your magic."

"Lackwit fool!" Erejzan exclaimed. "This is different! Can you see anything at all, Tyrus?"

"Not . . . not yet." Tyrus shivered under a fresh wave of hurt.

"I warned you once, acrobat, to hold your insolent tongue," Aubage said with heavy menace.

"We have no time to see who is the better man in this," Erejzan said, his momentary anger lost in greater concerns. "Rof's men are still confused. I think we can elude them, Tyrus, if we keep behind the wreckage. Even without the glamour, it can be done. Can you walk?"

Jathelle said anxiously, "No, he must rest."

Tyrus pressed her hand against his cheek. That warm contact gave him ease from the torment in his eyes. "No rest. Or we will all be Vraduir's victims. Help me up, Erejzan."

Jathelle resisted, arguing softly, anguished for Tyrus' sake. Finally Erejzan said, "He has the right, LaRenya. Would *you* be kept from LaSirin Ilissa's side—by anything?" It was the only counter that reached her and she reluctantly aided Erejzan, propping the injured sorkra on his feet.

Severely disoriented, Tyrus swayed. His eyes were being stabbed by tiny lances dipped in flame. He reached out instinctively, his hands become his vision.

"This way . . ."

"Lieutenant, Miquit, quietly. All of you, keep to concealment," Jathelle whispered.

She and Erejzan walked beside Tyrus, guiding him. Again and again, as his boots slid on the frozen plain, raw panic churned his belly, worsening his plight. Though brain and body were in turmoil, he did not fall.

Many times he flinched beneath the fire in his eyes. Jathelle and Erejzan would steady him, then lead him forward once more.

Erejzan kept up a murmured commentary on their progress. "An open patch here, Tyrus. We must wait until the bandits are looking in another direction. Now! Quickly!" When they had reached another broken wagon or form of shelter, Erejzan went on, "A heap of ancient chariots, this, from the Traecheun empire, side by side with her enemy Ryerdon-yan. A strange ending for the traitors of both realms . . ."

As he talked, he and Jathelle crept on stealthily, protecting Tyrus and helping him through moments when he could not think for pain. Sometimes they would gently push down his head or instruct him to move bent over, lest his height reveal him to Rof and the searching brigands. From Jathelle's remarks, Tyrus knew the magic light had vanished completely, more proof that Vraduir was equally bereft of his powers. Dimly Tyrus heard Rof and One-Ear and the others hallooing back and forth.

"Find them!"

"We must, or the new master will give no gold!"

"Turncoat clenru," came a closer voice Tyrus recognized as Lieutenant Utaigh's.

"Yet they served us bravely enough in the Ice Forest and the haunted mountains," Jathelle said softly. "Perhaps I should have offered them still greater rewards."

"They would not have believed you, LaRenya," Erejzan said. "Vraduir made them his puppets. Hurry! Another ten lengths and we will be into the open."

Those around Tyrus trod carefully, trying to muffle their footsteps. This hid them from Rof, but it also confused Tyrus, the sounds occasionally so soft he feared he had been left.

His wits were clearing, slowly, slowly, wax melting in the autumn sun. Would his strength never be whole again? Tyrus strove to reach a part of his mind which lay suffering and dormant, useless to him. How many candle-marks before he could call upon his arts? Each time he stretched toward that special talent within himself, the source shriveled away like a living creature fearing worse hurt to match the agony in his eyes. Yet he tried repeatedly, enduring the pain, determined to have his wizardry as soon as possible.

"LaRenya," Erejzan was saying, "let go his hand." Tyrus did not have the will to brush Erejzan's mind, but he knew a time of great danger was upon them. "Tyrus must run in pace with me. We have done this before, when we were lads hunting the hurnbul and whantola."

With regret, Tyrus felt Jathelle's hand slip from his. He heard the cold slither of metal emerging from a baldric, knew Jathelle was drawing her sword, her breathing heavy, that of a battle maiden ready to face death. "Take my sword," Tyrus said suddenly, deciding. "I cannot wield it, and it is proof against Vraduir's imps, should any come against us."

Jathelle did not hesitate or make any counter suggestion that Erejzan should take the weapon instead. Skillfully, she took the enchanted blade out and sheathed her own in the baldric Tyrus wore. Through the mist of his injury, he sensed a part of his being—the magic which had transformed the wood and gold into a sword—moving off a trifle, though not far. Jathelle was close beside him, and so was the sword, that extension of his magic.

"The gate is closed," Aubage muttered, and other men seconded him. Apparently they were looking ahead, toward the citadel's main entrance. "If we leave this shelter and go into the open, and the gate is locked . . ."

"It is not locked," Tyrus said tonelessly.

"How . . . how can you know this, sorkra?" Tyrus

was familiar with all these voices now, after their days spent on the quest. Sirai Miquit did not doubt him, yet wondered if Tyrus' wounding did not muddle his wits.

"It is the Death God's citadel," Tyrus said. "Vraduir built it for him, but the god owns it. He has no wish to prevent anyone from coming to him and would not bar the gate against them."

The implications silenced them. For a long moment, they huddled and waited. Then Erejzan was pulling on Tyrus, growling instructions softly in his ear. Boyhood games were reborn, their strides almost matching, as Erejzan galloped along with the sorkra. Tyrus' pain made him less quick and the pace was quite even. A few times, Tyrus gasped and stumbled and Erejzan dragged him forward bodily. Off balance, Tyrus fought nausea, blood pounding in his throat and throbbing eyes.

"There they are!"

"Rof . . . there!"

"I see them! After them, you bejits!"

A groaning thunder overruled those distant voices then, the noise of a massive door swinging back ponderously on great iron hinges. "Hetanya be thanked!" Jathelle cried. "Tyrus was right! It *is* unlocked!"

Tyrus was pulled along, scraped against a splintery series of planks. The door smelled of crumbling decadence, even though the citadel was newly built by Vraduir's slaves.

Howls and curses rang out all around him and men grunted and objects thumped sharply.

"A bar! Get something to bar the door against those brigands!"

"Nothing here! No lock, no bar . . . as the sorkra said!"

"Here they come! Niyah! Hai-yan Hetanya! For

Couredh! Stand fast to slay the enemy, soldiers of La-
Renya!"

"Strike! Keep them out!"

Scent and sound and touch assailed Tyrus. The door's
roughness seemed to rip at his flesh. The stench of
sweat and blood-stained garments filled his nostrils.
When blades clashed through what must be a narrow
gap in the doorway, the sound was a weapon striking
his tortured mind.

A small hand grasped Tyrus' shoulder and jerked
him to one side. He felt air rush past his face and heard
the blow that had missed him—it must have been an
axe, embedding its keen edge in the door instead of
his skull! Beside him, Jathelle screamed, "Attack someone who can see you, you spawn of a sea-snake!" She
pushed against him, lunging, and there was a cry as a
brigand reeled back, cut by Tyrus' enchanted sword.

Jathelle was pulling Tyrus away from the door, to a
place of greater safety. She was panting, still cursing
the man who had tried to kill Tyrus. "So would my
father have dealt with such treachery as theirs," she
said grimly.

There were other cries, some mortal, and grief
stricken outrage as one of Jathelle's people was evi-
dently hurt. The brigands' score was instantly answered
with other blows and triumphant shouts. "That for our
brave comrade, you Bog' cursed thieves!"

"Run, LaRenya!" Sirai Miquit was shouting. "We
will hold them back. Go! Find LaSirin Ilissa!"

"Ai! For Couredh!" The lieutenant and other soldiers joined in.

Tyrus was surrounded by a bewildering din of weapons and voices. Erejzan was saying, "Take him, La-
Renya. I will stay with them."

"You have no weapon, acrobat," Miquit protested.
"This is our fight. Go with LaRenya. Keep her safe.
The gods of Clarique help us all!"

"Erejzan!" Jathelle added her plea to the fray. "I cannot find Ilissa alone, not with Tyrus hurt like this. Come!"

It was the command that mattered, and Tyrus was being pulled forward once more, two hands steering him—one slender and feminine, the other rough and very strong.

"They will not be able to hold them for long," Erejzan muttered. As he did, a rumbling crash reverberated hollowly through stony corridors. Tyrus winced, battered by the sound, and Erejzan said, "A ram! Those brigands must be using part of those broken wagons to force the gate."

"So many corridors," Jathelle said, distraught. "How can we know which way to go?"

Footing was no longer slippery, as it had been on the frozen plain. To replace that, however, Tyrus was beset by new difficulty, an unnatural cold. It was far different from anything he had experienced. It was no chill of clime or weather. His veins and sinews were wrapped in an insidious and deadly embrace, the Death God's grip beginning to steal over him. How long would it be before this unbearable cold congealed their blood and took their lives? Would they become as the peasants and other hapless denizens of the plains—the Death God's minions, damned to wander this realm forever?

To the rear, victorious howls and rending noises echoed. The brigands must have breached the gates. And some of them must surely elude the young queen's gallant forces. Any of Rof's men who survived that murderous fight would come stalking their new master's prey, greed riding them with spur and lash.

Tyrus blinked and wiped at tears, straining his agonized vision, hoping some glimmer of sight was returning. It seemed there was a lessening of the all-enveloping blackness, but he could not be sure. He blinked again and feared that Vraduir might achieve full sight before he did.

"Where, Tyrus?" Jathelle was asking. Her words came brokenly, forced through chattering teeth.

"This way, LaRenya," Erejzan said.

"Trust him," Tyrus encouraged Jathelle. "He has . . ."

"Many arts and talents, like you." She cloaked her knowledge in diplomacy, following Erejzan's lead willingly. Her arm linked through Tyrus' left and she drew him along gently, warning him about steps or corners.

Tyrus gasped with exertion, his abused faculties complaining as he made himself keep pace with Jathelle and Erejzan. "He . . . Vraduir . . . will be in his sanctuary . . . in . . . in the citadel's heart."

"It has one?" Erejzan wondered, bitter. "Vraduir does not, nor does the Death God, I think. But we will find them."

They hurried on, turning and twisting, helping Tyrus along. The cold intensified, apparent to Jathelle and the acrobat, too, by now, as the menacing brush of Nidil Who Steals All Breath.

"Torches," Erejzan said suddenly, sounding relieved. "Now you may see as well as I, LaRenya. Why are there torches, though? Vraduir's fixtures? Nidil would need no light. The god can come to take human life in the darkness."

"I think we must have outdistanced any of the brigands," Jathelle said. She slowed her steps, shivering.

"Not all," Erejzan warned, and Tyrus felt his friend turning about abruptly, tensely on guard against attack from behind them.

"Aubage!" Jathelle said in surprise. "Where . . . where are the others?"

"They are holding near the gates. Two of the brigands have been slain and another sorely hurt."

"But some are still alive?" Erejzan guessed angrily.

"And the queen's men?" Tyrus judged Aubage's shrugging response by Erejzan's annoyed snort. "They could use your sword. Why did you leave them?"

"LaRenya needs me more," Aubage defended himself, covering his fear with strong boasts. "You would be no help, without even a decent blade in your hand. And the sorkra is blind. My sword will guard Jathelle from—"

"Still!" Tyrus demanded. A fragment of his arts shuddered and recoiled far within his mind, alarms jangling through his lungs and head. There were choking sounds, Aubage's revulsion. Jathelle gave a disgusted yelp, and Erejzan's fingers bit hard into Tyrus' forearm. " 'Ware," Tyrus said, squinting through a blur of burning tears. "I . . . I can see it . . . a little . . ."

In truth, he was grateful his sight was misted. The form approaching them was immense and hideous, writhing with tentacles like some bloated sea-crawler. No fisherfolk would take *this* thing in their nets! Harvesters of the deeps would row as fast as they could to make away from the monster. The reek staggered Tyrus. He blinked again, discerning the ugly mass as it wavered before him, blocking the passageway. Then slowly, with peculiar grace, the creature undulated and swayed, snaky limbs wobbling sinuously, and it stretched forth tentacles toward the four fugitives.

Tyrus forestalled any impulses, even Erejzan's desire to match the alien thing with his man-ecar powers. "It is no illusion, but it is not Vraduir's slave, either." Aubage was retching noisily as Tyrus went on. "This is another of the Death God's pets, but one too difficult for us to kill. We must avoid it, if we can."

"There . . . there is another corridor to one side, here," Jathelle said. Her voice was distorted by horror, but she held her stomach better than Aubage did. She took Tyrus' hand, ready to lead him.

"Put my hand upon the wall and walk before me,"

Tyrus said. "I can see the beacon of your hair. You must have your hands free to use the sword, if need be."

Tyrus kept hidden his anxiety—that if he could see that small amount of the outside world, so could Vraduir. Magic was yet beyond the son, and it must be so for the father, the wizard-king, as well. But soon . . .

"It is after us!" Aubage exclaimed, brushing by Tyrus. He stumbled backwards by Jathelle's side, trying to keep his sword pointed at the shambling monster, yet not be laggard. Erejzan was behind Tyrus, also backpedaling, far more steadily, maintaining a wary watch on the Death God's beast.

As they turned into the corridor Jathelle had chosen, the tentacled thing went on by, its mission and purpose unknown. Sighing with relief, the four waited a while in the shadowy hall, and Erejzan bent his keen hearing and other senses to decide which route they should take. At length, he led them on down the corridor, saying this aimed toward the citadel's northernmost section.

From without, viewed across the frozen plain, the citadel had appeared like a sprawling city clad in high towers and thick walls. Within, it was a confusing warren of interconnecting rooms and halls. The four prowled through these cautiously, stopping often to listen and wait until some threat or unfamiliar noise had passed them by in an adjacent hall. In whispers, Jathelle and Aubage speculated on how and why such a godlike citadel had been built. Erejzan made no comment, intent on following his guesses, tracking for the citadel's center. Tyrus was trying to listen to another awareness, still fighting the hurt searing his eyes and will, clawing his way back to his strength.

In the distance, now and then, they heard sounds of battle. Did men fight beasts? Or had the brigands and Jathelle's people both escaped that fierce encounter at the gates and entered the citadel, too? From the clash of metal on metal, ringing through the frosty halls, Tyrus suspected that was so and hoped Jathelle's men were winning. It was possible, also, that brigands and soldiers and Sirai Miquit had come upon others of the Death God's creatures and had sought to slay them, with disastrous results. Tyrus shoved that awful idea out of his whirling thoughts.

How long and how far had they walked through the corridors? Time was numbed by inexorable cold. Tyrus clenched his jaw to quiet his jittering teeth, then said, "There is another of the Death God's beasts, that way. But it is going in the opposite direction. I feel illusions as well, some of Vraduir's slaves. Their power will be as limited as his. He will have little control over them until his pain eases. Only if he stood very close to them would his magic have any effect upon them now."

"Ilissa," Jathelle said suddenly. "Hetanya! I . . . I know she is here! Somewhere! I know it!"

"And we shall find her," Erejzan said without hesitation. Almost as an afterthought, he said, "Tyrus?"

"I agree. She is the key to Vraduir's scheming. We shall go on as we have. My hand upon the wall, La-Renya before me to show me where to walk."

They began to descend. The staircase was very long and winding. In some places, Tyrus' head brushed the ceiling, so low-pitched was it. Along the stairs there were landings and other staircases or halls branching off. At one of these, they halted, stupefied by the noisome draft blasting from a black passageway to the right.

Tyrus delicately called on his arts, grimacing, enduring the hurt. He traced, none too closely, the thing that had left the sickening scent. "Another alien animal . . . it . . . it seems asleep, in there."

"Will it come back?" Aubage asked worriedly.

"Who can fathom Nidil or his creatures?" Erejzan said with scorn. "Only such as Vraduir would even try."

As they went past the reeking opening, Aubage's curiosity made him peer inside despite the awful odor. "What does it look like, this one?"

"You do not want to know," Tyrus assured him. "I wish I did not."

The stairs leveled and became a corridor, then gave onto a series of small chambers. As they crossed the threshold of the first one, Aubage and Jathelle braced, pointing their swords. But they had learned from previous encounters and made no move to strike, awaiting Tyrus' judgment. He had been leaning heavily upon the door jamb, mopping away his tears and sucking in icy air. After a moment, Tyrus said, "This . . . this one is none of the Death God's making."

"It is quite ugly enough," Erejzan said. "An ugly creation of an ugly master."

"Jathelle, please step aside," Tyrus asked. "I must see it straight. I think I have enough skill to work a countercharm, at this range."

The thing that occupied the chamber was a beast travesty, kindred to the pitiful creations Vraduir had conjured on Qamat when he first attempted wizardry beyond any yet known. Tyrus knew its like and had probed how it was made. He considered what spells would best serve to send the brute to oblivion. "Bogotana must have thee," he said soberly. "You should have perished with the others of your ilk, when the innocent people of Qamat died. Now you will meet the fate you escaped then. Annoint you and enfold you in bright fire . . ."

Jathelle and Aubage did not understand the gibberish that followed. Erejzan did not know these magic phrases, either. But through long acquaintance with sorkra, he had learned when serious wizardry was under way, for good or ill. He grinned when the bug-headed winged wolf thing started to waver into transparency. As it clicked its ferocious mandibles, the acrobat thrust his forearm into the creature's maw. Aubage boggled at his courage and Jathelle tried to pull him away, frightened that he had gone mad. Then both of them laughed as the demon bit futilely on Erejzan's flesh, drawing no blood nor giving hurt. In a few moments, it had vanished, leaving not even a stench behind.

In the chambers beyond, there were other concoctions, none of them real but all of them terrible to see and hear and smell. Tyrus' pain was still great. Yet at these quarters—no more than a few arm lengths—he could work magic effectively. One by one, he spellcast out of existence a slurching sea slug, a scab-coated brute resembling a gigantic golhi, and a snake covered with steel scales and sharp spines.

Faintly, in the background of their hearing, that struggle between brigands and Jathelle's people went on. Tyrus could spare no concern for that. The perils facing him were unforgiving of distraction.

Edging past the spot where the metal snake had melted into fog, the four crossed the stone-walled room into a larger chamber. Erejzan slammed to a stop and forced Jathelle and Tyrus behind him, shielding them with his own body. "If this be no illusion . . . !"

Tyrus was tall enough to see past his friend. His sight was unclear but showed enough to explain why Erejzan was braced to attack. "No, mai fiyel. It *is* an illusion. This is Vraduir's puppet, not Vraduir himself."

Tyrus knew by his companions' reactions that the puppet was very convincing and lifelike. Vraduir—tall, broad shoulders, hair pale in the torch glow—paced to and fro, seeming to take no heed of the intruders. Tyrus squeezed by Erejzan, going toward the simulacrum.

Indeed! How lifelike it was! As he drew near enough

to make out details, Tyrus' emotions wrenched. Urges warred in his soul. He longed to act out youth's affection, to greet and embrace his sire. Yet hatred consumed him, too, a fire countless times hotter than the hurt in his eyes and brain.

"Being, imitation of Vraduir, begone . . ."

"I am Vraduir," the illusion insisted. Tyrus could not tell if it answered him or spoke a reflexive response to any interruption of its methodical pacing. "I am Vraduir, master of wizardry, wizard-king, lord of knowledge. I am the Death God's loyal servant and his inheritor."

"What will you inherit, imitation of Vraduir?" Tyrus held his magic. Wonderment drove him to ask, "Why will the Death God choose an heir? What need has he of any mortal servant? He is Nidil."

"And he shall be god above all gods. I shall make him gifts past price, sacrifices greater than any god has known. And he shall make me master, ruler, to create the world as it should be," the illusion crowed. "I shall rule time unending, undying, Nidil's honored servant, safe from assassins and death and age."

The copy aped Vraduir's manners faithfully, now clenching a fist and shaking it in the air, now clasping his arms across his chest as he strode back and forth. Awesome intelligence and lust for more knowledge shone in the handsome features and blue eyes. Each movement and expression brought a pang to Tyrus, love and betrayal chains cutting into his soul.

"Immortality!" Jathelle breathed, her piety offended. "It is not possible!"

"I will be immortal and assure that my wizardry shall always hold sway," the imitation Vraduir said. He was talking to himself rather than to Jathelle. Tyrus realized Vraduir had transferred his resolve-making to this illusionary guardian, a kind of constant worship of Nidil, and of the bargain he hoped to make with the Death God.

"A god cannot be bound with magic," the copy said, shrewdly laying a finger along its cheek. "This I have learned. Ah! But a god is a god, and a god relishes sacrifice and can be made content thereby. I could not enchant Bogotana. Could not be done. But when the conjured beasts and the people were taken in his fiery hands, Bogotana accepted the sacrifice and let this servant live."

Jathelle turned away, hands over her ears, as if yearning to shut out this blasphemy. Tyrus stood it, ice and fire in his blood, reliving the past with every word.

There was a nuance of regret in the expression of the imitation Vraduir. "I had not intended it to happen that way. My subjects, the first to know my rule . . . but mistakes are made. I will be more careful now. Not easily bought, a god. Favor must be won gingerly. Ah! True sacrifices. Not the rituals and common offerings of ordinary mortals. For Nidil takes everything. The key! Things given before their time. Then . . . *then* he will smile and grant me dominion. I shall be his ally, master of life and death, wizard-king of all realms, all provinces—*my* realms, *my* provinces! I rule life, as Nidil rules death!"

"Begone!" Tyrus roared, flinging up his hands to gesture the image away, lashing himself with wizardry his will was not yet healed enough to take well. Pain shook him violently. "Rasven aid me! I cast thee out, as thy master cast away his people. Sacrifices! He threw them away to save his own life, for all his talk of ruling! Ruler of death and agony! A world we will not let him have."

As Tyrus chanted his most powerful charms, the illusion of Vraduir staggered in apparent pain, clasping breast and throat. Still it showed no awareness of

Tyrus' presence or that of the others. This confirmed
Tyrus' suspicion that the simulacrum was mere vanity,
constructed to parade and echo Vraduir's own being,
a sorcerer's boastful fancy, a living statue in honor of
himself.

The copy was falling, writhing in death throes while
Tyrus struck it again and again with magic, venting
fury he had nursed for more than a year. Erejzan
grabbed him, breaking through the anger. "It is not
him. Save your wizardry, Tyrus. Save it for the true
Vraduir."

Tyrus faltered, wobbling, and Erejzan held him until
the waves of hurt and rage passed away. Frozen in its
agonized sprawl, the copy lay at his feet. Tyrus made
a negligent motion, completing the charm of banish-
ment. "I send you forth forevermore. Come never again
to the walks of earth. You belong to eternity, creature
of Vraduir."

Like dew, the illusion drew up into nothingness and
was gone. Tyrus sighed and rubbed his forehead wearily. Jathelle came to him and said, "I know something
of what you suffered, Tyrus. I wanted to run him
through. Worse, I wanted to torture him, as the barbarians tortured some of our people they captured in
the wars." Jathelle was aghast at her own reactions.
"I . . . I thought myself civilized, and yet . . . Never
have I known such hate! And this was but his illusion!"

"His exact image," Erejzan said, watching Tyrus for
further signs of hurt or weakness. "You would hate him
even more, if . . ." The acrobat broke off and bit his
lip, unwilling to confess the curse Vraduir had laid
upon him.

"To rule the world with his ruthless magic," Jathelle
murmured, thinking of what the image had said, horrified.

"What is this?" Aubage went past the place where

the illusion had been, around a screen of cunningly-worked small stones. His footfalls echoed from the outer walls. Then Aubage stopped short, staring.

The others followed him. Jathelle took a torch from a wall bracket and held it high. They gathered around the thing within the antechamber. "What can it be?" she wondered. "It shines like the Death God's snow upon the mountains outside."

The thing was a large cube, twinkling with that same eerie iridescence that had filled the night around the campfire. Though the surface seemed rigid, the contents swam and danced incessantly with that holy light.

Suddenly, Jathelle choked and said, "Tyrus . . . there . . . there is a man trapped within!"

At those words, they became conscious of sweet music, soft and flowing. It was swelling gradually, wafting all about them. Unlike their words and footsteps, the music made no echoes at all. Pure and unaltered, plangent notes floated. These formed into the sprightly melodies of Clarique, the islands' laments and joy-takings. Tunes of fisherfolk, drovers, farmers, and nobility hung in the cold air, perfect and haunting. Tyrus had never heard such music. The songs were so godlike they wept at the sheer beauty of these.

Spellbound, they listened, staring at the man within the crystalline cage. He seemed to be suspended in the twinkling interior, the alien light dancing and swirling around him.

The man was holding a themshang, his hands locked in position on the glittering strings. His lips were parted, as if he were frozen in the moment of singing one of those matchless notes. His voice and the harp's were one. Sublime and flawless—man and themshang blended into one marvelous instrument.

Tyrus' eyes were teared from the explosion of his vision-glass. But now fresh wetness clung to his lashes.

He wept with the others, deeply moved. Tentatively, he spread his fingers against the crystalline cage. To his surprise, he felt no vibration nor any other indication that the singer or the themshang were stirring the transparency or air within the cube.

"We are hearing him as he was," Tyrus said, gazing sorrowfully at the man floating amid the lights.

"Sacrifice," Jathelle said, shaking off the mood the harper had woven around them. She rushed to the same terrible conclusion Tyrus had reached and remembered things the imitation Vraduir had said.

Wary of his pounding skull, Tyrus nodded slowly. "This was the famed harper of Atei. Vraduir's enchanted ship kidnapped him last fall." Tyrus pressed his forehead against the cage. The cube was icy, a surface as cold as death itself. The chill should have eased the pain in his head, but it did not.

"Poor musician!" Jathelle mourned. "The gods be kind to him." Her tears fell anew, in grief now, not because of the lovely music. The sweet tunes had turned to a dirge for him who had brought the perfect music into being.

"Why was . . . ?" Then Aubage answered his own query. "He was killed to please Nidil?"

"One of Vraduir's sacrifices to gain rule and immortality," Erejzan said. The acrobat gazed at the harper, a vein in his temple throbbing visibly. To Tyrus, it was apparent his friend was fighting a powerful urge to shape-change. Here, such angry eruptions could serve no purpose, since Vraduir was not yet within their grasp. They could not help the harper of Atei. No mortal could.

"Sacrifices," Jathelle said. "All the things you said he stole, Tyrus. Sacrifices to gain his ambitions and the Death God's favor. And Ilissa? *Ilissa?*" Jathelle sank to her knees as she would before an altar. Tears streamed over her cheeks as she looked at the terrible cage. "We cannot be too late! Oh, Hetanya! Do not let Ilissa have been sacrificed, too!" And Jathelle thrust her hands against her lips, muffling a scream of utter despair.

XV

Sorcerer's Greed

❋❋❋❋❋❋❋❋❋❋❋❋❋❋❋❋❋❋❋❋❋❋

AUBAGE AND EREJZAN BENT TO HELP THE YOUNG
queen, but Jathelle shrugged away from them, rallying
her emotions. "No! It is not so! I will not let it be so!"
She scrambled to her feet, confronting Tyrus. "I know
she is still alive, not sacrificed in . . . in one of these
deadly cages. I *know* it!"

Honesty would not let Tyrus reassure her without
reservation. "I have no arts to tell if she has been lost
to us." He added gently, "But bonds of blood are very
potent."

"And such a one joins my sister and me, the blood
of our parents! Ilissa is alive," Jathelle said firmly. She
lifted Tyrus' enchanted sword and vowed upon it,
"Mother of Earth, guide me to her and the third of my
harvest shall be given your temples all the years of
my life!"

Erejzan said suddenly, "That puppet spoke Vraduir's own plans, did he not, Tyrus?" When Tyrus
nodded, the acrobat built upon that fragile foundation.
"He said Nidil could not be swayed by common sacrifice, and LaSirin Ilissa is truly perfection. Then . . . he

cannot have slain her. Vraduir has not gained the full
favor of Nidil, yet."

Jathelle swung around, her face pale, awaiting Tyrus'
answer. Tyrus himself was half persuaded to his friend's
argument. "Indeed, it seems not. If the god favored
him, we would already be dead, and the world forfeit,
the power Vraduir wants now in his hands." Jathelle frowned over this as Tyrus went on, "The best
proof that Ilissa lives is the fact that we are still alive.
If Nidil had given Vraduir his dominion, we would
have been slaughtered at once, the first prey in his taking rule of all Tyta'an's provinces. For some reason,
he has not given her to the god's crystalline cage—yet."

Jathelle's fear for Ilissa did not harden her soul to
the possible danger to all humankind. "All realms hang
on Ilissa's life. It is not merely my selfishness that
wants her safe."

"It is not selfish," Erejzan said most fervently. "We
all want that."

Aubage took the torch from Jathelle and led the way
around the musician's glittering cage. Erejzan offered
a hand to guide Tyrus, but the sorkra waved away his
help. His vision was somewhat obscured, though. He
walked slowly over the frost-covered bricks patterning
the floor. They left the antechamber by a portal opposite the one where they had entered.

A hall beyond opened onto another stair, an ascending one. At the top there was a cramped area with
many staircases leading off from the junction. Tyrus
dipped lightly into the fringes of his arts to choose
which way to go. It brought less pain than he anticipated. Erejzan read his expression and guessed what
was happening.

"Ai, mai fiyel," Tyrus said. "But Vraduir is healing,
too. He was not ready for the explosion, as I was,
and will recover more slowly. But he will be whole
again. This way!"

Inwardly Tyrus exulted, human joy greater than this proof of his magic. Sight! How precious it was! There had been long, bitter candle-marks when he had not known if that sense would be returned to him. Even were it marred or affected by the desperate gamble with the vision-glass, he would be able to see *something* again! His spirits were lifted by that, despite the grim situation.

He led them ever deeper into the citadel, this bastion-city Vraduir had built with much wizardry and the blood of hapless peasants. Had he borrowed labor from Nidil's legions of the damned as well? It seemed so. And now some of those cursed shades and creatures wandered the vast corridors and rooms of the Death God's citadel.

Tyrus could not describe how he knew which direction to take. All normal choices were muddied by cold and danger. The skill he used had no comparison with hunter's craft or reckoning by star or sun. This lore came from arcane wells, taught him by a master of these sorceries—Vraduir. Now Vraduir was the lodestar upon which Tyrus focussed, pulling Tyrus to him. And Vraduir was at the dark core of the citadel.

They met with more illusions and a few imps, leavings, of Vraduir's conjuring on Qamat. Jathelle slew one of these gibbering demons with Tyrus' sword, while Aubage slashed futilely at the same wolf-sized thing. Once they shrank back into the shadows on Tyrus' command and watched wide-eyed as a skeleton warrior strolled by their hiding place. It paid no heed to the frost issuing from their noses and mouths and steaming from sweat-damp patches of their clothes. Yet Tyrus waited, distrustful, fearing another black lightning from those bony fingertips. However, the grue-some relic of bygone wars did not strike. Intent upon business none living could comprehend, it rattled the length of the corridor. Armor of wadded quilting and bronze studs shifted over a rib cage where lungs had long ago rotted. A helmet of an empire whose name was lost in dust capped an eyeless skull. Spurs dangled from boots which were no more than leather rags. Ghostly, terrible, the warrior disappeared around a corner and was gone. The four lurked in the darkness long minutes until they were certain the skeleton would not return, then once more made their way toward the citadel's interior.

The sorkra skills were strengthening, bit by bit, and Tyrus relied on these. Northward, ever northward, as the quest had led from the beginning. North, to the end of life, as far from the citadel's gates as they could go . . .

They came through a wide arch and tensed, on guard. Jathelle and Aubage readied their swords and Erejzan scuttled along the shadowed wall to Tyrus' right. No illusion or imp or skeleton warrior, this. A man stood within the chamber.

"Hold! All of you! Stand still or I will put a dagger through your gullet!"

It was the brigand named One-Ear. He was near another of the crystalline cages, his stance predatory, avarice bright in his eyes. One-Ear had a belt full of knives, his own and those taken from fellow thieves and perhaps from Jathelle's men. He held a keenly-honed dagger in his right hand and a sword in his left.

"That is Miquit's sword!" Aubage shrilled. "If you have killed him . . ."

"Stand back!" One-Ear growled again.

"There are four of us and one of you," Jathelle said, a menacing tone in her words. She took a two-handed grip on the enchanted sword.

"Ai, LaRenya! We outnumber him! For the honor of Couredh!" Aubage sidled forward a step.

"Back! I am man enough to deal with several of

your kind, Sirai. And you, Clarique queen, keep your distance or I will put out your pretty eyes."

"He does not play at killing," Tyrus said. "He is as good as he claims with that dagger. He can throw it and slay you before you could reach him with swords. Do as he says."

"Lesson them well, sorkra." One-Ear said with less belligerence, "No need to bleed you, if you leave me to my work. Rof's the one intent on taking you to the other wizard. I have found my reward here, and enough."

It was plain One-Ear had been in furious combat. He was wounded in several places and his already-filthy garments were further dirtied with his own gore and that of others.

"How many of my men did you kill?" Jathelle demanded. But she obeyed Tyrus and made no effort to move against the blood-stained throatslitter.

"I do not count," One-Ear said with a shrug. "Stay away. This is mine . . ." He turned, reaching for an object behind him.

Until he had stepped away, he had blocked a clear view of the thing. It was another crystalline cage, much smaller than the one containing the harper of Atei. As One-Ear revealed the sacrificial cube, Tyrus shielded his hurt eyes from a bright glare and the others gasped. Squinting, Tyrus defined the shape inside the crystal amid his tears. There were gold and emeralds and other brilliant stones and metal, dazzling in their purity and quantity.

"Hetanya's crown!" Jathelle cried. "Stolen from her temple on Sersa-Ornail!"

"The goddess has no need for it, and it will keep me rich for many a year," the brigand retorted. As Erejzan shifted his weight, the mutilated killer darted a glance at him. "Stand still . . . whatever you are! I am taking the crown! No one stops me."

"Do not strike it!" Tyrus yelled.

Too impatient to stay his hand, One-Ear brought down the captured sword on the edge of the shining cage. Sirai Miquit was a wealthy lord and the blade was of finest Krantin steel. The blow was a mighty one, driven by One-Ear's greed. Had the crystalline cage been merely the beautiful glass it appeared, surely the sword would have cracked, if not shattered, it.

But this was not glass. And the Death God did not intend to give up sacrifices rendered him. The chamber filled with god-light, a terrible crackling blueness, limning One-Ear, racing up the blade to the hilt and into his body. Transfixed, his mouth agape in a silent scream, One-Ear was rigid in agony. As abruptly as it began, the blue light vanished. One-Ear slumped away, sprawling onto his back, sword and dagger falling from lax fingers.

As Tyrus and the others approached the body, the corpse twitched a few times. But the eyes were vacant and lifeless. Aubage stepped over the supine form and reached for the fallen sword.

"Touch nothing!" Tyrus said emphatically.

Sobered by One-Ear's punishment for ignoring such an order, Aubage jerked away as if burned by that unearthly light which had killed the brigand.

"I . . . I only meant to return the sword to Miquit's kindred," Aubage said.

"Meager fare for the Death God, compared to this," Erejzan said, looking in awe on the Hetanya crown. The cage had no mark upon it, no sign to show the sword had ever struck it. The famous crown floated in iridescence, locked away from the world.

"But . . . but you touched the cage that held the harper," Jathelle said, and she eyed Tyrus worriedly, fearing a belated punishment might befall him.

"I took a risk I did not realize then. It must be that

I escaped because I had no covetous intent. One-Ear meant to steal the crown, and it cost him his life."

Jathelle made an obeisance to the holy object, shaping Hetanya's sacred triangle with her fingers and thumbs. "How the people of Sersa-Ornail must mourn for this priceless treasure," she murmured.

The heavy gold was intricately carved, the work of Sersa-Ornail's finest artisans. Reliefs of flowering trees and ripe grain fields encircled the glittering band. Figures of priests and priestesses paraded through golden woods and pastures, honoring the Mother of Earth. There were the black pearl and the rare stones of blue ice Tyrus had described to the gem merchant in Couredh; these dangled from a delicately meshed gold chain set with many carnelians, a lacy drape below the crown's brim. The leaves of trees were individual tiny emeralds, and on the crown's top stood a single, stunning emerald of great size, radiantly faceted, cradled amid golden petals. The crown was too large for a mortal woman, for it had been made for Hetanya herself.

"No longer to be seen by humankind," Jathelle said sadly. "No longer Hetanya's. We are in the snow-clad lands of Omaytatle, but the crown is Nidil's now."

"We must not linger here," Tyrus said. "There could be other brigands also seeking treasure, and Vraduir's eyes are mending fast."

They needed no prodding, quickly leaving the chamber and continuing through the citadel's maze of rooms and halls. Time and again they dodged the Death God's minions. Fortunately, for Tyrus disliked taxing his returning powers, they met no sorcerer's illusions. He wondered if Vraduir was nursing his blindness and too pained to control his slaves or send them in a logical search for the fugitives.

They found other chambers and other sacrifices.

Each discovery made Jathelle's worry the worse. There was a cage holding the renowned tapestries of Arniob, from far in the South Clarique Sea. The tapestries had been the first irreplaceable prize taken by Vraduir and the crew of the ship, nearly a full turn of the seasons ago. How long Vraduir had worked to his present evil scheme! He had stolen this delicate weaving while Qamat's ashes were still smoldering with fresh-spewed lava.

Another chamber held the silver fish net of Aza-Dun, he who had come from the sea, the dweller-in-water. Like the Arniob tapestries, this was a treasure from the times of Traecheus, legendary, priceless.

Lives had been lost in these thefts, temple guards and valiant soldiers of the islands of Arniob and Bendine, who had sought to protect their people's honor. Enchantments and the merciless will of Captain Drie and his sailors had killed any who opposed them, leaving a trail of blood and frightened tale-telling which Tyrus and Erejzan had followed doggedly.

They were not surprised when they came upon yet another stolen glory. The stallion had been taken from Gros-Donaq's temple grove on Tor-Nali and the animal, too, was forfeit to Nidil. Aubage gazed admiringly at the godlike brute within the crystalline cage. "A charger kings would war to own," he said. Then he remembered One-Ear's fate and added hastily, "But no man will ever ride him, now that he belongs to Nidil."

Frozen, its eyes gleaming as if it still lived, the horse was in its way as flawless a sacrifice as the harper, the crown, the tapestries, and the man-fish's net. They thought they could hear its hooves drumming and breath whistling through the flared nostrils. The red coat of the magnificent dredis stallion shone like sunset and tricked their eyes till they imagined the head was turning, those soft eyes returning their stares.

"Vraduir stole it from the Storm God and his holy sons," Aubage marveled. "Even if it was to please another god, does this sire of yours fear nothing?"

"He fears Bogotana," Erejzan answered for Tyrus, very grim. "Vraduir believes that if he wins Nidil, all other gods are his allies. With Nidil's favor, he need not fear even death."

"And will take many another sacrifice, before the time appointed by the gods," Jathelle said. Tyrus gently urged her to leave the chamber of sacrifice, but she pulled away, distracted. "Ilissa? I . . . I hear Ilissa!" She whirled and ran back toward a door they had used earlier, the men at her heels.

Jathelle stopped in the hallway beyond, turning to a dim staircase which was half lost in shadows. The steps wound down into blackness. "There! The cry comes from there. Tyrus, it *is* Ilissa! I know it is!"

Danger was tangible, and Tyrus felt an ominous and steady building pressure. Vraduir, reawakening. Yet Jathelle's hope bound him and became his own. The hatred which drove him after Vraduir was not so strong as this newer link with Jathelle. Her will overcame his reservations.

Erejzan started to add his arguments to Jathelle's. "Tyrus, I hear it too. I had not thought anyone's senses were keener than mine. But LaRenya's heart gives her the advantage. I am sure it is the LaSirin."

"Ai." Erejzan gawked with pleased surprise as Tyrus agreed. "Time grows sharp. Now!"

Jathelle plunged down the stairs recklessly, into the blackness. Tyrus and Erejzan caught up with her, restraining her lest she fall to her death. They looked back at Aubage. The courtier hesitated on the topmost level, his complexion gray in the wavering torchlight. Tyrus and Erejzan urged him to follow but he did not stir until Jathelle exclaimed, "It is your betrothed! You swore to go through fire and ice for her. Is darkness such a challenge? Come!"

He swallowed audibly, then trotted after them. He showed no eagerness to go to the front and lead the descent. Erejzan grabbed the torch from Aubage and took the perilous assignment for himself. With feral grace, the acrobat ran down the stone staircase, Tyrus and Jathelle following as rapidly as they could. Aubage did not relish this excursion into the depths, but did not want to be left behind. He crowded so close upon Tyrus and the young queen that he nearly pushed them down the precipitous steps.

Foul dampness clung to the walls and Nidil's unnatural cold was everywhere. The torch lent little warmth. Their breath was fog, floating above them like a misty flag. They took care not to touch the walls with bare skin showing through frayed gloves, fearing flesh would adhere to the icy stones.

Erejzan paused on a landing, cocking his head and listening intently. Three more staircases branched off, two of them descending. "How much deeper can we go?" Aubage grumbled, flapping his arms about himself and stamping his feet. "I hear nothing."

"Silence!" Jathelle snapped.

A heartbeat after she had spoken, they all detected the faint noise. Tyrus could make no words of the plaintive wail, but Jathelle teetered forward and cried, "Little one. I am coming, Ilissa!" She turned this way and that frantically, trying to select the correct staircase, confused further by echoes.

Erejzan held out his hand courteously. "This one, LaRenya."

As they descended once more, the torch sputtered and started to go out. Tyrus gestured and a bright, sorcerous light took the dying torch's place. The brilliance separated into four smaller, bouncing glows.

These hovered, one to light each traveler's way. Jathelle and Erejzan looked apprehensively at Tyrus, fully knowing what this demonstration of his powers meant. Without discussion, they rushed down the staircase Erejzan had chosen, scuffling over the bricks and stones.

The air became very close, barely enough to sustain life. Tyrus gulped for breath, supporting Jathelle as she stumbled in her haste. The steps spiraled first in one direction, then swung around dizzyingly in the opposite pattern. There were no landings, no places to rest; nor dared they stop. The magic tapers bobbed above them, lighting their path into the bowels of the Death God's frozen realm. By now they must be far below the plain, and below Vraduir's sanctuary in the heart of the citadel.

That arcane pressure Tyrus had sensed a short while earlier was ever increasing. He drew upon his arts and added a shield to the lights. The effort brought pain but was bearable. Eventually Vraduir would be strong enough to find the shield and possibly to break through it. He would learn quickly, fathoming Tyrus' new knowledge, as Tyrus had once learned Vraduir's own wizardry.

Without warning, the steps ended. Ahead was a heavy wooden door formed into massive bars. Beyond there was light and warmth and abundant air, a haven in the depths.

"Ja—Jathelle! Oh, Jathelle! You *did* come!"

Ilissa was on the other side of the barred door, groping desperately through the openings. Jathelle flung herself upon the obstacle, embracing her weeping sister as well as she could through the barrier.

"Ilissa?" Aubage seemed disbelieving, as if despite his boasts, he had never expected to see Ilissa again.

Erejzan immediately began shaking the bars and

looking for a hinge or catch. He took the enchanted
sword, which Jathelle had dropped in her desire to have
both hands free to touch Ilissa, and pried at the door.

"It is sealed by spells," Tyrus said. "Jathelle, Erejzan,
LaSirin Ilissa—stand back. I must break this enchantment with a countercharm. When it gives way, it is
likely the door will fall."

It was most difficult for the sisters to separate so
soon after being reunited. But there was the promise
of the barrier's destruction. Jathelle smiled encouragement and let go Ilissa's hands with a lingering touch.
"Soon, my little one. Just a bit more. Tyrus will have
you free at once!"

"Or as soon as I can," Tyrus said honestly. "This is
a well-charmed lock." He pressed his knuckles against
his temples, hurling his power against the door. There
were numerous seals, invisible to the others but quite
apparent to Tyrus. He identified each one. Vraduir's
presence was a brand on each latch and unseen bar.
And each spell was familiar to Tyrus. He re-enacted
boyhood tests Vraduir had set him. Another sorkra
might have found the task impossible. Certainly none
could have mastered and deciphered the keys so quickly. Unerringly, his memory sharpening by the moment
and his mind accepting these demands upon it, Tyrus
broke all the spells.

"Magic," Aubage whispered. "Always it must be
magic. I would cut away ordinary locks with my blade."

"Good magic to destroy evil," Jathelle said, watching the door.

The heavy bars creaked and the door thumped on
hinges that were not there. It fought him. With hands
that were not hands, Tyrus pulled. A strong pull resisted—Vraduir's sorcery. Again Tyrus countered, overcoming the reluctant barrier. Slowly, it gave way.

Fearful of being crushed, the others stepped back still
farther.

Erejzan glanced over his shoulder and his expression
tightened, as if he heard something amiss on the winding staircase. Whatever had distracted him, he forgot it
when Tyrus' wizardry proved champion. With a booming crash, the door fell flat, leaving the portal open
wide.

Jathelle ran over the threshold, wrapping Ilissa in her
arms and hugging her close. "I told you! Tyrus did it!
You are free!"

Tyrus felt like an intruder on this tender, personal
scene. Laughing and crying with happiness, Jathelle
cried, "Mother of Earth bless you all the days of your
life, Tyrus, and you, Erejzan. You have brought me to
Ilissa, just as you promised you would!"

The acrobat was grinning shyly and blushing, much
affected by the sisters' reunion. He enlarged his joy to
include Tyrus. "Hai! Traech sorkra! He always said *he*
was that, but you deserve the title instead, Sirin Tyrus."

Tyrus shook his head, refusing such a rank, studying
the cell. He noted a second enchanted barred door at
the far side of the room. There were a number of special accoutrements and adornments, things Vraduir had
provided for Ilissa's comfort, here in this citadel of ice
and death. She was Vraduir's prisoner, but he had
made certain she had heat and light and luxuries befitting a princess. Light globes, similar to those Tyrus
had conjured, made the room cheery. Flameless heat
radiated from lumps of obsidian set in braziers, an
arcane device Vraduir had originally employed on
Qamat when he sought to tame the smoking mountain's
fire. Silver pegs studded the walls between layers of
fine tapestries. Costly garments of velvet and grir fur
and delicate Irico woolens hung from the pegs. There
were clothes chests everywhere, brass-bound volumes of

writing and pictures, and plate and goblets. Tyrus knew there must be a regular delivery of food here as well, brought by Vraduir's slaves. There was even a thick carpet. And there was a bed, one as regal as that in Ilissa's own bedchamber in Couredh palace.

With sinking dismay, Tyrus grasped the significance of all these things. A helpless young woman, beauteous, innocent—in a room locked by Vraduir's wizardry. The triumph of rescuing Ilissa was tinged with bitterness. In one sense, they *had* arrived too late. Erejzan's smile was fading, too, as he comprehended what had happened.

"Ah! Let me see you," Jathelle was saying, brushing Ilissa's tangled hair from her lovely face. Jathelle's happiness dissolved into horror as she peered into Ilissa's red-rimmed eyes. There was a haunted look in Ilissa's expression, that of a fragile woman who had held madness at bay only with desperate courage. Her will was battered, still trembling on the edge of panic.

She wore the same clothes she had when the skeleton warrior abducted her. But now the garments were even more torn and rumpled. Ilissa had tried to mend the damage. The nature of these darnings told a story of outrage and degradation. Her breeches had been badly ripped and repaired without much success. Several panels of her slashed skirt hung askew. Her bodice lacings had been cut and then knotted together in a pathetic attempt to shield her modesty. Thus ravaged, her breasts were partially exposed and bare skin showed through gaps in her breeches and skirt. She cowered as if expecting a blow—and in her present state, a harsh word would be a blow as terrible as an executioner's axe. Somehow, miraculously, she had clung to sanity through her ordeal. Now, confronting Jathelle and the others, she shivered despite the magic heat from the obsidian lumps. "Oh, Jathelle, I . . . I could not de-

fend myself. He spoke some strange words and . . .
and . . ."

Jathelle embraced her again and shook with wrath.
"What manner of beast is this wizard Vraduir?"

"Say not a beast, LaRenya," Erejzan begged. His
stricken countenance revealed his torment on Ilissa's
behalf. "Only men so abuse the laws of decency."

Ilissa wept bitterly. But she seemed to take heart
from Erejzan's defense of her honor. She gazed at him
and Tyrus, and recognition bloomed in her beautiful
eyes. "You . . . you are the amusers. Ai! When . . .
when you came to the cell, I feared it was . . . *him*
again," she said, gulping tears, and Tyrus winced at
the pain in her innocent face. She *was* innocent, for all
that Vraduir had done to her. Her fear eased and she
said, "But you never hurt me with your magic. And
you are Erejzan." Ilissa forced a sweet smile and went
on with growing trust, "You saved me from the cutpurse. And you leaped onto the skeleton warrior's
horse. Oh, you might have been killed! How brave you
are!"

Erejzan knelt, impulsively taking Ilissa's hand and
kissing her pale fingers. "I would have died to keep
you safe, LaSirin. Know that I am your servant in all
things. And I will be your avenger. I swear this to
Gros-Donaq and all the powers of sky and sea!"

Tyrus added his vow. "And by all the arts of sorkra.
You are free. Vraduir will not touch you with his evil
any more."

Ilissa continued to search Erejzan's eyes, trying to
believe he did not think her shamed past understanding. "But . . . but none of this can change what . . ."
She buried her face on Jathelle's breast for a moment,
struggling for composure. Jathelle stroked her hair
soothingly as the younger woman sobbed. "He . . . he
said I would henceforth be his queen. And he bade

me put on those garments." Ilissa pointed at the silver pegs and the beautiful clothes, royal robes and dresses for the consort of humanity's conqueror. "I would not wear them! I would not have anything from him! Nothing! I have slept on the floor, not where . . . where he . . ." She broke off, turning away from the luxurious bed that had meant such brutal hurt for her.

"Hush! Gently, it is all over. You are safe now," Jathelle crooned. She cradled Ilissa's head on her shoulder, rocking her, looking at Tyrus.

The bond that linked him and Erejzan with Jathelle was joined by a delicate and fragile life—Ilissa's. Tyrus fought off the looming pressure of Vraduir, sharing Jathelle's anguish, matching it with his own. "My mother," he said in a constricted voice. "He . . . he has dishonored her noble memory past any redemption by this crime. And there was a time when Vraduir hung pirates who dared force our women during their raids," Tyrus went on, genuinely bewildered by this. "How can he so turn his heart against all that . . . Rasven! I wish my blood were not his! I am ashamed to call him my sire!"

Ilissa clung to Jathelle, murmuring, "So strong. His magic. If I only had a knife, I might have . . . I feel as if I can never face the sun or Hetanya's temples again."

As Jathelle softly argued against Ilissa's self-loathing, Erejzan added his pleas to hers. "Do not weep, LaSirin. Do not hide your beautiful face from us. There is no shame for you in this. The shame is Vraduir's. And he will pay for his crime with his life!"

Jathelle nodded to him gratefully. She beckoned Aubage and said, "Come and comfort her. She needs her betrothed to dry her tears and make her forget these cruelties. What is the matter with you? Aubage?"

When there was no response, they all looked at the

young courtier. Warning forces were thundering along Tyrus' veins and bouncing within his skull. His emotions, though, were still tied to Jathelle's. Sudden suspicion made him examine Aubage, probing his features and his mind. Once, briefly, he had thought Aubage might be Vraduir's tool. Tyrus had long since put that possibility away. Rarely, the lord of the border lands had shown some bravery and pride befitting his rank and breeding. Far more often, he had been what Jathelle warned—an ambitious seeker after titles and properties. He was, as the court's servants proclaimed, the least of his household and all pretty words without substance. Now, too vividly, Aubage revealed his emptiness.

Tyrus had not thought he could be more angry for Ilissa's sake. Now Aubage's cold stare sent fire through Tyrus' soul.

That reaction, however, was mild compared to Jathelle's. She laid a hand upon her dagger. "Aubage? Say something! Speak to us!"

"And what would you have the Sirai say, LaRenya?"

As one, they shifted their attention to the open portal. Rof leaned against its side, grinning at them. He had arrived so silently that only Erejzan might have heard him approach—and Erejzan had been completely preoccupied with Ilissa. Like One-Ear, Rof was armed with more weapons than he had owned when they had left him. As Erejzan jumped to his feet and started for him, Aubage turned and pointed his sword at the bandit. Rof countered with a sword and an axe, one in each hand, stopping them in their tracks. The grin widened into a wolfish leer.

"Hold there, lads, and no harm done, for now. And for later . . . well and at that, we must see what my new master wishes for you all!" He winked at Tyrus, and the pressure that had shoved against Tyrus' mind for a quarter candle-mark rose to a menacing power, ready to fall upon him, while Rof the bandit lord barred the only escape from this cell in the depths of the citadel.

XVI

The Death God

"How did you find us?" Tyrus asked with decep-
tive calm. He knew the answer, but juggled for time.
The air was a weight, greater and more burdensome
with every heartbeat. Tyrus' vision was fully cleared
now. Deliberately, he took slow breaths, matching
pressure for pressure against Vraduir's gathering attack.

"My new master guided me here," Rof said with
a shrug. "I go where I am paid, remember?"

"Your reward will be dust and your own death."

Rof pretended not to hear Tyrus' warning. He looked
at the scene within the cell as if it were a performance
staged to amuse him. For just a moment, he seemed
taken aback and sympathetic as he gazed at Ilissa and
grasped why she was captive in such a place. But he
quickly turned his black eyes toward Jathelle and the
men. "Eh, m'lord Aubage? LaRenya is waiting. Why
do you not speak? You were ever good at that, during
our journey."

"Shut up, you whoreson!"

Unoffended, Rof laughed. "That I am, m'lord, and
no apologies. I am no mewling fop full of boasts about

311

my rank and titles, like you. You have much thought for your rank and for words instead of courage. No courage to tell her the truth?"

"What are you saying, bandit lord?" Jathelle cut in. "Aubage, are you stricken dumb or witless? Tyrus does not enchant your tongue this time. I will have an answer!"

Stung, Aubage blurted, "And I will no longer tolerate being treated as a page boy by the house of Fer-Sro. My lineage is Irico and nobler by far . . ."

"And your blood thinner, border-man," Rof taunted.

With growing consternation, Ilissa stretched forth her pale hands. Her exquisite face was bejeweled with tears. "Aubage, you must understand! He . . . he is a wizard! He used magic . . ."

Though she was well out of his reach, Aubage shrank away in loathing. Ilissa might have been a diseased beggar. He acted as if she could contaminate him with her touch, his revulsion obvious. Coldly correct, he said, "LaRenya, we will discuss this in a more proper setting."

"What? How . . . You gold-seeking toady!" Jathelle gripped her dagger while Ilissa struggled with her, pleading for patience. Even now, Ilissa made excuses for her betrothed, taking his side against her enraged sister.

Foolishly, Aubage would not be still, rising to the challenge Jathelle had flung. "I am kin-brother of the sons of Huil-Couredh. It is not our custom to take other men's concubines. We are second family. By rights, when the Fer-Sro left no sons, one of us should have had the throne, not you!" A deeper truth crept into Aubage's soft, handsome face, a dread of being scorned by his clan. "My . . . my kin-brothers would not acknowledge such a joining. By honor, Fer-Sro is betrothed to me, and there is yet blood of your house they *would* bid me wive."

He was past reasoning, blind to the danger in Jathelle's expression and the murderous posture of the
acrobat. Erejzan was nearest the courtier and his hands
curved into clawed vises, eager to fasten on Aubage's
throat.

Tyrus shouted, trying to bring them all to their
senses. But as he did, a tremendous blow landed at the
base of his neck. No ordinary hand dealt it and nothing
was seen. Yet he was knocked to the carpeted floor
and clutched his head, severely shaken. He concentrated all his will desperately, hurling Vraduir away.
Stunned, unable to spare further strength to use his
voice, Tyrus gawked at the others.

Everything was moving with unusual slowness. Words
were distorted. Rapid gaits were crawls. Reality was
grossly changed as Tyrus' sorcery and Vraduir's met in
a powerful collision.

"Rip his heart out, shape-changer!" Rof was yelling.
"Fang him, handri!"

It was the only thing Rof might have said that would
have broken Erejzan's wild fury. With superb control,
Erejzan mastered a lunge half begun, teetering on the
balls of his feet. He stopped a hand-span away from
Aubage's sword-point, which aimed at his belly. Warily,
Erejzan withdrew a pace. He looked from Aubage to
Ilissa and back again several times, in an agony of
indecision.

Tyrus' enchanted sword lay on the carpet a length
away—as far away as Sarlos!—where Erejzan had
dropped it after trying to pry open the door and rushing
into the room to greet Ilissa.

Tyrus knew the cause of Erejzan's hesitation. So did
Jathelle. Rof pursed his lips, following Erejzan's frus-
trated glances at Ilissa. At times the shape-changer's
curse had been a tool which served them against the
Death God's pets and saved lives. Now it was a bane.
Chagrined, Erejzan could not bring himself to alter his

nature, even to kill Aubage. If he did, Ilissa would see him as the beast Vraduir had made him.

"Hai! Fihar!"

With no warning but that, Rof tossed his sword to Erejzan. The acrobat snatched it out of the air, hefting the solid Clarique blade, turning the edge toward Aubage.

The moment Rof gave up the weapon, he supplied himself with another from his accumulated store. Still ready to deal with any who would come at him, Rof exhorted Erejzan, "You can kill him as a man would. Do it, acrobat! Finish his whining and bragging. You are far more man than he is, whatever form you take!"

Tyrus crept toward the wall, hanging to the cracks in the stones, forcing himself painfully to his feet. The air seemed vivid with coruscating color and exploded in countless tiny stars. Through the rainbowed space filling the cell, he saw Erejzan advancing, striking with a skilled beat, driving Aubage's sword point aside. Rof was cheering him on, for all his earlier taunts at Erejzan's expense.

Panic seized Aubage and he backed away, sucking in his belly as Erejzan slashed violently at his gut. Frantically, Aubage countered and parried but was out of his element against Erejzan's furious, hacking blows.

"No pretty, courtly contest, this, eh, m'lord?" Rof cried gleefully. "No dancing and bowing or shamming. The fihar is a fighter! Put it through his gullet, Erejzan!"

"Jathelle! Stop them! I beg you!" Ilissa screamed. She would have run forward and thrown herself between the swordsmen. Jathelle restrained her absently, her strength more than a match for the much-abused younger woman. "Jathelle, please! They will kill each other!"

Though Rof was enjoying the battle, it was plain he would not object if that were indeed the outcome. He watched the swordplay with keen appreciation, applauding Erejzan and calling advice whenever Aubage managed to avoid a killing stroke.

Tyrus gritted his teeth until he thought his jaws would crack. The exploding lights divided into two sparkling lines—one green and fiery white and the other an ugly black. Tyrus thrust at Vraduir's magic and hurled it back, first in one place and then in another. Age was matched against youthful determination, desperate pride with righteous anger.

But part of Tyrus' consciousness was his again as he followed Erejzan's attempt to wipe out Aubage's insults with blood. "Stop . . . it!" he roared through his charms and counter spells. "Stop! Vraduir . . ."

The warning was costly. As he took breath to speak, Vraduir's wizardry overcame Tyrus' at two critical points. The walls of the cell started to move apart. A massive stone block dropped from the ceiling and landed directly between Aubage and Erejzan. It came so close to crushing them both that Erejzan's sword was smashed out of his hands and Aubage's cloak pinned under the block, ripped from his shoulders as he squirmed out of the way.

Jathelle instantly swept Ilissa tightly in her arms, pulling the smaller woman with her, running toward Tyrus and seeking his protection. He braced himself against the heaving wall, battered by far more than the crumbling stones.

In the doorway, the lintel suddenly collapsed, and with it came the staircase beyond. Rof dived into the room, rolling to evade the descending storm of stone and brick.

Erejzan and Aubage gaped at the ceiling and walls in fright and confusion. Sorcery overwhelmed reality and became hopelessly entangled. Walls and floor and ceiling had life, hopping about ludicrously and popping forth birthlings of rock or timber, showering these on those in the cell.

Jathelle knelt by Tyrus and covered Ilissa's head. Then, struck by inspiration, she left Ilissa in Tyrus' sole care for a space of a few heartbeats, scurrying through the falling debris, retrieving the enchanted sword. She hastened back, once more enfolding Ilissa in her embrace with one arm as she held the sword out, seeking an enemy to fight. There was no target for the enchanted blade, though, only the constantly shifting wall stones.

The way they had entered was now hopelessly blocked, filled with the ruins of the staircase and the portal. Tyrus swiveled toward the door opposite. It was still intact, but sealed with magic. He forced his will toward it, cords in his neck taut, sweat streaming. Intuitively Erejzan fathomed what the sorkra was doing and came running, forgetting his hatred for Aubage. He twisted nimbly this way and that as the stones bounced around him. Vraduir sought his death and the massive stones were missiles!

"Rof! Aubage! To me!" the acrobat cried. "We have to help Tyrus open the door. He is conjuring, but he needs our weight as well!"

Jathelle dared not leave Illissa again. The younger woman was too distraught to protect herself, and Tyrus was focussing his being on the locked portal. But she added her voice to Erejzan's. "We have to escape from here. Tyrus has found the way. Help him! *Help him!* Rof, your new master is a treacherous demon! He will kill you with the rest of us! Where is your reward now? You cannot buy your way free of this!"

As suddenly as he had been bought on the frozen plain, Rof turned his coat again. He was as lithe in spirit as Erejzan was in body. "Reason is yours, La-Renya! Sorkra-y! By Bogotana, I am sorry I ever dealt with the wizard kind!"

He danced out of the way as a ceiling timber tumbled
down the length of the room. Ilissa shrieked, some of
her long hair snagged by the splintery beam. Ruthlessly,
Jathelle severed the tresses with the enchanted sword.
She sacrificed Ilissa's beautiful hair without hesitation.
Shorn, but otherwise unhurt, Ilissa flung her arms about
Jathelle's neck. Together they edged toward the door.
Then Jathelle saw that Tyrus was not moving from
his place and guessed, "He cannot stir. Everything is
magic. Ilissa, with me!"

Tyrus raked with his mind, ripping with frenzy at a
descending mesh none but him could see. To Jathelle
and the others, he was rigid and staring at nothing, his
eyes glittering with peculiar fire. Yet to Tyrus the
world teemed with colors he could not name and traps
springing into existence from the realms of bright webs,
bottomless chasms, and things of sorcery. He saw two
worlds—the world of Vraduir's magical assault and
his own valiant defense, and the world of the collaps-
ing cell, with his friends and Rof and Aubage trapped
inside. Some of the falling stones were illusions. But
some were real—and his companions had no method of
knowing which stones were deadly and which could
do them no hurt.

"To . . . to the left," he heard himself say, his voice
seeming to come from beyond the Death God's lands,
so faint was it. There were hands touching him, wom-
en's hands, two pairs, girdling his waist, tugging at
his tunic and cloak and arms. He was being pulled,
forcibly led toward the door opposite. Erejzan and
Rof were already there, locking Rof's axe and sword
into a lever to give them more purchase on the bars.
They leaned on the barrier and Tyrus felt his energy
swell, gaining strength, more than matching Vraduir's.

"Aubage? This way!" Jathelle's shout was hollow,
echoing erratically through Tyrus' mind.

Laboriously, he craned his neck, peering through

sparkling lights into the cell, seeing Aubage. The noble-man had not moved since he lost his cloak under the ceiling stone. Dumbfounded, he stared at the dis-solving walls. His face was empty, witless.

"Left . . ." Tyrus mouthed. Then the door gave way a bit more under his efforts and those of Erejzan and Rof. "Left . . . avoid the stones to the right," Tyrus managed to warn them.

"That side is loosening!" Rof exclaimed, grunting. "On your side! Now, shape-changer! Push hard!"

Erejzan did not answer, ramming his full weight on the point of his shoulder, heedless of pain. The door shook on unseen hinges and Tyrus drove his will into the gap, opening the portal still wider. Rof whooped in excitement. Then he too struck the door with his shoulder on his side as Erejzan repeated his attack.

Vraduir's magic locks burst with a sound of shatter-ing glass and a rain of black sparks. This time the others saw the proof of sorcery as well as Tyrus; in failure Vraduir's enchantments were revealed to the mortal world, the mask of wizardry torn away as the spell collapsed.

Rof and Erejzan fell over the threshold. Then Erej-zan quickly turned and held out his hands to the women. "If you are LaRenya's man again, help me!" he demanded of Rof. Belatedly, Rof obeyed. Erejzan grabbed Tyrus and dragged his friend through the newly-created portal. Tyrus was still gripped by sorkra, holding Vraduir at bay, unable to initiate much action or speech.

"Aubage . . ."

For all he had said, Ilissa still feared for her erstwhile lover. She looked back, calling to him weakly. Erejzan picked her up and carried her to a safer spot beyond the broken door and Jathelle willingly relinquished her sister's care to him.

Tyrus now was past the worst of Vraduir's focus, and

as Vraduir paused to collect fresh magic after losing the door, Tyrus spared his own energies to look where Ilissa was gazing. He shouted to the terrified courtier, "Go to your left, Aubage. To the left! You . . . you can make it!"

There could be no glamour, as Tyrus had used it previously. Vraduir had penetrated that device. They were wizard warriors, each knowing the other's shield and weapons, a deadly balance.

"Left! Go left!" Tyrus repeated urgently.

Aubage roused from his stupor at last, his lip curling in a sneer. "You would lead me amiss, conjurer. You want Jathelle for yourself! A pact was made. I will not be tricked, by you or her." With calculation, he stepped to his right, heading toward the door.

Illusionary stones crashed thunderously along his left. They seemed to shake the floor, crushing furnishings—or was that but an illusion also? Tyrus narrowed his eyes, seeing a shimmer behind the place where the stones had broken chairs and the bed, seeing the wood and fabric still intact. Illusion—all illusion, there!

But to the right the rain was far less, and Aubage ran along that side, keeping his sword out in case Erejzan attacked him again. Though Tyrus' vision was clear, matters still appeared to move slowly. The ceiling brace was coming loose, falling with feathery lightness, falling . . .

Aubage ceased running, walking at leisure, cocky, heedless of the threat. Malicious triumph ruled him. "I knew you had lied . . . again!" he crowed.

And then the toppling brace buried him amid the rubble.

Ilissa's scream was a knife, piercing Tyrus' sick horror, shifting his view of the world into normal speed. The grief-stricken princess beat on Erejzan's chest with her tiny fists, weeping and crying that they must return and help Aubage. Then she saw what the others al-

ready had seen—a spreading puddle of blood beneath
the collapsed brace, too much blood for any man to
lose and survive. With a pathetic sigh, Ilissa went limp
in Erejzan's arms, sinking into merciful unconscious-
ness. Erejzan lifted her, holding her close.

Jathelle jammed a hand against her mouth to choke
back her vomit and Tyrus hastily motioned to Erejzan.
He took Jathelle, forcing her ahead of him up the
staircase beyond the door. "Quickly, before Vraduir
can overturn these stones!"

Rof squirmed past them, taking the steps three at a
time. "Magic!" he panted. "No trusting it!"

More stones were falling, but most were illusions.
Tyrus shunted them aside angrily, dimly aware that
they were melting into nothingness as Vraduir's aims
were foiled. The staircase was cramped, spiraling up
and up, retracing that route, through the darkness, out
of the depths. Tyrus conjured lights to fight cold and
black, reaching the corners of his arts for more power.

As they reached the top of the steps, they found all
corridors leading south blocked by fallen stones, and
most of those were real. It became apparent why Vraduir had relaxed his striving to crush them. He had
worked a different tactic, shutting them off from any
chance of retreat. Tyrus shook his head in amazement.
"That effort strained his wizardry much," he said.

Jathelle was rallying, a bit of color coming back to
her ashen cheeks. Ilissa was coming to herself and
Jathelle fussed over her tenderly. With some reluctance,
Erejzan set the LaSirin on her feet and he and Jathelle
supported her. Of them all, Erejzan was the least
winded, even though he had carried Ilissa up the full
length of the long staircase. Rof's breath came out in
frosty gusts as he declared, "This is the last time I ever
bind my cause to a sorkra, mark me!"

"You have no choice henceforth." Tyrus was amused
despite their grim dilemma. He pointed to the blocked

passageways. "That is the route to the gates. He has pinned you along with us, bandit lord. Decide which wizard to follow and keep to the bargain, for once."

Rof chuckled. "So I will. What an army we are!"

"We can expect no help but our own. If any of your men or Jathelle's live, they cannot get through that barricade in time to aid us," Tyrus said. The wall stones about them rumbled and Tyrus muttered in grudging admiration, "Still strong. Deeper into the citadel. He is trying to box us there."

"And will we play his deadly game, Tyrus?" Jathelle asked fearfully. But she was helping Ilissa, following Tyrus with the rest. "He drives us. And you take us where he wishes us to go?"

"Where we must go! We shall see who hunts and who is hunted!"

They hurried up and down small flights of steps and through twisting halls, always moving away from the gates and the depths where Ilissa's cell was buried. Ilissa was still dazed. A dreamwalker, she dragged her feet and leaned on Jathelle and Erejzan by turns. Tyrus could not help them with this. He was gathering, walking in two halls, real and unreal, anticipating what must come. All their beings were weighed in the scales of the gods.

"His sanctuary," Tyrus said to himself, uncaring if the others were listening. "The innermost chamber, where he has reared an altar to Nidil. He wants us just outside the barred doors at his whim, his slaves, where we must await his judgment."

"Does he?" Rof said with sudden heat. "And what of your will, sorkra?"

"Equal to Vraduir's," Erejzan broke in.

Grateful for the praise, Tyrus tempered that warily. "So I believe. So we will discover the truth. Gods of Clarique—help me!"

Stones shivered and rock dust sifted down from the

disturbed ceilings of the halls, chastening reminders of Aubage's fate. Tyrus wasted little energy fending off the rain, wanting no delay, not even at the risk of letting Vraduir marshal some of his sorcery. He was not surprised when imps and specters took form before them, materializing from the icy dust. As they had done on the plain, they held out gems and gold and silver and sought to hire Rof's loyalty. The brilliance of sham treasure warred with the bobbing lights Tyrus used to lead them.

"Bandit lord! Riches! Riches from earth and sea! Riches to make you Renya of Brigands, master of all things . . ."

Rof took an axe from his belt and slashed through the specters' bony hands and scattered the false gold and jewels. "Go back to your wily wizard kind! His bribes are lies, like his promises!"

Jathelle said cynically, "Are you lessoned at last, Rof? Or will you come at our backs when you may?"

Shameless, Rof exclaimed, "Not till a far safer reward is offered me, LaRenya. In a war of sorkra-y, I must gamble with him who will spare me."

The corridor widened, and this hall was lined with guttering torches. Tyrus extinguished all but one of his magic lights but kept that in reserve, distrusting Vraduir. It was not unlikely Vraduir would snuff the torches, if he thought that would confuse his victims. Tyrus had done this same trick often and knew it well. It would be a petty harassment, and yet . . .

They rounded a curve in the hall and Tyrus staggered. He was braced and ready, but the awesomeness of Vraduir's wrath took him off balance. At the end of the corridor were immense doors, hingeless and without any latch, as those barring Ilissa's cell had been. Ahead of the five, filling the length-wide passageway, were hordes of man-things, demons, and imps. All these were slinking, creeping, flying . . . toward Tyrus and his companions!

"Tyrus . . . ?"

"Real!" Tyrus warned his companions. "The Death God's beings and Vraduir's true slaves!" He clutched his head, fighting crumbling walls at their back and the locked door ahead. "Vraduir! Inside! It is the last . . . last barrier!"

The opposing army of hideous creatures launched at them. Jathelle and Erejzan pushed Ilissa down against the wall opposite Tyrus and met the first wave of monsters. Rof was nearly borne down by a wave of the fiends. Stabbing and cursing, he wriggled free. Erejzan ran to help him, tossing aside a red-eyed golhi that was about to disembowel the brigand. Sparing no breath on thanks, Rof handed the acrobat his axe to replace the sword lost in Ilissa's cell.

Tyrus lifted his hands, gesturing, magic flowing from his fingers and his mind.

Vraduir! He could *see* him! The doors separated them, but Tyrus beheld his sire, standing directly on the other side of that barricade! Like Tyrus, Vraduir's hands were raised, conjuring with all his might.

There was another presence, hovering, coalescing, coming upon them with inexorable force—gray and omnipotent and beyond wizardry . . .

"Slay them! Drink their blood! Slay them all!" Vraduir was chanting. He mixed his vengeance with cold sorkra incantations, spells most terrible. He called upon things forbidden, as when he first sought to beguile the Fire God himself.

"Not Qamat," Tyrus said tensely. "Not ever again!" He slumped on the wall, his limbs quivering as his will met Vraduir's in headlong combat. Charm matched charm and sorcery balanced sorcery. "Not ever again. The door! We . . . must . . . breach . . . that . . . door!"

"We cannot get *to* it!" Jathelle wailed. She was

covered with the ichor and splattered brains of the demons she had slain, but still hacked and lashed murderously with the enchanted sword. The battle maiden proved her courage with every breath and blow, fiery in her desire to reach her sister's defiler. Ilissa cowered behind her, her eyes wide and bewildered. Then, as ice snakes slithered between Jathelle's legs and hissed and spat at Ilissa, the beautiful LaSirin reacted. Pent-up rage exploded and she seized a snake behind its hideous head, holding it from her throat.

Erejzan raced to her, hurling the other serpents into pulp on the wall stones. Jathelle leaned down, pressing a dagger into Ilissa's fingers; with surprising strength, Ilissa killed the snake attacking her.

"Hai, little one! We are one blood!" Jathelle shouted. "We will win!"

Rof was skidding on ichor he had spilled, dancing comically, all his fighting skills in play even so. He tried to use his whip, but a scaly winged demon had bit the tough leather in two, nearly taking Rof's good hand with it. He artfully flipped his sword over into his left and went at the brute, spearing its wing until Jathelle's enchanted sword took its life. "Bogotana, they are spawnings of earth's guts!"

The air burst with incandescence and everyone could see the clash of wizardry. Tyrus' will collided with Vraduir's above their heads, drenching them in gouts of cold flame and miniature stars. An arrow shaped of green light sprang from Tyrus' brow and eyes and stabbed at the distant door. Halfway there, Vraduir countered with a shield of black wizardry. Arrow butted shield again and again, a silent siege, each blow jolting Tyrus to the very marrow.

He felt himself sliding to his knees, held up only by his shoulder upon the wall.

Ahead, the doors were holding, but the arcane nature

of them was becoming transparent and tenuous. Ilissa pointed and cried in dread, "It is the enemy!"

Vraduir was visible through the doors!

He was on his knees, as Tyrus was, shuddering as the wizard arrow rammed against his barriers. So far away, Tyrus should not have been able to see such details, yet everything was strikingly clear. Sweat poured from Vraduir's fair hair and down his shaven jaw, staining his kingly garments. Tyrus felt that strain in every sinew, a mate for his own near exhaustion.

A beam fell from a wall strut, almost hitting Ilissa. Jathelle and Erejzan leaped to pull her out of the way, then wheeled to cope with a new wave of demons and beasts.

"Cannot . . ." Tyrus gasped. "Door . . . must get to the door . . ."

Rof did not break the pattern of his cutting and thrusting, but he called wearily to Erejzan, "We are done, shape-changer."

"No!" Erejzan looked at Ilissa, fury in his eyes. The women were bitten and bruised and bleeding, suffering as imps and monsters evaded their weapons and struck.

With sudden decision, Erejzan thundered, "Not done yet, Rof. I will take them. Get to the door. Help Tyrus!"

Deliberately, he accepted the curse Vraduir had put upon him. Heedless of witnesses and his shame, Erejzan changed before their eyes. In an instant, that powerful, furred body, clad in rags of torn garments, was springing at the foremost of the demons, rending them with fang and claw.

The Death God's pets and Vraduir's slaves were dangerous but dull of wit, made to kill, not to think. They had been made to affright humankind and not other beasts, and particularly not a beast that fought with a man's cunning.

The noise was terrible, a mad tangle of keenings

and yowls and screeches, as Erejzan snapped bone and ripped flesh and scale and leathery wings.

After a heartbeat's shocked staring, Jathelle and Rof waded into the fray close behind the shape-changer, striving to help the man-ecar. Tyrus crept along the wall, his fingers half-numb and bleeding as he clung to the frosty stones. Without pause, he countered Vraduir. The vision beyond the door—no, *through* it!—pulsated and glowed alarmingly. His magic and Vraduir's were warping the very existence of the citadel.

The floor ran with stinking ichor, and there was Erejzan's blood mixed with it as well. Rof seized the beam that had almost struck Ilissa and dragged it forward, matching pace with Tyrus. Jathelle stayed with Erejzan and was his ally, finishing brutes he dragged down or crippled. Ilissa crawled in her wake and she too found courage and dealt many a blow with the dagger.

Imps and demons tried to escape the shape-changer by scrambling up wall stones. Erejzan leapt for them with lithe ease, batting them down with murderous paws and sending them to Jathelle's enchanted blade. The magic which cursed him and which transformed the sword dealt death again and again.

"Door . . . door," Tyrus moaned, an entreaty he could not be certain anyone had heard.

But they had. Rof waded through severed heads and limbs and butchered tentacles, avoiding Erejzan's swath of destruction. He could barely lift the makeshift ram, but he propelled it as hard as he could against Vraduir's wavering image. The door, now totally transparent at the center, blocked the way. The impact made Rof lose his grip on the beam for a moment. The boom reverberated through the corridor, drowning the gibbers and screams briefly.

Rof gulped and heaved the beam up to his shoulder

once more, then rammed the barrier. Sparks flew, scatterings of ensorceled wood and ice.

Tyrus progressed by measures of a finger, a hand, and then the length of his forearm. Winning! Moving! Forward! He felt bloodless, his belly a pool drained dry, his lips cracking and no spittle to wet them. Yet he was heartened. "Again!" he begged Rof. "Again!"

The brigand's beard and proud mustaches were drooping and his clothes were in ichor-stained tatters. But he obeyed, and Jathelle helped him. The demons were slain, and she somehow got her slender arms about the bulky beam and lifted the far end. Together the LaRenya of Couredh and the bandit lord ran through slime and blood, smashing the ram into the unseen door.

There was a strange, soundless explosion full of materials unknown in the mortal world. Tyrus had been pressing with all his might against the immovable barrier—immovable, but he was moving it!

And it gave way. Drunkenly, he reeled forward, almost sprawling his length, clutching the door jamb for support.

The doors were gone, crumbled into air, the magic that had made them vanquished. Rof knelt on the threshold, sucking in air in wheezing gulps, his hands still locked around the beam. Jathelle lay across the other end of the ram, gazing around in astonishment. Then she turned and sought anxiously for Ilissa.

The LaSirin was close by, on hands and knees, moving through the charnel house that had been a corridor. No imp or demon or hideous beast stayed her. All were slain or fled. Jathelle watched her sister in wonderment, then her expression shifted, warm with compassion.

Ilissa sat beside a huddled form lying amid the dead army of demons. Erejzan was changing back to a man again, his terrible task complete. The acrobat was bleeding severely from tens of wounds, his eyes bright with shock and pain. His clothes were gone, torn in his shape-changing and the combat. Too hurt to move, he could not even hide his nakedness.

Tyrus stumbled toward him, leaning over his friend, squeezing Erejzan's shoulder. A hint of a smile twisted the wounded man's mouth. Ilissa was wrapping Erejzan in Jathelle's cloak and gently caressing his brow. "You have saved me again, Erejzan," she whispered. Then she bent down and kissed the one spot on his face that was not bruised, cut, or abraded. His smile widened at that. Ilissa's small hands became dabbled with Erejzan's blood as she began to staunch his hurts. She did not seem to notice.

Much affected, Tyrus brushed Erejzan's hair, and the shape-changer said weakly, "For . . . for Qamat . . . and for Ilissa . . . finish him, Tyrus."

New strength and determination surged through Tyrus' body and mind. "Ai! I shall! Revenge is ours, mai fiyel."

He strode into Vraduir's sanctuary. It was the chamber he had seen in the vision-glass. Now it was real, a windowless hall, vast, the ceiling lofty. There were other doors, through which slaves had arrived and exited on Vraduir's errands, as Tyrus had seen in the glass. All doors save the one he had broken were still closed. By ordinary bars and latches, or by magic? It was a wizard's lair—and a god's altar room.

Vraduir was there, badly disoriented by this setback. He was scrabbling painstakingly toward an immense stone altar which sat in the room's center. Alien fire, without sound or heat, burned on the sacred table. Vraduir reached the foot of the altar and groveled, murmuring incantations to protect himself. From what? From Tyrus? Or from the wrath of the divine presence whose citadel this was?

Above, a shape was gathering, looming, a thing blotting out Tyrus' view of the cavernous ceiling and

the darkness in the high corners. It was rising, rising . . .
human and bird and beast all in one, incomprehensible.

Nidil, the Death God, He Who Steals All Breath,
came into his citadel. He was always here, yet he had
not been here while the battle from the gates to Ilissa's
cell to the doors of the sanctuary had raged. Now, in
his fearsome majesty, he was the presence Tyrus had
sensed in the vision-glass, grown in power a thousand-
fold and more.

He was clad in gray cold. As he arrived from those
immortal regions where only gods might go, he brought
with him a sweet, sickly odor of decay and life long
lost. Nidil was Death, the god everyone must face but
none would hurry to find. With chill, merciless interest,
those black, fathomless orbs that might be eyes peered
out of the seething cloud, lowering toward the humans,
impaling them with a stare.

XVII

The Bargain Fulfilled

❊❊❊❊❊❊❊❊❊❊❊❊❊❊❊❊❊❊❊❊❊❊

THERE WAS A VOICE. BUT IT WAS *not* A VOICE. THE
gigantic lips did not move. They heard his words,
though, a thrill within their minds, awesome power
probing their innermost beings.

"Who are you who come into my citadel?"

Tyrus sensed what he must do. In every thing, he
must be Vraduir's master, not only in sorcery but in
common wit. If not, the world and their lives were
gone. "We are the enemies of Vraduir," he said, surprised at his audacity.

"Vraduir is my servant," the Death God said, a
rumbling that made Tyrus' bones shudder with cold.

"I *am* your most loyal servant, O Puissant Lord of
Death!" Vraduir exclaimed hurriedly. He heaved himself up to his feet, leaning on the altar. Radiant shards
of the magic door bespattered his tunic and breeches.
His hair was tousled and wild. He pointed malevolently
at Tyrus and the others. "They are truly my enemies,
Lord Nidil. Mine and yours! Take their lives, for they
defile your sanctuary!"

Jathelle came forward and stood by Tyrus. The enchanted sword hung slack in her nerveless fingers as she

330

looked upon the god. But she faced him bravely, and Vraduir with hatred. "Nidil! He Who Steals All Breath! We did not come to defile your altar. We came to end Vraduir's blasphemy and treachery!" Jathelle said loudly, interrupting Vraduir's tirade. "We reverence Nidil and the gods. It is Vraduir we want. Only Vraduir!"

"You are intruders! Invaders! It is *you* who blaspheme!" Vraduir said. "Strike them, Lord of Death!"

Tyrus felt an opening in the web of sorcery. Vraduir had poured vast quantities of his skills into weaving the magic doors and in ordering up the demons and the Death God's pets who had threatened the invaders. Now the door was broken, and he was trapped. Very much on guard, Tyrus wondered what spell Vraduir would try next. There was a chink in the master wizard's armor—or was it a ruse to trick his son into a fatal attempt against the enemy?

For now, Vraduir beseeched the god, begging Nidil to slay his enemies and end Vraduir's peril for him. Then there would be no need to call further on his arts.

Ruse or not, it was a weakness in the wall Tyrus must dare. He shielded his mind from Vraduir's constant lancing search and readied himself to attack.

Father and son looked at one another. Mere lengths separated them. A few lengths . . . and the entire meaning of magic and decency. The cold fire was a moving curtain behind Vraduir, highlighting his golden hair and kingly features. Once he *had* been a king, until his son became his equal. And then . . .

Time was crawling once more. Time, eddying around them, ripples at the fringes of sorcery, a battle rejoined anew. Time filled with grief and pain and shattered love.

Qamat—serene, prosperous, loyal, the realm of a wizard-king and his pious queen.

Time crawled, and the good queen was taken to

Keth's holy portals. Bereaved, the king took no carnal solace for a long while, then only with such women as were pleased to sell their favors for a king's generosity. The king occupied himself with rule and with sorcery, teaching his young son as the boy grew into his gifts.

Time, and dangerous sorceries were found, a rivalry born, a rivalry the boy sorcerer had not meant to create. Ambition and fear, fear of age and death that had taken his queen and would take the king himself and leave his son to his throne. Sorcery was his weapon, delving secrets locked from humankind—for wise reasons!—since remembering had begun.

Time, and rebellion, a courageous young clan son, the king's own beastmaster, challenging the king's unholy experiments. And the king's son learning, late, demanding—and taking the blow unfairly dealt.

Time. And Tyrus was confronting Vraduir, as in that time more than a year past. Love and devotion broke over the truth. This was not the man he had known. As Vraduir sought forbidden knowledge, his very nature had altered, far more than the curse altered Erejzan. A gulf yawned between father and son, forever, as deep as the waters rolling where Qamat had been. Unprepared, once Tyrus had entered his father's sanctuary and spoken of Erejzan's imprisonment, of the wicked things Vraduir was doing. He had hoped to warm that ember of pity he thought remained in Vraduir's heart. Instead, there was cold, cold like Nidil's embrace. As he pleaded for Erejzan's freedom and a repentance of the awful experiments, Vraduir had struck, and Erejzan had a companion in that unnatural cell within the rock.

"I will not plead." Tyrus realized he had spoken without intending to do so. Since it was done, he said it again, with emphasis. "I will not plead with you ever again. I am far older and wiser now. I know I cannot touch you. You slew that which was Vraduir and gave

yourself to evil. You enchanted me and cast me away.
So shall it be. I am my mother's son but I am no
longer yours."

"Ah! Your son, my servant Vraduir?" the omnipotent voice rattled in their minds. When Nidil addressed one of them, they all heard, with brain and with
soul. Tyrus could not look squarely upon that churning
shape in the ice smoke. From the corner of his eye, he
studied the god, pondering what might convince Nidil
to heed his arguments.

"He . . . he *is* my son, O Great One," Vraduir admitted reluctantly. *"Was* my son. I showed him pity.
I let him live, thinking he would learn to know his
folly, that I was his better. But he raised sorcerous
weapons against me. Me who taught him! Now he is
my mortal enemy!"

Tyrus would have laughed in bitterness. Pity? Was
that why Vraduir had not killed him and Erejzan outright? Not pity. Pride. They were the spirit of Qamat,
his son and he who would be next clan chieftain of the
island people. Vraduir had assumed they would cease
fighting him, come to adore him and honor his blasphemy. And this he called pity, that he had cursed
them and spared their lives to earn their frightened
worship!

"Yet he is your son," Nidil said. "And you have
sworn to take each other's lives. Interesting." If Nidil
was interested in this terrible conflict, it was in a way
no human could understand. A thread of amusement
ran through his words. "So often is man's seed his joy
and his sorrow. You should have joy that your son
learned so well, my servant Vraduir. Here is a most
impressive sorkra. He bested you many times in his
quest and has broken your doors, your every barrier.
Is this not so?"

"Trickery, Lord of Death. I wanted him to come
here," Vraduir said quickly. He glanced at Tyrus. Was

there a suggestion of regret in his eyes? Tyrus did not—
could not—believe that. His memories were scars that
would never quite heal. Vraduir had looked at him this
way once before, a moment ere he cast the dark spell
which bound his son in the prison rock, chaining
Tyrus' sorcery while Vraduir continued his experiments
with Bogotana's powers.

Regret, a flickering remnant of the man Vraduir had
been. Regret drowned in envy of Tyrus' youth and
strength and ability.

"Trickery, my servant Vraduir?" Again there was
that thread of chilling amusement. Nidil was laughing
at these puny mortals and their games of life and death.
"These others are not sorkra. Why are they here?"

Vraduir glared with undisguised contempt at Erejzan. "That one in the doorway is a former subject of
mine, Lord of Death. He dared rebel against my rule."

"Against your heartless tyranny!" Tyrus hotly defended his friend. "Against rituals that enchanted brutes
and made them demons."

"He was my subject, my beastkeeper! He had no
right to speak so rashly to the traech sorkra of Qamat!"
Vraduir shrilled. "He is a beast himself, as I have made
him, with Bogotana's favor. The form suits his animal
temper." Vraduir peered at Ilissa, who was still tending
Erejzan's hurts and paying Vraduir no attention. Nor
did Erejzan seem to hear him. Uneasy, Vraduir turned
away, focussing on Jathelle. "And she . . ."

"I am LaRenya of Couredh," Jathelle announced,
taking the words from his mouth. "This evil wizard
invaded my realm, using your skeleton warriors to steal
my sister and wound and slay many of my people.
I have come to see him punished, Lord of Death. That
is my right!"

"She does not like you, my servant Vraduir." A
sepulchral chuckle sent jagged waves through Tyrus'
mind.

"She is no longer in her realm," Vraduir said, cleverly shifting the attack from himself to Jathelle. "She is
in *your* realm now, Lord of Death. You alone may
choose or have rights *here*."

"So I will. And that dark man there?"

"Him?" Vraduir's gaze skipped over Rof. "An insolent braggart, of no importance, Lord Nidil . . ."

"Bogotana shrivel you, accursed wizard. I am Rof
of the bandits." Rof had apparently made up his mind
to die with bravado, if he must. Arms akimbo and feet
firmly planted, a bloody weapon in each hand, Rof
shouted, "You know me well, sorcerer. It was you who
sent the Death God's minions to hire me away from
LaRenya and your son, hire me with treasure made of
dust and rock. No fair bargain, that. And then you
tried to slay me."

"No dust, this," Vraduir said, negligently gesturing.
An emerald of startling luster appeared on his palm.
"I have the arts, bandit. You will enjoy them, if you
come back to me. Kill my son and these others and
we shall rule all the provinces together. I will make
you my warlord when I am lord of Tyta'an. Or would
you prefer your own little realm, to be my viceroy?
Krantin, perhaps? That blood is in your veins, I guess."

"And it taught me never to trust a liar twice," Rof
said. He grinned as if daring Vraduir to strike. "I am
a liar myself and admire a good one, and you are the
best. You would not let me keep that emerald long,
nor my life. Bogotana take you to the depths with the
emerald, sorcerer."

Vraduir spread his hands and the emerald twinkled
out of existence. He grimaced, his bribery dashed to
the earth by a rude peasant. "I withdraw my offer,
then. They are all yours, Lord of Death, sacrifices, as
I promised you. Even that noisy brigand is a sacrifice,
though of poor quality, I fear. Let them join the other

precious things and be their attendants, the harper, the stallion, the crown . . ."

Nidil had been listening. It was impossible to be sure, but it might be that the god was on the verge of deciding their fates. The time that was spinning through Tyrus' memories stopped. Life, too, would stop, if he did not act. With tremendous force, he shot gathered sorkra power against Vraduir, catching his father as the elder wizard started to speak further to the god.

Such a simple trick, the first Vraduir had taught him, so many seasons ago. A boy sorcerer's magic. Vraduir would have disdained it, thinking it beneath him. Tyrus did not, willing to use whatever would win.

As he had stopped Aubage's tongue, now he gagged Vraduir. The charm was immeasurably more potent than that he had used against the dead courtier, of course. Vraduir was no foppish young lord, but the most deadly wizard who had ever been born.

Incredulous, Vraduir grappled with an unseen device fastened snugly over his mouth. He had protected himself with countercharms against far more intricate assaults, but he had not expected such a direct and plain enchantment. He was marshalling his will to master Tyrus' spell, though. Tyrus must speak fast or lose his chance.

Vraduir's eyes bulged with fury as he twisted this way and that and fought the gag. Distracted by the main problem, he allowed still another chink to open in his magic, an opening Tyrus rushed through. With another sharp gesture, Tyrus rooted Vraduir's feet in place. This would preoccupy his foe a bit longer and keep Vraduir where he stood, slowing his return to full speech and movement.

"Hetanya go with you," Jathelle prayed, knowing what Tyrus intended. She clasped his hand in hers, giving her heart and strength to his.

Tyrus said soberly, "I must hurt us still more. But it is the only way I can succeed."

Trusting him, Jathelle nodded, ready to endure whatever might come. Slowly, with a lingering touch, Tyrus released her hand and approached the altar. The cold which held them all was thickening his blood and breath. He steeled his will, looking into the boiling cloud, his gorge rising at the constant stench of decay and corruption.

"Nidil, Death God . . ."

"Son of Vraduir." Nidil was laughing, a heavy, divine wave of pressure, chilling as the air. The reason for his mirth became obvious as he went on, "I Am He Who Steals All Breath, but you have stolen Vraduir's breath, and his tongue. Vraduir said he played you with trickery and was your master always. I think his game has gone awry."

"It has, Lord of Death. But Vraduir will not care, if he wins what he has bargained for. He *has* bargained with you, I know. It is his way. He treated thus with mighty Bogotana," Tyrus said. He wished he had time to choose his words more carefully. So much hung on what he said!

"Bogotana is not so mighty," Nidil retorted. "He terrifies you mortals. But it is *I* who takes you from life. That is my realm."

"Indeed! Or it was, until Vraduir lusted for your prerogative." Vraduir flailed wildly, choking in his helplessness. His rage was Tyrus' weapon. Under most circumstances, Vraduir would have calmed himself and concentrated to break the charm. His fury and his fear were so great that they rattled his wits, to Tyrus' benefit. All too soon, though, he would likely come to his senses and be free.

"My prerogative? What say you, son of Vraduir?"

"The ability to control life and stand off death. Is this not what Vraduir begs for? He envies your power."

Tyrus spoke earnestly, his thoughts racing. "It is because of this he has brought you sacrifices from throughout Clarique, treasures locked in those cages . . ."

"They are mine," Nidil said with a hint of petulant possessiveness.

Vraduir was rallying, thrusting against Tyrus' spell, each shock jolting his son. Tyrus maintained his position. "And in exchange, he would be your ally, Lord of Death. He has used your realm, your Ice Forest and forbidden lands and their beasts, your armies of the damned and lost to attack us. *Yours,* Lord of Death, not his. But he wants them to be his, his minions and subjects, as would be all humankind. He has lied to you, however. Such pride! How well I know it! Only Vraduir would be so bold as to cheat Nidil or covet the sacrifices he promised to the Death God."

"How am I deceived, son of Vraduir?"

"Aaar! Aaar . . . !" Vraduir had one foot free and part of the gag torn away. His eyes burned and one hand went out, sending streaks of sorcery at Tyrus.

With a fragile portion of his skill, Tyrus fended these off, ducking others that got through his shields. The streaks seared along his flesh and gashed at his ice-encrusted clothes while he hurried to finish his conversation with the god. "He cheated you! He kept a promised sacrifice for himself. And now it cannot be given to you. The sacrifice is flawed and no longer perfect. Vraduir despoiled it."

The floating black orbs that could be eyes turned from Tyrus to Vraduir. The stare was terrible. Tyrus retreated, even though he was not the target of that ominous gaze. He drew upon his powers anxiously, shunting aside the rest of Vraduir's vicious darts, resisting his flagging strength. They were both nearly spent in this lengthy duel of magic, their wizards' arts lowered to a crucial level.

As Nidil's dark attention fell upon him, Vraduir

abandoned attempts to slay Tyrus with magic. "No! It is not true!" His denial echoed the length of the immense chamber and back again. "He is lying!"

"Father! This is a god! You cannot lie to a god, not again!" Tyrus exclaimed. "Tell the truth. It is your only hope."

"No! He lies! I am ever your loyal servant, Lord of Death! I delivered to you every sacrifice. Every one!" Vraduir said desperately. He clasped his hands in prayer and lay across the altar, peering up at the wavering god-mist.

Once, Tyrus had hoped for pity from Vraduir. Now, strangely, he was the one who pitied. He looked at this spectacle and shuddered. Desire for knowledge and immortality was consuming all that had been Vraduir, all honor and courage of the wizard-king of Qamat. Only a shell was left, a shell reeking with envy and lust, and with Vraduir's still-awesome sorkra gifts.

Morosely, Tyrus turned toward the broken door. Jathelle trembled and anticipated what Tyrus must do. Her pain was his, but there was forgiveness in her eyes ere he struck the blow. "Lord of Death," Tyrus said, "there is the sacrifice Vraduir stole for himself." And he pointed to Ilissa.

Erejzan was clinging to consciousness, his lips moving in voiceless protest at this cruel revelation. Ilissa stiffened, a hurt little fawn. Her lovely face was reddening with shame as Tyrus described her ordeal to the god.

"This woman, a gem among mortals, incomparable in her beauty and innocence—this woman was stolen by your skeleton warriors, Lord of Death. Intended as a sacrifice for you. She was to enter one of your icy cages and be forever yours, perfect in her loveliness, unchanging through eternity. But Vraduir wanted her—wanted *your* sacrifice. He hid her with his magic, here, within your own citadel, sealed behind wizard's locks, a victim of his carnal pleasure." Tyrus took a deep breath, cold air burning his lungs. "He is a man, Lord of Death, not a god, nor fit to be the ally of a god. He yielded to his lust, though he swore to serve you. Instead he used your property and ruined it."

"Tyrus, look out!"

Jathelle's scream came too late. Tyrus fell under Vraduir's weight. Amazed, he realized that his father had attacked him bodily, letting go for an instant all sorcery.

"Betrayed me . . . traitor!" Vraduir howled, slamming the younger man's head against the stones. "Should have smothered you when you were a babe. Never should have taught you . . . taught you . . . ungrateful whelp!"

The blows glanced off Tyrus' jaw and brow, the jabs of a man worn by many candle-periods of the most extreme sorcery, and of a man long unused to physical combat. Vraduir had grown soft in mortal strife, and the lack of practice showed. Tyrus shook off the lights dancing behind his eyes, bringing up his knees and grabbing handfuls of Vraduir's tunic and cloak. Smoothly, he upended his sire and sent the master wizard sailing over his head.

Vraduir landed hard on his back, the wind knocked from him. Tyrus rolled onto his side, getting up, and saw Rof running forward, a knife out and ready to cut Vraduir's throat. Tyrus flung himself into the brigand's path, tripping Rof. They sprawled together, legs tangled, stunned.

"Stay back!" Jathelle ordered. She stepped between Rof and Tyrus as they pushed themselves apart. The point of the enchanted sword was at the bandit's belly. "We will do what Tyrus says."

"This is our chance to kill that—"

Tyrus chopped down sharply with his hands, silencing them both, intent on Vraduir.

The evil wizard had recovered enough breath to plead with the god. "I . . . I am your . . . servant . . . he is my son, Nidil . . . my own son . . . I taught him . . ."

"The woman was promised to me," Nidil said. Death's unshakable embrace was in each throbbing syllable. "She has known your body. There was no mortal joy for her. But you had your will and your desire. It is as your son told me."

Vraduir's face was slack, his urge to match sinew and bone with Tyrus gone. But there was craftiness in his sky-colored eyes.

"I warned you not to lie to a god," Tyrus said. He collected his will and cloaked himself and the others in the last vestiges of his magic, a final barrier, nothing else at his command. Would it be enough? His eyes still hurt and he ached in every muscle. It *must* be enough!

"No more lies. I swear, Lord of Death, no more lies. It is so!" Vraduir groped along the altar, finding purchase, a supplicant very much aware of what was at stake. "I repent my sin most sincerely . . ."

"You lecherous clenru! Repent? You rape my sister and think to wipe away the crime with words?" Jathelle roared, forgetting that Tyrus had cautioned her to be still. He swept her in his arms and held her fast, trying to smother her fury. Jathelle fought, the battle maiden blooded and eager to strike. Tyrus restrained her with difficulty.

Vraduir had not ceased talking during her outburst, seeking to make his peace with the hovering god-smoke. "But . . . but there could be a far better sacrifice, Lord of Death! A much better sacrifice! As incomparable as the woman ere she lost her maidenhead. No other god could own this thing. You would have a matchless prize for one of your cages."

"I am listening, my servant."

That invitation excited Vraduir and made him glib.

He gulped air and pressed his side, nursing hurt ribs. "My son! Behold! A master wizard! A sorkra more skillful than any of our kind! He has even bested *me!* You yourself said it, Great One. He is the most powerful sorkra who ever lived, and he is yours, a most worthy sacrifice."

A lifetime ago, Tyrus would have laughed at the jest. How long he had striven to emulate his wizard sire, copying and learning and trying to please Vraduir with his arts. And Vraduir bade him be humble whenever Tyrus sought praise. No, Vraduir had always said; he was not yet quite the equal of his mentor. In time, perhaps, in time. Until Vraduir was lost to corruption and father and son turned onto separate paths.

Tyrus' strength at last quieted Jathelle, and she controlled her anger. They became as one. She was nodding. Tyrus let her go, facing Vraduir and the god.

"I *am* skilled, Nidil Who Steals All Breath. I do not pretend otherwise. But if I am skilled, it is because I was taught by the master of all wizardry—Vraduir," Tyrus said tonelessly. His gut was a frozen lump and his legs shook with painful spasms. These were the hurts of life, while death hung over them all. No pain, and no pleasure. The end of existence, for them. And . . . immortality for Vraduir?

"He was an apt pupil, true," Vraduir retorted. "So very clever, this son of mine. He . . . why he broke out of my enchantment and got himself and the shapechanger free of a prison when I had thought no mortal could escape the spell. Bogotana himself gave me that shape-changer's enchantment. Yet here they are. As I say, my son is a master wizard . . ."

"But Vraduir never taught me everything he knows." Vraduir was stricken by Tyrus' praise. Tyrus went on calmly, "His last words, when he bound us in that prison, were: 'Foolish cub. You have much to learn before you begin to rival me.'"

Vraduir shook his head, frantic. "I but chastened him to make him modest. *He* is the greater wizard, Lord of Death, greater than I am."

Sickened by the lie, Tyrus said, "If I were the greater sorkra, I could have come against him alone. But I was helped." He glanced with love at Jathelle, Erejzan, and Ilissa. "I needed their help. Without them, I could not have breached Vraduir's doors nor entered the Forbidden Lands nor your citadel, Lord of Death. Yet Vraduir has stood alone against me. The slaves were his minions, magicked by him, acting through his will and without strength of their own. Judge, Lord of Death. Which of us has more power? Only a wizard of peerless gifts could perform the wonders Vraduir has. *I* did not try to harness Bogotana. *I* dare not try to grasp life's secrets and master them. I could not even save my own subjects." Tyrus ached as he spoke that poignant truth. "Look deep into my soul, Lord of Death. Know my grief and helplessness, that I was pent and enchanted while my people died for want of a protector from Bogotana's wrath. Know that if I were the sorcerer Vraduir claims, I would have spent every one of my skills to keep Qamat safe and to prevent Vraduir from making the sacrifices he already has . . ."

"Not me! My son is the true sorkra," Vraduir said. "Take him, and we will reign together, Nidil! I will sacrifice the world to you, all the world, my realm, my kingdom, to work my wizardry. A plan, I have a great plan, new forces, new ways to govern, to build. All the stupidities, and waste put aside. Tyta'an—mine! Every province, laid at your feet, O Great Nidil! My son is the sacrifice you seek, and then we are allied, forever!"

Tyrus could not move. A stunning brilliance engulfed him, an ocean of light that was all the universe and its gods. Jathelle nestled close to him, her silken hair brushing his cheek.

Were they dying? Was this how death felt? Had Nidil taken them in his icy grasp?

He saw himself, and he saw Vraduir. Where? Where were they? How could he see his own form, unless . . .

He was on Qamat, reliving a fateful encounter for the last time. Enchanted, bound, and Vraduir gloating. "If you were not so timid, if you dared to reach for hidden lores, I would have shared. We would rule all, even the gods, even death itself! But you will die, and I will go on to learn death's secret and become its conqueror. I alone have the wisdom, I, the traech sorkra of Qamat, the wizard who will never have an equal!"

The light was ebbing. Tyrus and Jathelle were two beings amid a storm of godlike dimensions. They were on a prominence, tossed between sun and moon. And then the cold and blinding radiance melted, liquid falling from them like water.

A stillness lay over the great chamber. Nidil was waiting in the cold altar fire, a not-shape, a not-voice. Eternal . . . waiting . . .

Tyrus licked dry lips, savoring the ability to move. Jathelle was stirring in his arms, saying faintly, "Ty—Tyrus? What has happened?"

"Bogotana! What struck us?" Rof said, looking around furtively for the vanished unearthly ocean. "Sorkra?"

Then Rof, like Tyrus and Jathelle, stared at the altar. Another crystalline cage now stood before the stone table. It was filled with the same twinkling iridescence as were those in the sacrificial rooms. This cube was not so small as those holding the Hetanya crown or the man-fish's net or the Arniob tapestries, nor so large as that penning Gros-Donaq's sacred stallion. It was suitable for the harper of Atei or for Ilissa, had she been slain. Instead, it held Vraduir.

"Hetanya guard us," Jathelle whispered in horror.

"She does, my own." Tyrus veiled his tear-blurred

eyes in Jathelle's golden hair a long while. Then he steeled his will, looking at the cage once more, his heart bleeding with numberless wounds old and new.

Vraduir was frozen in the act of gesturing, the last wizard's gesture he would ever make, a sorkra's final, magnificent effort to challenge holy powers. His arms were upflung, his head back, his lips parted. As the harper's lovely music had surrounded the cage which imprisoned his mortal form, so Vraduir's arcane words encircled his cube. Endless, futile, meaningful only to another master sorkra such as Tyrus, the words and incantations rang. Spells that had been Vraduir's key to ultimate sorcery swarmed about him.

"My sacrifice," Nidil explained. "The traech sorkra of Qamat is mine. The bargain is fulfilled, as he has wished it. He wanted to fathom the secrets of life and death. With this, he achieves his goal. Now he knows. He understands what no other mortal has learned. He alone possesses it—he and I. Together, we shall share it. Allies. I trust he is content. He will reign here through eternity, my servant Vraduir—my most priceless treasure of all."

XVIII

The Abandoned Citadel

━╫━╫━╫━╫━╫━╫━╫━╫━╫━╫━╫━╫━╫━╫━╫━

TYRUS WAS A PUPPET, WALKING TOWARD VRADUIR'S crystalline cage without will or spirit. Jathelle walked beside him, her victory muted with pain, pain for Tyrus' sake. He stopped at the shimmering cube and gazed at Vraduir.

It was done. The blasphemies, the rivalry gone mad, the sorceries no wizard should have sought—done. The quest ended. Vraduir was sealed away from humanity forevermore. And with Vraduir died the man he once had been, king, sorkra, husband . . . and father.

Tyrus leaned his head, resting his temple against the icy cage and staring into Vraduir's unseeing eyes. Jathelle had respected his agony, but now she pressed his arm gently. "Tyrus, it had to be."

He nodded and said, "I know. The lash of Kida drove him, took his sanity." Tyrus glanced at the god, hoping for proof of this. Had Vraduir been insane? It would be a reason, a forgiveness, and a hope the divine ones might grant the sacrificed wizard a chance at another existence. Nidil gave no reply, imperturbable. Tyrus moaned, "For Vraduir, this was the only escape. He . . . he had to die. Yet I am half slain, too."

346

Jathelle drew him away, not letting him look any more at the cube. "Give yourself measure to heal. We all need that."

Rof shook himself, waking from the dream of that unearthly sea of light. Distracted and restless as a nervous steed, the bandit prowled the length of the chamber, staying close to the walls, as far from Nidil's altar as was possible. Tyrus saw this without curiosity, allowing Jathelle to lead him. Then Ilissa called to them, breaking through his mourning. The LaSirin still crouched beside Erejzan, plainly much concerned for the acrobat. Goaded by her cry, Tyrus and Jathelle ran to them.

Tyrus lifted Erejzan's shoulders, turning his friend's head so that Erejzan could see into the great chamber. He forced himself to speak dispassionately, as if Vraduir were a defeated enemy he had never known and loved. "Qamat is revenged at last," he said softly.

"Ai, it is over . . . over . . ." Erejzan's pallor was alarming. Ilissa had used the acrobat's ruined clothes and panels of her skirt to bind up his worst cuts, but many still showed, seeping and ugly. Tyrus' worry lessened, a trifle, however, when Erejzan looked up at him steadily and said, "I felt it when he . . . when Vraduir died. The curse truly linked my being with his, and now . . ." Erejzan reached out and Tyrus clasped his hand strongly as the injured man said, "I am sorry . . . for you . . ."

Tyrus was swept by emotion, his fingers tightening gratefully about Erejzan's. Behind him, Rof cleared his throat noisily and said, "Do not fret, sorkra. He is too much for those demons to kill. Best tie up some of those gashes, though, ere he turns pale as an Irico."

"Cease your babbling!" Ilissa said with unexpected anger. She laid small fingers upon Erejzan's blood-smeared mouth. "Talk no more. Rest. Pay no attention to that rude fellow. And you, sorkra, ease him back down. You encourage him to move about and make the bleeding worse. I need more bandages. Give me your mantle."

Pleasantly startled by her brusque manner, Jathelle began to assist the younger woman. Tyrus obediently stretched Erejzan his length once more, then unfastened his cloak. He jerked a thumb at Rof. The bandit saw what was needed and shrugged. Amiably he thrust his sword through one of many rents in the fabric, ripping it in pieces. One of these Tyrus wadded into a pillow for Erejzan. The other the women cut into smaller sections, tending to the acrobat's wounds.

"Women are skilled at this sort of thing," Rof said. "The healers of my people are always the women." He prodded at a nasty cut on his thigh, as if debating whether to ask for nursing by the royal sisters. "Fah!" he said. "Cast one of your spells, sorkra, to be sure this will not poison me, and I am content."

"I will, in a moment," Tyrus assured him. He had almost forgotten he still carried the pack under his arm. Hastily, he took it off, rummaging about for laidil root, thinking this might ease Erejzan's weakness.

Then that not-voice filled his brain. "Your sacrifice has pleased me. What will you have in exchange for Vraduir, my servant Tyrus?"

They all had heard the god. Erejzan tried to sit up, but Tyrus and the women forbade this. Rof cringed, not hiding his dread. Jathelle and Ilissa were frightened, too, their eyes wide as Tyrus walked back into the god's altar chamber. He stood well away from the cage and could not bring himself to look at Vraduir—the sacrifice which had pleased Nidil.

"I . . . I did not intend to ask for anything, Lord of Death."

"All mortals do." The not-voice was colder than ever, without any amusement now. Fear for himself and the others pulsed through Tyrus. "Mortals pledge gifts to me, all manner of gifts, if I will but stay my hand a while and let them live. You have sacrificed most worthily, far more than most of them, my servant Tyrus. No pledge, but honest fulfillment of a bargain made with Vraduir. What reward will you take?"

Battered by events and sorrow, Tyrus sagged. "He . . . Vraduir was my sire, Lord of Death. I cannot profit by this . . . sacrifice."

"Fathers, mothers, sons, daughters—all kinships and every mortal meets me, in time. That is the way of it. Your father's time had come." Tyrus lifted his head, heavily struck by that inexorable logic. Had Vraduir's death been fated? Was it not, then, his fault but the gods' own design? "By laws of mortals and us divine ones, he died," Nidil explained. "It is right that you should be recompensed for the pain he dealt you. Ask!"

His thoughts whirled. Tyrus felt he was robbing Vraduir's corpse like a scavenger to gain this boon. Yet he said, "Then . . . then if you would, Nidil Who Steals All Breath, give us . . . safe passage out of your realm. The perils of the frozen plain and the Forbidden Lands and the Ice Forest are many. My sorkra arts have been sorely taxed coming to your citadel. I do not know if I can protect us when we return to the lands of life or heal the wounds your beasts and skeleton warriors have dealt us."

The not-voice was silent. Tyrus considered this, guessing that the god knew his wants better than Tyrus knew them himself. With some hesitation, he went on, "And . . . freedom for Erejzan. I beg you to take away the curse Vraduir bought from Bogotana and laid upon my friend. Only a god can banish another god's evil spell. Erejzan's bravery made it possible for me to . . . to sacrifice Vraduir to you. He deserves reward, too."

Still there was no reply from the shifting form in the smoke and the fire that gave no heat.

Tyrus plunged on. "And freedom for those poor

damned souls who wander the frozen plain outside the citadel—the peasants and specters and even Captain Drie. Give them to death and peace, please."

Had he sought too much? Vraduir overreached, fatally. Tyrus met the blackness, the god-eyes hovering beyond Vraduir's shimmering cage. Would they all be slain because of Tyrus' presumption? Were they, too, to be encased in crystalline, deadly beauty?

At last, an answer came. "The first two requests I will grant."

Tyrus started with joy, scarcely believing.

Jathelle hurried to him, embracing him, at one with his delight. "Safe passage! The horrible beasts and cold and the Skull Breakers . . ."

"None will touch you. You are under my protection," Nidil said within their minds. "Wounds given by *my* minions will be whole."

"And Erejzan . . ." Tyrus looked at his friend. "Did you hear, mai fiyel? The Death God ends Bogotana's enchantment."

Ilissa was tucking Jathelle's cloak about Erejzan, comforting him. She whispered to him. Erejzan smiled faintly and Ilissa said, "He heard. He knows."

Tyrus faced the god again. "And the third request, Lord Nidil?" Did he tempt the immortal's lightnings?

"In part." Tyrus and Jathelle puzzled over this. Nidil was not quick to end their confusion, for time had no meaning to him. When they had begun to think there would be no further words, Nidil's not-voice shook their skulls. "The peasants I release. They will go to Keth's portals and the wheel of existence."

Jathelle wept and said, "Countless thanks, Lord of Death. Their misery is at an end. I praise your generosity."

"I am not generous. I took them, as I take all life. But the peasants committed no hurt or sin. Vraduir enslaved them and their souls do not belong here."

"Captain Drie and his crew?" Perhaps fatigue and the shock of triumph made Tyrus bold.

"They must remain. They chose Vraduir of their own will, hoping to share his power. They are traitors. Keth will not receive them at his holy door." The ever-moving shapes that might be eyes centered upon Vraduir, admiring the wizard within the cage as a jeweler might gaze on a gold morsel locked in ancient resin. "He built well, my servant Vraduir. I do not judge evil. I take life. He took life, too. He reared this citadel for me and worked many a slave to death. But Keth tells me they may enter his divine lands. Vraduir and Captain Drie and the others may not. They will serve me forever, they and the betrayers of Traecheus and Ryerdon and Benrigu and Tredeno . . ."

Nidil chanted a litany of names, most of which meant nothing to Tyrus and Jathelle. Were these lands lost in time and dust or lands yet unknown to the provinces of Tyta'an? They dared not question, accepting, taking what Nidil granted.

"Mine. All is mine. I will keep the citadel. It pleases me, as his sacrifices and yours do. Go forth under my protection with what you have received, my servant Tyrus," Nidil said. "But come no more to the Death God's realm. I shall show any other intruders no mercy at all." They shuddered, contemplating the nature of Nidil's mercy, tendered unto them—and to Vraduir. "Come no more, till the time shall be when age severs your life and you must depart to Keth, my servant Tyrus."

Uncertain if he was expected to say anything, Tyrus stammered, "I . . . I thank you, Lord of Death."

Again came that hint of unworldly laughter. "No thanks are necessary! I will claim you, too, some day. But not as a sacrifice, I trust. I leave you now. My realm is wide, and the citadel but a tiny portion of my domain. I rule all, as Vraduir will see. All . . . all . . . all . . ."

The sound was fading, and so was the heatless flame and the smoke. The altar fire did not sputter and sizzle like a normal fire being put out. Like the Death God's voice in their minds, the fire dissolved in a blink of an eye, leaving the stone table utterly bare and unsmudged by any ash or residue.

They became aware of their own breathing and heartbeats. The silence was profound once the god had left. Gone, too, was the scent of decay and the cold that numbed the will. It was still icy in the room, but it was the cold of the far north, deadly, but part of the world they had always known. Wary, Tyrus and Jathelle withdrew from the altar, back toward the doorway where Rof and Ilissa and Erejzan were.

Rof shook his head, wiped his eyes, and said, "Did it really happen?"

"Vraduir is the proof," Tyrus said grimly. "He has been left as an ornament for Nidil to admire when next he visits his citadel." He hunkered beside Erejzan, touching his friend's brow. There was no fever yet nor chill. But such wounds were bound to cause bad after-effects. Tyrus made plans how to care for the acrobat throughout the journey. Even with Nidil's promised protection, the trip would not be easy. Erejzan was too hurt to walk.

Erejzan roused, peering up at him dully. "I dreamed that . . . that he said I was no longer cursed."

"No dream," Tyrus said.

"It is really so?"

"That god has no need to lie!" Rof was fast regaining his cockiness now that the Death God's presence was vanished. "And he lets us go through his realm unharmed, even past the Skull Breakers. Hai! By Bogotana, you drove him a canny bargain, sorkra. A fair challenge, fairly won!"

"Be quiet," Jathelle chided him, eyeing Tyrus sympathetically.

"Well and at that, LaRenya. As you say. I am your man."

"Are you?" Jathelle said, arching a pale eyebrow. "How long and how far are you my man?"

"LaRenya! You wound me! I vow I am your subject. And I am eager for my reward," Rof said ingenuously. "The reward was the only reason I guided you to the Ice Forest and went on into the Death God's realm at your side."

"Reward?" Jathelle was outraged. "You tried to kill us! You *have* killed my men!"

"Not I!" Rof's expression was one of studied innocence. "I never shed their blood. No need, when One-Ear and the others were willing to take the risk for me. In fact, your men are good fighters. I give them that. Two of them yet live. They are prowling this citadel, looking for you and LaSirin. I had no little problem eluding them when Vraduir sent me on your trail."

"Hetanya! Do you expect me to believe you?"

"I think he may be telling the truth for once, Jathelle," Tyrus said.

The brigand indicated the bristling array of weapons he wore. "You read me aright. If I wanted to kill you, I would have. While you warred with Vraduir, your back was to me, sorkra. I could have used it as a target. It was most tempting. The acrobat would have been easy prey then, and LaRenya and our pretty LaSirin."

Tyrus smiled and said, "Yet you were my ally against him. Why?"

"The bargain was better on your side, as you yourself told me."

Jathelle exhaled sharply. "It was not so when you betrayed us on the frozen plain!"

"That was then, LaRenya. This is now." A grin

split Rof's scarred face. "You said when your sister was rescued, I would get my reward. She is with you once more. We are even, eh?"

"And it helped sway your choice of sides, no doubt, when Vraduir tried to crush you with the wall stones," Tyrus said with sarcasm. "Why do you think we will not repay you in kind for your treachery earlier?"

"Ah! You, unlike your sire, are a man of honor. And LaRenya of the house of Fer-Sro is from a line that keeps their bargains, too. I can tell these things. I must, if I am to survive and win gold. That is my calling, you remember."

Rof was affably unashamed. He twisted his unkempt mustaches into their former sharp-tipped elegance. His clothes were torn and bloodied and his jaunty cap long gone, his baldric hanging by one frayed strap. But he was the same merry and confident bandit who had accosted Tyrus and Erejzan in the streets of Couredh.

"You came rather late to your loyalty," Tyrus said, chuckling.

"In time enough to save my skin. That does well enough."

Jathelle looked from one man to the other, bewildered by such cheer and concord. "Tyrus, he betrayed us . . ."

"And helped us when we most needed it," Tyrus reminded her gently. "Without his weapons and strength, we could not have broken into the sanctuary. For once, Rof aided the cause of justice and right."

Rof was embarrassed to have that pointed out. "Fah! No matter. Play herb-healer to these paltry nips and bruises of mine, sorkra, and I will take my leave—ere LaRenya's men find us. They might not be so understanding as you."

"Leave?" Jathelle waved at the corpse-piled corridor and the rubble blocking its far end. "How?"

"There are other doors out of the chamber, LaRenya.

A wise thief always makes sure of his escape path, lest the battle turn against him. While you and the sorkra were talking, I peeked through one of those doors and found the passageway clear. I can find my way to the gates, no fear."

He bowed low, edging away. Jathelle moved as if she might try to stop him and Rof raised a warning finger, still grinning at her. "Let us part friends, La-Renya. I like you and the sorkra. Do not push my loyalty too far. I would be truly sorry to be forced to kill you."

"We can pursue you, bandit lord." It was apparent, though, that Jathelle's resolve in this matter was faltering.

Rof looked toward Erejzan and Ilissa with something resembling kindness in his black eyes. "I think not. You and the sorkra are linked to those who need your help. You will be too busy to chase me. Vraduir might have left them to freeze and bleed. You will not. Eh, Sorkra?"

Bemused, Tyrus said, "You read me well. It may be I too am a brigand at heart."

Paling, Rof cried, "Never! And forget I ever offered to hire you! We are even and done, sorkra. I want nothing more to do with the wizard kind, not even your honorable sort. Come. Mend these bites and I will . . ."

Tyrus made no gesture, but Rof's mind and tongue stopped. Dumb and unthinking, he was a statue. Jathelle stared at the Krantin thoughtfully. Tyrus waited, knowing what she would say before she spoke. "Tyrus, he did help us. And if it is true that he did not kill my men . . ."

"I do feel other human presences in the citadel besides our own," Tyrus said. "Rof knew lesser prey would bring him no profit from Vraduir. And he does not kill for malice, only for pay."

"His reward," Jathelle murmured. "The spell?"

"It does him no harm. I merely hold him for your pleasure . . . LaRenya." Tyrus grew sly. "He is your hireling. He took your hand upon it. Now the LaRenya must decide if he has fulfilled his bargain, or shall be punished as a villain and an outlaw."

With a sigh, Jathelle said, "Let him go, Tyrus. He earned his reward and his freedom, for now." Her chin went up stubbornly and she added, "But once he is back in Couredh, and the reward is his, let him take care. He will be fair game for any thief-taker, as before."

"I would not wager too much on the thief-takers," Tyrus said. A sound that might have been a soft laugh rattled in Erejzan's throat. Tyrus peered down at his friend. Ilissa pillowed the acrobat's head in her lap, stroking his brow, scolding him for resisting sleep so long. It was plain Erejzan had heard the exchange and was amused, silently mouthing approval of Jathelle's decision to let Rof go.

A milky film swam over Rof's eyes as Tyrus addressed the bandit lord. "Hear me, Rof. You will own what I tell you, and no more. You came with us to the citadel. There was a battle, and you changed sides and back again. You helped us defeat Vraduir in the end, and for that you shall be paid. But you never saw Erejzan change shape. You have no memory of that at all. Nor do you remember what has happened to Ilissa here. These things are lost to you, never to be found. Webs and water and fire, closing and upon him and sealing memory fast. It is so." Tyrus nodded, and the milky film disappeared, leaving Rof's mind and will free.

Frightened, Rof tensed, demanding, "What . . . what have you done to me?"

"Made certain you will not act as our enemy. You see, we do not entirely trust you," Tyrus said lightly.

Rof groped at his face and breast, as if fearing to discover some lingering evidence of magic chaining him.

Finding nothing, he did not know whether to be encouraged or not. "I am whole?"

Tyrus reached in his pack and cut off a lump of sticky dried sap from his hoard of wizard's cures. He tossed the stuff to the bandit. "That will make you so. Use it upon your cuts and bites. The enchantment is already in its nature and will serve to heal the evil dealt by Vraduir's minions."

"But none of this will help you if you slew my men and lied to us," Jathelle said grimly.

"Two of them are alive. I swear it," Rof exclaimed. "I swear it by Bogo . . . by my beard and by the Death God and his citadel!"

Tyrus twisted his head and said, "So it would seem. One oath you have kept." In the distance, they could hear shouting. Someone was hammering at one of the alternate doors to the sanctuary, not the one Rof had indicated as his escape path. The voices were human and familiar. Jathelle ran to the door, searching for a latch, calling through the cracks in the panels. "Is that you, Miquit?"

"LaRenya! We are here! Utaigh and myself! We will save you from the wizard!"

Those within the chamber laughed at those earnest pronouncements. Rof acted hurt that anyone had doubted his word. "You see?" He pocketed the magic cure Tyrus had given him and turned toward his chosen exit.

"Take nothing of the Death God's," Tyrus warned him. "Leave his property here. All of it. And leave horses for us, or I will enchant you further."

Rof rolled his eyes at this threat, then smiled. "Willingly! I can always steal more horses—no! Buy them, with the coin LaRenya will pay me . . ."

Tyrus brushed Rof's mind while the bandit's guard was down. The sorcery was thoroughly successful. The Krantin's brain was emptied of knowledge concerning

Erejzan's banished curse or Ilissa's rape. If necessary, he would work the same forgetfulness on Jathelle's men, and on Ilissa herself, perhaps, if the princess wished it. With this, Vraduir's evil would truly end. The cruel reminders of his wizardry would be left here in the citadel with the sacrificed sorcerer.

The door gave way under battering. Only stout wood and metal hinges had barred the way to Miquit and Utaigh. The force that had locked the sanctuary earlier was gone. Doors were merely doors now.

The men hailed Jathelle, their voices tangling as they both described the fierce battle they had fought against the brigands and Vraduir's beasts. They grieved that Sergeant Neir and troopmen Ris and Xan were slain. So were the outlaws. Rof's name did not enter the tale, Tyrus noted. In truth, the bandit lord must have abandoned that fray as soon as possible and gone on his own quest for prey and gold. Utaigh was swaying, weak from blood loss from a badly-cut arm. Miquit was bruised and gory and complaining that he had lost his sword in the melee. But they were alive, and Rof's promise was proved.

Tyrus walked to the door Rof had thrown open—as Miquit and Utaigh had been entering by another portal. Absently, Tyrus heard the chatter between Jathelle and her faithful followers. They were coming after him, the babble abating as Jathelle asked, "Where is the bandit . . ."

There was a staircase at the end of the hall beyond the doors. Rof had stopped on the topmost step, and he called back to them. "LaRenya, remember! Send my reward to the Inn of the Cutpurses! I guarantee no harm will come to your messenger, no harm at all! On my oath!"

Miquit and Lieutenant Utaigh would have pursued him, but Jathelle ordered them not to. They heard Rof's footfalls pattering down the stairs and away into

the vastness of the citadel. Belatedly, the courtier and
Utaigh saw Ilissa kneeling in the other doorway and
whooped for joy. "LaSirin! She is safe! Safe!" Neither
man was so cruel as to comment on her torn dress and
bruises. Indeed, all of them were in rags and hurt, and
they gallantly pretended this was the whole cause of
Ilissa's condition.

Jathelle, too, was aware of their kindness, fear for
her sister's reputation gradually fading. She was starting to laugh, the bubbling escape of relief after trials
nearly past enduring. "Rof of the bandits! Such insolence! He will have his reward, but not from a single
messenger. I will send a well-armed troop, lest my men
be robbed as well as the reward delivered! Tyrus,
will . . . will he still be lord of bandits if he is the only
one of his brigands left alive?"

"Of course. His survival and the reward will prove
him strongest among his kind. They admire such a clever
braggard. Watch! He will soon have other thieves flock-
ing to his rule, hoping the next time they will be fortunate, too!"

"For gold," Jathelle said wonderingly. "Ah! Well, it
is his calling!"

And they embraced, their laughter an intertwin-
ing sound, rising to the lofty ceiling, chasing away fear
and cold, for a while.

XIX

The Wizard King of Couredh

REALITY WAS THE PERSISTENT COLD, QUENCHING THE brief moment of celebration. They had won, at great cost. And now they must leave the citadel. Nidil had set no time for them to depart, but none was anxious to remain long within his realm.

Tyrus started to draw within his mind. Then Jathelle caught his hands firmly. His eyes snapped open and he met her knowing gaze. "Not alone," Jathelle said, in that stubborn tone Tyrus had come to expect. "You seek out more magic."

He nodded at Erejzan and Utaigh and Ilissa. "They need it. So do we and Sirai Miquit—strength to sustain us through the journey."

"The herb brought from wizard's realms? I remember the danger involved. Erejzan did not approve. He is too weak to argue with you, now. I am not."

Tyrus was touched by her concern, pinned by her stare. "I must," he said, insistent.

Jathelle repeated, "Not alone."

As before, they were one. Jathelle's courage was an extension of his will, and hers, that spirit that had led

360

him through such perils on this quest. Despite the situation, Tyrus smiled as he sank into arcane depths.

He had drained his reserves earlier. Some power would have returned to the fount, however, when the battle with Vraduir ended. Tyrus had not been sure he had arts left to search out those sources again. Now it was surprisingly easy. He was weary, yet he moved without mishap across the webs and bottomless chasms with the alien eyes, hurtling obstacles with his mind, eluding the grasp of jealous beings who dwelled in the world below and beyond.

Tyrus was coming to the surface, entering existence once more. Safe. Jathelle peered up at him anxiously. For her, no time had passed at all. But she understood Tyrus had undertaken the journey and returned unharmed. Her smile was the sun, welcoming him. "Never was that done so quickly," Tyrus said. Then he sobered and knelt beside Erejzan.

"Help him, please," Ilissa begged softly.

"I will, LaSirin, with the gods' favor." Tyrus touched the acrobat's cold fingers. "The rest of you—join your hands with mine."

Lieutenant Utaigh and Sirai Miquit did not understand, but they followed Jathelle's lead. There was no need for Ilissa to move; she was stroking Erejzan's brow, and the magic herb's influence would flow through Erejzan's body and thence to the woman who held him so tenderly. Jathelle and the others gazed wonderingly at their linked fingers as strange sensations poured into their veins. When the transfer was done, Tyrus cautioned them, "This energy will not last indefinitely. But it will take us, I hope, as far as the campsite in the valley of the ridges."

"And then you will conjure the black-stemmed flower to counter this magic," Jathelle said grumpily. "I wish you would let me help you more."

"Perhaps I will, in time." Jathelle seized on that

vague promise like an eager child; Tyrus remembered how he had anticipated sharing his world of sorcery with her. In time, he repeated silently, cherishing that possibility.

"I will treat us all with a substance to cure Vraduir's evil," Tyrus said, displaying more of the sticky sap he had given to Rof. "It should be proof against bites and hurts we suffered from his demons and slaves, and Nidil has taken away the deadly wounds his minions gave." Jathelle was worrying over Lieutenant Utaigh's cut arm, a result of his battles with the throatslitters. Tyrus frowned, acknowledging this problem. "Wounds dealt us by true men are . . . just that. I fear I have no arts of surgery."

"Deal with the magic," Jathelle said brusquely. "The rest we must handle as we would any hurts in an honest war, for the struggle through the corridors with those turncoats was surely that!"

Tyrus did so, moving as swiftly as his aching body allowed. At one point he offered some laidil root to Erejzan. To his surprise, not only did the medicinal root give no help but it nauseated his friend. Disgusted and retching, Erejzan spat it out. He roused a bit and moaned aggrievedly, "I am become my grandmother's heir at last . . . I . . . I cannot stomach that . . . that foul root."

Ilissa looked as if she blamed Tyrus for causing this upset. In sincere apology, Tyrus threw away the now-useless remedy, saying to Erejzan, "It means more than that you are grandchild of a Destre, mai fiyel. Before, you said you rather liked the taste of it. Matters have changed." Erejzan blinked and tried to comprehend what Tyrus was saying but could not. Tyrus' happiness in finding the curse was truly lifted was lost in fear. "All these cuts and bites he endured are too many for the sap to overcome. The blood is thinned badly. He cannot walk."

"Most certainly not!" Ilissa flared, outraged. "We must make a litter for him. But . . . but how? There is nothing here."

"We must take nothing that belongs to the Death God out of his realm at any rate," Tyrus said. "But the weapons—those are ours. Put them in a pile, here."

Utaigh and Miquit hesitated only a moment. Even as the courtier expressed mild doubts, he was obeying. "Will we not need arms to fight imps and warriors as we leave the citadel, sorkra?"

"Tyrus has won us a truce from Nidil's armies," Jathelle said. The men eyed him with awe, much impressed. Miquit surrendered an Irico sword he had confiscated from a bandit to replace his stolen one. They put that with the axe Rof had loaned Erejzan and various daggers and knives and other blades. Atop all, Jathelle gingerly placed the enchanted sword.

Around them, the citadel was changing—Vraduir's work, being erased. Illusion divided from reality, his beasts vanishing and the sham toppled wall stones winking out of sight.

Tyrus ground his knuckles into his forehead, concentrating. Fiery green light lanced into the weapons. Wooden haft of the axe. Wood within the enchanted sword. Gems, studding Jathelle's dagger and Miquit's eating knife. Krantin steel and Clarique iron. The gold coin Tyrus had used to form the magic blade. All these things Tyrus reshaped into a different sort of tool of survival. When he was done, the green light flowed back into his being. In place of metal and wood, there was a strongly-made litter frame.

They secured Miquit's cloak in place, then Tyrus and the nobleman carefully picked up the acrobat and laid Erejzan upon the new-made stretcher. As they covered the wounded man in the queen's mantle, Tyrus could not resist looking toward Nidil's altar one final time. The impulse brought him agony, for his grief was fresh and an open wound. Vraduir's crystalline cage shone with Nidil's radiance, vivid and deadly, a vision branded in Tyrus' mind.

"We are ready, Tyrus," Jathelle said, leading him away with the golden strands of her voice and her soul. Willingly, his heart twisting upon sorrow's spear, he turned away.

Tyrus and Miquit picked up the litter. As they did, other illusions melted. All at once, the questers saw that the way to the citadel's gates was far straighter than they had supposed. Many of the maze-like halls and rambling steps which had shunted them aside were part of Vraduir's trickery. There was a direct path, it appeared, now laid plain as the snares to delude the infiltrators faded and were gone. Much of the rubble was disappearing, too—debris that had never been there at all.

Even so, they were forced to walk slowly. Despite Utaigh's claims that he was steady, his complexion was ashen and pain made him wince often as he made his way up and down steps and through corridors. Erejzan was a heavy burden for Tyrus and Miquit. They weaved along, calling instructions to one another, matching their pace so that they would not jostle the acrobat any more than necessary. Ilissa trotted beside the litter, asking again and again if she could not do something more to help Erejzan. Jathelle and the men assured her that her presence was enough, and this was so. When his wounds troubled him, Ilissa's caress seemed all that was needed to calm the man in the litter. Barely conscious, Erejzan would lie back, gazing at Ilissa and smiling faintly.

Their way out of the citadel was lined with silent, grotesque rows of spectators. Gruesome armies of skeleton warriors and hideous animals from ages and places unknown watched Tyrus and Jathelle and their companions. The scrutiny was frightening, as all the denizens of the citadel came forth and hulked along the icy walls.

Yet none of this horde threatened them or made any move against the humans. The chieftain of the skeleton warriors swiveled his helmeted skull as they passed, empty eye sockets apparently tracking their path. But there was no bolt of Vraduir's black flame to strike at Jathelle, no magic Tyrus must counter with desperate effort. The warriors were Vraduir's to command no more. Chained by Nidil's promise of safe passage, they waited on either side of the corridors, they and the dreadful, stinking creatures of the death realm. It was a peculiar parade, with Tyrus and Jathelle leaders of the procession, surrounded by cheerless, soundless crowds of unliving beings.

They lost count of time. There was no way to tell if it were day or night or how many candle-marks had gone by while they fought Vraduir through the citadel to the sanctuary. Doggedly, the questers continued on their way toward the gates. When they went by the skeleton warriors, Ilissa repressed a shudder and hid her face, refusing to look at her abductors lest the memory steal her reason.

They found human bodies amid the tumbled wall stones and rows of silent death beasts and damned warriors. The brigands and the brave soldiers had died locked in combat. Rof had turned his coat again to help Tyrus, but Utaigh and Miquit cursed the slain bandits and said none of them had shown pity, even when it was becoming apparent that Vraduir was losing his power. With honor, they removed the bodyguards to separate halls and buried them under cairns of broken wall stones. The bandits had shown no loyalty and none of the survivors felt any toward their corpses. They made no cairns for the dead thieves, and they stripped the bodies to give warm clothes to Erejzan and Ilissa and replace the others' badly-frayed cloaks, tunics, and gloves.

The last of the three burials took place just within the citadel's gate, where Sergeant Neir had fallen as he tried to protect his queen. "Hetanya guide him to her holy realms," Jathelle mourned. With fervent prayers, she swore to inscribe his name and those of Troopmen Ris and Xan in the Adril-Lur, Mother of Earth's most sacred book. "Ai! When we have come again to Couredh, all the realm shall know of your valor, brave soldiers of Couredh. And we shall sacrifice to you and Troopman Halom and Sirai Dorche, too, who died on the trek that the rest of us might win free to the citadel."

The others piously seconded her and spoke loud praises of their dead comrades. They had set the litter by the doors, and Ilissa was sitting there beside Erejzan, absently repeating the prayers as she fussed over the wounded man. Miquit glanced toward the princess, then lowered his voice and asked judiciously, "LaRenya, what of Aubage?"

Jathelle also looked at Ilissa and said in a whisper, "He will have prayers." She endured Miquit's quizzical stare a while, then went on curtly, "He died as he lived." Miquit asked no further questions. His expression told that his suspicions regarding Aubage's shallow nature had been confirmed. He shook his head wearily.

Ilissa took no notice of this soft conversation, though if she had strained her ears she could have heard them. Jathelle wondered on this, raising an eyebrow at Tyrus. His smile was comfort, very gentle.

Gifts. Sorkra gifts, to be used for good. And what was good? Was it not kindness, the kindness of forgetting? Tyrus brushed Ilissa's thoughts and discovered her forcing away memories of Aubage—of his insults, and of how he died. It took but slight pressure from Tyrus' arts to aid Ilissa in this. A great part of her spirit was running away from Aubage's cruelties, and

hurrying toward new-found yearning, concern for Erejzan, admiration for his loyalty and courage. Tyrus
guided her in that wishing and in the forgetting. He
could not—would not—wipe all of it away. He did not
have that right. But for now, Ilissa did not hear Aubage
mentioned, did not think about him at all. She leaned
over Erejzan, wiping cold sweat from his face, brightening when he was able to murmur thanks.

Tyrus and Miquit picked up the litter once more, and
Jathelle helped Utaigh past a sprawled corpse on the
threshold. Tyrus recognized the brigand—the one called
Breg, who had been first, ever, to pounce on any spoils
left by the dead. It seemed fitting he was now stripped
of all he had worn, a traitor going to meet Bogotana
without garment or gold.

In the back of his mind, Tyrus had been counting;
with Breg the tally was complete. Breg, One-Ear,
Branded-Hand, Ouar, Bloody Axe—all the bandits,
dead. All save Rof, and Rof they had bought again. He
was their man, no threat, at least until his reward was
delivered.

The gates of the citadel stood open wide, a mute
suggestion that they leave Nidil's realm. It was an invitation they accepted with alacrity, hurrying forth.

Their boots squeaked on the ice. The cloaks they
had taken from the bandits kept them warm and elim-
inated any need for Tyrus' glamour to hold in heat,
nor was there need to hide from danger. Vraduir's probing light was gone. The brigands were slain. Even the
ice-fog lifted to let them see their way clearly to the
ridges. The Death God's hand seemed to draw up the
mist, a coldly polite gesture to make certain they left
as quickly as possible. The foggy shroud floated above
their heads, an eerie blanket which made their footfalls
echo. This time there was no wild dash for cover or
hiding behind ruins of ancient vehicles.

But the ghostly legions still haunted the plain, waiting for them. Like the skeleton warriors and the Death God's pets, the specters lined their route. They were not silent, though. They groaned and sobbed in hollow chorus, frantic to reach the travelers' hearts. Ilissa had not seen these gruesome spirits before and she gasped in horror and turned this way and that, wanting to flee. Jathelle sheltered her sister within her cloak, letting Ilissa hide her eyes from these things. She could not shut out the sounds, however, and Ilissa trembled at each keening cry.

Jathelle dared express her anger to the looming fog, the personification of Nidil. "He said his minions would not harm us, yet their laments and pleadings are a torment as awful as demons' fangs and the skeletons' lances!"

"I cannot enchant them away," Tyrus said ruefully. "I can stop the tongue of a mortal, but this is beyond any sorcerer's power."

As he spoke, he felt the ponderous touch of the Death God's distant presence. Distant, yet it was everywhere in this frozen land. Nidil's not-voice seemed to rattle within Tyrus' skull. "You are humble, my servant Tyrus, far more humble than Vraduir. He would have sought such power—my power. Listen!"

At that command, the pressure lifted abruptly, and the dismal wailing died to an indistinct susurration. The sound was still depressing, wafting around them as they trudged, but now it was bearable, the steady murmuring as of countless lost souls.

Ilissa was unsteady on her feet despite the strengthening magic Tyrus had brought from the webs. She leaned on Jathelle, stumbling along, her head down, her face emptied by weariness and terror. She did not fall, though. And the others found the will to shut the pleading and entreaties from their minds.

The pleas did not cease, ever. Captain Drie and his crew knelt beside the track the litter must pass, arms

stretched forth in supplication. Tyrus skimmed them
with his gaze, struck by Drie's strong resemblance to
Erejzan. Kinsmen of his friend, several of them had
reddish hair, and they were but recently dead; their
flesh had not decayed, leaving their square features
and the greenish eyes of the Qamat clans as yet rec-
ognizable. Men of Qamat's clans, but lacking Erejzan's
faithfulness and honor. Those they had thrown away,
if they ever owned them. Without remorse, Tyrus passed
the sailors by, their muttered words never reaching him.

Kings of conquered realms and pirates and evildoers of every land were left, unheard, unheeded. No-
tably absent were Jathelle's enslaved peasants. True to
his promise, Nidil had released them from this eternity
of wandering. Their souls and their forms were gone,
safely on their way to Keth's portals, the country folk
freed at last. Jathelle saw this and turned to look at
Tyrus, gratitude bringing tears to brim on her pale
lashes. He nodded, glad for her sake and for the peasants, and they plodded slowly on toward the base of
the northernmost ridge.

Armies of the dead lined the plains. They had no
ability to deter the companions nor to affright them
any more. No one needed to brush them aside. The
specters were mist, as ethereal as the fog, and as helpless. Bit by bit they were forgotten, melting, even their
soft noises swallowed in natural sounds of booming ice
and the rustle of garments and creak of the litter frame.
When the travelers reached the place where the horses
were tied, they were alone once more. The emptiness
was daunting, but it was better than the mournful
hordes of condemned who were trapped in the Death
God's region of eternal night.

It *was* night, or fast becoming so, a subtle darkening
of the perpetual overcast from deep gray to fathomless
black. Tyrus conjured light for them, a warm, cheery

magic taper to hang in mid-air while they readied to ascend the ridge.

Rof had taken three of the horses and, they found, not surprised, all the coins and gems he and his fellow brigands had carried from Drita Meadows the length of the trek. Now he was taking them with him back to Couredh, the inheritor of all the plunder, because he had turned his coat one particular time. This discovery brought the travelers some amusement. They forgave his greed, for he had also been generous enough to leave them the packs containing most of the provender. "He took but enough to feed him and his mounts through the barren country," Miquit said, assessing the stores. "But no more. You lessoned him well, sorkra Tyrus." There was much respect in his manner, a regard Utaigh echoed.

"Likelier he knew there would be little sale for any extra grain of this quality, or for the motge meat. He can afford to be generous. He owns enough treasure to insure his position among the brigands even without Jathelle's reward," Tyrus said absently. He gathered his sorcery again. This time Jathelle did not protest, too troubled over Ilissa's shivering and half-delirious mumbling. Erejzan was also feverish and Tyrus worked to ease the climb for them.

With magic, he altered the litter into a sledge and made some of the captured gloves and boots taken from the bandits' corpses into harness. Jathelle and Ilissa rode the steadiest horse. Utaigh was weak, but he would not consent to take the best mount, still sworn to serve LaRenya and his princess. They could not move with any speed. Tyrus walked behind the sledge. Miquit rode close by, now and then dismounting and helping Tyrus lift the awkward conveyance around rough spots and sharp turns on the path. Ilissa woke from frightened dreaming again and again, hearing the wind in the jagged peaks. Jathelle would soothe her and urge the puffing horse on up the ridge.

There were no awful howls from the ice-covered rocks and snowy tors. Occasionally, those who had crossed these haunted heights on the way to the citadel listened and wondered, unsure if some sound were the wind or a muffled yelp from one of the Death God's pets. Dully, Tyrus decided this too was a favor granted them, as Nidil had hushed the pleadings of the ghosts. No slavering brutes or abominations from time's dawn leaped out of the swirling flakes or from hiding behind rocks. The creatures stayed at a distance. Perhaps they were watching hungrily. Their master, however, chained them firmly and kept his promise.

The travelers were forced to stop many times, despite the comparatively gradual ascent. The strange, iridescent snow added to Tyrus' magic light and showed them the turns in the trail they had left earlier. At the crest they halted to rest, gazing back over the frozen plain, for the fog had parted. It was as if Nidil wished to show them his domain, his glory, and his awful citadel. Shaken with cold and dread, they saw an omnipotent glow under the entire field of ice, unending, a gleaming expanse reaching outward east and west. The citadel hulked above it, the Death God's castle that Vraduir had made. So much blood had been shed to build it and to rescue its lovely prisoner. Uncaring, eternal, the property now of Nidil, Vraduir's citadel bade them farewell. The sight urged the exhausted travelers on, driving them to new efforts. They moved over the crest and started the difficult descent to the valley.

When they reached the foothills, they could go no further. It was some distance from the place where they had made camp with the stone wood. But Tyrus called a halt. He assumed command, for Jathelle had no wish to rule, too tired and anxious for Ilissa's health.

Again Lieutenant Utaigh and Miquit followed Tyrus'
decision, tacitly accepting him as leader of their small
band. He returned the sledge to its former materials,
giving them back their blades and bidding them dig in
the snow for more of the stone wood. He kindled
smokeless fire in the hollow of rocks, wondering if
Nidil were controlling the weather. Where had this
shelter been when they had fought their way up the
slope toward the citadel? Now, the bargain made, the
wind softened and the blue flakes heaped in banks
around their tiny camp, giving them much protection
from the cold.

They slept, posting no guards, no one able to stay
afoot or awake any longer. Tyrus shared the black-
stemmed flower with them all, countering the stress of
previous magic. He shuddered within, his brain dull,
demanding rest; with the others, he sank into long and
dreamless sleep.

It was impossible to judge time, still. They thought a
full day passed while they camped in the hollow. The
snowbanks made of it a blue-white fort girded in ice-
encrusted rocks. Though they yearned to leave the Death
God's realm, it was not possible yet. Utaigh was sick
from his cut arm and Erejzan out of his wits from
fever and chills. Ilissa wanted to help them, but she
herself was too weakened from her captivity and the
abuse she had suffered. Tyrus used the webs' powers
as often as he dared; but, for some of their injuries,
magic served little. They must wait and pray and minister to the worst hurt with moss and simples.

By what seemed like the beginning of the third night
since they had left the citadel, matters were better.
Tyrus began to hope by morning they might try crossing the valley and the second ridge. Utaigh's festering
wound had showed signs of draining and Erejzan's fever
was less. The magic herbs and devoted care were healing the casualties of the battle of the citadel.

He sat by the arcane fire, musing on the best way to scale the final ridge, when Jathelle edged closer to him and said, "You should get some sleep. You have been busy all day, conjuring our ragged clothes into fresh weaving, mending split boots. Wasting your energies, again." But her scolding had no weight, and her eyes twinkled.

"I am not the only one spendthrift with energy, nor are we the only ones who are wakeful." Tyrus unobtrusively indicated the scene opposite them across the fire, and Jathelle smiled fondly.

Utaigh and Miquit were asleep, but Erejzan and Ilissa were not. The acrobat looked haggard and thinner than before, yet he fought rest. He was propped on a saddle, swathed in cloaks and blankets, sweating out the remainder of his fever. Ilissa was pale and edgy, recuperating gradually from her encounter with evil wizardry. She, too, seemed to resist sleep and took an unusual form of cure from their on-going conversation. They were heedless of Tyrus and Jathelle, wrapped in each other's words and longings.

". . . I kept his bestiary, you see, and managed his hunting preserves. I was always strong, and I suppose that is why he made me . . ." Erejzan was explaining, a bit flushed at that shameful memory.

"Marvelously strong! But you are no longer cursed. Tyrus says so." Ilissa's faith in the acrobat's sorkra friend was childlike. Her attitude toward Erejzan, however, was that of a young woman finding a new belief in manly honor. As she would not let Erejzan recall his former bondage, so he would never let her mention what had happened in the citadel. Together, with mutual gentleness, they helped each other out of the dark past.

"Shorn away, your curse," Ilissa murmured, then added sadly, "Like my poor hair! Jathelle cut it off. I know it was to save me from the beam but . . ."

"It is still beautiful, silken sunlight and moonlight interwoven." Part of the brightness in Erejzan's eyes was lingering fever. Much of it was not, though. His soul was in his stare, and Ilissa answered it silently, her tiny hand enfolded in his.

"I wonder what they are thinking," Tyrus said idly as the silence across the fire lengthened. He drew up his legs and rested his arms on his knees.

"They are thinking about the future, and how wonderful it will be, now that they have found each other," Jathelle replied. She peered up at Tyrus and her smile widened.

Bemused, Tyrus asked, "How do you know that?"

"We sisters have a bond of the soul. Do you not have such a link with Erejzan? I have sensed it many times on this quest." Tyrus admitted this was so, his heart warming. Jathelle went on, nodding at Ilissa and Erejzan. "She has made the right choice, finally. An honest clan chieftain of great courage. No pretty speeches, but will and strength to keep her safe and love her all her days."

"You read the future for them," Tyrus said softly. "Is it all decided?"

"Do you not think so? Look at them. Erejzan has tried to shape-change since the fever slacked. I saw him, saw his face when he found he was truly free. And I saw Ilissa's delight in his victory." Jathelle doted on her sister and Erejzan, her affection a pulse beating in pace with Tyrus' own wishes. "She has learned, through pain, and so have I." She cocked her head, studying Tyrus, her expression sly.

He hid a laugh, "Is that decided, too?"

"Ah! Is it, my sorkra prince?"

Tyrus grew solemn. "Erejzan is free. And I have given Ilissa the forgetfulness she wants." His voice was hoarse with emotion.

"And your burdens, Tyrus? Burdens are easier to shed with the love of those who have shared them."

The future. She spoke of the future for Erejzan and Ilissa. Another and similar future was in Jathelle's sharp face and blue eyes. There were clotted cuts in her scalp, her golden hair was dotted with snow, and bruises stained her cheeks. But to Tyrus her greatest beauty had always been her intelligence and spirit, that union with his own being, at one with him. Now she invited him to the times that would be.

"Burdens . . ." Tyrus took a deep breath. "The curse Erejzan endured, the guilt I felt because I did not challenge Vraduir sooner . . ." And suddenly the weight, a year and more old, lifted away from his mind. Jathelle knew at once, exulting with him. "It is gone," Tyrus said slowly, incredulous. "They are avenged. And the burden is gone."

His soul was soaring, a hawk on the wind. There was another hawk beside him, matching him in every shift and emotion. Erejzan and Ilissa were oblivious to anything but their own happiness. Ilissa was speaking of her favorite tales of quests and heroes, and Erejzan was her legend come to life, adoring her, as in the stories.

Jathelle furtively pointed to them and said, "They are alone. Why should we not be? Once you wove a glamour within a glamour to shield us from prying eyes. It was dangerous, then. Now?"

Tyrus' smile widened into a delighted grin. "It would call for use of magic. And . . . desire can weaken the tightness of such a spell."

"Perhaps you might dispense with magic, for once. After all, the quest is done. Even a sorkra prince should be allowed a mortal weakness at times," Jathelle said. She leaned closer with every word, teasing. It was not coquetry. She was too direct for that.

"What do you suggest, LaRenya?" Tyrus asked, playing her game.

"Titles? Ah!" Jathelle eyed him warily. "Very well then, a title. Not prince. Not Sirin. Be Renya, Tyrus—Renya of Couredh."

He blinked, his thoughts in a wild jumble. "I . . . I had not considered past . . ."

"The victory? I know your will as well as my own, remember. We are one, sharing that bond," Jathelle said, growing earnest.

"I will think on it. It may be time to put away amuser's disguise."

"And put on a new one. Being a monarch is your calling," Jathelle mocked him in friendly fashion.

He silenced her then, but she made no objection. They were sure Erejzan and Ilissa would not be shocked. As Jathelle had said, they all were people who had met in disguise, their loves forged in terror and triumph. And now they could reveal their true identities at last.

The following day, they crossed the final ridge and made camp again. The extra rest did much for Utaigh, Erejzan, and Ilissa. They were not yet whole. But with each candle-mark they strengthened. Utaigh could ride easily now, and even Erejzan could sit a saddle with little trouble.

Miquit and Utaigh were not unconscious of the attachments of the princess and the redheaded clan chieftain, nor of Tyrus and Jathelle. The leadership they had acknowledged in the citadel was still Tyrus' to claim, and Jathelle did not protest when Tyrus chose their route or took the van. More and more the courtier and the bodyguard gave Tyrus his due as a wizard and as a prince, honor Jathelle paid him in a subtler form but just as plainly.

Despite Nidil's pledge, they waited a long while outside the Ice Forest before venturing into its depths.

Ilissa was very frightened. She had flown above this terrain and it had been only a blur. Now Erejzan insisted she ride before him on his horse, for him to comfort her. Jathelle archly asked if Tyrus would suggest the same for them.

"For the battle maiden of Couredh?" Tyrus returned, shamming amazement. "Pity the Skull Breaker which dares strike at you! You will scatter his brains!"

"So I shall!" Together, Tyrus and Jathelle led the way into the black wood, side by side, until the narrow path made them follow one another.

The Skull Breakers did not appear, however. And the stone branches fell far to either side of the way they rode. Ilissa peered around in confusion, asking why the place was supposed to be so perilous. Her innocent query made Erejzan, Miquit, and Utaigh chuckle with relief. At a jauntier pace, they hurried on, their fears gradually diminishing.

Erejzan pointed out fresh hoofprints ahead of them. "Rof has already made his way through."

"And is heading for his reward at the Inn!" Tyrus called back over his shoulder. "Well, he has earned it."

"We all have," Jathelle said decisively. "Times of peace and warmth and the cheering light of Iesor-Peluva, a time when clouds bring only rain to freshen the earth, not Nidil's brutal ice and snow!"

"It is all there, LaRenya," Miquit said, snapping his reins along his horse's flank. "Waiting for us, in Couredh."

They burst out into the sunlight, cheering spontaneously. Even the horses frisked, beasts sensing escape from danger that had slain their herd-mates. As they left the Ice Forest, an ominous darkness settled over the trees and the sky to the north. A door seemed to have slammed, a tangible if unseen presence lowering.

Tyrus reined his mount, staring into the brooding woods. "We must block the way to the Death God's realm. No more must venture there, until the god summons them to Keth's portals."

"It shall be done . . . Renya," Jathelle said.

He opened his mouth to reply when a shout and a blare of horns and drum rattles cut him off. Utaigh was pointing to the south. A troop of soldiers was riding rapidly toward them, crossing the last mountains of the barren country. Banners snapped in the brisk air and pikes waved.

"An army?" Erejzan wondered uneasily. "Barbarians?"

"Lord General Zlan," Utaigh said, adding his cheers to those of the on-coming troopmen and officers. "Those barbarian standards are ones they have captured. They have lessoned the barbarians while we have rescued LaSirin! Hai! Niyah!"

A roar of greeting and triumph came back. "Haiyan Hetanya! Couredh has conquered!" The general was riding forth ahead of his men, waving his cap like a jovial boy. "The feint succeeded, LaRenya! Hetanya be praised! LaSirin is safe! Couredh is safe! LaRenya . . . welcome!"

The troops crowded around the weary questers, whooping and laughing. They gave wineskins to those who had had nothing but melted snow, fresh grain cakes to those sated on stale fare. Some soldiers looked past them at the Ice Forest and shuddered in horror, full of sympathy for those who had dared so much. There were moments of sorrow when they learned of the deaths, but they raised such loud praise, even for Aubage of Huil-Couredh, the gods would surely hear and acknowledge the losses with honor.

"Tamed the whole frontier, LaRenya," General Zlan boasted to Jathelle. He could not contain his pleasure at seeing them all safe in his protection once again. "Those wild tribes did think to use LaSirin's abduction as an excuse to cause trouble. We have quieted them down for many a season, no fear. All this, and our little Ilissa safe! Keep her safe, Erejzan of Qamat! Long life to you! Hai-yan! Couredh!" He wheeled his horse and rode among his aides as they set up new cheers.

They readied to escort the questers back through the hard lands, strong men and many arms to keep them well.

Jathelle turned to Tyrus. "Safe. And we are going home to Couredh. You said you would think upon my wish." Pride shone in her face. "I will not have a Rasil-yan. I am not a woman to share my man with any other. And I have met the lords and princes of my neighboring realms. None has touched me . . . until you, Tyrus."

"I have a doubt . . ."

"Not about being a sorkra?" Jathelle exclaimed in exasperation, reading him astutely.

"To some degree. Vraduir was wizard king of Qamat. How would your subjects feel about a king who was a sorcerer? My blood is Vraduir's. If I should fall prey to the same ambition that ruled him . . ."

"You will not." Jathelle brooked no opposition. "Because you will have me at your side." She enlarged her embrace to include Ilissa and Erejzan. "You will have many to remind you of what we dared and won, and why. In humility, you won our lives and all the world from Nidil. I do not believe the man who did that can ever yield to ambition. And furthermore, I will not let you!" Her chin went up defiantly.

General Zlan was spreading the news of the defeat of the enemy wizard. Throughout the escort, cries arose. "Sorkra! Tyrus! Hai-yan Tyrus!"

Troopmen took the questers' bridles, leading them southward toward the rocky hills, toward warmth and green fields and lands where summer came after winter's snows. Utaigh and Miquit greeted friends and comrades among the soldiers and officers. The happy shouts included Tyrus and Erejzan as well as the royal sisters, Sirai Miquit, and the army's own Lieutenant Utaigh. All of them were welcomed as heroes and heroines, the beginning of a legend.

Jathelle let the soldiers guide her horse, intent on Tyrus. She asked hopefully, "My Renya?"

"There is something I must know."

Jathelle drew back, apprehensive, for Tyrus' countenance was very serious.

"I have not known these cold lands ere I came to Couredh. I do not know how well I can bear your winters."

"You will find them invigorating," Jathelle promised him eagerly.

"Like Couredh's women?"

She began to guess he was feigning his hesitation, watching him narrowly, a dangerous glint in her gaze. Tyrus could scarcely hide his amusement.

"I will teach you to like our clime and all else you need to become Couredh-yan, my Renya." Jathelle pleaded, "I trusted you at Drita Meadows. Can you not trust me, Tyrus?" She had reminded him of that again, most earnestly.

"Can you handle a tiller?" he asked abruptly, in a stern tone.

Jathelle's fair eyebrows lifted toward her hair line. Then she grinned. "As well as you, I wager. I am a Clarique, am I not? We shall see how you can handle the tiller yourself, sorkra—of the *Wyolak*, my flagship. I grew up aboard her each of my girlhood's summers. You must prove you are my equal at her helm."

"I will."

Jathelle flung her arms about Tyrus' neck, almost pulling them both from their saddles. General Zlan and the onlookers laughed and applauded loudly, enjoying the embrace. Jathelle joined their laughter. "And you shall then have to show me the secrets of those tricks that so mystified me, my sorkra. If I am your wife, I will have that right, ai!"

Regally, cloaking himself in that hauteur that he had used so often in his travels as a magician, Tyrus said cryptically, "Why, battle maiden, a magician never reveals all his arcane lore." Jathelle was about to rail at him as an unfair bargainer when he added gently, "Except to a very few, my queen."

Her hand met his, their fingers interlacing. Bloodied and ragged but victorious, they rode south, to Couredh, and to the many seasons and long years that were to come.

Glossary

Arniob one of the most ancient of the Clarique deities, a Pan-like nature god. He is worshipped largely in the southern islands, the largest of which bears his name.

Bogotana the evil god, monarch of the realm below the earth, particularly of volcanoes and their fire.

Clarique the island province of Tyta'an, easternmost of the peoples and kingdoms.

dredis the favored breed of horses in Clarique, generally rangy animals with chestnut or sorrel-colored coats and manes.

ecar a large wild feline, ranging throughout the provinces.

fihar the Krantin term for redhead. The Clarique equivalent is handri.

fiyel literally "faithful," an affectionate epithet usually reserved for close kindred or sworn friends.

golhi a ferocious carnivore, gradually becoming extinct, but still noted in most realms for its courage and deadliness.

grir   member of the weasel family. Its fur is prized for its warmth and luxuriousness and is a principal export of Couredh.

Gros-Donaq   Lord of Storms, Clarique god of sea and sky. He is abetted by a pantheon of his sons: Qlitos, Rorsa, and Wyolak.

Hetanya   Mother of Earth, the Clarique goddess of fruitfulness. She is known as Ethania and Hethys in some parts of the province.

hurnbul   an exotic member of the deer family, hunted throughout the central and southern islands.

Iesor-Peluva   the sun god.

Irico   the province north and west of Clarique, noted for its rigorous climate and valuable timber forests. Genetically, the people are closely related to the Clarique.

Keth   the Dreadful, guardian of the gods' portals, he who allows the dead to enter the lands beyond or condemns them to wander eternity as unappeased spirits.

Kida   demigod of madness. His lash takes sanity from his victims, for varying durations of time, occasionally until the victim's death.

Krantin   the province west of Clarique, populated by emigrants from the ancient city-state of Ryerdon. The people are predominantly dark-haired and shorter than the Clarique.

LaRenya   Queen. (The other titles of nobility in Clarique are: Renya, King; Sirin, Prince; LaSirin, Princess; Sirai, Lord; LaSirai, Lady. Plural: Sirai-yan, etc.)

Lorit-yan   the dominant tribes of central and northern Clarique.

motge   a bovine species providing meat and leather. Some wild herds still roam Krantin and Irico, but in Clarique the motge has been domesticated for many generations.

Nidil   the death god, who comes out of the regions of eternal night, from far beyond even Irico's coldest lands. He Who Steals All Breath.

Omaytatle   god of snow and ice, an Irico god also worshipped in northern Clarique.

Qlitos   god of winds, particularly of sea breezes and hurricanes. He is one of Gros-Donaq's sons.

Rasil-yan   coastal Clarique tribes which have intermarried with the border clans of Irico. Among other customs, the Rasil-yan have adopted the Irico polygamous marriage.

Rasven   reputedly the first human to recognize within himself the gifts of white wizardry. He is the patron of all his kind, a model for their sorcery and its uses.

Rorsa   god of rains and the ocean currents. He is another of the divine sons of Gros-Donaq.

Ryerdon   the original city-state of the people who became the Krantin-y. It was located on the site of present-day Alen-Sal, in Clarique.

Sarlos   southernmost province of Tyta'an. Her people are very short and have dark complexions and curly hair.

sorkra   a sorcerer, a practitioner of the arcane arts, ideally for good. Also, the art of sorcery.

Soronos   the moon god, who causes the changing phases by driving his herds of white mares from one lunar pasture to another as the nights progress through the month.

themshang   an intricately-strung and tuned harp, the most favored instrument of Clarique musicians.

Traecheus   once known as the Empire of the Eastern Islands, this ancient kingdom fell because of civil wars and natural disasters. Its people were the an-

cestors of the Clarique. Laril-Quil on the coast
stands on the site of Traecheus.

whantola a bird much resembling a peacock, prized
for its plumage.

Wyolak god of lightning, son of Gros-Donaq, the
storm god.

ABOUT THE AUTHOR

JUANITA COULSON began writing at age eleven and has been pursuing the habit off and on ever since. Her first professional sale, to a science-fiction magazine, came in 1963. Since then she has sold thirteen novels, several short stories, and odds and ends such as an article on *Wonder Woman*, science-fictional recipes, and a pamphlet on how to appreciate art.

When she isn't writing, she may be singing and/or composing songs, painting (several of her works have been sold for excessively modest prices), reading books on abnormal psychology, biography, earthquakes and volcanoes, history, astronomy, or almost anything that has printing on it, gardening in the summer and shivering in the winter.

Juanita is married to Buck Coulson, who is also a writer. She and her husband spend much of their spare time actively participating in science-fiction fandom: attending conventions and publishing their Hugo-winning fanzine, *Yandro*. They live in a rented farmhouse in northeastern Indiana, miles from any town you ever heard of; the house is slowly sinking into the swampy ground under the weight of the accumulated books, magazines, records, typewriters, and other paraphernalia crammed into it.

Most of Juanita's books to date have been science fiction, but she has also written two historical romances, *Dark Priestess* and *Fire in the Andes*, available from Ballantine, and *The Web of Wizardry*, her first fantasy for Del Rey Books.

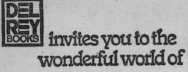